SO BEGINS THE TALE OF THE

When the Revery falls to Corruption's seed
The dragons shall come with fire and endless fury.
The Black Wind's son shall rise again,
After kingdoms fall under the sign of his name.
The Balance shall break and the angels will fall
And Astasia will reign with the coming of the Grey Dawn.

— *"The Days of Astasia," taken from The Portents of Olerune*

For more information about the literature and music of Lorenguard, visit:
www.Lorenguard.com

A LORENGUARD NOVEL

EVE OF CORRUPTION

BOOK ONE OF THE DAYS OF ASTASIA

By Brady Sadler

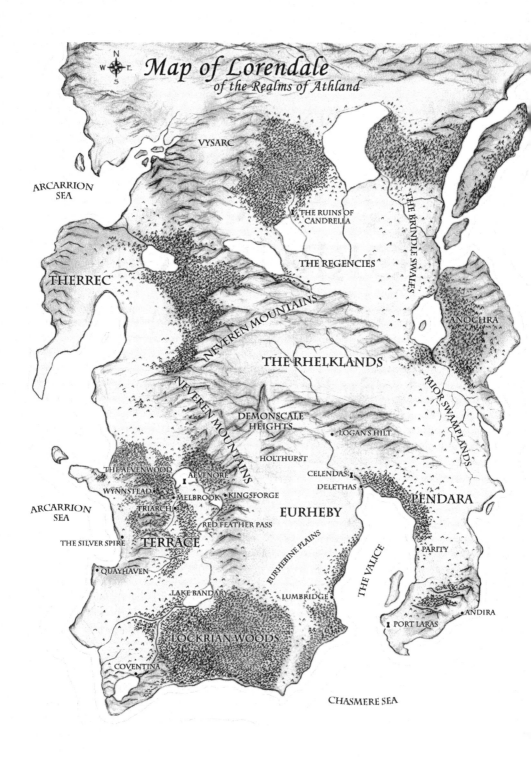

Map of Lorendale
of the Realms of Athland

ARCARRION
SEA

VYSARC

THERREC

THE RUINS OF
CANDRELLA

THE REGENCIES

THE BRINDLE SWALES

ANOCHRA

NEVEREN MOUNTAINS

THE RHELKLANDS

MIOR SWAMPLANDS

DEMONSCALE
HEIGHTS

LOGAN'S HILT

HOLTHURST

NEVEREN MOUNTAINS

THE ALVENWOOD

AEVENORE

CELENDAS

DELETHAS

PENDARA

WYNNSTEAD

MELBROOK

KINGSFORGE

ARCARRION
SEA

TRIARCH

EURHEBY

THE SILVER SPIRE

RED FEATHER PASS

TERRACE

PARITY

QUAYHAVEN

EURHEBINE PLAINS

THE VALICE

LAKE BANDARY

LUMBRIDGE

ANDIRA

PORT LARAS

LOCKRIAN WOODS

COVENTINA

CHASMERE SEA

For my wife Sarah,
here is a mere fragment of the inspiration your love has given me.

For my daughter Rylie,
with hopes that you'll read this someday.

And for my Lorenguard brothers,
for giving me a reason to do this.

I'd like to draw attention to the following fans who have gone above and beyond to show their support for Lorenguard:

Timmy Foley from Australia, Michael Johnson from Middle-earth, Graham Morgan and his wife Sammi (you guys have stuck with us!), little Harper Konieczka with her parents Corey and Shannon, Daniel Millard from Black Wind Metal, Michael Barnes from Fortress Ameritrash, Victor Hernandez from Spain, Power Metal Dom from Germany, pretty little Harper Griest, and Juan Carlos Mariño from Uruguay.

You guys are making this a reality, and we thank you deeply!

PROLOGUE

Andira, down the east coast of Pendara

Two cloaked figures walked through the dead streets of Andira. One wore ashen robes while the other was wrapped in pitch black. Both moved with a sense of urgency and purpose. The figure in black—a woman—removed the hood of her cloak to reveal a head of long, dark hair. It spilled to her shoulders, thin and straight. Her suspicious eyes darted around, surveying the ruined city, and, while she did see several rats scurry into the ruins of a church, she did not notice the great galley on the distant horizon, rocking on the gentle waves of the sea.

"Where is everyone?" she asked her companion, while following him through the remains of the once-proud port city.

The taller figure threw back his hood to reveal sharp, regal features, his eyes more certain and knowing than hers. He pointed down to the crude streets underneath their feet. "Below, my love. The ceremony is to begin soon. We must hurry," he insisted as he took her hand.

But she slowed her pace, stopping him short. "I don't know, Mathias. Something feels wrong…"

Mathias turned, his eyes suddenly narrowing.

With their attention on each other, neither noticed the small skiff departing the large galley, slowly making for the rotting harbor of Andira. The silhouettes of two figures rowed their way toward the battered remains of the docks.

"Rya," Mathias began, malice creeping into his voice, "you said you believed." He released her hand. "After everything we've been through…finding the lost fragment of the Binding Ritual, tracking down the one scribe able to translate it…after all that, do you really want to return to the Spire so that old coward, that conjurer of lies, can claim the Shackles for his own?"

Rya Kindell, an Entrusted of the Silver Spire Academy, stared at Mathias as if he had just asked her to betray everything she had ever known…which was exactly what he asked of her. Before she met Mathias, she was blind, just another mortal swayed to believe that Sol Saradys and his followers were nothing more than vile parasites, seeking the world's destruction. Rya's eyes had been opened to these and many more of the Cult of the Burning One's ideas over the course of her adventures with Mathias. Love has a strange way of opening one's mind.

The cult's teachings said that the Balance was merely a restraint placed upon mortals by the tyrant gods of the Heavenly Realms. They believed Sol Saradys was the savoir who could free them from their prison so they might harness the hidden magicks that were denied to the world.

Rya could not deny the temptation these beliefs presented. As a student of the Silver Spire, the only institute associated with magic study in all of Lorendale, she wanted magic more than anything: real magic, no more alchemy or rituals. Upon meeting Mathias, the teachings of the Silver Spire slowly became a memory as the possibilities of love and magic set a fire under her heart. Yet, here she was—in the ghostly streets of a city that was once glorious—and doubt choked her like a serpent coiling around her neck.

"Do you?" Mathias asked her again, challenging her new faith. "Do you really want to go back to the tower?"

Rya shook her head, her eyes searching beyond Mathias as though to make sure no one else witnessed her denial.

Mathias took her hand again, drawing her eyes back to his. "Then let us make haste." His other hand rose up to brush Rya's cheek. "We must let the congregation see who was responsible for bringing them their salvation."

As the two held each other's gaze, neither saw the two shadowy figures dock their skiff at a vacant dock. Mathias and Rya exchanged a few more whispered words as the intruders crept through the tattered alleys. A swelling chant could be heard coming from the center of the city, summoning all the devotees of the Cult of the Burning One. Mathias and Rya turned in that direction, holding hands as they made their way toward the awaiting masses.

One of the shadows—dressed in deep crimson—stopped long enough to watch the two cultists march off to their master's call, before he turned the other direction to follow his companion to a different doom.

Einrist was busy at his scribing table when the eyeless priest walked in. They were deep in the bowels of the old baron's estate in Andira, where footsteps would echo like whispers from the Abyss. Einrist had been confined to his study for more days than he cared to count, partly out of his scholarly desire to finish his work, but more so to remove himself from the disturbing company of the cultists. If it wasn't an undulating chant at sundown to honor the Burning One, it was a dark ritual at midnight to turn men into beasts. Sometimes it was an act of perverse debauchery in which all of the cultists were invited to share. Whatever ritual this night brought, Einrist cared not to witness it.

"We sail for Vhaltas in three days," hissed the priest from his drawn hood, the shadows forming dark pools where his eyes had once been. "The congregation is waiting." He was robed in colors of ash—as was the custom of the cultists—with a dark red sash to signify his rank, and a flaming staff in his grimy hand. Einrist knew the only wood that burned indefinitely was harvested from the malign trees of Vhaltas, yet these Burning Priests treated their staves as if they were recovered from the very forests of Nekriark. "The rites must be ready."

Einrist set aside his quill in favor of the old chalice on his table that was filled with Pendaran red. He drank deep, keeping his back to the priest as he spoke, "I believe these dead languages would have been translated days ago if it were not for these incessant interruptions." He let his voice echo as he took another long drink. "Correct me if I am wrong, but the Burning One has slept for over 600 years. I do not think that another few days, or a week, or even a year would vex him much at this point." He drank again. "And do not propose to rush my work. I need not remind you of the importance of these documents, without which your people have no reason to sail." Einrist turned and motioned toward the door. "Now if you would be so kind…"

The priest did not move, silently contemplating the brash words. He stared at the old scribe with the hollows of his eyes, his flaming staff flaring brightly. Defeated, the priest turned to leave in silence.

Einrist set down his wine to return to his work, but the sizzling sound of a dying flame caught his attention, followed by the sound of a man choking on his own blood. The scribe spun in his seat, his arm knocking over the chalice and spilling red wine across his table. Dark liquid crept down the slanting wood, narrowly avoiding his work. In the dimly lit hall outside,

Einrist could see the priest's body sprawled out on the floor, his staff extinguished. Above the lifeless body stood a thin man dressed in bright crimson with long blonde hair, a dripping dagger in hand.

The scribe's heart began to race, not because he mourned the priest's death, but because he did not want to join him on his way down to the Abyss. Einrist was not employed by the most honorable of men, and many enemies quite literally hid in the shadows of Andira. A quick scan of the room assured him that there were no weapons with which to protect himself. He had only his wits—which was a blessing, as they were much more polished than his abilities with a sword. "You are not a cultist."

"No," answered a voice from the darkness. The voice was not the assassin's, who remained standing above his kill wiping his blade clean. "I am a godless man, such as you, Scribe, and I am fascinated by your recent findings."

Einrist positioned himself between the voice from the darkness and the scattered parchment on his table. "How do you know who I am?" Einrist asked, intrigued. He was well known in Lorendale for his contributions to the religious world and for his knowledge in language and translating texts. However, this stranger didn't immediately strike Einrist as a man of the Faith, meaning he was either a scholar or an agent from the Silver Spire. Einrist liked neither prospect.

The stranger stepped into the light. He was young. His long, dark coat, along with the rapier at his waist, told the scribe that the man was a merchant sailor from Pendara. Einrist had spent enough years at the ports of Laras to know how much the Pendara traders favored their fashion.

"Would you believe that you and I are in the same trade? Procuring of holy relics, dealing in ancient texts…we both profit off of the faith of others."

Einrist grinned slightly. "Well now, I would absolutely agree with you if you hadn't just murdered one of my employers. I seem to be suddenly lacking patronage."

The stranger's face was impassive. It was unsettling for Einrist to see such a young man appear completely emotionless.

The stranger spoke again. "I have come to present you with a more rewarding offer than whatever the cultists promised you."

"Well, the cultists promised me a new carriage, two steeds to haul her, and enough currents to fill her. What do you have to offer, boy?"

Not even being called 'boy' seemed to affect the stranger. He simply replied, "Illumination."

Einrist chuckled slightly, disguising his own unease at the stranger's demeanor. "I am too old for illumination, my friend. I profit from ignorance, anyway."

The stranger pointed to the parchment on the scribe's table. "If you complete the deciphering of that ritual for me instead of for the cult, I will be able to show the world that the Balance is a myth." He held up his hands innocently. "Or the gods will smite me for my blasphemy. Either way, we shall all have illumination."

Something crawled up Einrist's spine—a cold sensation that could have been doubt or fear, or both. He forced a smile. "This ritual is quite valuable, boy, and the only one of its kind. Though, I'm sure you know that. Why else would you be here?" The scribe paused as if expecting an answer. When he received silence, he prattled on, hoping to disarm these villains. "Written by the Four, it is said, and used to bind Sol Saradys to the Stratovault. The cult went to great lengths to secure it, and they will go to even greater lengths to recover it again. Would you risk offending the Burning One's legions?"

The stranger smirked and called to the assassin behind him. "Scarlet." The man in crimson turned his back to Einrist and promptly began urinating on the dead priest whose hollow eyes drank the faint torchlight.

Despite the haunting fear that these men inspired, Einrist could not restrain the laughter. Yet, the mirth died, quickly becoming nervous laughter.

"I plan on defying the Burning One himself," the stranger said matter-of-factly. "I care little for his legions."

"Very well," said Einrist, desperately trying to maintain his composure. "And if the ritual succeeds and you wake the Corruptor? It is said that he shall claim a champion once more and return to this world as a mortal. What then?"

"I will kill him."

The bluntness of the statement should have made Einrist laugh again. But he couldn't even smile. He knew he was staring at a dark soul, strangely capable. Regardless of Einrist's faith, he was also a historian, and he knew very well of the destruction wrought by the man who called himself Sol Saradys during the War of the Scales. That power was real to Einrist. All he could ask was, "How?"

"I do not have to tell you the story of Sol Saradys' imprisonment and the Shackles that bind him," the stranger began, tucking his hands behind his back as he began to pace around the study. "But I may have to remind you that if he were to awaken, the bindings would still hold him in his prison. He would be unable to take mortal form again unless a willing vessel surrendered to his will. What if such a willing vessel did not exist?"

The blonde assassin called Scarlet stepped forward, straightening his belt that held an assortment of exotic blades.

Einrist understood. These men meant to ensure no cultist lived to welcome the Burning One's possession of their body. He wrinkled his brow in interest. "So you plan to take war to Vhaltas? Maybe you could employ the witch hunters of the Sect to help you with that." He turned to refilled his chalice, feigning boredom. "But you do not believe any of this will matter? You do not believe in the Balance…"

"I do not." The stranger stopped pacing. "And neither do you. Yet, much of the world does, and I mean to change that. Much like you once did."

Einrist gave him a confused look.

"Before you killed my parents."

Einrist stared at the brazen youth for a long moment until realization slowly sank in. When it did, the wine decanter slipped from his hand and shattered on the floor, splashing red wine all over his cream colored coat. "Donovan…"

"And spare me your denials," Donovan continued, emotion now finding its way into his voice. "I was there. The Spearitans may have executed them, but their deaths were of your making, Einrist."

Sweat began to collect upon the scribe's wrinkled brow. He remembered the days when he sailed with the Marlowes on their excursions to the lost islands of the Chasmere Sea. Those expeditions had made Einrist an extremely wealthy man for a time, selling relics of Chaos to the Spearitan churches and the secret traders of the Silver Spire.

The Marlowes were left to take the blame when the Spearitans turned their backs on the business and accused the ship's entire crew of heresy. Einrist served as a guide for the Marlowes' campaign, as he was the most knowledgeable of the lost tombs they raided. So, he was the first to be approached by the Spearitan paladins. In exchange for the information Einrist provided about the expeditions, his life was spared. The rest of the crew were burned as heretics, including Donovan's parents.

Einrist remembered seeing young Donovan on the day of the execution, spared on account of his age. Those dark eyes of his hadn't changed. They were forever seared into Einrist's soul.

"Donovan, I could not prevent it," the scribe began. "The Spearitans hold too much sway in Pendara..."

"The past is done," Donovan said plainly. "I am not here to speak of it. You will finish the ritual for me."

Einrist felt a surge of relief that Donovan cared only for the translations, not for revenge. The scribe could part with parchment and heresy, and even forgo the cult's payment, in exchange for his life. He reasoned that he could end this business respectably. "You are in luck, Donovan. I have had these works completed for days. I only meant to postpone the priests for another week so that I might negotiate additional currents from them once they became impatient." He smiled weakly.

Donovan stepped forward to peer at the desk behind Einrist. He seemed content at what he saw. "Very well."

In a sudden flash, Donovan's rapier was unsheathed. The thin blade slid silently between the old man's ribs. Einrist choked on his breath as the blade pierced through his back. He looked up into his killer's eyes. They were dark and certain. Of all the thoughts that ran through the dying scribe's mind, only one was spoken through his broken gasps.

"What...if the Balance...is real?"

Donovan withdrew his blade and looked on Einrist's work. The faintest hint of a smile flashed across his face. "Then call me Skall, for I shall usher in the Days of Astasia."

Einrist's final thoughts were of Skall, the Son of Chaos, who was said to be the harbinger of Astasia. He almost smiled as he died, watching Donovan and his assassin leave the study as his vision faded. He looked down at his bloodied hands. The blood that seeped from his wound mixed with the wine that stained his clothes. His final coughs sounded almost like laughter.

He had taken part in the destruction of the gods. There were worse ways to die.

CHAPTER 1: THE SILVER SPIRE
The Silver Spire, West Terrace

"Astasia," said Grand Adjurer Marakus, "is a theory, young Master Rutherford, not a governance. If we were to abide by every theory we heard, then we would all bury our dead in the ocean so they could not hear the calls of Nekriark to wake them from the dead. Or we would sleep standing up, so the marons of the Revery could not sit on our chests to give us nightmares." Marakus animated these exaggerated beliefs by waving his old arms in the air in mock horror. The class shared a quiet laugh.

Anerith Zathon watched Rutherford's face redden, obviously embarrassed that he raised his hand in the first place.

Anerith heard Demitri and Xavia snicker behind him with the rest of the class, but he simply turned a page in *Book IV of Astasia*. Rutherford's question wasn't necessarily idiotic, but Rutherford was, so Anerith tended to ignore the boy's incessant questions. However, since today's lesson was on the writings of Uresiphe and his beliefs on the Balance, Anerith supposed that Rutherford's question was covered in the readings—which Rutherford surely had not read. Anerith skimmed ahead to refresh his own memory.

"Yes?" Marakus began, "Miss Maldroth?"

Anerith stopped reading, suddenly forgetting what he was looking for. He turned slightly so he could see Xavia seated behind him. She was leaning over her lectern with her arm raised high into the air, eager yet graceful. Xavia was older than Anerith, nearing her twenty second year. She had long dark hair that always seemed to float, and her mouth had a way of captivating a young man, no matter what she was using it for.

Demitri sat next to her, as he always did, his black hair streaked with unnatural white. He gave Anerith a cross-eyed look while motioning to red-faced Rutherford. Demitri and Xavia rarely tired of poking fun at young Rutherford who, unlike them, came from a wealthy family.

"Grand Adjurer," began Xavia, her voice sharp with an eastern accent. "I have heard that our own Luminary has many writings about the Balance and Astasia in his personal library. Perhaps if we were to—"

"That will be enough, Xavia," Marakus commanded, his scratchy voice carrying authority. "I have told you before: the Luminary has no such secret library, nor does he drink wine with the Underlords, nor does he keep pet dragons. May we please return to our lesson?"

Xavia gave a resigned sigh and leaned back in her chair.

"Now," said Marakus, brushing the long white hair from his sweaty forehead. "While Rutherford's assumption blatantly conflicts with today's assigned reading, he does make a valid point. Many people are led to believe that Astasia is the apocalypse, which is not necessarily a falsehood, but quite a leap nonetheless. Astasia is the idea of living in a world that is left unchecked by the gods, which some may consider the end of the world..." Marakus looked over his moon-shaped glasses at the ever-pious Evelyn Truman seated in the front row, a sixth year Accepted that was quite open about her beliefs.

Most of the class, including Evelyn herself, shared another laugh.

Marakus almost smiled before continuing. "It all depends on your religious sensationalism. For the sake of argument, let us all assume that the Balance is fundamentally proven: there is magic in the world and the Balance governs how the good and bad magic is to be divided. If you worship the Four as Miss Truman does, then you are probably of the belief that the Balance is inherently good: Athlas clearly crafted the Balance to ensure equality among the inhabitants of the mortal realms. However, there are others that believe the Balance only encourages holy wars. Since Order and Chaos are cursed to always be at war with one another, the Balance only ensures that neither side could ever be defeated by the other. Thus, in this light, the Four are nothing more than tyrannical forces that must care only to watch mortals kill each other."

Evelyn's hand shot up with such force that it made a nearby silken tapestry dance against the wall.

"Easy, Miss Truman," Marakus said, slightly raising his hands in defense. "I am not preaching; these are only theories. Your theology Adjurer will no doubt gladly hold religious debates, but this is neither the time nor place. Are there any more questions regarding Uresiphe's writings on Astasia?"

Anerith raised his hand then, not even knowing what he was going to ask.

A small look of surprise washed over Marakus' face, but the shock faded as quickly as it had come, and he nodded for Anerith to speak. The class turned to the youngest Adept in the Spire.

Anerith bit his lip and looked down at the page he was reading. It was a worn tome, and, judging by the stains on the leathery pages, had obviously seen use by many students before him. The chapter was entitled *Magicks Governed by the Balance*. Anerith looked back up to Marakus; the smoke from the burning incense on the Adjurer's podium gave him the look of a pensive god. "If Astasia is the absence of Balance in the world, and you believe there is no magic in the world to be kept in check, wouldn't it be safe to say that we live in Astasia now?"

Marakus smiled. "Insightful, Master Zathon. The thinkers dwell in silence, so it seems. However, your hypothesis is based on my beliefs, which are irrelevant. Beliefs have no place in logic, and this course is designed to teach the *Books of Astasia* from a logical standpoint." Marakus fell silent for a moment, looking at the class that he held in rapt attention. "And yet, I will answer your question, Anerith, for I think it is a perspective that is important to this study. No, I do not think we live in Astasia, because I do believe in magic and I do believe in the Balance. But, my beliefs should not have any bearing on your own, mind you," he said, waving his crocked finger at the whole class. "I believe that magic—*true* magic—is a resource, and the world was bled dry of it a long time ago. And, I believe the Balance is a property, one that cannot run out, but can be destroyed." He raised an eyebrow. "I will leave you with that today."

"Thank the gods!" exclaimed Demitri as they walked out of class. Xavia laughed, holding onto his arm as Rutherford and Anerith followed. "Marakus is the only thing duller than the readings he assigns."

Anerith hefted the heavy *Book IV of Astasia* in one arm as he tried to slide his other into his red robes. "At least I'm starting to enjoy his course more than Elementology. If I have to set one more thing on fire…"

"Of course you'd enjoy it," Xavia said mockingly. "You actually do the readings. I hate theories and philosophy. Give me fire and alchemy any day."

"Look!" Rutherford exclaimed suddenly, pointing toward the Adjurer's dormitory hall. A huge door could be seen at the end of the hall. All the students of the Spire shared the belief that the huge, menacing iron door led down to the 'dungeons,' but none had truly been down there. "Someone went in!"

Demitri and Anerith scoffed in unison.

"What did you see?" Xavia asked, taking a step toward the dormitory hall, clearly intrigued.

"A shadow," Demitri said, pulling at the sleeve of Xavia's robes. "Let's go get some food. I'm famished."

"I want to see…" Xavia began.

"Now, now," said a deep voice from behind. They all spun around to see Adjurer Marakus waving a crooked finger. "Unless you want to clean my quarters, young lady, you know the rules. No students allowed."

The four solemnly took the stairs down to the main floor. They took their lunch in the courtyard where they usually ate and shared a meal of hard bread, cheese, dried meat, and an exotic fruit from Rokuus, the name of which none of them could pronounce, but all agreed it was delicious. They spent their meal discussing their lives at the Spire: classes, Adjurers, and the recent disappearance of their friend Rya Kindell, who wore the black robes of an Entrusted. After awhile, the sonorous bells rang out, announcing the next half of their day.

They were all about to return to the Silver Spire when Rutherford leaned in and whispered to the rest of them.

"Who's that?"

Anerith squinted against the sunlight to see what Rutherford saw. The outer gates of the walls surrounding the Spire had been opened and the Vigilants on either side had their bows out with arrows notched. They only did so when visitors came. The visitors that now strode into the courtyard were armed men, led by a man in a satin black cloak with silver heraldry that Anerith could not make out from this distance.

The leader was younger than his retinue, but walked with an unmistakable air of nobility.

"That's Baron VonAnthony!" Xavia hissed. Anerith could smell the fruit on her breath and he leaned away from her, shifting uncomfortably. "His wife used to be an Entrusted here, one of the Luminary's black robes." The Spire had a ranking system with its students: red robes were Adepts, blue robes were Agravites, white robes were worn by the Accepted. Each specialized in a certain study of lore. Black robes, however, were only worn by the most elite of the Spire's students, excelling in all lore. They personally trained under the Silver Spire's Luminary, Vanghrel Thondrane, who ranked above all others. "I heard she went missing a while back while on a quest for the Luminary. Just like Rya." They all exchanged worried looks, but Xavia quickly changed the subject. "I wonder what the baron is doing here."

"Maybe looking for a new wife," Demitri offered. In return, Xavia offered him an elbow in the ribs.

The group watched intently as the baron walked along the silver stone path, winding through the elegant shrubbery that decorated the courtyard. His company was flanked on either side by Vigilants, the black garbed watchers of the Silver Spire. Rumor had it they were all Rokuusian assassins, but they wore masks and gloves, revealing none of the olive skin and elongated features the Rokuusians were known for.

"More secrets," Xavia said under her breath.

Anerith sighed quietly. Xavia was certain that something sinister was afoot in the Spire, and she was determined to find out what it was. She had easily dragged Rutherford into her conspiracies, since the fool was desperate to be a part of anything that distracted him from his studies. Anerith could tell Demitri was also on the verge of joining her campaign...compelled by other motives, of course.

"He's just here to pledge support," Anerith said, returning to his open book. "The Spire can't survive without noble patronage. Barons, dukes, and even kings visit now and again. We've all seen them."

Xavia shook her head and watched the baron's company disappear into the Silver Spire, her mouth tightening.

"They are late," Myriad grumbled as he peered into the dark orb. He was a short creature, barely able to see over the Luminary's table, but he carried an exceptional amount of confidence and malice in his small, dark-skinned frame. "You said they were suited for this task, Luminary." His eyes glowed violently green.

Vanghrel busied himself with the cluster of maps littering the table in front of him, avoiding the stare from those fathomless voids that seemed to oversee every move he made in his tower—*his* tower, not the demon's. Vanghrel had been Luminary of the Spire since its conception and construction, though the demon Myriad had been a resident of the depths below for even longer, giving the creature the notion that the tower was his.

"The realms are wide, dear Myriad," the Luminary said as he smoothed out a rather large map depicting Athland and the vast Arcarrion Sea to emphasis his point, "but my wyverns know the way. And my Entrusted know better than to return empty-handed." Scattered across the map were several black stones used to track Vanghrel's agents. Rya's stone was on the southeastern shores of Pendara, near the ruins of Andira. Benegast's stone was still north in Therrec. Vanghrel had not heard from either of them in days, but he did not inform the demon of such troubling news. "They know failure is not accepted. Their lateness bodes well, in my opinion." Vanghrel's voice was raspy and malicious, but it did not hold a candle to Myriad's.

"That is all well and good," Myriad offered, "but for too long has this campaign been halted." He paced about the wide chamber. The long, black table in the center was flanked by high-reaching bookshelves lined with countless tomes. The elegant furnishings clashed with the slick stone surroundings, but they served their purpose. An eerie blue light illuminated the space, provided by the mystical flames that were known as cold fires. The demon stared in contempt at his surroundings. "I do not know how much longer I can endure this place, Vanghrel." Myriad suddenly sounded more like a whining child than the demon he was. This caught Vanghrel's attention, and the Luminary's eyes followed Myriad's pacing. The demon looked like nothing more than a small and wrinkled man. His dark, ashen skin spoke the truth of his ancestry, born from the wicked depths of Volkris in the Abyssal Realms. His wiry hair was silver and hung down past his shoulders. Two small tusks protruded from his lower jaw, causing his forked tongue to occasionally slip through his sharp teeth.

Myriad turned and stared into Vanghrel's eyes. "To live this close to the surface of your world and remain as a prisoner below dishonors my kind. I mean not to bear it much longer."

Vanghrel caught the desperation in Myriad's voice. "The time will come, Myriad, you have my word, which you know to be of worth. The Shackles of Heaven will be ours, the Balance will crumble, and the Gates of the Abyss shall be opened wide. All has been foretold in the *Books of Astasia*."

Myriad's eyes met the Luminary's and Vanghrel saw in

them a spark of subtle contentment. The smaller figure nodded.

"Very well, Luminary. See it done." He turned to leave and motioned toward the dark orb upon the table. "And see to your guests."

The Luminary frowned and gazed into the orb. The shadowy mists parted in the orb to reveal the Spire's underground passageway lined with bones. Six men, led by two Vigilants, shouldered their way through by torchlight. Vanghrel noted one of them as Baron VonAnthony from Wynnstead. The Luminary's eyes narrowed.

"Demons. Everywhere I turn."

"The old man is blind, Anerith!" exclaimed Rutherford. After realizing how loud his voice was, Rutherford immediately lowered his head, ducking below the high hedges of the courtyard as if to escape the hearing of any passing Vigilants. Rutherford lowered his voice and moved closer to Anerith, raising the hood of his yellow Alchemist robe. "Xavia took me up to the Luminary's study three times! I bet we could have walked right in and he still wouldn't have noticed."

Anerith was reading from a large volume on the history of the Vysarcian Empire, pretending not to hear. Demitri and Xavia had another class after midday, to their fortune, leaving Anerith to deal with Rutherford on his own. He continued reading, hoping the younger student would move on and recruit someone else in the Spire's courtyard for his foolish nocturnal adventure. However, the Alchemist was not one to take a hint.

"You should come tomorrow night, Anerith, after the Adjurers retire," Rutherford said, peering over the book to get

Anerith's attention. "Demitri might come this time."

Anerith raised an eyebrow. "Did *he* say that? Or did Xavia tell you that?" Anerith wouldn't be extremely surprised if Demitri began to participate in Xavia's mischievous endeavors. He thought bitterly about how much time the two had been spending together lately. Perhaps she had finally gotten the best of Demitri. However, Anerith did find it a bit curious that Demitri would sacrifice his standing as an Agravite to cater to the whims of a girl.

Then again, Xavia was an exceptionally beautiful girl.

"Why does it matter?" asked Rutherford, frowning, suddenly entranced by the nearby fountain.

"He just made blue three moons ago," Anerith said with annoyance, referring to the blue robes worn by the Agravites, learners of gravity and the astral lore. "I highly doubt that he even associates with the Adepts anymore."

"You could make blue as well, Anerith," said an approaching voice from the other side of the fountain. "But you seem to prefer those red robes." Demitri threw a small pebble into the waters of the fountain as he passed.

"I prefer to stay grounded," replied Anerith, closing his book. "Don't you and Xavia have class?"

Demitri raised an eyebrow and flashed a mischievous smile.

Anerith shook his head, his insides twisting. "Forget it. Are you actually going to romp around the Spire at night with Rutherford and Xavia?"

Demitri gave the Alchemist a quick scowl.

Rutherford's eyes widened as he gathered himself to leave. "I have to return to Metallurgy. See you tomorrow, Demitri."

Anerith couldn't help but grin slightly. "How long did it take her to turn you into one of them, Demitri?"

Demitri gave his friend a rude gesture as he took a seat next to him on the stone bench. The noon sun beat down above them, and Demitri leaned back to feel the warmth of it on his face. His exceptionally long, white-streaked hair fell over his shoulders. "I think I love her, Anerith. I keep having these dreams...of me and her." He closed his eyes. "You know where I come from, Anerith. I could never take her as wife, but the dreams always feel so real."

Anerith's smile faded. He did not cherish having to discuss Xavia with Demitri, but Demitri was his closest friend. "Dreams are no reason to throw away any chance you have at Entrusted. I know how much that means to you. Let her and the other Adepts have their fun, just don't let her drag you in to it."

"But what if she's right?" Demitri asked, turning to face Anerith. "What if there are things hidden in the Spire? What if there are secrets?"

"To the Abyss with them," Anerith said. "If there are things hidden, they are probably hidden for good reason. Don't go digging in snake holes."

Demitri shook his head. "It's different." He looked around. Three other Adepts walked by and a Vigilant paced around the fountain. Demitri waited until the sentry was walking away from them. "I had this dream the other night. This... man told me that I could become an Entrusted by uncovering the Luminary's secrets. He told me I would be with Xavia and not have to hide our affections..."

"So you think snooping around the Spire is going to explain something about these dreams?"

Demitri ran a hand through his hair. Anerith remembered asking his friend about the sudden appearance of the pallid streaks in that hair. Demitri was too young to be losing his dark color, but the only reason he would offer was: "Experiments have their prices".

"The Luminary is old, Anerith," Demitri noted, "older than anyone else in the realms, I'm sure of it. Like it or not, Xavia's right. There is something more to this place, and he's hiding it."

Anerith exhaled pointedly. "Even if there is, why do you feel the need to be a part of it? There is more world out there than just the Academy." Anerith motioned beyond the walls of the sprawling Spire's courtyard. "Who cares if this place was founded on some witchery? It's not doing the world any harm staying secret. Just let it be."

"I can't."

Demitri spoke the words with such conviction that Anerith was taken aback. "Do you actually believe in the magic Marakus speaks of, Demitri?"

"I can't believe in what I don't know," Demitri said solemnly. After a moment, he smiled and turned to his friend. "Just like you." He stood up and looked at the Silver Spire as the wind caught his hair.

"But, unlike you, I have to know."

The Vigilant pacing around the fountain moments before was now gone, nowhere to be seen.

"I do not think you know what you are asking, Baron." Vanghrel sat at his black table across from his guests. "This is no small thing."

Baron Gabriel VonAnthony sat next to Toland, a balding man with burn scars across his face. The other five men-at-arms waited silently in the stone halls beyond the study doors. "I do not ask this on a whim, Vanghrel," the baron replied. "I have spent the last seven days preserving my wife's remains in preparation for her return. I know what must be done and I know the consequences that may arise. I do not ask you to involve yourself in any way, aside from aiding me in the means needed to perform the ritual."

Vanghrel restrained a fit of mocking laughter. *The means.* VonAnthony spoke of a necromantic text as if it were available in any nobleman's library. The fact that the baron implied that he were entitled to whatever resources the Spire had to offer made the outlandish request that much more entertaining. Before the Luminary could offer an appropriately contemptuous response, the baron continued.

"Of course you will be exceptionally well-compensated for assisting me in this endeavor. I am not known to be unkind to any ally of my house."

Vanghrel gave the man an arrogant smile—the kind of smile bestowed upon a begging man. "As generous as your offer sounds, Gabriel, the Spire is in no need of financial assistance at this time." The Luminary had recently accepted a sizeable donation from King Garrowin of Aevenore for inducting his nephew into the Spire. Under other circumstances, Vanghrel might have fulfilled the baron's wishes. However, his treasury was full and he didn't care for Gabriel's excessive confidence. Vanghrel would gladly sacrifice a few currents at the expense of annoying VonAnthony.

The baron's face was a mask, betraying no emotion. "I do not speak of coin, Vanghrel. The coffers of my house have been sparse as of late. However, I do possess other items of worth, if you would be willing to barter."

Vanghrel regarded his guests silently, awaiting the offer.

"I assume you have a bit of interest in artifacts of a spiritual nature," the baron began as he shot Toland a glance. The burned man reached to the pack at his side. "It has also come to my attention that you have dedicated yourself over the years to the recovery of the Shackles of Heaven."

Vanghrel's face tightened and he instinctively clenched his fists. He watched as Toland produced a small scroll case and set it in front of the baron. The Luminary had no idea why the baron seemed to know so much of his affairs, and it was far from pleasing. Vanghrel wanted to set the scroll case aflame along with the cocky baron that grinned at him from across the table. He would not, however, risk such things on this trivial man.

Gabirel laid a hand on the scroll case. "Surely you are asking yourself how I know of this campaign. However, it is in your own favor that I know such things. I offer you assistance in your quest, in exchange for a small favor from the Spire in the form of my wife's resurrection."

Vanghrel's eyes narrowed. "Is that..."

"That," said the baron, patting the case with his hand, "is the only remaining document of the Binding Ritual, written with the coals of Prythene, upon the parchment of Uldagard, cleansed in the waters of Acrivas, and delivered by the winds of Sollum. I am sure you possess a copy of the other half, written by the Underlords. Those circulate in the slums of any major city. Yet, as you know, the Heavenly language cannot be duplicated, making this one of the rarest artifacts in the world."

Vanghrel tried to retain his skepticism, but his sheer optimism—or desperation—had won him over. "How?"

The baron shrugged. "A shaman in Therrec was robbed and killed. These things happen. Do we have an accord?"

"Would you truly offer me this, in exchange for a mortal life?" Vanghrel began to collect himself. "You hold in your hands the key to undoing the world, and you would trade that to undo a death?"

The baron's face soured, as if he swallowed bitter wine. "I would gladly trade the world for my wife, Luminary. In all honesty, she would want you to have this. I offer you something that serves both our purposes. My wife was one of your best students, and she died in pursuit of magic. She would want this. And I want her."

Vanghrel tried not to laugh. Helena was far from his best student, and she had killed herself trying to usurp the Revery. She got what she well deserved, yet he chose not press the matter.

"Let me locate the necessary text," Vanghrel said as he left the table and headed toward his hidden libraries. On his way, he contemplated the possibilities now presenting themselves to him. He had wanted to wait to secure the other Shackles before daring to disturb the bindings on Sol Saradys. However, things have a way of changing course. As he slid the stone wall away that hid his more precious volumes, a small demon the size of a cat scurried out of the alcove and into the darkness. Vanghrel couldn't help but smile. Soon, he could loose them upon the world to forever serve him.

On a shelf rested a book that was encased in death. The skin-like material that bound the tome was withered with age, and on the cover was scrawled the title *Permissions of Nekriark*. He retrieved the book that would serve the baron's purpose and turned back toward the study. Suddenly, Vanghrel realized he needed another Entrusted to carry out his new plans. The others were probably dead. Young Xavia Maldroth was the first to cross his mind. Like Rya, she was a cunning and hungry Adept, but he quickly decided against it. Xavia was too willful, which was probably what led to Rya's demise.

Yet, there was another who showed a certain promise. What was his name?

Anerith?

CHAPTER 2: THE PRINCE OF DOOM
Celendas, the kingdom city of Eurheby

The towers of Celendas reached higher than any other in Lorendale. Atop the highest of these, King Alastair Galvian stirred from a nightmarish sleep. He rubbed the weariness from his eyes while reflecting on his dreams. They were filled with memories from his youth, of swordplay and adventure—things he saw very little of these days. He yawned and stretched as the morning sunlight poured in.

Behind him, the bed was empty.

"I dreamt you were taken by dragons, Magdalene," Alastair mused aloud to the specter that shared his bed. The queen had been dead for over twenty years, yet he spoke to her every morning. "The Dragon's Dawn had come and the wars had started anew. I rode out into the mountains on a white courser to rescue you." He betrayed a smile. "Theodric and Cedric rode with me."

Through the open balcony doors, Alastair could see the sun peeking over the horizon, the morning light shimmering on the waters of the Valice. It was early, earlier than he usually woke these days. Something was amiss. He thought he saw ship sails on the far edges of the Valice, but as he stretched his legs and walked out into the open air, he saw it was only a flock birds taking flight in the distance. Below, he could see his city waking to the dawn. Smoke poured from the chimney of Rault Bridger's bakery, and Waldron Thace's river flats were already carrying goods down the Celedine River to the ports of Delethas.

The king ran calloused hands through his thinning gray hair and paced back into his chamber. Something made him uneasy.

Alastair was about to cross the room to don his robe when he heard a faint hiss from outside of his chambers. He went to the heavy oak doors to investigate, opening them but a little to prevent them from creaking. Out in the hall, he noted that one of his guards had been relieved, and the remaining sentry was being scolded by a frail figure in a heavy velvet robe. The king's High Councilor was an older man, and his voice had become serpentine from years of speaking in whispers.

The king opened the door, surprised that it did not creak as much as usual. "Gledra?" Alastair asked, stifling a yawn. "Where is Myron? And what has Kessley done to deserve such wrath?"

Geldra peered at the king from below his hood and bowed his head. "I am sorry if I woke you, your majesty." He turned back to the guard with fury in his old watery eyes. "It was your watchmen's duty to wake me before dawn. However, it seems that Myron has lost his way to my chambers this morning. He no doubt found his way to the kitchens instead."

The king smiled. "Does your ward no longer wake you in the morning?"

Geldra removed his hood and approached the king. "No, your majesty. Camry has more important business. We had visitors last night, near midnight. Camry has been attending to them since their arrival. I asked these two sots to wake me before sunrise so I could inform you of their presence as soon as you woke."

Alastair nodded. "Very good, Geldra. I have been informed. Now, perhaps you can tell me what sort of business our visitors bring with them." The king turned toward his room, stretching his arms. "Have some Pendara merchants broken another of their ship's ornaments on our docks? We will not pay them for their own mistakes. Just send them to Geyer. I am not awake enough to discuss currents, and I am to see to Captain Nol from the Hilt before supper."

Geldra followed the king into his chambers, taking a moment to bow at the threshold. "Your majesty, these visitors have come from Aevenore with urgent tidings."

Alastair paused after donning his robe and turned to face his councilor. "Aevenore?" He furrowed his brow. "Please, Geldra, tell me the king has finally come to his senses and sent us aid. The Rhelklanders threaten their lands as well as our own. Logan's Hilt cannot stand against these constant assaults."

Geldra shook his head. "As to that, I know not. They wished only to speak to you. But this was no contingent of knights; only a few minor lords. The king's cousins or retainers no doubt." Geldra looked somewhat nervously at his hands. "They carry with them ill news; I do not doubt it."

The king sighed. "I can always count on you to brighten my mornings, Geldra. Go. Summon the councilors. Do not bother calling on Geyer; let him tend to the treasury. Fetch Tanith and Carthys."

The king strode toward the balcony to shut the doors as Geldra retreated from the chambers. The king shouted after him, "And find my son!"

The crown prince of Celendas choked on a mouthful of wine as his chair began to topple. Laughter erupted from the table as he fell backward, staining his purple tunic with the finest that the Celendas vineyards had to offer. The morning bells were chiming beyond the keep's walls, but they could barely be heard above the merriment.

"And she never even knew I was in the bed as well!" Kable attempted to finish his story over the laughter, but it was too overpowering. The spectacle that Cedric had made drew all attention from Kable's latest tale of conquest. Kable shook his head at the sight of Cedric rolling on the floor, the prince's long dark hair spilling into a puddle of wasted wine.

Stroman Hale, the wharfmaster of Port Cray, stood up and slapped his bulging belly. He could hardly speak through his coughing laughter, but he managed to compliment Kable on another fine victory. When the other lords got over their merriment, Stroman bid them farwell. "Well, the sun be up now, I reckon. Another night of hard work with you fine men, and now I must face another morning of retching and sleeping. Good morrow, good sirs!"

Cedric, still lying face-up on the floor, raised his empty goblet to Stroman. "Good morrow, fine sir! May the waters flow as well as your own!"

This brought more laughter from the remaining men around the table. Kable Orton straightened his tunic and rose from his chair. Although he had laughed with the others, he now wore the usual resigned face he saved for whenever the prince stole the floor from him. Kable was one of the few nobles that still referred to Cedric as the Prince of Doom merely out of spite, but never within the prince's company.

"I must retire as well, my lords," Kable said with a slight bow. "I have a few companions awaiting me this morning, so I will bid you all farewell." He grabbed his remaining ale from the table and finished it in one gulp.

"Do take the lift, Kable," Cedric said, still lying on the

floor and trying to drink what was left of his wine. "I would not like to see you roll down the keep's stairs again."

Kable gave the prince a slight grin to hide his resentment and nodded. "Good morning, my lords."

Only the prince, his good friend Lord Raymun Landover, and the lift operator's young son, Durrek, remained around the table. Trying to contain his laughter, Raymun stood up to help the prince to his feet while Cedric hummed a tuneless melody and rolled across the wine-soaked floor. Durrek, who had been hiding his shy smile for the entire morning, began to clean up the emptied flagons left behind by the departed lords.

"Arise, my prince!" Raymun announced mockingly. He took Cedric's hand and pulled the nearly limp prince to his feet. "I must away myself, before my father sends the dogs after me."

"Oh, come, Raymun!" Cedric said drunkenly. "Let us have another glass: a toast to the morning. Let our fathers wait." Cedric held out his empty glass toward the busy lift operator's son. "Boy! The king's son commands you to–"

"Go and see to your father, Durrek," Raymun ordered him, motioning for the lad to forget his cleaning. "The lifts no doubt need attention."

Cedric fell back into his chair once Raymun had stood him up. "Let them take the stairs!" Cedric said lazily, almost falling asleep in his chair. "The prince shall not drink alone!"

Durrek looked confused, unsure of exactly whose command to obey.

"Do not stall, Durrek," Raymun said sternly. "If the king is forced to take the stairs down from his chambers, he will no doubt be in a fiery mood. Go."

Durrek bowed without a word, and turned to leave the room. A glass fell from the table and broke.

Prince Cedric had fallen asleep.

Not a moment after Durrek had closed the council room doors, they were thrown open again as the Tower Guard Myron Sties stormed in. Myron's eyes narrowed on Raymun from beneath his ornamented helm.

"Was that the lift-hand's boy who just ducked out of here?" Myron asked, with fury buried in his strong voice. "I had to march down every bleeding step of this keep last night because no one was answering the damned bells! Were you giving him drink again?"

Raymun gave Myron an apologetic grin, and then stepped aside so the guard could see his prince. Cedric was fast asleep, drooling.

"Ah, Dhullus take me!" Myron growled, trying to keep his anger contained in presence of the prince, sleeping or not. "Has he been at it all night?"

"Mostly just this morning," Raymun said. "I'll clean this up, Myron, don't you worry."

"Pardon my curtness, my lord, but be quick about it. Old Geldra has called a small council this morning and the king means for his son to attend." Myron pointed toward the snoring prince. "Sober him up and I'll get the kitchen to clean this place. Just don't let the king see him."

Raymun nudged Cedric. "Come on, duty calls."

Cedric groaned and shifted in his seat. Raymun sighed and threw the prince's arm over his shoulder and forced him to his feet.

Myron cursed under his breath as he turned from the sight. "The kingdom is surely doomed."

Tanith Elton studied the body. The eyes had been gouged

out and the mouth mutilated. This was an obvious attack against the Cult of the Burning One, whose presence in Celendas has been the subject of local rumor lately. Tanith's armor creaked as he reached up to scratch his thick neck. *They always take the eyes*, Tanith thought to himself. He found that ironic, considering that was the practice Burning Priests used to initiate a new member into their order. He recalled the old saying: one does not need eyes to be led by corruption.

The body laid like some slaughtered animal in an alley not a stone's throw away from the keep's walls. Tanith tilted his head slightly and determined that the victim was once a woman. Beautiful, probably, but that hadn't stopped the Sect of Halcyon from performing such atrocities on her. This was definitely not the first unsanctioned execution that Tanith had stumbled upon in Riverside.

"I cannot have this, Captain," stammered Marl Keys, proprietor of the Lock & Key Tavern. He was a middle-aged man with the composure of a beardless boy. "This is the fourth murder this moon. Soon, my customers will think I run a cult refuge."

Tanith narrowed his eyes. "Keep spouting off nonsense like that and I'll post a burning tongue on your door myself, innkeeper."

A voice came from the street behind Tanith. "By Athlas! Did you have to kill her, Captain?"

Tanith turned around, his hand ready to draw the sword from his back, but he relaxed when he saw old Felix peeking around the corner of the Lock & Key. Tanith set his large form between the dead woman and Felix's peering eyes. The old man slumped in disappointment. "Was she a thief?"

"Nothing to worry about. Back to your wagon, Felix," Tanith urged, moving him out of the alley. "Grigg! I told you not to let anyone back here."

Grigg was across the street, bent over three other men who were playing at dice. At the sound of Tanith's voice, Grigg hurriedly slipped a handful of currents back into his purse and returned to his post by the alley's entrance, much to the dismay of the other gamblers. "Sorry, Captain! Just breaking up some trouble."

Tanith let Grigg escort Felix away from the Lock & Key and then returned to Marl. Tanith pointed to the innkeeper. "Listen, we already have too many mouths flapping on about holy wars and Astasia and the like; what we do not need is more kindling to keep the fire rising. I do not have enough men in the garrison to hold off a riot against the Church or any such nonsense." Tanith was a huge man, able to intimidate anyone in Celendas. Marl was no challenge. The captain of the Tower Guard motioned to the dead body. "This *whore* was killed for swindling a customer, Marl. Do you understand?"

Marl looked behind Tanith, nervously nodding. Tanith looked back at what drew Marl's attention. Three of the Phoenix Guards—in their shimmering purple armor and velvet cloaks—were speaking with Grigg as he motioned down the alley toward Tanith.

Tanith knew he was needed in council. The Aevenore envoys were no doubt already hounding the king. He looked back at Marl and nodded to the body. "Take care of the *whore*," he said, emphasizing the last word. Tanith walked out into the street toward the purple knights, his armor catching the morning sun and nearly blinding Marl.

The innkeeper turned to the body and wondered if Pandry's pigs would still be hungry.

Cardinal Carthys and Captain Nol were the first to gather in the council chamber, joined only by the two guards flanking the main doors. Both men kept to themselves as they waited at the large table. The Cardinal drank from a glass of wine as he patiently wrote in a leather journal. The scratching of his quill was accompanied only by Captain Nol's tapping fingers.

"How fares the Church, Cardinal?" Nol asked suddenly. His voice was rather deep and commanding for a man of his age and stature.

Carthys looked up from his writing, his old eyes kind but arrogant. His mouth tightened into something that resembled a frown. "We have begun to feel the strains of our recent expansions, Captain. This past winter, we began to spread the Lady's teachings beyond our own walls, and in doing so, we neglected the needs of the chapel here in Celendas." The Cardinal looked down at his book, as if reading his writing aloud. "There have been killings."

Nol looked up from his tapping fingers, intrigued. His bushy eyebrows rose with curiosity. "I had not heard."

Carthys nodded. "I do not doubt that, Captain. The grievances of the past few months have been kept quiet. In all honesty, it pleases me to know that word of such ill deeds has not yet reached the Hilt, as all the priests below me have worked tirelessly to keep rumors from spreading."

Nol nodded. "Perhaps you could entrust me with such delicate matters?"

The Cardinal closed his book. "It seems that agents from the Sect of Halcyon have infiltrated the Church and spread tales of witchery and heresy in our own streets. Unfortunately, I was away in Lumbridge at the time, helping with the construction of a new chapel dedicated to our Lady. You see, the rangers of Lumbridge have long dealt with ravages of beastmen from the..."

the Cardinal caught himself and smiled. "Sorry, I digress. As I said, I was away and unable to stamp out these foul mistruths while they were merely rumors. Upon my return to the keep, I found the lower levels of the Temple of the Lady being used as a slaughterhouse." Carthys stared blankly at a tapestry on the far wall behind the Captain. "My own clerics were performing unspeakable evils on the innocents. Removing their eyes, burning their tongues...and the women..." Carthys trailed off, his hand slowly covering his mouth. "The Sect had poisoned their minds."

"What barbarism." Captain Nol's forehead creased as he stroked his short beard and listened intently to the Cardinal's report. Of course, Nol had spent the last few years defending the realm from the Rhelklanders to the north and was no stranger to much more barbaric deeds. He tried to keep the bitterness from his voice as he began to console a trouble that seemed to him petty when compared to his own. "I am sorry to hear that, Cardinal. The Sect is a lot of doomsayers bent on bringing on the Days. If it were up to me, I'd strap them all to the hull of a ship bound for Vhaltas and let them save all they believe needs saving there." Nol cracked his knuckles. "It'd save the rest of us a whole lot of trouble. Let the Sect and the cult slay one another until Astasia comes." Nol almost grinned at the notion, and he wasn't a man who grinned easily.

The Cardinal nodded in agreement. "A fine notion, Captain. But tell me, how fares the Hilt these days? I assume things are not satisfactory considering your presence here."

Nol's face darkened. "Far from it. The savages do not rest. They live to kill and die, like no other beast I've known. While your enemies of the Faith are no doubt troublesome, Cardinal, I'm afraid I bring much more dire news from the north." Nol let the words sink in. Part of him knew it would be difficult to convince the king to spare men for the Hilt, but if he made his point clear to the Faith, perhaps it would help his cause. Or, it might just piss the old man off, which Nol had no problem with. "If we do not strengthen the garrison at Logan's Hilt, the Rhelklanders will tear apart all of Eurheby."

The Cardinal eyed Captain Nol as though he were an insolent child. "I see," Carthys said, nodding. "I hope the king understands the severity of both of our plights."

Captain Nol was inspecting his mail bracers, hiding his worry. "I am sure his majesty will ensure the safety of his realm." His response was nonchalant, but he quickly stiffened when the doors to the great chamber creaked open.

King Alastair Galvian strode into the council chamber. He wore a long purple cloak embroidered with golden phoenixes. Atop his golden crown, sat a phoenix with its flaming wings spread wide. At his heels came his high councilor Geldra and two armored guards.

The king looked at the Cardinal and Captain Nol, both men standing to acknowledge his presence. The envoys from Aevenore were nowhere to be seen, but the king only asked: "Where is Prince Cedric?"

Cedric vomited once more into the running waters of the otherwise crystal clear Celedine Canal. Raymun whistled and nodded to passing courtiers. They had been there most of the morning, Cedric retching up the last of the morning's merrymaking and Raymun ensuring the prince didn't choke.

Lady Orton had stopped by to inquire about Kable's whereabouts, but Raymun played the fool. The jester Berex stayed to juggle a bit until Cedric threw up on him.

When the Temple of the Lady's bells rang out, Raymun began to grow impatient. "My father is going to have my hide, Cedric, and you need to get to council. I already saw Tanith and those nobles from Aevenore head into the keep."

Cedric sat slumped against the stone spandrel, looking half asleep. He managed to raise a hand to shoo Raymun away. Raymun kicked him lightly. "Come on, Prince of Doom. Your kingdom waits."

"Do not call me that!" Cedric snapped, shielding his eyes from the rising sun.

Raymun was taken aback by the outburst. The prince did not stand for that name being uttered in his presence by most people, but Raymun had always been given leniency. That was his privilege as the only noble able to tolerate the prince's erratic behavior.

Cedric sniffed and Raymun realized the prince was crying. Raymun looked around, confused. When he saw the statue, he felt like a complete fool.

Just below the bridge, Magdalene Galvian stood vigilant over the courtyard, the morning sun framing her stone form. The statue had stood there for Cedric's entire life, Raymun's as well. Raymun silently cursed himself for his rashness and sat down next to Cedric. He was about to apologize to the prince, but Cedric spoke first.

"My father spends all of his mornings out there, standing with her and talking quietly so I cannot hear. But I know what he tells her." Cedric wiped his nose with his soiled tunic. "He tells her how much he misses her. How much he misses Theodric. He tells her how good a king their son would have been."

"And watching your father mourn the dead angers you?"

Raymun asked. "You would rather he move on, marry a bedmaid, and praise his living son?"

Cedric narrowed his eyes at Raymun. There was a hint of amusement behind his dark eyes. "It would serve better than being constantly reminded of what I took away from him." Cedric laughed weakly. "The Prince of Doom." He tried to fix his matted hair, throwing it over his shoulder.

Raymun stood up and scoffed. "The way I see it, you did not force the king and queen to birth another son. You did not inflict Theodric with the plague. So, stop taking credit for it by acknowledging that name. It's unbecoming to steal cruel fate's thunder."

Cedric turned and spat into the river behind him as he stood up. "Go see to your father, Lord of Landover. The sword yard is calling my name." The prince's mood was noticeably lightened by the proposition of swordplay.

"Prince Cedric!"

Raymun and the prince turned to see Geldra, red-faced and panting. The high councilor was motioning for Cedric to hurry into the keep. The guard Myron was behind him, looking abashed.

"The sword yard looks furious, m'lord," Raymun said, stifling a laugh.

Cedric didn't bother stifling his own as he staggered toward the morning council.

Cedric changed his clothes quickly, sobered himself up with a few mouthfuls of rheystone oats, and hurried to the council that was already underway. As he approached the doors to the chamber, he heard raised voices and a fist slamming the table. A sudden wave of excitement passed over him. This wasn't a council to discuss the spending of the kingdom's ample treasury or which portion of the city should hold the New Season Festival this year. This was something else.

Cedric pushed the doors open and assumed his best regal pose.

The voices ceased as attention turned to the prince. Cedric saw that his father sat at the head of the table, his eyes weary and his mouth firm. He motioned for the prince to take the seat reserved at his right. As Cedric made his way to his seat, he noted that the Cardinal and the grumpy captain from the Hilt exchanged venomous glances across the table. Two strangers sat next to the Cardinal, dressed in green tunics and darker green cloaks. The cloaks bore the sigil of Aevenore: three birds soaring over three green valleys on a field of blue sky. Cedric found it curious that nobles from the west were here this early in the morning with no notice yesterday.

Tanith began speaking as Cedric claimed his seat, apparently rebuking a statement from the Hilt's captain. "And just this morning another body turned up, all eyeless and such. I am sorry, Captain Nol, but I must support the Cardinal in this matter. Without enough men for a city watch, I fear the Sect will take hold and turn the small folk against each other, seeking Chaos in every shadow. The Hilt must find their men from the northern houses."

"Wetnurses and bean farmers are all you'll find in the northlands, Tanith!" Captain Nol exclaimed, clearly losing the argument for whatever he had hoped to attain.

"Silence!" the king said sharply. He slid a goblet of rheystone milk toward the prince, obviously no stranger to

Cedric's nocturnal habits. "Let us hear our visitors speak of their need, and then we shall discuss the Hilt's request."

Cedric drank deep. The milk was thick and bland, but he drank it all before the strangers began.

The younger of the two men spoke first. He was a brown-haired man with the definite air of nobility. "Thank you, your majesty. My name is Errol, royal scribe and herald for my cousin the king." Errol motioned to the older man on his right. "And this is Rennig, one of King Garrowin's advisors. We do apologize for our abrupt arrival, but we are gracious to be so well accepted. Our news is dire, and we can now see," he said with a motion toward Captain Nol, "that it comes at the worst of times."

Rennig interrupted, leaning over the table toward the king. "Perhaps, your majesty, we could discuss this matter in private."

King Alastair brushed the suggestion aside with a wave of his hand. "My council will hear any matters that affect the kingdom."

Rennig sat back slowly, as if shocked by the refusal. "Very well, your majesty. However, I implore the council to understand that King Garrowin has kept word of our tidings extremely discrete in Aevenroe, as to avoid panic among the smallfolk." He eyed each member of the council. "I would advise the council do the same for their kingdom's sake."

Errol nodded in agreement. "Pardon my abruptness, but we need to return to Aevenore before the next moon, so allow me to present the king's request in order to give the council reasonable time to consider a course of action." The council motioned for him to continue. "There has been talk of late in our lands of the killings in the Neveren Mountains. The town of Kingsforge has taken the brunt of the violence, but even there, we have no leads as to who...or what...is responsible for these brutalities."

Cedric was more than intrigued. The Neveren Mountains were home to various kinds of unsavory beasts, and as a boy, Cedric had read countless books on the matter. Not only did clans of nomadic greks—the horrid beings that lived to terrorize—reside in the shadows of the mountains, but wyverns hunted from above and enormous cave worms lurked below. It was a dangerous place to be sure, even in these times, with the dragons having fled to Rokuus. Cedric suddenly found himself wishing that he had taken more interest in affairs outside of Celendas so that he might have some insight into these rumors.

Errol continued, "The dead are usually found savagely mutilated, which suggests that whatever is killing them is primarily bestial. However, the bodies are left behind, not consumed, which suggests either territorial killing or…or simply primal rage."

Captain Nol scoffed. "The mountains are a dangerous place. Why does your king trouble himself with lackwits who get killed for wandering into the wild?"

Errol's expression hardly changed. He seemed to have expected some skepticism. "Those who were killed were reportedly taken from town…snatched from their homes or outside their farms without leaving a trail, as if something flew in and carried them off."

The council was silent for a moment. But then, Nol interjected again.

"We all know that wyverns don't carry off children like in the stories. You're sure these deaths were not a result of drunks or angry wives?"

Alastair answered this time. "That will do, Captain." He said it coolly, but Nol was obviously abashed. The king motioned for Errol to continue, "What does Luther think may be responsible for these killings?"

The Cardinal and Tanith both made to speak, but the Cardinal won the floor. "Do the dead still have their eyes?"

Errol's expression finally changed, not expecting such a question. "As to the dead, I cannot say. King Garrowin believes there is some evil at work in the mountains. Some of the reports from Kingsforge speak of a man in black, wandering Neveren and speaking of dragons. The king has put a bounty on the man. Others have spoken of other sightings that worry the king."

"Dragons?" asked Cedric. He hadn't even realized he spoke out loud until everyone turned their attention to him. He could feel his face reddening when Captain Nol grunted a small laugh.

"Not exactly, milord," Errol replied. "However, whisperings of drakes have made it back to the king. And King Garrowin does not take such things lightly."

Rumored to be the offspring of dragons, drakes hadn't been seen since the days of Adratheon, the terrible black dragon that was slain by Cedric's great grandfather, Ausfred Galvian, with the help of the cursed blade Dragonsbane. Cedric had always been fascinated by that part of his family's history. The legend of Ausfred and the Dragonsbane was the main reason Cedric kept up with his swordplay. As a boy, he fantasized about being Ausfred or one of his legendary knights of the Eurheborn. Yet, suddenly, the proposition of facing a horde of dragon spawn seemed much more terrifying than it had when he was younger.

"Drakes," repeated Alastair. It was not a question, but it sounded unsure.

"That is what brings us here, your majesty," Rennig finally chimed in. He had a scholarly look about him as he spoke. "King Garrowin is aware that it has been over sixty years since the denouncement of the Eurheborn, however, his majesty is also aware that the noble houses of Celendas still train their knights by the traditions of your people. Which, speaking bluntly, is the tradition of killing dragons." The statement seemed so surreal that Cedric wondered if he was still drunk. "The king has dispatched us here in hopes that you would consider his official request for Celendas to aid Aevenore against a common threat between our borders."

The council was quiet as the words sunk in. Dragons and the Eurheborn: two things barely spoken of in Celendas these days.

Cedric reached for one final foul drink from his goblet, but found it was completely empty.

CHAPTER 3: GREENSTONE
Outside of Lumbridge, southern Eurheby

Lacey Renevere crept silently through the Murdock Woods. His dark green leather armor and leaf-covered cloak helped him fade into the budding foliage of spring. His bright blonde hair would have given him away, but it was tucked into the hood of his cloak, which was drawn close to shadow his face. Although Lacey dressed the part of a woodsman, his face belied his occupation. He was beautiful, elegant, and lithe, like a prince from a fairytale. Yet in reality, he was the son to the patron of the Lumbridge Ranger's Guild, and a master woodsman.

"Lacey," a voice hissed from the leaves, "I don't see nothing."

Lacey bit his lip, as if someone had just knocked over a house of cards that he had been building. "Then you see *something*," he whispered back.

"Huh?"

"Hold your tongue, Fesk," Lacey ordered. He sniffed and continued forward, lowering himself to the ground. The scent of blood was in the air as he approached the clearing ahead, parting the leaves for a better view.

In the clearing, the morning mists surrounded a cave on the side of a rising hill. Lacey had scared more than a few beasts from that cave in the past, and now he cursed himself for never having the damned thing filled in. Milling about outside the cave's entrance was Lacey's quarry.

Werelings.

Mysterious and vicious, werelings were the main source of Lumbridge's trouble. They were wicked little creatures that hunted in packs. They walked upright like men, but stood just a little taller than children. Covered in coarse hair and dressed in whatever crude clothes or jewelry they procured from their victims, werelings were the epitome of savagery.

Lacey heard a choked breath from his right and he tensed, afraid that Fesk and the others might have given away their position. Fortunately, the werelings were preoccupied.

There were eight of the beasts near the cave, with the promise of more inside. Two bodies lay mangled on the ground, holding the werelings' attention. They were the broken remains of embrechauns, the small greenfolk from the Locrkian Woods to the west. Lacey bit his lip as he watched the beasts feed on their prey.

They look like children, Lacey thought to himself. The embrechauns were a reclusive people, cut off from civilization and shrouded in folktales and superstition. Lacey had been raised close enough to Lockrian to know they were not dangerous; they were simply people of the wild.

As he watched the grisly spectacle before him, a fury began to rise inside—the fury that takes hold of the righteous witnessing supreme injustice.

Lacey notched an arrow to his bow and pulled the string taught. A reasonable voice in his head—his father's—told him to alert the others and ready an attack, but as he watched the werelings tear an arm off the female embrechaun, he forgot reason. Rage was the careful hunter's bane. Lacey leapt into the clearing, fired his arrow, and notched another before his feet hit the earth.

The wereling holding the embrechaun's arm dropped it

and fell over as an oaken shaft embedded itself in his mouth. The other werelings responded instantly, standing guard against the rival scavenger that came for their feast. Lacey fired again before they could attack; another wereling fell shrieking to the ground. The remaining six beasts bent over onto all fours, snarling and drooling, and bounded toward Lacey. After missing the mark on his next target, Lacey dropped his bow and drew two short swords. As he prepared to receive the attack, Lacey heard the lovely tune of bowstrings singing from the trees behind. At least Fesk, Brody, and Case hadn't fled in fear as they so often had in the past. Only one wereling fell before the pack closed in on Lacey, the other arrows of his comrades either flying erratically overhead or dropping weakly over the shrubs on account of poor notching and drawing.

Lacey crouched and readied himself. His swords spun as he opened up another wereling. The creature fell to the forest floor, bleeding and screaming, but still alive. The remaining four split up. Two of them surrounded Lacey while the others dove into the brush to attack Lacey's less-than-efficient companions. Lacey cursed aloud as he heard Fesk sound the retreat. He would have to clean this up himself.

Lacey began to wonder why in the name of Dhullas he had only taken three rangers with him on this hunt. But the snap of a wereling jaw reined in his attention. He swung his blade and missed. These two were quicker than the others.

Lacey heard more growls as five more beasts emerged from the cave. His eyes widened in panic.

Eat the greenfolk, Lacey thought to himself. He no longer felt sympathy for the broken and bloody bodies in the middle of the clearing. *Better the dead than the living*. Lacey's thoughts were little comfort as the werelings focused in on the slayer of their pack.

One of the werelings nearest to Lacey leapt and snapped at his throat. Lacey agilely stepped back and dodged the bite, then brought down the hilt of his sword onto the wereling's skull. The blow knocked the wretched thing down, but another beast took the opportunity to sink its teeth into Lacey's exposed arm. The ranger screamed in agony, dropping the sword from his left hand. He fell to his knees and bashed the creature on the nose, bloodying it and releasing its grip on his arm. It was ravaged; the damned thing's teeth sunk in to the bone. Lacey could barely stand due to the pain exploding from the wound, and the two dazed werelings were already on their feet joining their pack.

Lacey saw his own death in that moment: the two beasts he pummeled would circle behind him while the rest of their pack would close in for the kill. They would tear him to shreds and the town of Lumbridge would be left vulnerable. His ailing father would be left to lead the Ranger's Guild and the creatures of the wild would slowly become too much. Murdock Woods would swallow the town.

No! Lacey thought, gripping his remaining sword with both hands, his left arm nearly numb from the pain. "Come on, you foul shits! I will not flee!"

One of the bigger werelings—this one wearing much more decoration than the others—stepped forward and established his dominance over the pack. He let out a howl that made Lacey's skin crawl, but he did not cower.

Just as he thought the beasts would make their attack, a falcon burst from the western trees and soared into the clearing. It let out a piercing cry and dove for the nearest wereling.

Lacey stared dumbfounded at the bird as another shape leapt into the clearing. This one a was man, dressed in green and nearly as graceful as the bird of prey that was now sinking its sharp beak into the neck of the alpha male. The stranger in green landed in a crouch, a silver dagger in each hand, poised to strike. He had shaggy brown hair tucked behind his ears and an arrogant grin on his face. The werelings did not hesitate, suggesting they knew this foe well. Even the two beasts surrounding Lacey ignored him in favor of the newcomer. The man in green rose to meet the challenge.

"Come!" he shouted, spinning his blades. "You can't flee this time, you filthy dogs!"

The first two beasts to accept the invitation met a quick end as the stranger flourished his blades. One wereling fell to its knees, savage claws clenching its slit throat as the other rolled to the ground with a dagger buried in its chest. Another blade flashed through the air as the nimble man threw a knife into the back of the alpha still being tormented by the falcon. Lacey watched in awe of the man's grace. He was flawless in his movements, as though he anticipated every attack. He spun and struck as if this were a dance he had known for years.

Before Lacey could blink three times, the battle was over. The werelings lay dead or dying, strewn about the forest floor in quivering heaps. The strange falcon flew to perch on the man's shoulder when he arose from gathering his blades. He caught sight of Lacey, who was still kneeling and bleeding at the edge of the clearing.

They stared at each other in silence. The stranger wore dark green like a ranger, but his clothes were old and ragged, and the hilts of more than a dozen daggers and knives could be seen about his person. No bow. He was no ranger. Daggers were the choice weapons of thieves and highwayman, knaves of the wilderness. Yet, something else caught Lacey's eye. A large green jewel entwined in silver leaves hung from the man's neck, roughly the size of a plum. The beauty of the pendant greatly contrasted with the rest of his attire.

Then, realization struck Lacey.

The Emerald Scout! Lacey didn't know whether to thank the man or slay him. Many tales were told about a man who wore an emerald around his neck. Those stories spoke of him slaying werelings and greks and other woodland lurkers. However, the tales were not all pleasant. Some said that the Emerald Scout was as likely to rob you as he was to protect you. He had once been a thief who tried to steal Lockri's soul from the embrechaun's forest. When the dryads caught him, they chained a shard of the stone around his neck to bind him to the forest, cursed to serve their will forever...or so it was said.

No one knew his name, or much about him at all, other than he walked the hidden paths of the woods, guided by the shard of Lockri's soul. Some even said that he knew the way through the Burrow Gates, but Lacey didn't bet his currents on alehouse legends.

The Emerald Scout looked mournfully at the bodies of the embrechauns and then back to Lacey. He opened his mouth as if to speak, but stopped short as a bough broke in the distance. The Emerald Scout quickly drew a small blade and whipped it toward the noise.

However, there were no other werelings. Fesk stumbled into the clearing, the hilt of a throwing knife protruding from his chest. He fell to the ground coughing. Out of pure reflex, Lacey snatched his bow from the ground and readied an arrow to loose at the attacker. But, when Lacey took aim, the man was gone, and his bird as well. Behind him, Fesk coughed and moaned as the other rangers stepped into the clearing to help him. Fesk was still alive, but from the look of the wound he would need a healer soon. Lacey considered pursuing the Emerald Scout, but he knew Fesk was his responsibility.

"Who was that?" asked Brody, the young boy's eyes wide with fear.

"Get him up," Lacey said fiercely. "We don't have much time."

Gwyndalin watched the East Brim vigilantly. As an embrechaun, she was not permitted to pass beyond any of the natural borders of Lockrian Woods. That law pertained to Raiken as well, though he often feigned ignorance on the matter.

Past the East Brim, the trees thinned and the ground gave off sharply, creating the cliffs that overlooked the beaches below. Gwyndalin could see the Murdock Woods in the distance below, dark and expansive. There was no movement.

Raiken had been gone for hours. They had both tracked the werelings to the edges of Lockrian, and when Gwyndalin pleaded for him to return with her to tell Fyrechel about the missing embrechauns, Raiken refused.

"I'm not going to leave them to those beasts!" Raiken had said as they neared the Brim. "They are your people, Gwyn. How can you just sit here while those bastards drag away your kin?" Raiken's falcon, Valcorse, cawed in agreement. Two days had passed since the young lovers Myra and Thoun had gone missing, and neither Raiken nor Gwyndalin had given up looking for them. Their search had led them to believe that werelings had abducted the lovers.

"You know I cannot leave the forest, Raiken!" Gwyn shouted at him. "And neither can you. As long as you wear the

Greenstone, you are bound here as well!"

Raiken did not hear her. He was already free of the trees and bounding toward the cliffs, Valcorse soaring right behind him.

"You stubborn knave!"

Now that her anger has passed, Gwyn wished she had not yelled at him. Thoughts of his death overtook her mind and she did not want the last words between them to have been said in scorn. She hugged her knees to her chest, her green skin melding into the leaves around her. She fought off the tears she felt coming. Raiken was the only human allowed to dwell alongside the dryads and embrechauns of Lockrian since the druids of before Loren's Coming.

Gwyn remembered the day she met Raiken Belrouse more clearly than she remembered any other moment in her life. He had stumbled into the forest with his twin brother, Sebastian. Both of them were desperately lost, spending days trying to navigate the mystical forest. Gwyndalin did not engage the men, as the council forbade embrechauns to reveal themselves to outsiders. However, when Gwyndalin saw that one of them carried a shard of Lockri's soul, she called for their apprehension.

She smiled at the memory, but as the sun slowly began to descend, she felt the tears coming again. Wereling assaults were not uncommon in Lockrian, but Raiken had ventured into Murdock, where worse things than werelings dwelt. Even with the Greenstone to aid him, he might not survive.

Just as her thoughts were blackening, Gwyn heard the beautiful sound of Valcorse's piercing cry. She jolted out of her seat and grabbed her bow. She notched an arrow and leapt from her current tree to one that provided a better view of the cliffs. She caught sight of Raiken immediately, climbing over the last ridge. He looked tired and covered in scratches from the climb, or from something worse. A darker shade of blood stained his vest and arms. Wereling blood.

He killed them, Gwyn thought, *he killed them all*. She smiled brightly, and then it occurred to her that no one followed him. Her smile faded quickly. *Myra and Thoun...*

Despite her exceptional camouflage, Raiken's eyes found Gwyndalin's easily. The Greenstone made it nearly impossible for her to hide from Raiken. His look was apologetic and sullen, with no trace of his usual arrogant smile. She knew the embrechauns were as dead as the werelings. There was no use in speaking of it.

As Raiken neared the trees, Gwyndalin leapt down from her high perch. Her bare feet barely made a sound upon the leaves of the forest floor. She shouldered her bow and waited for Raiken to enter the woods. She was ready to embrace him, to kiss him and hold him for as long as he had been gone. Just like they used to.

When Raiken stepped into the shelter of the green, his eyes were distant and he seemed not to even take notice of her. He allowed Valcorse to perch on his shoulder, but he did not take Gwyndalin into his bloodied arms. He knelt down so that their eyes met. She was nearly a head and a half shorter than him, yet she was proportioned much like a human woman. Despite this, Gwyn couldn't help but feel like a child when Raiken knelt down to her level. It always made her shutter with a passing weakness.

They said nothing for a long moment. Raiken reached out and pushed a tuft of green hair behind Gwyn's pointed ear, running his finger down the length of it. Gwyn knew it as one of his nervous ticks, and she felt a heavy burden through his touch.

"It wasn't your fault, Raiken," she said gently. "They knew the dangers of the East Brim..."

He opened his mouth to speak, but suddenly a voice came from behind Gwyn.

"Raiken," Leyis said in his shrill voice. "The council has been looking for you." The young embrechaun stepped around Gwyn and saw the ruin all over Raiken. His eyes widened and he was about to ask what happened, but thought better of it. Instead, he said, "Fyrechel wants to see you."

Valcorse took to the air and Raiken swallowed whatever it was he was about to say, standing up to answer to the council. The Emerald Scout left Gwyndalin there at the edge of the forest.

"You have been forbidden to take the Greenstone from the safety of these woods," Fyrechel stated calmly, her voice as subtly strong as a raging rapid. "And you have been reminded of that on more than one occasion, Raiken."

Raiken nodded, staring down at the jewel that he wore around his neck. The stone contained a swirling pool of green that easily hypnotized any that stared into its depths. Raiken knew that vastness well and was able to lose and find himself with ease. As much as he wanted to lose himself now, he looked back up to the council, feeling strangely ashamed.

Fyrechel stared down at him from the dais. She was a dryad, able to take the form of whatever she pleased. However, in the three years that he had lived under her rule, Raiken had only ever seen Fyrechel as the human woman she appeared as now. She was elegant and common at the same time, beautiful and earthly. She dressed like the embrechauns, in the colors of their surroundings, with little regard for modesty.

Raiken felt the eyes of the rest of the council on him.

Therrus, an elder embrechaun, crossed his arms and gave Raiken the same knowing grin he always did, holding his authority above him. Therrus would not be sad to see the Emerald Scout depart the forest forever. Raiken knew that the elder embrechaun abhorred the idea of Raiken's relationship with Gwyndalin, or with any embrechaun for that matter. He did not trust the race of men. Raiken also knew that Therrus coveted Gwyndalin, and he was an exceptionally jealous creature.

To the other side of Fyrechel sat the younger dryad, Audrea, whose cold stare always hid her true emotions. She usually appeared in her true form, dark skin the texture of tree bark with leaves for hair. Yet today she appeared as a woman with sharp features and pointed ears.

The last member of the council was Genis, a creature smaller than Therrus. He was a broan, one of the last of his kind. Raiken heard that he had come from the Burrow Gates years ago, fleeing from Anochra when the embrechauns there had aligned themselves with the darker aspect of Lockri. Genis was about the same size as a human child in its sixth year, but parts of his body were covered in coarse patches of hair and two distinctive horns protruded from his brow. He smiled, as he was much kinder than Therrus, and lashed his tail about behind him. In spite of the broan's amiable demeanor, Raiken had always found something sinister about him.

"Correct me if I am wrong," Therrus began, addressing Fyrechel, "but was Lord Belrouse not informed of his punishment should he misuse the shard of Lockri again?"

Fyrechel nodded, tiredly. "Thank you, Therrus."

The embrechaun pressed the matter. "And was that punishment not the relinquishment of the stone?"

"That will be all, Therrus," Fyrechel said sternly. "Raiken, the council is aware that you left the borders of Lockrian Woods this day. Our scouts see all. While you are more than free to venture beyond the forests at your leisure, the Greenstone must not leave the Brims. I was under the assumption that you understood this."

"As was I," added Therrus, "considering that you have a reminder of it hanging around your neck."

Audrea finally spoke. "Not only did you leave Lockrian, Raiken, but you carried the Greenstone into Murdock. There is no place worse I could think of to take the stone, aside from maybe the Burning Isles."

Raiken's eyes slowly narrowed with contained rage. He heard the words, but his focus was on the memory of those mutilated bodies and the stench of the werelings. The dead girl's face had become Gwyn's in his mind, and he could barely stand closing his eyes. He was sick of councils and he was sick of their rules. He wanted to tear the Greenstone from his neck, throw it at their feet, and return to his own life. But, he could not take Gwyndalin with him. Just as he could not take the Greenstone.

He knew he had no life to return to. All he had was Lockrian. All he had was the Greenstone.

"The embrechauns?" Genis asked hopefully.

"Dead," Raiken spat.

Therrus scoffed, as if their deaths had been Raiken's fault.

"They were taken by werelings," Raiken glared at Therrus. "I tracked them with the Greenstone and killed them all."

"That did not save Myra or Thoun," Therrus said, his voice rising.

Fyrechel stood up from her seat and stepped down from the dais. "That is not the point and you know it, Therrus. We have no responsibility to interfere with the doings of the world outside of our forest." She approached Raiken, standing nearly a head taller than him. "Lockri bound himself to these trees for a reason, and that reason lies in the world out there. We need only concern ourselves with our home."

Genis stood up too, leaping off the dais. "In young Raiken's defense, Lockri guides his conscience, whether he realizes it or not. He wears part of the stone that contains Lockri's soul, a part of the stone that the dryads entrusted to him. He is an anointed scout of Lockri, thus he does the forest's bidding. Perhaps the forest drove him to chase after those embrechauns. Thus, can he be blamed for carrying out Lockri's will?"

"Most certainly!" commanded Therrus.

Before he could continue, Audrea added her reply. "Regardless, the Greenstone cannot possess its bearer. Raiken knew that he was going against the orders of this council when he left the borders. Also, it is quite possible that he could misinterpret the bidding of Lockri. He is not a child of the forest and it is not in his true nature to speak to the wild."

Therrus nodded. "As was my argument upon his anointing. He is not fit to carry such a gift. He is a man."

Genis laughed. "Men are fit for just about anything these days, Therrus, if only you could see beyond the trees."

"It makes no matter," Fyrechel said, her commanding voice ending the argument. She was the Heiress of the Druid's Council, and her words held all the power that mattered in Lockrian. "Raiken, three years have you dwelt beneath these trees. For your bravery and valor in returning the missing shards of Lockri's soul, you were given a boon in the form of the Greenstone. With it, you have learned empathy and you have guarded the forest valiantly with the heightened senses it provides you. However, you have repeatedly gone against this council's wishes to keep the Greenstone within the safety of these borders. Lockri's soul needs to be kept together; thus, the Greenstone must remain near Heartheald where the rest of the shards are kept. You have failed to acknowledge the importance of this matter. For that, I must ask you to relinquish the Greenstone to the council."

Raiken had sensed the words coming, but they still felt like a dagger in his stomach. Everything he had known of happiness and home for the last three years slowly dissolved. Without thinking, he reached up to remove the clasp that held the Greenstone around his neck. But Fyrechel motioned for him to stop.

"Not now."

Raiken gave the dryad a questioning glance.

Fyrechel's face betrayed a hint of sympathy. "When you are ready to depart, I will accept the Greenstone."

Raiken was about to argue the matter, but he realized that she was right. Without the Greenstone, he would not stay in Lockrian. It was the Greenstone that brought him here and its power kept him. Without it, he would not belong. He would be an outsider.

Moments ago, Lockrian Woods had seemed a prison, binding him to a life of heavenly seclusion. Yet now the doors had been thrown open, and all Raiken could think of were Gwyndalin and the Greenstone. They both bound him here. *Where else do I belong?* Raiken thought, staring at the polished wood below his feet, wondering where he should go.

Perhaps Sebastian will have a place for me. He hadn't seen or heard from his brother in years, but Sebastian was the first person Raiken thought of whenever he felt alone or unsure. *Perhaps he will forgive me…*

CHAPTER 4: A KNIGHT CAUGHT IN THE CIRCLE
Melbrook, a small town in the heart of Terrace

The waters of the Glimmeraine River flowed down from Mount Arkia, trickled through the valleys of Terrace, wound around the kingdom city of Aevenore, and eventually found their way to Melbrook. Laurel Darcy bent over the river's sloping bank to let the water run through her fingers, her dark hair bound up tightly underneath a blue wrap. The waters were said to be the purest in Lorendale. The mountains of Arkia stole the rain from the sky, kept it cool in its springs, and then fed it to the land. According to legend, the waters ran all the way down to the hidden caverns of Coventina, where Celecy kept the tears she wept for her dying lands.

Laurel cupped her hand and drank of the cool water. She did so every morning, letting her mind focus on the purported healing powers of the Glimmeraine. It made her feel closer to the gods—a comforting feeling of insignificance that far outweighed the one she felt from working in The Raine Song Inn. Lennick was a fine man to work for, but the patrons of the tavern were some of the worst Laurel ever had to serve. This was to be expected, however. Melbrook was a popular stop for nobles, minstrels, and merchants traveling between Terrace and Eurheby. Bad apples were bound to fall off the tree that caught the most wind. Laurel had a much more pleasant time when she had served patrons of The West Wind in Aevenore, where the king's law was more closely obeyed. This was not the case for the lands surrounding the city.

Laurel splashed some of the cold water on her face, letting it drip slowly around her tired eyes. She was certain that her nights at The Raine Song were the cause of her dreams of late. That bastard-born Vance Mandary fancied himself an entitled nobleman, free to take any maid of his liking, and he had set his sights on Laurel as of late. She tried to keep her distance, but he continued to find ways to corner her and force himself upon her. His advances had yet to lead to anything more than groping and horrid, unwanted kisses, but Laurel had become increasingly frightened of him. To make matters worse, Lennick would not lift a finger against the noble for fear of losing business.

So, Laurel dreamed nightly of fire and blood, and Vance's terrible demise, and a flaming hand offering her a knife. If she had somewhere else to go, she might have left The Raine Song by now, but this was her life.

However, Melbrook did have its subtle graces. She turned at the sound of hoof beats.

"Morning, Sebastian!" Laurel called as she saw the priest riding over the bridge into Melbrook.

Sebastian Belrouse reined in his horse when he caught sight of her. He smiled brightly. He was bare from the waist up, wearing only the bronze Sacred Circle medallion of his order around his neck, his heavy mace at his side. He was covered in sweat. His horse, called Aldarion, wore heavy saddlebags from which a pickaxe hung. Laurel knew that Sebastian had been mining in the hills and training in the woods. He did so nearly every morning before the rest of the town awoke. His dedication to all he did was just one of the qualities that she admired about him.

"My lady, I did not expect to find anyone at work this early." Sebastian nodded toward the pails at Laurel's feet. In truth, she had not even intended to fetch water. She had a habit of bringing the pails along whenever she went down to the river.

"I forget that you are the only one that gets to rise before the sun," Laurel said, charmingly. "How fares your work?" she asked, motioning to the heavy sack that hung from Aldarion's saddle. Laurel knew of Sebastian's growing desire to become a knight in service to Aevenore, just like his late father. However, all knights needed to acquire their own suit of armor. Being a journeyman priest of such a remote branch of the Faith, Sebastian was far from able to acquire the necessary currents to purchase armor worthy of a knight. But, instead of giving up, he made a deal with the local blacksmith, Barrid Lupke, who had once been an armorer in the port city of Quayhaven. Barrid would forge Sebastian a full suit of plate mail as long as Sebastian gathered the necessary supplies, such as ore and leather.

Sebastian dismounted and laid a hand on the sack, "Ever since Kingsforge opened up those mines in Neveren, most of the prospectors from Valemor packed up and left the hills free for the taking. After a few more loads this size, I should have Barrid well supplied for at least two seasons worth of horseshoes."

"And your armor?" Laurel asked.

Sebastian nodded with a smile. "I hope to bring back a little more tomorrow. I've heard some trouble in the mountains caused several miners to return empty-handed. The hills might be swarming with scavengers again before the moon changes."

"And the tourney is next week, isn't it?" Laurel asked, though she knew the answer. The New Season tournament in Aevenore was the same time every year, but Laurel liked to watch Sebastian's face light up whenever the tourney was mentioned.

The priest nodded, hefting his mace. "Barrid should have the armor fitted by then. It shall serve for the melee, but I will not ride in the joust, that is for sure."

There was an awkward pause while Laurel and Sebastian timidly smiled at each other.

"What sort of trouble?" Laurel asked suddenly, not quite sure why. "In the mountains, that is."

Sebastian shook his head, looking distantly behind her. "Probably some mountain cats taking up residence in the mines."

Laurel turned to see what had caught Sebastian's attention; Barrid Lupke was shouting at his young apprentice in front of their shop.

"If you'll excuse me, my lady," Sebastian said, courteously, "I must away."

He's going to make a perfect knight, Laurel thought to herself with a smile.

He began to lead Aldarion away, but turned around as Laurel collected her pails. "You will be at this afternoon's Recitation, won't you?" Sebastian asked her.

Laurel gave him a smile. "Only if you save me a seat, kind sir."

Sebastian made a show of bowing deeply and then hurried toward the blacksmith's shop. Looking at the smoke rise from Barrid's smithy, Laurel felt more at home than she had since her days in Aevenore. Still, while she watched Sebastian leave, she knew it was a fleeting moment. She would soon have to return to her duties at The Raine Song…and face Vance. She let her eyes drift skyward and wondered if Sebastian would take her to the tourney and fight with her favor hanging from the hilt of his mace.

Just then, Lennick stepped out of the tavern and called for her. She turned back toward The Raine Song. While she felt foolish dreaming of such things, she let the romantic wonderings of knights and ladies drift through her head.

Hope would be her armor.

As Sebastian approached the shop, Barrid was shouting at his apprentice, Orris, to fill the water basin.

"I want enough to last me through the day this time, boy, or you'll be fishing my hammer out of your—"

"Morning, Barrid," Sebastian interrupted with a smile, ducking under the low awning that covered Barrid's workshop. The blacksmith's shop had three walls, a massive water basin by the forge, and a row of anvils. Hammers, horseshoes, tongs, and other smithy supplies hung from the walls, as well as a large bronze symbol of the Sacred Circle that Barrid had crafted himself. He was a deeply pious man, which probably led him to making such a fine offer to a young priest in need. "Supplies from the Creighton Hills." Sebastian began to remove the heavy bag from Aldarion who stomped his feet and snorted, announcing his thirst.

Barrid, whose mood changed more often than his chimneys smoked, let out an abrupt chuckle, and walked over to take hold of Aldarion's reins. "Come, Al, there's fresh water in the trough. And I have something for you too, Sebastian."

Barrid led the horse to the side of the shop and tethered him next to the trough. "I think you've far outdone yourself, Bash," the blacksmith said motioning to the heavy sack that the priest had set down next to the forge.

"I *am* a man of Olerune," Sebastian said with a smile, making the sign of the Oath Keeper over his chest.

Barrid laughed and patted the priest on the back before leading Sebastian into the interior of the shop. "I've been waiting to show you until it's completely done, but you have been working so hard lately…I'd also like to see if it is up to your specifications…"

A heavy wool curtain hung in front of Barrid's self-styled armory, where he kept all the tools that he crafted. Barrid pushed the curtain aside and bright blue steel caught Sebastian's eye.

Sebastian stared at the armor for a long moment, speechless.

The suit was blindingly beautiful. Sebastian had seen knights ride through Melbrook and once had the chance to see the Vale Knights gather when he was in Aevenore. Their brilliant armor had always stuck in his mind. This armor was different. This was made for him, and its beauty was indescribable.

The armor hung on a wooden bust. It was gilded blue steel, with bronze inlays depicting the arms of the Sacred Circle on the breastplate—a circle that was ornamented with the devices of the Four: the Hammer, the Flame, the Spear, and the Winged Blade. Sebastian had not requested the armor to bear a device, but now that he thought of it, all knights were pledged to a house. What better house to be pledged to than the House of the Four where he was raised? Not only was it appropriate, but Sebastian had never seen a better rendition of the Sacred Circle's crest. Barrid was a master artisan, and Sebastian cursed himself for never fully appreciating the man's talents.

"I know it's not customary anymore for churches to house knights," Barrid said defensively, walking to the armor and polishing the breastplate with a rag, "ever since that damned Silverguard made a mess of the business. But I figured times have changed enough…"

"It's perfect," Sebastian said, still hypnotized by Barrid's work. "I couldn't think of a more fitting suit of armor."

"Don't say that," Barrid laughed. "You haven't even tried it on yet."

With that, the blacksmith helped Sebastian into the breastplate. It fit perfectly, the leather padding molded to his body in an instant and the steel fit over him like a second skin. He moved around in it, feeling its reassuring weight. After raising his arms and pulling them backward, he nearly laughed in disbelief. It was as if the metal was nothing more than a wool garment.

"It is perfect," Sebastian said with certainty.

"Let us have a look," Barrid said as he adjusted a tall mirror, the frame of which he forged himself. "You might just be the first Knight of the Circle."

Sebastian liked the sound of that, and he liked even more what he saw in the mirror when it was finally adjusted. He saw in that mirror everything he had been striving for these past few years.

"You look like a knight if I have ever seen one," Barrid said with a proud smile. Sebastian knew that the smith had seen his share of knights in Aevenore, and the priest was honored to be counted among them. "Ah, 'tis a shame you will not get to break it in at the tourney."

The words cut into Sebastian like a dagger that found a gap in his new armor. "Will it not be ready by then?" he asked weakly.

Barrid looked at the priest, his head cocked to the side in confusion. "You mean, you haven't heard? Well I hate to be the bad raven, but word came from the throne just yesterday. The king has announced that the tournament will not be held this spring."

The words sunk in like poison coursing through his veins.

Barrid continued through Sebastian's pain. "The court says that the treasury will not be able to support a festival that the New Season deserves. But there will be a grander celebration to make up for it next year."

Sebastian's mind was a mix of anger and complete depression. He had spent all of winter in preparation for this tournament, and he knew it would be his best chance to make a name for himself. The New Season tourney was the biggest in Lorendale since the Tripartite. Before that time, the Emperor Loren held legendary tourneys at his seat in Candrella. But now, Aevenore had become the proving ground for knights from all three kingdoms of the Tripartite, as well as from across the mountains and seas.

Barrid looked to make sure Orris had yet to return from the river, and leaned closer to the priest. "Speaking from my own sources, Bash, I hear there is trouble in the mountains. Three knights from South Terrace passed through here a week ago and paid me with a bag full of currents to repair their arms and armor. I'm ashamed to say that I overheard them at their drink in The Raine Song afterward. They talked about King Garrowin calling for worthy knights to take into Neveren to answer some threat. I did not hear much else." He ran a hand through his thick beard. "But if I had to bet a current on it, I'd say the king canceled the tourney because something in those mountains scares him. And we all know Garrowin is a man to chase shadows."

Sebastian wondered if this was the same trouble that had begun to scare the miners from the new mines. He would have inquired about it then, but there was no use. He was no knight, so he could not answer the king's call, and he could not become a knight without competing in the Trials at the tourney. Defeated, he removed the beautiful blue armor.

Barrid misread Sebastian's sour mood. "No worries though, lad. The mountains are far away. We're safe here."

Sebastian returned to the church in far lower spirits than he had departed. He took Aldarion to the stables and slowly made his way back to his quarters. On his way, he squinted against the rising sun as it climbed over the church. His thoughts went to his brother, Raiken. Mornings outside the church always reminded him of their eleventh birthday when he woke up and Raiken had runaway to Quayhaven looking for adventure.

He began to wonder if he would be a knight today had he left Melbrook with Raiken. It was a feeble thought, since he could not undo the past. Despite the anger his brother had caused him by abandoning his responsibilities to the church, he couldn't help but be a little envious thinking of Raiken living in the freedom of Lockrian now, able to come and go as he pleased. If it weren't for his sense of duty to the church, Sebastian was sure he would have been knighted by now.

However, unlike Raiken, Sebastian was not one to run from his duties.

Sebastian hung his mace on the wall as he entered his quarters. He stared at the weapon and thought of Raiken again. Four years ago, the twins had recovered the missing shards of Lockri's imprisoned soul in the ruins of the Vysarcian Empire, where Sebastian discovered that mace among the undead legion's hoard of stolen weapons from the glory days of Candrella. Sebastian still had nightmares about the things he had seen in that hellish place: the walking dead, the power of the Corruptor, and the prices that had to be paid to uphold the Balance.

He turned away. It was too early in the day for such dark thoughts. He quickly dressed himself for the Recitation and headed upstairs to see Father.

Father Vincent Cruland was the head priest of the Church of the Sacred Circle. There were almost a dozen small churches throughout Lorendale dedicated to worshipping the Sacred Circle, and Vincent was the highest-ranking priest among all of them. Other religions like the Faith, the Sect of Halcyon, the Spearitans, and the wretched Cult of the Burning One possessed greater numbers, but the Sacred Circle was the only religion that never incited a holy war throughout Lorendale's long history. All Circlists took pride in that. The Circle upheld the Balance and only used their strength to fight against Chaos' advances, never to seek out conflict.

Sebastian took the wooden stairs up to the vestibule overlooking the monastery. The small windows of the winding staircase afforded a view of the church grounds, and Sebastian spied some acolytes in the gardens outside. The church housed several monks who kept up with the routine maintenance of the church. Vincent, Sebastian, and Martin were the only practicing priests. Sebastian reached the top of the stairs and noticed the door to Vincent's chambers open. Inside, he saw Martin's bald head reflecting the sunlight. Sebastian entered, seeing that Vincent had yet to rise this morning. Martin sat next to the elder priest, his head bowed in prayer. Vincent's health had been slowly declining, and it seemed that today he would again be bedridden. Sebastian's mood darkened further.

When Sebastian entered, Vincent, who had been staring out the window, turned to welcome him. Sebastian knelt on the side of the bed opposite Martin.

"How are you, Father?" Sebastian asked.

"Never you mind that," Vincent answered stubbornly. He had always been a willful man, which Sebastian found amusing. "Martin here was just telling me the rotten news about the New Season festival. I am sure you have heard…"

Sebastian nodded.

"I tell you, if that Garrowin ever catches the usurpers he sees in every shadow, it will be a fine day indeed!" Vincent began coughing violently.

Martin offered the ailing priest a cup of water, hoping to calm him.

Vincent took it, drank, and coughed weakly before handing the cup back to Martin. Then Vincent turned and patted Sebastian's hand, "I know you had your heart set on competing in the Trials this year, Sebastian. Do not let this set your path astray. You are on a fine course, and you should take this time to enjoy the frivolity of small town life before you enter the royal court." Vincent smiled and coughed again. "I will be glad to see you here for another year. Also," he added, "I'd hate for the beautiful Laurel Darcy to have to find a new reason to attend Recitations."

Sebastian laughed softly and tried not to blush like a boy.

"Sebastian," Martin began, "Father Vincent will be unable to perform the Recitation this afternoon. I have one prepared, but I must away before noon. Would you care to act in my stead?"

Sebastian was taken aback. He had yet to carry out a Recitation. Martin and Vincent were elders and it had not yet come to Sebastian to perform such an honored ritual. Before Sebastian could answer, Vincent explained.

"A courier from Wynnstead brought word from Baron VonAnthony's estate. Apparently, that noble head of his isn't large enough yet. He wants to host a requiem for the dead. As if any of those sots buried in his crypts deserve recognition."

"Father..." Martin protested.

"Do not be foolish, Martin! There is more than just one of those VonAnthony's that worshipped the Burning One." Vincent coughed again. "Do not pretend." He squeezed Sebastian's hand a little tighter. "And that Helena of his...she died a blasphemous death. I dreamt of her…in the Revery…" Vincent was trailing off, eyes wandering.

His rambling had worsened as of late.

Martin addressed Sebastian now. "I must be our envoy to carry out the rites. Either one of us or a Sectary of Halcyon could perform the ceremony, but I do not dare let VonAnthony align himself with the Sect. Duke Berrymore of Romney has already fallen in with them, and I care not to see more of Terrace fall under their influence."

Sebastian nodded in agreement. He would hate to see the Sect gain more footing in Lorendale. They were a dangerous organization of witch hunters bent on the absolute destruction of Chaos. The Sect of Halcyon went against everything the Balance stood for. They were known to burn anyone they suspected to be aligned with the Burning One. Sebastian was sure he was not the only man that found the practice highly ironic.

"Would you lead the Recitation?" Martin asked again.

Sebastian nodded in agreement. His mind went back to the times when he and his twin brother practiced at Recitation. They loved the stories of the god Lucrid and his Winged Blade, but Raiken always focused on the angels, like Dameon, Mereketh, and Lockri. Strangely enough, Raiken had always been fascinated with Lockri—the archangel who fled the Heavenly Realms at the urging of Sol Saradys—even before he had discovered the Greenstone. Sebastian loved all the stories, which was just one of the reasons that he remained with the church when Raiken fled. He took Vincent's cold hand in his, *just one of the reasons*.

A small sense of regret crept into Sebastian's heart. With his aspirations of knighthood suddenly threatened today, he finally found a bit of understanding as to why Raiken had left. He winced at the memory of all the anger he had directed toward

Raiken. Sebastian suddenly missed his brother more than he had since Raiken first ran away.

Sebastian nodded again, oblivious to the fact that Martin and Vincent had begun their own conversation. It didn't matter. Sebastian wouldn't even need the Recitation Martin had prepared.

He had a story of his own to tell.

The altar was arrayed with the tools that Sebastian would use for his Recitation. A small diorama of miniature scenery was split into four sections upon the altar: a lush and verdant forest to represent the Heavenly Realm of Uldagard, fiery plains for Prythene, blue waters for Acrivas, and a sea of clouds to represent the windy realm of Sollum. Scattered about the scenery were the miniature statues that represented the gods, angels, and other characters that appeared in the stories of the *Mythos of the Four*.

The Church of the Sacred Circle used visual story-telling as the primary source of worship, a practice that was carried on from the warrior priests who used their military maps and markers to tell each other stories from the *Mythos* so they could remind themselves why they fought in the War of the Scales. After the war, many of the monks and priests of the Circle became master craftsmen in the carving of miniature sculptures, an art form that became widely popular in many royal courts.

Sebastian approached the altar as two young acolytes in soft blue robes finished placing the necessary pieces on their respective sections of the diorama. Lockri, wreathed in leaves and vines, was placed in Uldagard with the hammer-wielding Joacim, Sol Saradys and Olerune in Prythene, Athlas in the center, and Mereketh in Sollum with Lucrid. These were the players

Sebastian would need for his tale.

As Sebastian lifted his chalice from the altar, another acolyte—a young girl with sapphire eyes—hurried over to fill it with wine. As she did, the attendants arose and began to serve each other wine from the trays in the aisles. Sebastian caught sight of Laurel—alone as usual—at the front of the assembly. They exchanged smiles. The assembly left their pews, gathered around the altar, and knelt upon the cushions. Laurel made sure she had a close seat.

"To the Hammer and Flame, the Spear and the Blade," Sebastian began, "let us drink to the Balance, to which we adhere, and to the Order which we forever serve." Before drinking, Sebastian added, "And to the staying of Astasia, a world without Balance."

Astasia was a term commonly misunderstood in Lorendale to mean literally 'the end of the world.' In truth, it was an old word that meant 'to be without Balance,' and in the religious world, it was a foretold era in which there would be no Balance to protect Order or Chaos from destroying each other.

Sebastian motioned for everyone to drink with him. The congregation raised their glasses, some more eagerly than others, and drank. And so the Recitation commenced.

"Long ago, many of the Faithful considered Lockri's Flight to be the First Day of Astasia," Sebastian began, "the first of the final days. As it was understood by the Faith and by the Spearitans, Lockri was the harbinger of Astasia: the fallen angel who would destroy the Balance. However, Lockri's Flight merely helped to strengthen the Balance and to rid the Heavenly Realms of the Corruptor, Sol Saradys. So begins today's tale, Lockri's Flight..."

Sebastian set down his ornamented chalice and moved

the Lockri statue to the edge of Uldagard. "Long before Loren's Coming, and since the Division, angels watched over the Mortal Realms, lending their prayers to the mortals in their everlasting fight against Chaos, or weeping at the sight of mortals succumbing to the mysterious force of corruption. After a time, Lockri grew tired of watching the constant wars and strife, and his attention was captured by the subtle wonders of nature upon Athland. He watched the woodlands grow, the rivers divide, and the mountains rise. He soon longed for the ever-changing landscape of the Mortal Realms. However, he knew that the Balance forbid him from crossing the Black Sea. So, Lockri remained in Uldagard, wondering how he might someday sate his desire.

"Over the years, Lockri watched the forests fall as the cruel greks learned to make fire and steel on a much more destructive scale than men. This made Lockri weep and he longed even more to descend upon Athland to defend his beloved trees against the monstrous savages. He soon decided he must do something, and so he approached Athlas the Spearbearer in the Hall of the Four."

Sebastian moved Lockri to the center of the altar, where the borders met in a circle that represented the Hall of the Four. A much larger statue represented Athlas, carefully painted to represent the Crafter of the Balance in his brilliant white armor and wielding his legendary spear, Fulcrum.

"Lockri spoke of his concern to Athlas and presented his solution: the creation of a Warden. The Warden, Locrki insisted, should be as beautiful and as wrathful as nature, assigned to protect the forests. Athlas considered this, and eventually brought it before the rest of the Four. Olerune the Enlightener found truth to Lockri's concern and pledged his fire, Lucrid the Defender admired Lockri's desire to protect the green and pledged his blade. Joacim the Justicer slammed his hammer down in agreement, and the Four were of sound mind. Lockri was sent to Sollum to deliver word to the Creator, Celecy."

Sebastian moved Lockri to the clouds and placed him next to the Keeper of the Wind, Mereketh. "There, Mereketh gave birth to a mighty wind to send the Four's decision to Celecy, and the dryads were soon born. Lockri returned to Uldagard, satisfied that his will had been carried out."

Sebastian moved Lockri and Sol Saradys to Uldagard. "Yet, soon the Thane to the Flames, Sol Saradys, ventured from his throne in Prythene to call upon Lockri. Sol Saradys had secretly made pacts with the Underlords and longed to begin his campaign of corruption upon the Mortal Realms. Lockri, who still yearned to venture across the Black Sea, would become the Corruptor's unwilling instrument in breaking the Balance."

Sebastian went on to tell the tale of how Sol Saradys seduced Lockri with whispered promises, how they could sail the Black Sea in secrecy. Sol Saradys knew that the Balance would not permit him to pass to the Mortal Realms alone, because his intentions were impure. However, he knew Lockri meant well and his intentions were genuine. Thus, if they crossed the Black Sea in harmony, the Balance would permit it. After much urging, Sol Saradys finally persuaded Lockri to join him, bringing about their Descent.

"And thus ends the tale of the Lockri's Flight," Sebastian said, raising his chalice again. "And so begins another tale for another time." He drank.

The congregation drank, applauded, and arose from their knees. Barrid came over to commend Sebastian's first Recitation with a strong pat on the back. Seeley Finch, the young baker from Crescent Ridge, gave Sebastian a basket of fresh basil bread that he baked that morning and called the day's Recitation "better than the book." The widow Yvette Langley gave Sebastian a rather moist kiss on the cheek before leaving.

Last to approach Sebastian was Laurel, whose smile took Sebastian's mind off of the mouth-watering aroma wafting up from Seeley's basil bread.

"I've never heard Lockri's Flight told so well, Sebastian."

"Thank you," Sebastian said with a slight bow. "It was my brother's favorite story." The statement made him suddenly sad, and he looked at the small figure of Lockri on the altar. The statue was fashioned after the popular depiction of the Forest Lord: vibrant green skin, three small horns protruding from his temples and the top of his head, and a broad jaw that was a mix between a wolf and a cat. Raiken had broken a sculpture of Lockri just like it when they were younger...

"...I dreamt of him, oddly enough," Laurel finished, looking down at the figure of Sol Saradys next to Lockri, her smile fading.

Sebastian realized that he hadn't been listening. "I'm sorry?"

Laurel looked up and laughed, "Never mind. I have to return to the Song. Will you come by later?"

"Of course, my lady," Sebastian said. He quickly remembered himself and handed the basket out to her, offering her some of Seeley's bread.

"So gallant," Laurel teased, taking a small piece. She turned to leave, but not before casting a cold glance at the small statue of Sol Saradys, wreathed in flames.

CHAPTER 5: PLANS, PROMISES, POSSESSIONS
Port Laras, kingdom city of Pendara

King Benedict DeSatho sat at the head of a massive table. Atop his balding head rested the crown of Pendara—one even larger and more ornamented than the legendary one that sat atop Emperor Loren's head. Upon the table, sat a feast the likes of which could feed an entire village, but only Benedict's closest vassals were gathered, licking their fingers clean of their lord's decadent offering. Plucking his fine harp on the raised stage behind the king, the bard Jaryd Fawn let his voice rise over the merriment. He styled himself "The Greatest Bard you are Bound to Hear" for good reason, as his powerful voice could be heard even at the back of Shingle Hall—possibly even down at the docks.

Jaryd sang The Raven and the Dove as his fingers danced lightly across the silver strings of his harp. Many of the guests had abandoned the feast and gathered around the stage to witness Jaryd's playing, drawn to his beautiful voice and assured bravado. This was not the bard's first time in Pendara. In fact, he had a tendency to outstay his welcome in the kingdom's port city of Laras. Yet, whatever bad reputation he garnered, he was still the most famous bard in Lorendale, from the Brindle Swales to the western shores of Terrace. And Jaryd was not one to let anyone forget that fact.

His song carried out over the broken conversations around the table.

Divided by war and denied their love,
The Raven took wing to a new land, never to see home again
Never to see his Dove

"And furthermore, you majesty," Jassily Constance said to the king, although he may as well have been speaking to himself. Benedict was in no mood for council. "I think it would be wise to consider these requests from both the Spearitans and the Regents. The Reclamation is at hand, and the kingdom of Pendara could very well stake a claim in the new Loren Empire."

Benedict tore another bite of lamb from the haunch he held. He glanced up at Constance as he chewed, a sign that he was only partially listening now. Then, from the corner of Benedit's eye, he spied his queen, Amarie. Her eyes were fixed on the bard, her lips spreading into a smile. He turned his head to watch the bard, who was directing his song toward a tan-skinned woman beside the stage. The king took a long drink of wine as he stared at the dark-haired beauty. The woman was Kaireth, his mistress from Aushua.

"Bard!" he shouted suddenly, jolting not only Constance and the queen, but quieting nearly all other conversations around the table. "Play a new song."

Jaryd looked up, long blonde hair spilling over his eyes. His merry expression soured and his fingers slowed. The chords of The Raven and the Dove slowly faded into silence. Despite Jaryd's towering presence, he suddenly looked like a scolded child.

Queen Amarie's smile faded as well, but she merely lowered her head and returned to her meal. The king was continuously short with her for her inability to give him a son.

Their daughters, Bella and Reyna, sat at a distant table with their handmaidens, playing chips with two of Benedict's young wards. King Benedict barely even acknowledged his daughters as his own children, but Queen Amarie could say nothing. This was Pendara, not Terrace or Eurheby where women shared power. So, Amarie drank of her wine as Jaryd Fawn began to strum his harp to the tune of Walking in Feathers. The lively and bawdy drinking song heavily contrasted the prior ballad. Amarie always found the song harsh and grating. Her husband, however, let the music liven his spirits.

"Drink, my queen," the king said, as he did so himself. "Let us be thankful for the coming harvests. Our friends to the north are not as fortunate as we." He chuckled and glanced at Constance, who hailed from the north himself. "And do not talk of matters of state tonight, Constance. 'Tis New Season, and the Reclamation can wait."

"Very well, your majesty," Constance said with feigned resignation, pushing a lock of dark hair from his eyes. He had traveled far to speak with the king about this matter, but DeSatho was not a man to be challenged. Constance drank his wine, hoping he could bide his time in order to sway the king's position on the Reclamation in the morning. If Constance were to return to Dratherford without at least a small contingent of Pendara knights, Lord Eyra would have him flayed. Constance's responsibility as the Regency's ambassador was to strengthen their forces for the Reclamation. Pendara had been his first hope, knowing that King DeSatho would want a formidable slice of the new empire. However, the king seemed quite distracted.

Benedict ordered a young Aushuin boy to pour him more wine as Jaryd finished the final chords of Walking in Feathers. As the applause died down, many requests were called out to

Jaryd, most of them drinking songs. When an older man begged for The Man of the Dale, Jaryd immediately took the opportunity to present his take on the classic anthem of Loren the First. The bard's eyes, full of mischief, were fixed on the Regency ambassador during the song.

When the land was left to blood and ash
Savagery thrived in the wake of the clash
The Balance restored as the Burning One slept
Loren would come n' dry tears the Dale wept

Benedict seemed intent on the words, as if they spoke to his conscience. "Constance," the king said suddenly as he set his goblet down, "tell me of this rebellion of yours."

"The Reclamation," Constance corrected Benedict, eager that the king had gained an interest from the bard's clever urging. "The Regency has aligned all of the northern houses under the Imperial Flags, finally putting an end to the Small Wars. Dratherford, Karrek, Veylore, Lhark, Sorentha," Constance counted the Five Houses off on his fingers, "have all pledged an alliance to carry out the Reclamation, your majesty. We mean to cleanse the Loren Empire of the rotten greks and retake Candrella. They will answer for the villainy they carried out all those years ago…"

The king drank. "And who will sit the throne? Will Lorendale once again have an emperor, uniting the Tripartite?" Benedict made it sound like a dire proposition.

Constance shook his head. "The Loren line was lost with the death of Loren IV. Queen Venora and the princess fled Candrella before it was sacked by the greks, but they were never heard from again. They were not found in the Marus Tunnels, the only possible escape route, so they were pronounced dead." Constance leaned in closer. "This is not a play for power on the part of the Regency, your majesty. We are only interested in crushing the greks and purging them from our home. They are growing more ambitious from their seat in the Dale: raiding our lands, poisoning the earth, making the forests too dangerous to hunt. Our lands are suffering, and soon that will spread into the Tripartite. We cannot let the greks thrive. These are our lands."

"The treasury of Candrella must be quite formidable..." Benedict pondered aloud, drinking again.

Constance knew it would come to this. It was an old saying: *all currents find the Pendaran shores.* "Quite formidable indeed," Constance reassured the king. "And the Regency is willing to share that wealth with all who aid in the liberation of Candrella. Greks are drawn to gold and silver, and they seek it merely to hoard it. When we free the north, we will also free those currents. The more knights you send with me, the more currents can be carried back with them upon their return." Constance smiled and cocked an eyebrow, knowing he had the king.

Benedict gave one of his restrained chuckles and drank again. A shadowy figure approached the king before he could respond. It was an older man in a black robe with the silver anchor of Pendara over his heart. Quarris, the king's advisor, was a haggardly man, with a hooked nose and an eerie glass eye. He bent over and whispered into Benedict's ear. The old man's false eye regarded Constance, making the ambassador shudder. The king nodded and turned back to Constance. "It seems that everyone is intent on ruining New Season for me. I shall return." He nodded to Amarie, "My lady."

She did not respond as her husband departed. She looked over at Jaryd sitting on the edge of the stage near the tan-skinned daughter of the Aushuin prisoner. Benedict had been keeping the girl's father for unpronounced treasons. Jaryd was still strumming his harp, but singing quieter now, his words meant only for the young woman. Amarie smiled, strangely fond of the scene before her, even though she knew the king was bedding the girl.

"Your daughters look beautiful," Constance said, raising his glass to the queen. His stubbly beard made him look caring and worldly. "They shall one day make two queens nearly as lovely as you."

Amarie laughed. "So gallant of you to say so, Ambassador. Tell me, Jassily, will you fight in the Reclamation as well?"

He nodded, "With all my heart, your highness."

Amarie DeSatho smiled and turned to watch Jaryd Fawn serenade the Aushuin girl, who seemed to be in a trance, unable to take her dark eyes off of the bard. "I cannot think of anything better to fight with, Jassily."

Quarris led the intoxicated king down the broken stairs. Worn from years of use, the stairs led deep into the bowels of Castle Laras. Down in those damp, dark levels of the castle were dungeons used for various sinister purposes by the king's predecessors. Benedict had no taste for the grisly practices carried out by his ancestors, so he bequeathed those places to his father's most trusted councilor, Quarris Felgun, in exchange for the same lucrative advice that the councilor had given Severen DeSatho during his reign. In addition to being his councilor, Quarris was also a priest, but not of the Faith.

"Could you not tell me this dire news in a cleaner venue, Quarris?" Benedict asked as he ducked under a dripping collection of questionable black sludge. "You know I hate it down here."

"Your majesty will excuse the inconvenience," Quarris hissed through his nearly toothless mouth. "When I have told you of these tidings, you will return to your festivities much the happier."

"I was happy enough, Quarris." The king produced a sweetcake that he had been hiding in a belt pouch. When he bit into it, the honey filling dripped down his chin. "Did you know the Imperials are offering the currents of Candrella in exchange for killing greks? You never told me such news. I would have sent out half of the Shore Guard immediately."

Quarris stopped and turned to the king. "The Reclamation..." The old man thought for a moment while the king continued to eat his cake with a raised eyebrow. An idea came to Quarris and he smiled. "Do not send any knights to the Regency, your majesty."

Benedict stopped eating for a moment, and with a full mouth asked, "Mhy mot?"

Quarris smiled wider. "If the ambassador cannot procure enough soldiers from Pendara, he will be forced to travel to Eurheby and Terrace to help bolster the Regency's forces. If Luther and Alastair oblige, that would leave both kingdoms significantly weaker than your own, your majesty."

Benedict swallowed. "You starting a war, Quarris?"

"Not I," Quarris said with a grin, his glass eye shimmering in the torchlight. He turned to continue downstairs. The king hurried after him, no longer dragging his feet.

They entered a round chamber at the bottom of the stairs with halls that branched out in all different directions. Benedict heard moans in distant rooms, but he declined to inquire about them. Quarris performed strange and perverted rituals on the islanders that Benedict collected from Aushua, and wandering into only one such ritual was enough for Benedict to know that he would prefer ignorance of the matter. He kept himself blind to the fate of his captured Aushuins.

The business of slave trade had been a custom of the Pendara nobility since they began to rule the seas with their strong galleys. The Aushuins were a primitive people, constantly at war with their lizard-men hydrek enemies, and they were easily bested by the growing, ambitious kingdom of Pendara. Benedict kept some slaves, but many of his captive Aushuins were relatives of his mistresses, kept bound in the dungeons to ensure that his bedslaves would not flee Castle Laras.

Quarris walked to the center of his chamber. The walls were stone with stalactites hanging from the ceiling. The chamber would have looked like little more than a cave if it had not been for the expensive furnishings. The room was filled with towering bookshelves, exotic statues, and large, ornamented chairs. Quarris took a torch from the wall and lit the candles on the center table. A large map was spread over the table, with hundreds of small black stones arranged in groups upon it. The map read *Vhaltas* in a script that largely lacked elegance.

"Something is happening upon the Burning Isles," Quarris said, leaning over the table and arranging certain stones as though he were trying to create a piece of art.

A scream echoed from one of the long hallways.

"I do not doubt it," the king said sarcastically. "Why does that constitute *dire* news?"

"Sol Saradys has awoken," Quarris said, as plainly as if commenting on the weather.

King Benedict DeSatho held the cake to his mouth, stopping in mid bite. He lowered the cake, "What?"

"The Corruptor has been disturbed," Quarris said, looking up with his one good eye. "He came to me in a dream and gave me visions. Meddling forces from the west allowed Sol Saradys to overthrow Sand, the Dream Lord, in the Revery."

"You brought me down here to discuss dreams, Quarris?" The king was becoming less interested and increasingly annoyed with the old man. "You know, if it weren't for my father and the fact that you bring a fair share of coin to the coffers, I'd have had the Sect of Halcyon come and rid you of your tongue long ago." The king turned to leave.

"Celendas will fall," the priest said plainly.

The king stopped.

Quarris continued. "You must excuse an old man's ramblings, but you need to know of the Burning One's awakening to understand what is to happen."

The king turned, shoved the rest of the cake into his mouth, and sat down in the most lavish of the chairs. "Indulge me."

"Sand rules the Revery, where we go when we dream," Quarris began. "After the Shackling, Sol Saradys slept for many years and his influence began to wane. During his slumber, he was doomed to roam the dreamlands, searching for a way to influence mortals once more. But only Sand had the power to shape the dreams of mortals. However, under this very moon, I dreamt of Sol Saradys, who has somehow overthrown Sand for control of the Revery, a fact that I have confirmed with several of my…colleagues. The Burning One's sleep has been disturbed by some unwitting, yet commendable, mortal who has performed a deadly ritual that could have greatly shifted the Balance. Fortunately, we have yet to see retaliation."

"So, get on with it. What do your dreams have to do with Celendas falling?" Benedict began to pour himself some of

Quarris' wine, expecting to be there for a while.

Quarris motioned to the map of Vhaltas. "The cultists are restless. They have done nothing during the Burning One's slumber but worship his name and offer him sacrifices, yet nothing seemed to wake him. However, now he comes to them in dreams and unites them all." Quarris pointed to the different clusters of black stones, representing the cultists. "The Cult is amassing, and once the Binding Ritual is translated, a vessel will be chosen and Sol Saradys' right hand will be freed."

"His right hand?" the king asked with a smile. "What about the other?"

Quarris looked up, sudden fear painted plainly across his face. "The left hand carries the doom of us all. The Underlords did not bind that hand, the Four did, and with good reason. The ritual will not disturb that half of the *kropal*."

"Alright," Benedict said, telling the old priest to settle down with a motion of his hands. "So, the right hand is a vessel of Sol Saradys—a mortal who can wield his powers. I've heard the stories. Get to the point."

Quarris produced a piece of parchment and read aloud:

> *When the Revery falls to Corruption's seed*
> *The dragons shall come with fire and endless fury.*
> *The Black Wind's son shall rise again,*
> *After kingdoms fall under the sign of his name.*
> *The Balance shall break and the angels will fall*
> *And Astasia will reign with the coming of the Grey Dawn*

Benedict drank. He had been to church before. Being aligned with the Spearitan Faith required the king to make appearances at many ceremonies in the city of Parity, the Spearitan capital.

He knew the Prophecies of Astasia well. "So, you want to bring about the end of the world?"

Quarris smiled. "The end of *this* world, your majesty, and the birth of a new one. Astasia will bring about the demise of the Balance, which is clearly a device to work in favor of those who follow Order," he said spitefully. "All the lands are ruled by those who revere either the Four or the Lady. We," Quarris said, pointing to the clustered black stones that represented the Cult of the Burning One, "are not opposed to living under the restraint of the Balance, as it protects us from total annihilation. However, we can no longer live under *this* Balance. Our lord was chained for eternity for spreading his word, and we cannot abide by that. Lorendale needs a new law and a new ruler, one that is respectful of our worship."

Benedict knew that Quarris meant him to be the new emperor of all of Lorendale. He also knew that Quarris was absolutely mad, but he nodded anyway. "And this leads us to the fall of Celendas?" Benedict had often dreamt of expanding Pendara, and there was no better start than Celendas. The two kingdoms had warred in the past and there was a longstanding bitterness between Port Laras of Pendara and Celendas of Eurheby. Benedict could not deny his desire to take those lands as his own.

Quarris moved the black stones to the shores of Vhaltas. "The cult shall follow the prophecy to bring about the Days, and a kingdom shall fall. You are protected here by your family's allegiance to the Burning One and Aevenore is landlocked. This leaves Celendas, which is right on the shores of the Valice. Once we take Celendas, Aevenore will be next to fall. And you shall rule in the name of the Burning One."

The king smiled. *The Burning One, Nekriark, your mother's*

tits, I would rule in the name of any of them, you mad old fool. "Very well. I shall not send any of my men with Constance."

"Also," Quarris instructed. "It would be wise if we did not send any ships out into the Valice, as well as cut off land trade to Celendas. Those waters will not be welcoming in the next few days, and we should ensure Celendas is not well supplied."

Benedict narrowed his eyes and looked as if he were about to argue this decree. His trade to Celendas was a major source of currents for the crown, but the prospect of raiding the Phoenix Throne's treasury smothered any doubts he had. "I will inform the harbor master."

Quarris held up a finger to stall the king and produced a small ring. "One more thing, your majesty. The Burning One is quite unpredictable, and some who he…influences, do not handle it very well." The ring held a polished black stone. He handed it to the king. "If you encounter one of these unfortunately weak mortals under his influence, press this ring into their head or chest. It should purge them of their possession."

The king accepted the ring and gave Quarris an indescribable look.

Quarris shrugged. "You cannot predict pure Chaos, your majesty."

As the king departed the dreary chamber, he let the ring fall into the deep pocket of his coat, planning never to touch it again.

The next morning, Jaryd Fawn awoke with a splitting headache and an Aushuin in his bed. He groaned and rolled over as silently as he could, not wanting to wake her. He found a wineskin on the table beside the bed. He drank a little, hoping to remember last night. He wasn't sure, but he guessed that he was at an inn somewhere near Seaside. He remembered playing for that grouchy bastard of a king last night, but he hardly remembered the Aushuin girl. Many seasons had passed since Jaryd had performed while completely sober and this was not an uncommon result of his court performances.

"My lord," the young girl murmured behind him, rolling over and running her fingers down his back. "Will you play me a song?"

Jaryd drank, cringing slightly at her touch. He hated this part. "I can't, I have a ship to catch." A familiar tactic.

The girl sat up. "But my father…"

"He won't have to know, love," Jaryd said, having not the slightest care or notion who her father was. He stood up to find his trousers. "I'll be gone before he wakes, and just be sure to take some rillion weed. You're too young to have a bastard." He couldn't find his harp anywhere and he was beginning to panic. A good harp was hard to come by in the south.

"No…" she sounded confused. "You said you could help me save him. He's in the dungeons, below the castle. The king has him prisoner. You said you could pick the locks and release him for me."

Jaryd tried not to laugh. "I'm sorry, love, but if your father's below Castle Laras, then he's probably no longer in one piece. That glass-eyed priest down there likes to tear them up and see how long they can live through it. I hear he sometimes eats them." Jaryd threw on his shirt, still not even looking at the girl as he hunted for his harp. "Tell me, love, have you seen my strings or my blade?"

"You will save him!" she screamed from behind him.

The voice was terrifying. Jaryd turned, reaching for the dagger that wasn't at his belt. When he faced the girl, he saw why. She held it toward him, her eyes completely white.

"Careful with that, love," Jaryd said, raising his hands in submission. "Let's talk about this a bit." The girl was lovely, with spiraling tattoos adorning her bare flesh. Jaryd could see why he took her to bed, but with the life drained from her eyes like that, she looked absolutely frightening. Her absent gaze reminded Jaryd of his time in Andira, and he did not like to be reminded of Andira. He knew a possession like this could only be possible through a sleep ritual. "Tell me, did you have a bad dream?"

The naked girl stood up on the bed, still holding the dagger ready. "He said...he said if I bled you, father would be freed. He said you must die!" She leapt, slashing at the bard.

Jaryd sidestepped the swipe and brought his elbow down on the girl's neck. She slumped to the floor and the dagger went skidding under the dresser, out of his reach. He went diving for it, but then the girl was on him, clawing and biting. Usually, having a beautiful, nude Aushuin on top of him thrashing like this was the sort of thing Jaryd would have to pay for, but now he screamed in pain as she began to tear his flesh. He threw an elbow behind him that caught her in the temple. She fell back and Jaryd was able to snatch the dagger from under the dresser.

He jumped up and held it between them. "Now calm yourself! Do not listen to him!"

It was too late. The girl's eyes were pure white and pure fury. She dove toward the bard, heedless of the dagger. The short blade was buried in her chest before Jaryd could react. As she began to go limp, she widened her eyes and gave the bard a malicious grin.

"The Days are coming," she said, before coughing up

blood. A moment later, she fell to the floor dead.

Jaryd stared at her for a moment and then at his bloody blade until it began to blur in his vision. He reached over and drank what was left in the wineskin. Not nearly enough. He sat down on the bed to clean his dagger off with the sheets and thought that he had better hurry down to the docks before someone found a dead Aushuin girl in his room. He collected the rest of his things, finally finding his harp behind the door to the hall. As he picked it up and began to leave, he took one last look at the dead girl. Her eyes had regained their natural color, the influence leaving her. Sadness and pity washed over him.

Jaryd sat down on the bed and began to play A Night in the Revery, thinking she might have liked that one.

CHAPTER 6: THE SECOND SHACKLE
The Silver Spire, West Terrace

Vanghrel read the parchment again, this time spreading it across his desk to smooth the wrinkles out, so he knew he was reading it correctly. Though it was splattered with blood and ink blotches, the Luminary could still make out the words. The parchment read:

> *I have found the stone. The river shamans kept it*
> *secret, but I found it. I have been taken by the Sect and am*
> *being held in their citadel underneath Aevenore. I have*
> *hidden the stone and they must not find it. Send aid.*
> *-Benegast*

The raven that brought the message let out a loud call as it perched on the Luminary's windowsill, perhaps expecting payment for the delivery. Vanghrel, caught up in the excitement of this news, threw the bird a strip of undercooked boar meat from his midday meal. Usually, Vanghrel would have shooed the noisy bird away, as he had never cared for Benegast's bird of choice, but this unexpected message enlivened him. Right on the heels of Baron VonAnthony's boon, Vanghrel had just been given a second blessing. Yet, he must hurry. He was not sure what Benegast meant by being taken by the Sect, but he did know what stone his Entrusted wrote of.

The Stone of Acrivas—the Shackle of the Sea.

Only two more, Vanghrel thought to himself. Though he did

not physically have the *evathyste* or the *kropal* in his possession, these two possible leads brought him closer to his goal than he ever believed possible. *The Shackles will be mine*, he thought, smiling. *And the Underlords will be forever in my debt. Myriad's legions will be under my command...*

Vanghrel's smile widened, wickedly.

A knock came at the door, startling him. He reflexively rolled up the parchment and shoved it into his robes. "Enter," he said angrily.

A Vigilant walked in, shrouded and masked in tight, grey wrappings. A bow was strung on his back and a short blade at his waist. "You summoned me, Luminary."

Vanghrel relaxed. The Vigilants were his most loyal subordinates, even more so than his few Entrusted. They were privy to the secrets of the Spire and prided themselves on keeping their secrecy. Only assassins from the aptly named Quiet Isles were given the position of Vigilant, for they held their tongues and did not question any command. They were compensated handsomely for their services. Vanghrel snapped his fingers at Benegast's raven, sending it flying from the Spire. "Yes, Nyjien. Please shut the door." Vanghrel sat in the large ornamented chair behind his desk.

Nyjien Kast closed the door behind him, removing his hood and lowering his mask in the privacy of his master's study. His skin was relatively darker than most men from the Dale, as was common with the Quiet Islanders. His long hair was dark and thin, falling down to the middle of his back. A gruesome scar ran down the right side of his face, from his eyebrow to the corner of his lip. Aside from that, his face was a glorious work of art—beautiful and ethereal, standing before the Luminary's desk like an angel of death.

"I need you to bring me a student," Vanghrel commanded, "one that will serve as my new Entrusted."

"I know several that would serve well," Nyjien responded. "Xavia Maldroth has shown exceptional interest in the Lost Arts, and she has displayed great initiative in organizing other Adepts to sneak about the Spire at night. She has a thirst."

Vanghrel shook his head. Though he knew about Xavia's initiative and her potential, he did not want her. Not only did he not care to put such responsibility on the shoulders of such a young girl, he also distrusted Xavia's 'thirst.' Such ambition was selfish, and not a quality one looks for in subordinates.

Nyjien did not rebuke the decision. "Teylus Earrin healed a broken limb last month using…darker crafts than those taught to him here. He studies necromancy from books that he brought from Therrec."

Vanghrel had not given much thought to Teylus, a recent Accepted that earned his white robes at a much younger age than any other healer to pass through the Spire. Every so often, one of the Spire's healers naturally became fascinated with necromancy and resurrection. It, unfortunately, did not mean they were always willing to admit or pursue that fascination.

It must be Anerith, Vanghrel decided. *Anerith has survived so much…*

The Vigilant sensed the Luminary's doubt. "Just the other day, I overheard the young Agravite Demitri Dryce confide in Anerith Zathon. It sounds like he dreams of the Corruptor. Such happenings are signs. Sol Saradys lingers in the minds of those with an interest in the Black Winds, and even more interest in Chaos." Nyjien rarely revealed his emotions, but his face now hinted a smile as he caught the Luminary's attention.

Sol Saradys in the Revery, Vanghrel thought, remembering

the frequent visits from Helena VonAnthony before her death. She had come to him often speaking of interpreting an old text from beyond the Narrows to the north. She thought she found a way to dethrone Sand, the lord of the Revery. *Did she really usurp the dreamlord?* Vanghrel was suddenly astonished, never thinking Helena capable of something so...reckless. *If the Corruptor has taken over the Revery, I do not have much time.*

"Bring me Anerith Zathon, Nyjien," the Luminary ordered, deciding to go with his instincts. "He has shown that he can keep secrets by not reporting his friend's dreams to an Adjurer. And he has proven that he has the ability to survive hell."

"He quite literally walked through hell," Adjurer Mereth said as she motioned to the Abyssal Realm of Volkris on the hanging Chart of the Realms. "After helping bring about the fall of the Vysarcian Empire, Skall ventured into the Abyssal Realms, walking across the Ashen Fields of Volkris to confront Nekriark, the Underlord that allowed him to be born from the womb of a dead woman. Skall threatened to kill the Underlord, but Nekriark warned him that if he did so, he would be responsible for ushering in the Days of Astasia. So, Skall returned to the Mortal Realms where he and his ancestors were hunted by the Sect of Halcyon. Skall's bloodline was declared purged from the world when the High Sectary Leif Morrigan managed to drown the witch Malyse—the last of Skall's bloodline—in the holy waters of Coventina."

Anerith stifled a yawn, though it was not because he found the subject matter boring. On the contrary, he had spent the entirety of the prior night reading ahead in the *Life of Skall* and he was merely tired from the lack of sleep.

"Do you find this matter tedious, Adept Zathon?" Adjurer Mereth asked, craning her neck over the other students to address Anerith. She had an unnaturally long neck, Anerith always thought. Like a heron, only uglier.

"No, I—"

Mereth interrupted him. "Since we do have an evaluation on the history of Vysarc coming up, perhaps you would like to volunteer to give us a review of Skall's birth and the Fall of Vysarc?" It was not a question.

Anerith looked around at his peers; red robes, white robes, and blue robes alike all turned to stare at him. Demitri and Xavia gave him bright smiles from nearby. Xavia was so pretty when she smiled. Her dark hair fell over her face and her wide grin formed small wrinkles in the corners of her eyes. Anerith noted Demitri's hand on her thigh, and turned away. He stood up and walked to the front of the study hall as if he were walking to his execution. He hated speaking in front of so many people.

Mereth elaborately stepped aside and motioned to Anerith sweepingly. "Perhaps you will make history more exciting than I."

Anerith turned to the class, eyed the Adjurer, then sighed pointedly. "The Son of Chaos was born from a star nearly 350 years ago," he began. He recited everything he had read the night before. The story came out a lot easier than he thought it would. "The star was called down to Athland by the Vysarcian Archgeist Rhavael, who was a practitioner of the most ancient death magicks known in Vysarc. Together with the warlock Pulasia, who worshipped the Burning One, they were able to perform a ritual that manipulated the powers from beyond the Balance: the powers of creation." Anerith motioned to the surrounding blank space on the Chart of the Realms that represented the Black

Sea. "These powers were known as the Black Winds. Their ritual summoned the star that, when combined with the body of a holy Therrecian woman, Rhavael was able to craft into a magical being that would be unaffected by the constraints placed upon the mortals by the Balance."

Anerith looked at the Adjurer, hoping that was sufficient. She merely raised an eyebrow and motioned with her hand, signaling him to continue.

Anerith bit his lip for a moment before telling the rest of the tale. "The Archgeist named his creation Skall, meaning *unborn* in Vysarcian, and treated him as if he were a royal son of Vysarc. But soon, Rhavael grew greedy. He was not satisfied with merely wielding the powers of creation; he wanted to embody his creation. He wanted to wield the powers that Skall inherited. So, with Pulasia, he began to explore the powers of possession and, before long, he was able to impart his will upon Skall. He enthralled his so-called son, and used the boy to demolish entire villages and kill innocent people by the thousands. However, Skall thought he only dreamed these atrocities. When he discovered the truth, he assisted the Lockrian druids in destroying the Vysarcian Empire, which brought about the Fall of Vysarc. Since Skall was born from powers beyond the Balance, he could not be killed by forces born of Order or Chaos"

Anerith looked to the Adjurer again, hoping he could return to his seat. However, a Vigilant had appeared in the hall and was talking to Mereth in a whisper. The Adjurer looked up.

"Anerith, the Luminary requests your presence."

Anerith stood before the Luminary, trying as hard as he could not to stare at the old man's craggy face. Vanghrel was not one to make himself seen in the Spire, and this was the first time that Anerith had ever stood face to face with him. Before, he had wondered what the old man looked like. Now seeing him, Anerith was somewhat disappointed. He always imagined a withered and ancient old man that held infinite wisdom in his eyes. However, the man who sat before him looked barely over sixty, slightly balding on the top of his head, and his gaze seemed to hint that he was secretly planning Anerith's demise.

They both stood for a long and silent moment. Anerith could not begin to guess as to the reason of his summoning. Had he been promoted to Agravite? *No*, he thought, *I haven't even been to the observatory yet.*

Just when Anerith was about to inquire as to the reason for his presence, Vanghrel spoke, his old hand going to the bronze wyvern statue on the desk.

"Have you ever ridden a wyvern, Adept Zathon?"

The question took Anerith aback. The rookery in the western courtyard held Vanghrel's prized wyverns, but no students were permitted to ride them, aside from the Entrusted. Suddenly, Anerith feared that he had been falsely accused of sneaking into the rookery, an activity he could easily picture Xavia and Rutherford practicing.

"Sir, I have never—"

Vanghrel raised a hand to silence him, seeming to comprehend the denial. "Not one of the Spire's. I am merely asking if you remember your arrival to Terrace."

Anerith shook his head. He had never known his parents or of his reason for being enrolled in the Spire. At one time, he found this curious. However, many of his peers knew nothing of their own origins. So, after awhile, he found the subject to be irrelevant and he focused on his studies. Though why this concerned wyverns, Anerith could not say.

Vanghrel leaned back and stroked his chin. "You remember nothing before coming here?"

Anerith shook his head again. "No, sir. I have always assumed I was an orphan, probably from another land. In all honesty, I have never felt like a native to the Dales."

Vanghrel grinned. "No. You are not of the Dales. You came to us from the Therrecian peninsula, upon the back of a wyvern. You had barely seen your sixth year, but you somehow survived what had to have been a harsh journey." The Luminary waited for a reaction, but Anerith merely stared at him, taking in the information. "And as you know, wyverns are partial to the Dead Plains up north, near the ruins of Candrella and Vysarc…"

Anerith stared at something beyond the Luminary, trying to figure out what this old man wanted of him. He found it strange that he could not remember such a dramatic event of his life, but his past had always been a mystery. It was nothing new. "I did not know I was a Therrecian, sir. But, I thank you for taking me in."

"I had little choice," Vanghrel said, his smile fading. "No child of your age should have survived such a place or such a journey. I had to admit you into the Spire's Academy on pure principle." He pressed his hands together as if in prayer. "What I want to know is: what do you want to make of your time here?"

Anerith answered instinctively. "I am here to learn of the mysteries of the world, both the arcane and the natural forces."

Vanghrel waved a hand, motioning to the door. "They all are here for such purposes. Are you not here for power? To harness those forces you learn about?"

Anerith blinked, once more taken aback. *Is this a test or something?* "I have no desire to disturb the Balance, Luminary."

This answer seemed to displease Vanghrel, who looked down at his desk, pondering something important. After a long moment of silent consideration, the Luminary looked at a piece of rolled up parchment on his desk. He suddenly looked up to Anerith.

"Have you ever been to Aevenore, Anerith?"

Demitri walked beside Xavia through the courtyard. Both of them were nervous, but neither wanted to address their fears. Anerith was not an Entrusted, nor did he care to be one, as he was always quick to remind them of. The Luminary did not summon students to his chambers unless they wore black robes, or unless they had committed some sort of transgression against the Spire. While Anerith was not one to break the rules, some of his acquaintances were.

Neither Demitri nor Xavia spoke as they walked through the bustling courtyard. They did not touch each other either or walk too close until they reached their spot. On the far reaches of the courtyard, close to the aptly named Vigil—where the Vigilants kept their quarters—was a recess in the outer walls. The weeping limbs of a willow tree shrouded the hollow. Xavia brought Demitri here when they first began their courtship, and since then it had been their haven.

Demitri parted the hanging branches with his hand and remembered when she had brought him here in the middle of the night to tell him about her nightmare. It had been nearly a month ago, after Xavia's friend Rya was sent away on an errand for the Luminary. Xavia claimed she had dreamt of a man on a fiery throne whispering secrets in her ear, secrets that burned like flames. The dream sounded exactly like the ones Demitri had been having—but the whispers he had heard in his own dream were all about Xavia.

At first, Demitri did not believe her. He thought she was mocking him somehow, but how would she know of his dreams that he never spoke of?

"Did you tell him?" Xavia asked, as she entered the shelter of the tree.

Demitri nodded.

Xavia bit her lip. She did so when she literally wanted to bite back her words, a quality that Demitri was grateful for. He had seen her wrath unleashed on many Accepted during their younger years, and he loved her for holding it back on his account.

"A Vigilant might have heard," Demitri said, pulling a handful of leaves off the tree. He let them fall through his fingers, making a fist after they all fell.

Xavia rubbed her temple, thinking quickly. "I have heard of cultists being purged from the Spire," Xavia said nervously. Many stories filtered through the Spire about witches and warlocks who secretly worshipped Chaos being handed over to the Sect of Halcyon. Some said that the Luminary even falsely accused some of his students to keep strong relations with Aevenore and the Sect. Those students were burned at the stake like the witches of old. "Such dreams would be enough to get us sent to the Sect."

Demitri knelt down, pulling Xavia with him. "We are not the only ones having these dreams, Xavia. I have heard others whisper about fire and blood. Something is happening here, and surely the Vigilants and the Luminary know that. They will not burn the entire Spire over this."

"Why else would he summon Anerith!?" Xavia asked wildly. "He has never even stained his robes! Vanghrel wants a confession from him so he can send us away." She clenched her fist. "That old man is the real warlock! I know it!"

Demitri moved closer to console her, but she threw up her arms in refusal and stood up. "We have to prove it, Demitri!"

"What do you mean?"

Xavia pointed toward the Spire. "I know something is not right with this place. He's hiding something. Maybe he's somehow responsible for the dreams! He could be a cultist."

He shook his head doubtfully. "You have searched every corner of the Spire, Xavia. You know about his deals with the Sect and the nobility, but almost every establishment in Lorendale does these things. Where else could he be hiding his secret shrine to Sol Saradys?"

The question sparked an idea in Xavia, and she looked up at him. "Below," she said simply. "Something is through that door."

All the students of the Spire knew of the entrance to the 'dungeons' that was visible through the Adjurers' dormitory. The door was large and forged of black iron with stairs leading down to it. It was called the dungeons by the younger inhabitants of the Spire, and was the primary setting for ghost stories and the like. Nobody knew what actually lay beyond there, but many skeptics just claimed it was a storage chamber.

Before Demitri could respond, a Vigilant suddenly appeared and parted the leaves.

"Agravite Dryce," the Vigilant said, "the Luminary has requested your presence."

Demitri gave Xavia a quick look, wondering if, for some reason, this would be the last time he saw her beautiful face. "In my dream," he said, "that dark voice...he said I would give you everything you ever desired. I always liked to think that it was just me." He smiled weakly.

Despite her reluctance to avow any knowledge of their relationship, Xavia walked over and kissed Demitri in front of the Vigilant. She promised in his ear, "I will find his secrets here."

CHAPTER 7: AWAKENING
In the depths of Sleep

The Revery was a wondrous and dangerous place, sharing borders with the Abyssal Realms of Volkris and Enda. The atmosphere was insubstantial, changing constantly. One minute, a dreamer might be walking alone through a beautiful forest grove, and the next he could be in the center of a bustling metropolis, surrounded by thousands of other dreamers. As visitors of the Revery, dreamers came nightly to transform the realm to their will. However, the real natives to the Revery were the marons, demon incubi that lived and thrived in nightmares. These vile beings found joy in spreading their terrible visions to the dreaming mortals, though they were only permitted to give nightmares by Sand's decree. Sand was the Lord of the Revery, and he ruled over the marons from his palace known as the Hall of Mayrs.

That was, of course, until recently.

Skahgerok knew there had been a coup in the Revery; it was palpable. He searched for Sand, knowing that the Dream Lord was no longer ruling from the Hall. Skahgerok spent the last 600 years of his life becoming accustomed to the oddities of the dreamland, but until recently, he had not seen anything as unorthodox as what now took place. Marons ran loose, unchecked by their Lord. They captured dreamers and dragged them to the Hall of Mayrs, which now looked like it burned indefinitely wherever or whenever it appeared. Skahgerok dared not approach the Hall before discovering the Lord of the Revery's fate.

Once a mere Rhelklander, Skahgerok was chosen—or cursed, some would say—by the Four to dwell in the shadows of the Abyss. He was charged to wander the Revery in order to glimpse prophecies, and then to return to his body in the Mortal Realms whenever he needed to stay some coming storm. He befriended some mortals during his waking times, usually in order to prevent tragedy. This had earned him the title Eye of the Acrid Sky among those who knew his name, as he only saw darkness on the horizon.

He saw darkness now, enveloping the Revery.

The dreamland shifted from wilderness to ruined city while Skahgerok searched for any indication of Sand's power. As he passed several marons sitting upon the chests of mortal dreamers in that ruined city, Skahgerok wanted to snatch the demons up and tear them apart. Marons shared their nightmares by sitting on the chests of dreamers. Skahgerok knew that Sand would not normally abide this many nightmares spreading in the Revery. However, Skahgerok dwelt here by the grace of Sand. The Dream Lord would not permit him to interfere with the workings of his domain. So Skahgerok was forced to watch these atrocities as he continued through the ruined city and across darkening fields, desperately searching for Sand.

After what felt like days of wandering, Skahgerok finally came to a shoreline. The horizon was blue as far as he could see, with a small island in the middle of the pristine ocean. This was Sand's work. The Dream Lord loved the sea and sky, claiming he was a son to an angel of Sollum and an angel of Acrivas. Skahgerok dove into the sea and swam the distance to the island, the water cool and clean. Perfect. He made it to the shore of the island and saw Sand sitting on a small fallen tree. The remains of a fire pit were at his feet. The Lord of the Revery looked tired as usual; the hollows of his eyes were a hazy purple and his long, red hair was severely frayed.

"Lord Sand," Skahgerok said as he rose out of the water, his clothing already dry.

"Ah, the harbinger," Sand said, his voice dry and carefree. "Where were you when I needed you?" He smiled faintly, picking at the large piece of exotic fruit that he was eating.

"What has happened?" Skahgerok asked, forgetting formality. "The marons, they are taking dreamers to the Hall. What is the meaning of this?"

"Chaos," Sand said, his eyes lost in the surrounding blue of sea and sky. "Is there a purpose for Chaos to exist, Skahgerok? It just breeds destruction, change, and corruption. It is tiresome..."

Skahgerok knelt down so he could face the Dream Lord. "What happened?"

"Chaos," Sand repeated, his eyes finding Skahgerok's. "Not the Chaos found here in the Abyss, but corrupted Chaos. Your work is coming undone, Skahgerok," Sand said with a sad grin. "The Burning One is waking."

Before Skahgerok could question the Dream Lord, Sand waved his hand. Trails of sparkling dust were left in its wake, and Skahgerok's surroundings slowly changed. He was no longer on the peaceful island surrounded by eternal blue. He was now under a grey sky in the valleys of Terrace. Farms and villages were burning in the distance, and the walls of Aevenore were crumbling. Skahgerok ran toward those tumbling walls and found a lone figure wearing a red robe, his long hair dancing in the winds of his destruction. Skahgerok had never seen the man before, but he could tell instantly that he wielded terrible power.

Skall's descendant shall come, said Sand's voice in Skahgerok's head. *The Black Wind's son. And the kingdoms shall fall under the sign of his name.*

"Skall…" Skahgerok said aloud, but he could not hear his own voice over Sand's. *Skall.* It was a name Skahgerok knew well from his years in the Abyss. Skall was the child from beyond, able to work magic without fear of retribution from the Balance. But the man standing before Skahgerok, young as he was, did not look like the much-prophesied descendant of Skall. He looked unsure of himself, and awkward in sight of his own awesome power. Skall's descendant turned to Skahgerok and Skahgerok could see that he was weeping. *He is only a boy,* Skahgerok saw, *hardly past his twentieth year.*

The boy's face blurred with the crumbling castle. A dark cave rose up and swallowed Skahgerok. He was in Neveren, more specifically in the dark mountain caves of Demonescale Heights. Skahgerok knew what he would see before the figure in the distance even took shape. The cave was Scorn, and the figure materializing from the mists was the human form of Adratheon, the vicious black dragon that brought destruction from the mountains.

Adratheon descended the stairs from the altar that held his dragon form, pinned down by the legendary Dragonsbane.

The dragons shall come, Sand said in Skahgerok's mind, *with fire and endless fury.*

Skahgerok clenched his fists. He was awake when King Ausfred Galvian had done battle with Adratheon. Skahgerok had aided in the forging of the Dragonsbane. At that time, he had already wandered the Revery for years learning of the ferocity and lunacy of Adratheon. The black-hearted tyrant single-handedly bred a new breed of dragonkind after his own kindred fled to the lands of Ellanthra, where they would no longer be bothered by the trivial lives of humans. While other dragons cared little for humans, Adratheon's curiosity of them grew into a sickening obsession. He stole them, dissected them, challenged them, studied them, devoured them, loved them, hated them, and above all, terrorized them with a passion only a dragon can possess.

After seeing what Adratheon was capable of, Skahgerok had no choice but to wake and find other mortals to champion the cause of Adratheon's demise. He could think of no better place to find those willing mortals than in the kingdom of Celendas, which received the brunt of Adratheon's admiration.

Adratheon strode down the stairs and walked with a feline grace toward Skahgerok. His human form was beautiful and terrible: his skin lightly darkened like an Aushuin, his hair long and dark to match, and his eyes confident and cruel. As he approached, smiling, Skahgerok could no longer contain his rage. He let out a bestial growl and threw his hulking form at the dragon. But the visage faded as Skahgerok's arms wrapped around it. Adratheon's voice lingered, laughing at the dreamer's wrath.

The next vision came to Skahgerok as he rested on one knee, letting his fury fade. When he looked up, he saw the shimmering halls of Candrella with silver and emerald banners hanging from the high ceiling. The Lorenguard was gathered, lining either side of the throne, their various colored armors danced brilliantly in the sunlight that poured in through the high windows. On the floor, scattered about before the throne, were the mutilated bodies of humans, greks, angels, and demons—the remnants of a war. Skahgerok arose and faced the man who sat the throne.

He was Loren's heir; that was a certainty. He had the curly brown hair and vibrant green eyes of Loren the First. Across his lap rested an elegant grey sword. The blade looked as if it were carved of stone, not forged from iron or steel. The young heir's face was detached, betraying neither joy nor sadness. He merely sat, knowing he must rule. The Lorenguard, the legendary knights that were charged with the protection of the entirety of Lorendale, stood silently vigilant, watching the aftermath of the massacre that only they could have been responsible for.

In that silence, Skahgerok heard the Balance break, either in Sand's voice or in the indescribable feeling of doom produced by the scene before him.

The Balance shall break, Sand said softly, *and the angels will fall.*

Skahgerok knew the images for what they were now: prophesies of the coming of the Days of Astasia. Corruption had come to the Revery.

"Sand," Skahgerok began, still staring at the young heir who must have been dreaming the very same dream as he. "I must stop this…"

Sand did not answer. The image faded and suddenly a dark tower stood before Skahgerok, surrounded by drying marshland. The air was motionless and there was no sign of life. The grey clouds that hung above him were as still as stone. A black robed figure stood at the entrance to the tower, unmoving. His hand wrapped around a jagged stone.

The Stone of Sollum.

The Keeper of the Wind, Sand said distantly, as if he were fading from Skahgerok's mind. *The Shackle of the Sky is in dark hands, during dark times…*

"What about the others?" Skahgerok asked urgently. "Are the others kept safe?"

Sand did not answer. It was then Skahgerok knew that he was waking.

Deep in a hidden cave in the Neveren Mountains, Skahgerok's body had lain still for nearly fifty years while his mind wandered in the Revery. His mortal vessel was unnaturally preserved through years—decades—of hibernation, a part of his reward for banishing Sol Saradys from Athland. That body earned its rest. Now it twitched, softly at first and then violently.

His body still bore the appearance of a Rhelklander: a rough wool spun shirt covered his unnaturally thick limbs and barrel chest. He was big, even for a Rhelklander. His sword, Salvation, rested by his side, also preserved to survive the years of neglect.

A ray of sunlight broke into the cave, and Skahgerok began his Wakening.

He let out a roar that was more lion than human, and arched his back as pain shot through his old body. His limbs had not moved in over fifty years, and they screamed in defiance. The visions he had seen in the Revery only increased that pain. They had infuriated him, and his flesh could hardly contain the anger that now flowed through veins that had seen years of tranquil slumber. His body confused his emotions and his roar was broken into sobs of sadness. He rolled off the slate stone bed onto the hard stone floor. Unable to stand just yet, he reached up for Salvation.

It was still there.

CHAPTER 8: THE BLACK SHADOW OF NEVEREN

*Crestly, a town of little importance in the
Neveren Mountains, east of Terrace*

The old man sobbed like a child. "Please! Spare me," he begged, raising both of his bloodied hands in defense.

Anathu studied him for a moment, struggling to remember why his own hands were covered in blood and why this old man was begging for his life.

Where am I? The question was the only thing that seemed familiar to him at the moment, as if he had been asking it his entire life. Everything felt foreign. Even his own skin felt like it belonged to somebody else. *Who is this man? Is he an enemy?*

"I will give you all I have, sir!" the old man continued. "Thirty-five currents! Please spare me!"

Anathu noticed that he was in a strange position: crouched low, his body tense, poised to pounce on this defenseless man. He relaxed and stood up straight, not knowing how he had come to be in his situation. He looked down and saw that he wore a long, dark coat and his hands were shaped like talons, dripping with blood and gore. *What am I?* he asked himself.

The sound of coins hitting the hard stone floor answered. He looked down and saw the old man emptying his coin purse of currents. "Bless the Four, lad. I will tell no one! I will say it were the drakes, don't you worry none!" He scrambled to his feet.

Drakes. Anathu remembered them suddenly. He had been mining—he was a miner—in the mountains, and one of the other miners claimed he had found a bandit's cave. That was when they came, from every shadow in the rocks. The drakes came and all Anathu remembered after that was blood. Even in his confused state, Anathu knew that drakes should not be here. They are dragonspawn, and only the lands of Rokuus still saw dragons.

As the old man got up and tried to hurry past him, Anathu grabbed him by his dusty tunic and spun him around to face him. "Where are we?"

The old man's lip quivered. "Pardon?"

"Where is this?" Anathu repeated, digging his sharp fingers into the man's chest.

"Ah! It's Crestly, lad. In the Neveren Mountains, just a league up east from Kingsforge. Isn't that where you hail from?"

Anathu loosened his grip on the man's tunic, but did not let him go entirely. He looked at his surroundings. They were in a small wooden shack built into the stone of the mountain. The floors were flat stone and the walls were made of crudely crafted wood. Surveying his surroundings, Anathu finally noticed the bodies.

Two men lay facedown, drowning in their own blood. The gashes that tore their skin and clothing to shreds looked like the work of a giant bird with massive, sharp talons. Just like Anathu's hands. Three other men were dead from similar wounds, lying in different corners of the room. Anathu paid them no heed. His attention was fixed on the frail, slaughtered woman and the small dead child in her arms. Anathu turned away from their grisly demise before the torrent of emotions building up in his chest choked him to death.

"Mother," a weak voice said from behind. Anathu spun around, pulling the old man with him. "Father?"

It was a boy, no older than seven. He had wild, bushy red

hair, as if his entire head was engulfed in flame. Although he looked young, scared, and innocent, the boy was not crying. He simply stared at Anathu.

"What have you done?" the boy asked, his eyes fixed on Anathu's gory hands.

Anathu released his grip on the old man to stare at his hands. His fingers had shrunk and lost their sharpness. They were human again, but still covered in the remains of his victims.

The old man, ignoring the boy, bent to retrieve his currents while he still could, and then he darted past the man in black who had brought slaughter to Crestly.

Anathu fell to one knee, still trying to make sense of everything. He was on the verge of tears when the red-haired boy spoke again.

"Anathu," he said, stepping forward. "I won't hurt you. Not like they did. Please don't hurt me."

Anathu stared at the boy who apparently knew him. Who was this boy? Anathu's mind was burning with the unanswered questions. Why did he butcher these people? Had they done some evil to him?

"Do I know you?" Anathu finally asked the boy.

"It's me, Anathu," the boy said in a quivering voice. "Locksley."

The name struck a sudden chord in Anathu's heart. Was it remembrance? Or was it simply the guilt of killing the boy's family? Had his mother screamed "Locksley!"with her dying breath, as Anathu tore her to shreds? He couldn't say. Regardless, the boy seemed to know him well enough.

Anathu stood up. He tried not to breathe in the death from the room as he stumbled passed Locksley, unable to look at the boy any longer. He left the shack and stepped into the open mountain air.

Crestly was a small miner's outpost that rested under an alcove in the mountain, accessible only by navigating a winding path from the base of the mountain up to a high ridge. From there, the small town overlooked the rising peaks of Neveren.

But no town remained now; just a bloodbath with a name.

Anathu breathed deep and walked over to a small pond in the center of town. He knelt there and regurgitated into the grass by the water, unable to stomach the sight and smell of what he had done here. After a fit of coughing, he cupped his bloody hands and brought some of the water to his mouth. The pure mountain spring water reminded him of something from a long time ago, though he couldn't say what it was.

After drinking, Anathu stared into the waters until they settled and formed his reflection. He knew the face: lightly darkened skin and black hair. *They called me an Aushuin,* Anathu remembered. *This was my home once…*

The thought came to Anathu by surprise, and it knocked him from his knees. He sat on the hard ground looking at the ramshackle buildings that made up Crestly and he knew it was true. "Why?" Anathu asked aloud, trying desperately to rationalize this slaughter and his loss of memory.

An answer came as if from nowhere. *Because you are my fury,* said a joyfully malicious voice. *And I have your answers.*

Anathu stood up suddenly, his keen eyes darting in every direction, looking for Locksley. But the boy was nowhere to be seen. His hands tensed, and suddenly they resembled talons once more. Yet, he saw nothing. The voice was in his head. It was not his, nor was it Locksley's.

"Why?" was all Anathu could think to ask.

Come to me, my son, the voice whispered.

Anathu's eyes turned north toward the baleful black spire that rose up from Demonscale Heights. He could see Scorn...the blackened spike that jutted up from the heart of the cancerous wastes below. It was Adratheon's tomb.

This is what you're after.

Anathu recoiled as he felt a small hand take his. He looked down and saw Locksley now by his side, staring up at him.

"Are we going now?" the boy asked, clearly frightened and confused, looking for some small comfort from the violent stranger who destroyed his world.

"Yes," Anathu said nodding, clutching the boy's hand. "We have to find some answers."

The Revenants of Vysarc watched as Anathu departed Crestly.

"He's going," said Shaith, pulling her dark hood over her even darker hair. "The book is true!"

"Of course it is," Dora snapped, folding up a map of Neveren. "My Father was not a fabler."

Shaith nodded, declining to voice her displeasure every time Dora reminded her fellow Revenants that Pulasia was in fact her father, regardless of the lunacy of such a statement. Pulasia was over three hundred and twenty-five years dead, and Dora looked no older than thirty. However, Dora was a powerful noble of the Remnant Houses, so her insular behavior or maddening claims were rarely disputed.

"Well, let's move," said Feignly impatiently. The skeletally thin man spun the knife he had been sharpening and leapt up on to the ledge the others were hiding behind. "I'd like to get through Demonscale before the sun sets. I hear those mountain greks can see in the dark, and I don't want to be caught with my pants down." Dressed in light leathers and covered in small blades, Feignly Moss was the only one of the Revenants who was not actually born into Vysarc society. The others only wore their dark robes and carried their dark tomes because it was their duty as members of the Last Houses. Feignly, however, had chosen this life of shadows and death on his own, and he seemed to thoroughly enjoy it, always wearing a smile.

Shaith packed up their rations, or what was left of them. As it turned out, waiting for a half-blood to finish the slaughter of an entire town was an activity that made Feignly exceptionally hungry. She pushed her long black hair out of her face and watched Anathu disappear. "Will he know what to do?"

Dora opened up a small ornate box that had several recesses in it; one of those recesses held a brilliant red stone that matched the stone on her ring. "Father said that the dragon's blood is not something that can be ignored. The black dragon Adratheon will have total control over his son. The fury will drive him. He will take the sword and cleanse it, for that will be Adratheon's most urgent desire." She closed the box and tucked it into her robes.

Shaith nodded. She hoped that Dora was right. No one else could touch the Dragonsbane. Some said that it was forged in both the blood of Adratheon and the blood of Ausfred Galvian. Only members of those bloodlines could wield it.

Feignly drew a long knife from his back and spun it, and then spoke as if he were thinking the same thing as Shaith. "And if he doesn't, couldn't we just cut off his hand and take the sword out with it? What would be the difference?"

Shaith and Dora both ignored him and headed down the path to follow Anathu, leaving Feignly alone on the ridge.

"Or I'll just cut off that pretty finger of yours, put your Father's ring on mine own, shove that stone into *your* heart, make you get on top of me and—"

"Feignly! Away!" Dora called impatiently from the distance.

Feingly Moss laughed as he wondered if Pulasia had ever used his legendary jewels for such things.

CHAPTER 9: THE DECIDING FACTOR
Outside White Rock, Neveren Mountains, western Eurheby

The duke of Holthurst ruled from White Rock, a massive keep that looked like it was carved out of the mountain itself. The stronghold resided on the western borders of Eurheby, where, oddly, little out of the ordinary happened. Willem Conrad normally found this particularly unfortunate, but as he navigated his horse through the craggy paths of the Stairs looking for his sister, he wished it were just another ordinary day of hawking with his brother. His panicked mind tried to pretend that Bethany was back in the courtyards of Holthurst with her handmaidens, and not missing in the mountains for the past two days.

"The sun is waning, Lord Willem," said Farren, the heavyset kennel master, as his two leashed bitches panted heavily from the day's hunt. He was panting quite a bit himself. "We should retire and continue our search of the Southern Stair on the morrow."

"Aye," Serra, Willem's older brother, agreed. "You know as well as I, Willem, Beth is likely hiding in Hillside with that Karson boy. The girl is insolent, and it would not be the first time she ran away." He shouldered the heavy axe that never left his side and made to rein in his gelding and return home.

"No," Willem said, turning on both Farren and Serra. He would not return home to his mother and father without word of Bethany's whereabouts. Their looks were too painful for Willem to endure much longer. His own dread had begun to keep him up at night. Although Bethany had disappeared before, she had never been away this long without sending word or leaving some note for her handmaidens. "We keep searching until they light the walls. Would you like to be the one to tell the duke that his daughter is still missing because his two sons were too weary to go look for her?" He directed the question at Serra who grunted and kicked his gelding past his younger brother.

Farren dismounted and tended to the dogs, which were now as anxious as their master. "My lord, Kayce and Dally have not found a scent all afternoon. Perhaps Bethany was not in the mountains this time."

Willem shook his head. "Her handmaidens last saw her and Bory Karson taking the Stairs. Bethany paid Elsa and Valerie seven currents apiece to keep their distance." That fact angered Willem, but it also made part of him want to smile. His sister was such a rebellious girl that it was hard not to find it amusing. Yet, right now it frightened him. There were dangerous things lurking in the mountains, even this close to the foothills. Cave worms were known to claim land leagues away from the Demonscale Heights as their territory, and they viciously protected their boundaries.

The three rode further up the Stairs shouting for Bethany and the Karson lad. Farren caught up with Willem and offered him a drink from his wineskin. Willem declined. He refused to be a drunkard like his brother, so he rarely drank at all.

"You know, my lord," Farren said quietly, as if he didn't want his dogs to hear, "word has it some dark things have taken wing in Neveren. It might be proper to consider the safety of the duke's elder sons in addition to his missing daughter. The moon brings about strange happenings in the wild."

Willem pulled one moleskin glove tighter while he clenched his fist, a tactic he liked to use to reinforce his position when speaking to his men. *The drunken fool is scared*, he thought.

"I would not put much weight in gossip, Farren. They may be chasing dragon shadows in the Westlands, but I have yet to see any sign of them. And I would not underestimate the duke's sons." Willem placed a hand on the hilt of his jeweled sword. "The Conrads rule the mountains for good reason."

Farren nodded, raising his skin to his master's health. Willem could tell the older man was abashed, taking orders from someone so many years greener than he.

Suddenly, Kayce began growling, and Dally let out a howl. Farren did not swallow his wine.

Before Willem could ask the kennel master what the dogs smelled, Serra's voice bellowed from over a distant ridge. "The boy!"

Willem kicked his horse hard and it bolted. He could only hear the howling mountain winds and the yelping barks of Farren's bitches. Willem shortened the gap to the ridge quickly, and when he rounded the corner to the next ledge, he found Serra's horse, a discarded axe near its hooves. He panicked for a moment and dismounted, drawing his sword. "Brother!"

"Here." Serra's voice sounded distant and less assured than normal, yet he was nearby. Willem could see his steel leg guards protruding from behind a small shrub. He was sitting down, cradling the boy. Bory Karson looked like a child, not the nearly-bearded youth that he was.

Willem knelt down, about to ask if he was alive. He knew the answer as he neared. The boy's clothes were in shambles, his body covered in long, gruesome gashes. His left arm had been severed at the shoulder and his other hand cut off at the wrist. The blood had thickened. He had been dead for some time.

Serra held the boy as if he were his own son, cradling him carefully, heedless of the dark gore that soiled his gilded red armor. Willem had never seen Serra cradle something so lovingly, aside from his axe, which was now lying in the dirt.

"Brother..." Willem didn't know what to say. His own thoughts were on his sister, not the mutilated boy. "Where did you find him?"

Serra didn't answer. He just shook his head, vacantly staring at the ground.

The barking dogs came around the ridge followed by Farren's cursing. When the kennel master saw Serra and the boy, he reined in his horse and dismounted, his eyes and mouth wide. "Celecy's own!" he swore. "What could have done that?" Just then, a piercing, bestial shriek sounded in the distance. Kayce and Dally howled in answer.

Serra set the boy down gently and got to his feet. The Conrad's sigil upon his breastplate—the green oaken leaf on a field of red—caught the setting sun as he walked over to his discarded axe. "We have to find Bethany."

"What could have done this?" repeated Farren, both his dogs whimpering now as they sniffed and nosed at the corpse. "A wyvern?"

Willem looked at the boy. His face was completely mutilated. Large claw marks had left the flesh an unrecognizable mask. "Wyverns do not hunt people." It was well known. "And even so, they would not leave a kill for the crows."

"It does not matter." Serra said sternly. "Bethany!" he yelled as he mounted again. "Bethany!"

The sharp cry sounded again. Something was still hunting.

Serra turned in that direction and kicked his horse hard. "Ya!" His axe was raised.

"Serra!" Willem hurried to his horse. When he was mounted, he turned to Farren. "This was not a wyvern, nor a man." He spun his sword as his horse reared. "Perhaps your monsters are real after all, Farren. Ya!"

Willem galloped hard after Serra, but the elder Conrad had already disappeared from sight. The Stairs wound sharply this high up, splitting into many different paths. The only trail Willem had to follow was the rising dust left in Serra's wake. *The Steeps*, Willem thought as he reined his horse toward the plateaus. He could hear Serra shouting something over the beating of the hooves.

"Noooo!" Serra's voice suddenly echoed from the distance. Willem urged his horse faster, nearly standing in the saddle as he crested the final rise. Once he climbed that rise, his voice instantly echoed his brother's and he nearly fell off his horse.

Serra stood defensively over their sister's corpse, his axe raised high. Bethany's body was much less mutilated, but she was still as dead as Bory. She was wearing her favorite dress, Willem noticed through his teary vision. However, before he was able to mourn her loss properly, he caught sight of what his brother Serra was protecting their sister's remains from.

Taking to the sky, flapping its dark wings, was a beast about the size of a horse, covered in black scales. This was a creature from the heroic tapestries that hung in the walls of any of the noble Eurhebine houses, but Willem could hardly believe he was staring at one in the flesh.

Not a wyvern, Willem thought to himself assuredly. *Only drakes would kill for reasons other than food.* Reasons that were beyond the understanding of anything but a dragon.

Willem heard his brother roar and saw the dying sunlight reflect on his axe before blood was sprayed across the rocks.

Celendas, two days later

After many nights of solitary contemplation, King Alastair Galvian reconvened the council. The royal treasurer Geyer Ellis was called into attendance, as well as the young envoy from the Ranger's Guild in Lumbridge who had come earlier that morning to seek attendance with the king.

This time, the young prince was much more sober.

Cedric and Captain Nol were the first to arrive to the council chamber, both seeking an early meal. The kitchen servants were quick to array the table with spiced eggs, smoked ham, and fried bread, as well as Pendaran wine that Cedric did not refuse. He was well aware of the messenger lark from the Pendaran court stating king DeSatho's intent of postponing trade between the crowns on account of the draught up north. Cedric found this preposterous, but he knew that his opinion would do little to change the matter.

Nol and Cedric ate silently, which the prince considered a great relief. He found the captain rather unpleasant during his visits. The Hilt must be a dire place to breed such ill-tempered men. After a few bites of food, Tanith Elton entered, looking tired and sweating. He still wore his armor from a morning spent in the sword yard with the prince.

Cedric may have been a slouch in court, but he was far from it in the dueling circle. "I take it you are well enough for council, Captain?" the prince asked mockingly.

Tanith gave him a raised eyebrow but deigned to answer until he found his seat, as well as a boiled egg. "I shall be, after a glass of that Pendaran red."

Cedric smirked as he poured his instructor a glass of wine.

Soon after the rest of the food began to appear, Geyer entered with both envoys from Aevenore. The treasurer wore an elaborate yellow tunic accented with purple embroideries and a silk sash. He wore his customary smile while talking with Rennig and Errol.

"Morning, your highness," Geyer announced cordially when he saw the prince. His voice was smooth and thick like honey. "Ah, and Captain Nol. What a pleasure."

Nol gave the treasurer a sidelong look and returned to his meal without saying a word. Once Geyer and the others were seated, a young man with long blonde hair and dark green leather armor strode into the chamber: the envoy from the Ranger's Guild.

"You must be Master Renevere," Geyer said, rising from his seat. "I am Royal Treasurer Geyer Ellis. Welcome to the Phoenix Keep."

"Thank you," said Lacey. He was a young man—probably no older than Cedric—but he exhumed the bravado of a veteran tracker, along with the feminine look of a pompous courtier. "Where is the king?" he asked briskly. "I was told I would find him here."

Just then, Alastair Galvian entered the chamber followed by Geldra and Cardinal Carthys. The Cardinal walked with his eyes closed, as if the Lady herself guided his steps and he cared not of his destination. For some reason, the old man's unquestionable faith irritated Cedric.

"Have a seat, gentlemen," the king commanded, taking his own seat at the head of the table. "I will make this brief, as I know we all have pressing matters to attend to."

Cedric and Nol set their food aside as Geyer's smile faded into a complacent mask.

"Cardinal," the king began, "I am placing you in charge of a force of soldiers tasked to keep the peace in the chapel district of the city."

"Paladins?" asked Carthys incredulously, his eyes suddenly wide. The prince had never seen the old man betray such emotion. "Your majesty, we are not the Spearitans."

"Call them what you like, Cardinal," the king rebuked, "but they will be your new chaplains, hand-picked by the Faith from the available Tower Guard."

Tanith started. "Your majesty…"

"The Tower Guard will be hard-pressed," the king continued. "However, they are charged with protecting the crown, and that begins with protecting the city. The Sect of Halcyon presents an immediate threat to the stability of the kingdom. And that threat will be met." The king's voice brooked no argument. "Geyer, the festivities for New Season have been postponed indefinitely. We will need at least twenty thousand currents available to arm the chaplains."

"With all due respect, your majesty," Captain Nol began, visibly holding back his anger, "the Sect of Halcyon presents a threat to the stability of the Faith. It is the Faith's fault for welcoming ambassadors from all other religions through their doors and it is not the kingdom's responsibility to handle religious affairs. However, it is the kingdom's responsibility to meet the real threat to its realm: the barbarian bastards knocking at our back door!"

The king looked at Nol, maintaining his composure in spite of the captain's outburst. "The chaplains will be limited in number due to other demands on the realm. We will need at least five officers of the Guard to help train and command the new militias that will be sent both to Lumbridge in answer to the wereling attacks, and to the Hilt, to ensure the safety of our northern borders."

This quieted the captain, but not the treasurer.

"Twenty thousand currents will not come easy," Geyer said, rather nonchalantly. "Are we to impose new taxes?"

"Whatever it takes," answered the king.

"And the Guard?" asked Tanith. "Are we to lengthen the watches to make up for the waning supply of men?"

"Whatever it takes," the king repeated.

Cedric felt the waves of repressed rage that surrounded the table. *This is not wise, father*, he thought to himself. *What does this leave for Aevenore?* Cedric did not speak his concern, but he attempted to drown it in his wineglass.

Errol fidgeted in his chair, as if he didn't know whether to speak or not. Rennig, on the other hand, did not care.

"Your majesty, have you considered the threat in the mountains?"

The king finally softened slightly, sighing. "I have. I have considered gathering the nobles in an effort to reinstate the Eurheborn and answer this supposed threat. However, I cannot justify that decision right now. I do apologize to King Luther, yet I cannot offer him the aid he seeks."

Rennig bit his lower lip, his associate betraying no emotion by the decree. But this time, Cedric could not keep silent. The mention of the Eurheborn had rekindled his boyhood dreams of glory.

"Father, you cannot be serious. We must do something. Let me go. I will rally the men needed to—"

Alastair raised a hand. "Cedric, please..."

Before the king could continue, the council chamber doors were thrown open and two tall men armored in red platemail entered with several guards attempting to restrain them. One of the intruders carried a large, bloodied sack.

"What is the meaning of this?" Tanith asked as he rose, reaching for the sword on his back.

"They would not stop!" one of the guardsmen cried.

Alastair recognized them immediately as Jerome Conrad's sons. "Leave them be," the king commanded. "Lords Conrad, we are in a private council."

Serra Conrad threw the bloodied bag onto the council's table. "The baron's daughter—our sister—is dead, your majesty. We come seeking justice."

"Our father commanded us to abandon formality," Willem explained to the king, while bowing his head. "Your majesty will forgive the intrusion, but our father the Duke requires vengeance."

As Captain Nol reached over to open the bloodied bag, Cedric peered over his shoulder. The entire council, including the king, gasped when the bag's contents spilled out.

Cedric would never have guessed that such a small dragon would put into motion the rebirth of the Eurheborn.

CHAPTER 10: UPON THE BURNING ISLES

The island of Vhaltas, Chasmere Sea, south of Lorendale

The Stratovault—Sol Saradys' volcanic fortress— loomed in the distance like a terrible nightmare that Donovan Marlowe refused to wake from. It rose into the darkened sky like a smoldering hand, reaching up to disembowel the heavens. Donovan stood at the bow of *The Temptress* and steadied himself against the violent waves of the Chasmere Sea. His left hand rested reassuringly on the scroll case that hung over his shoulder and his other gripped the rigging for support, tightly, as if it were the last time he would ever embrace a lover.

The Temptress was not the most impressive of galleys. Its sails were unadorned, and the lurid mermaid who stood forever vigilant at the prow had been beheaded years ago, her elegant hand pointing forward toward the Burning Isles. Donovan remembered the altercation he had with the Royal Treasury of Celendas when he had tried to have the Phoenix Throne compensate him for that accident. The memory made him smile.

"Captain," said a quiet voice. Donovan turned and saw his First Mate Briar Hansel, his round face wearing a look of deep concern. He leaned in and whispered to Donvoan, even though there was no one else within earshot. "There are some talks of mutiny aboard. Noose says he will take command of *The Temptress* when you, pardon me for saying, sir, fall to your knees and...pleasure the Burning One."

Donovan grinned at that. Loose Noose was, of course,

not his first choice to replace him as captain of *The Temptress*, but the man did have a quick tongue, and Donovan always found him entertaining. That quick tongue had earned him his name in Quayhaven, where he escaped his own hanging by somehow slipping through the gallows' rope. "Noose will not survive Vhaltas," Donovan said plainly. "The cultists worship in silence, and it is said that anyone who breaks that silence will have their tongue torn out. Not cut out, mind you, but torn. And I do not think Noose can survive without his tongue."

Briar paled slightly. He was a little younger than Donovan, and an able youth, but he was shy and scared most of the time. The only reason that he rose to be Donovan's First Mate was because he had released Donovan from his cell in the Spearitan city of Parity some years ago. Donovan was sentenced to die for attempted assassination, but before the Archbason could identify him, Briar let him out of his cell asking only that Donovan take him away from the city. Apparently, the Archbason took advantage of the younger altar boys, and Briar was anxious to be away from her unwanted advances.

It was after that imprisonment that Donovan decided the death of the Archbason would not be enough to bring down the Spearitans.

He must bring down their foundation.

Donovan noticed Briar's discomfort. "Do not worry, Briar. I know the Isles well. I know the caverns of the Stratovault even better than the cultists who fear delving too deep there, afraid that they may find the truth about their sleeping lord." Donovan's hand gripped the scroll case until the wood began to creak. "I know the truth…" Yet he said it with uncertainty.

Briar watched the horizon, the captain's behavior making him even more uneasy than before. The sound of boot heels against the ship's deck announced Scarlet's approach from behind the First Mate.

"Noose plans on taking the ship," the blonde-haired man announced. He wore numerous blades on his belt, as well as the two short swords on his back. He looked ready for war, much to Donovan's pleasure.

"So I hear," said Donovan, still watching the coming darkness ahead.

"I wouldn't worry," Scarlet said, giving Briar a feigned look of terror. "We're all going to die anyway. Let the boy captain the boat for all I care."

"A little early for doubt, my friend," Donovan said, turning to his most trusted and least honorable man aboard *The Temptress*. "Or a little late, perhaps. Do you now fear the wrath of the Burning One?" Scarlet had been with *The Temptress* through its darkest hours, and Donovan could not imagine the man suddenly questioning their course.

"Doesn't matter," he said, watching the Isles as if he were watching a serene sunset. "We're all going to die on those Isles." He rested his hands on the pummels of his katars—punching daggers from the exotic lands of Rokuus. "But let it be known that I die for the promise of the gold that shimmers in the depths of the Stratovault, not on some fool's errand to piss off the gods." He spat over the side into the crashing waves of the Chasmere Sea. "The only power on the Isles is the power of lunacy and fanaticism."

Smoke plumed from various parts of Vhaltas. They were getting close.

You are wrong, friend, Donovan thought. His eyes were fixed on the Stratovault. His left hand was still clutching the key to his salvation, his revenge. The scroll case cracked and a splinter dug into his palm. He looked down as blood trickled through his tight knuckles. *My power lies there.*

"Anchors!" called a crewman. The deck suddenly exploded into activity.

Near the opposite shores of Vhaltas

Demitri gripped the reins tightly, trying not to look down at the never-ending black sea below. Part of him remained fascinated by the ability wyverns had to see in such darkness, but the other part of him was busy desperately trying not to abandon this quest, not to yank on those reins and guide the bird-creature back to Lorendale without the *kropal*. But he knew he could not, not now. He had gone too far.

Too far for her.

He pictured Xavia now, her dark eyes wide like they were when she became excited about anything relating to lost magicks. He remembered the last kiss she gave him, a promise of things to come should he return safely. She would no doubt give herself to him freely should she learn of his quick promotion to the black robes of the Entrusted. They would not have to hide their feelings anymore. *She will want to hear all about this.* He held on to that thought and it helped him stay his course.

But the course is so damned black, he thought, seeing only the dancing starlight on the water. While he could no longer see the coast, he did spot the dark outline of Vhaltas in the distance, a faint red glow coming from the volcanoes.

The wyvern pitched suddenly and Demitri quickly tightened his legs in panic. The creature leveled itself and made a noise that Demitri could have sworn was laughter. They were strange creatures to be sure, but they were remarkably able-bodied mounts. They had slender enough bodies for a man to wrap his legs around, and their wings were wide and strong, able to carry three armored men no doubt. Their heads were almost the same shape as a horse's head, only sharper and covered in thick black scales. Demitri briefly wondered why they were not common in Terrace or Eurheby, but quickly remembered that Vanghrel was not a man to share his secrets with anyone, and even Demitri had not known of the Spire's hidden wyvern rookery until his third year.

That thought sent Demitri's hand to his waist where he kept the scroll case. *The secrets of the Spire*, he thought to himself. He still could not reason why the Luminary had sent him so suddenly on this errand. *No doubt, I'm not the first Entrusted expended on such a foolish errand*, he thought bitterly. But what choice had he? This was the opportunity he had been waiting for, and he could not deny that the prospect of impressing Xavia had influenced his quick acceptance of the quest. Regardless, he was determined to succeed where the others had failed. The Luminary sought the Shackles of Heaven, and if they did indeed exist, Demitri would to return with the first of them.

Yet, in the darkness and solitude of the Chasmere Sea, he remembered his dreams, and he deeply feared where he was heading.

"Do not fear," Vanghrel had said, stroking the wyvern's long neck as Demitri prepared for his departure, "Kevrost knows the way well, and where he rides, no cultist would dare go. You will find the Shackle easily if you follow my maps and you will return it to me with no complications."

Demitri had little time to question his instructions before

he was already in the wyvern's saddle. The Luminary grabbed him by the neck of his new black robe and stared him in the eye. "Do not steer him from his course."

Those words now echoed in Demitri's head, and he tried not to pull on the reins too hard. But, as he neared the looming shadows in the distance, he knew it was too late to turn back anyway.

Donovan led his company through the coves below Vhaltas. He had scouted the Burning Isles before, and had mapped the secret paths that even the cultists did not use. He knew many hidden coves where pirates would meet to exchange vital information on trade ship routes, as he had sold such information to them in the past. In his quest for absolute vengeance for the death of his parents, Donovan had abandoned any sense of decency they might have taught him, had they lived. If he hadn't been blinded from reason for so long, Donovan might have found that ironic. Even so, he still held on to certain teachings of his parents.

"We might sell that which doesn't belong in certain hands to the same undeserving hands," his father Jonah had told him when the family had dealt old relics to the Spearitans, "but we keep those things from hands that would do far worse with them." Jonah had been sitting at the stern of their ship *The Godless Swan* with young Donovan on his lap. It was a pleasant memory, and a lesson that Donovan continued to apply. *Mortals may not be worthy to destroy idols*, he recited to himself as a mantra, *but it will prevent the tragedies perpetrated by those who revere those idols*.

"Captain," Briar said quietly.

Donovan returned from his subconscious and saw his men awaiting his command. They were lined up behind him, hidden in the shadows of the cave's wall from the firelight that came in from the mouth of the cove. Outside, cultists could be seen surrounding various campfires, hundreds of them. As Donovan had predicted, some ceremony or ritual celebration was underway. He signaled for Scarlet.

"Take your men down the paths through the Ashwood," Donovan said, motioning to the forest of barren trees along the coast. "You will find the caves to the north that lead down into the sacrificial chambers. Tell the men to loot what they can and make short work of anyone that gets in your way. When you reach the entrance to the chambers, I will create the diversion."

Just then, a hulking sailor by the name of Rahlla stepped forward with a huge barrel under each arm. He nodded to Donovan.

"You come with me," Donovan said. "Brair, bring the torch, but stay clear of Rahlla."

Both nodded, and Scarlet quickly led the rest of the men out of the cave. *The Temptress* rocked in the rough waters. Donovan took one long, last look at his home. Since his parents died, he had known no other life than aboard that ship. He secretly prayed— despite his lack of faith—a silent prayer to Athlas who watched the waters.

Keep her safe, he asked of the Spearbearer, *you bastard.*

With that, Captain Donovan Marlowe led his small remaining company toward the Stratovault, while the raging worship fires across Vhaltas began to multiply as if in expectation.

The Shackling was about to be undone.

The Stratovault, at the threshold of the Revery

Deep in the Stratovault, knelt Sinder, the Champion of the Burning One. He could be described in no other way than villainous; huge, cruel shoulders supported a sharp-featured head that wore a look of smoldering hatred.

Above him loomed the gigantic statue of the Corruptor, complete with long, flaming hair and the burnt angel wings upon his back. Sinder's body was bare, and the surrounding torchlight found all the grooves of his exceptionally muscled body. He appeared human, aside from the small bone fragments that protruded from his cheeks and jaw: the onset of horns that many cultists grew after years of serving the Corruptor. Sinder remained motionless, his arms held out at his sides, his fists clenched tightly. Yet he slept, unmoving except for his rhythmic breathing and his wordlessly chanting mouth. His body was kept in the Mortal Realms, but his spirit had already departed. The ritual had allowed him to enter the Burning One's court in the Revery.

Sinder walked through the enormous gates that led into the Hall of Mayrs. He did not fear this place, as he had been here many times before, even before Sol Saradys had claimed the throne. Back then, however, Sand had commanded Sinder to come before him as a subject. Now, as Sinder strode through the Halls catching the curious eyes of the lowly and enslaved marons, Sinder finally felt like the true champion he aspired to be. In this dream, he bore brilliantly gilded black steel armor lined with crimson. He wore an enormous sword across his back, but he strode lightly through the halls as if he wore nothing.

As Sinder reached the throne room, he was welcomed by

a swarm of perversely mutilated and contorted women. They were a mix of elegance, brutality, and utter disgust, yet in this atmosphere, they were exquisite and beautiful. On the raised throne sat Sol Saradys himself, looking tired and withered.

Sinder's heart raced, but he tried to maintain his composure. He had long been waiting for the moment that the cults would unite long enough to fulfill the rituals necessary for a champion to come before the Burning One. Now was that time, and he reminded himself to remain assured and confident.

Long had it been said that the Burning One did not abide weakness. Sinder found this rather ironic now, seeing the Corruptor in such a weakened state.

"Who dares enter my domain?" asked Sol Saradys, his voice like the crackling of a flame.

"I, Sinder, champion of your cause, have come to offer you a vessel to work your will."

Sol Saradys arose, studying the man before him. "You want to serve as my Hands? To do my work where I am forbidden to roam? You would give up your life to be a Shade?"

"Aye," Sinder said plainly. "So I may remove your Shackles, my lord, and you may return to the Mortal Realms to destroy the wretched Balance." Sinder had recited the lines in his head for years, and they came to him instinctively now.

Sol Saradys, once the Archangel of Prythene, laughed wickedly and sat back down on his throne. "I rule the Revery now, Sinder. What makes you think I want to trouble myself with the Mortal Realms? Here I can spread Corruption through the marons and their nightmares. I care little for the Balance and the old conquest for Astasia."

Sinder was taken aback, not sure how to answer. "Care little for the Balance?" was all he could ask. "The Balance was responsible for your imprisonment, my lord, and you care little for it?"

Sol Saradys narrowed his white eyes.

Sinder began to lose his composure. He was a wicked man at heart, and subservience did not come to him easy. "You have endless followers, my lord. They all call for the Days of Astasia, so that they may worship you without fear of retaliation or persecution from the followers of Halcyon. You must take mortal form and lead them in your conquest."

"I must?" Sol Saradys asked with a smile. "Do you command me, Sinder?"

"Yes," the word was out of his mouth before he could stop himself. There was no turning back now. He had committed his life to sacrificing himself to the Burning One, and he would not be denied his destiny. "You must take my body. I *will* be your Hands."

A vision suddenly appeared from the darkness of the hall. On either side of Sinder, the visages of two strangers materialized, kneeling on either side of a familiar altar. *The kropal,* Sinder thought, suddenly panicking. One man in black robes, the other dressed in prissy Pendaran fashion. *What is this?* Sinder thought, trying not to let the visions distract him from the encounter before him.

An explosion rocked the Hall of Mayrs, nearly knocking Sinder to the ground. No other creature in Sol Saradys' court moved. The quake did not come from the Revery, but from the Burning Isles, where his mortal body still slumbered. Even though he knew something unnatural shook the Stratovault, Sinder still refused to wake up. *Get away from the altars, you fools!* He clenched his eyes tight against the Mortal Realms, trying to ignore the scenes so he could focus on his once-in-a-lifetime meeting with

Sol Saradys. "You must, my lord."

Sol Saradys laughed suddenly—a knowing laugh that mocked the champion before him. He spread his wide, impossibly long-fingered hands. "I feel the pulling of cosmic threads—something I have not felt since the Shackling. Someone already frees my hands, Sinder, someone more worthy. You are too late." His laughter rang through the halls and sent all his subjects to their knees. All except Sinder.

The visions seemed to take over Sinder's mind. He had no choice but to watch the man in black robes, with silver-streaked hair, read a parchment. The frilly sailor read a parchment as well. *This cannot be*, Sinder thought. *They cannot take the* kropal! *I have to stop this! I have to…*

Sinder knew he must awake to prevent the ritual, but his fury kept him from opening his eyes. He drew the enormous blade from his back. "I gave my life to you!" he shouted as he charged the throne. Sol Saradys continued laughing, clenching and unclenching his fists in ecstasy, ignoring the champion that lunged toward him. Just as the Burning One brought his fists up, crossing his wrists over his chest, Sinder slashed with the mighty blade.

The hulking sword easily severed both hands in a single swipe. Sinder awoke to the sound of ungodly screams coming from two different directions. For a moment, Sinder wasn't sure if he was still in the Revery, but as another explosion rocked the statue of Sol Saradys, Sinder knew that he was back on Vhaltas.

He looked down to the familiar ground beneath his feet to find both of Sol Saradys' hands writhing, reaching for him.

After he finished reciting the words, Donovan Marlowe's ears rang with a demonic laughter that echoed through his mind. He dropped to his knees, letting the precious parchment that contained the Binding Ritual fall into the river of lava below the altar. He was unaware, but his scream was echoed from somewhere else in the Stratovault, as if another suffering fool had joined his painful choir. From the corner of his eyes, he could see Briar dropping to the ground dead, blood pouring from his ears. Bits of Rahlla were scattered around the entrance to the chamber, blast burns from his barrels marked the place where the explosives were set off by the dancing flames within the cavernous vault.

Everything had happened so fast. Donovan felt like he had already died, and bizarre scenes of his life flashed rapidly through his mind. But the pain was real. He felt a tightening in his chest—like flaming fingers wrapping around his heart. His unearthly howling carried over the churning volcano that was the Stratovault.

The entire fortress was about to erupt.

Donovan stumbled from the chamber and managed to find his way out. When he emerged, the cries of his dying crew could be heard between the hissing of the steam geysers around him. The Isles were alive with the savagery of war. Of all the thoughts tearing through his mind, there was only one driving him toward *The Temptress*.

I have brought about the Days.

However, he was unsure if it was even his own thought or if it belonged to something else that dwelled deep inside, hidden in his heart. As he made his way back to the cove, Donovan felt something burning in his left hand. He opened it up and found a broken shard of a black stone.

The left half of the *kropal* rested in the left Hand of Sol Saradys.

After the initial pain and confusion, Demitri steadied his breathing. The chamber was empty aside from himself. He knew who he was and where he was, but something unknown surged through his body, radiating from the black stone that he held in his right hand. He felt the power to dominate, the power to change. And suddenly, it was clear.

The realization came with a deep laughter that seemed to echo the sounds of the quaking volcano. Demitri hardly even noticed he was the one laughing.

I am Sol Saradys.

The thought only made him laugh louder.

CHAPTER 11: DEMONS AND DEPARTURES

The Silver Spire, West Terrace

Vanghrel jolted awake, his brow drenched in sweat and his fists tightly clenched. He rubbed the sleep from his eyes to take in his surroundings, reassuring himself that all of it truly was a dream.

As his eyes adjusted to the faint candlelight, he saw Myriad sitting at the foot of his bed. The demon was cloaked in a mist that hung around him like a shroud

"How long have you known that the Corruptor ruled in the Revery?" he asked plainly, as if he and the Luminary had been in the middle of a conversation.

Vanghrel swallowed, his throat painfully dry. He reflected on his dream, the parts that he could remember. He had been swimming through a sea of mutilated flesh only to reach the shores of a blackened isle. The solitude and the dread that he had felt was so real that his chest tightened, even in waking. "I was not entirely sure...until now."

Myriad's emotions were spread across his rigid face: a mix of restrained fury and anxiety. "My people have dwelt under your domain for nearly two hundred years, unable to leave the tower that you built upon the Calluses. And now that the moment of our salvation is at hand, you neglect to inform me that the Burning One has been stirred from his slumber?"

Vanghrel sat up in his bed, his legs stiff and his temper shortening. He reached for the glass of Rokuusian amber that he always kept by his bedside. "I do not make a habit of acting or speaking on my assumptions, Myriad. I have only recently begun to suspect that Helena VonAnthony might have successfully dethroned Sand by leading the marons in revolt. It should not have been possible, which is why she died in the process."

Myriad slid off the bed, the mists following him. "If Sol Saradys holds sway over the marons, he may soon be able to impart his will through them, meaning he may choose a champion among the cultists to serve as his Hand." Excitement had filtered into Myriad's voice. "We must act now!"

Vanghrel drank deep of the amber, letting it settle his nerves. He had grown more and more weary of Myriad as of late. He felt the demon did not respect the fact that he was at Vanghrel's mercy. "Steps have been taken, I assure you. I have sent my most capable Agravite after the Shackle of Flame, and he has with him a copy of the Binding Ritual. He should have no trouble retrieving the *kropal*."

This news silenced Myriad. His eyes seemed to glow faintly. "That is well."

Vanghrel set down his amber and climbed out of bed. Even at his frail age, he towered over the demon. "However, I shall remind you, Myriad: your fate and is in my hands now. I hold the key to recovering the Shackles of Heaven, and you will honor my generosity in using those holy stones in the aiding of your brethren. Is that understood?"

Myriad's eyes narrowed slightly, but they held no malice. Vanghrel couldn't decide what those eyes held. "Very well, Luminary. The Balance is in your hands." With that, the demon turned and left, the mists thickening.

Anerith found Xavia in the courtyard, at the same place he and Demitri would usually meet after the midday meal. She wasn't wearing her red robes. The crimson garments were resting in a pile beside her on the stone bench. Instead, she wore a simple tunic, brown with dark blue trim. She was reading the same volume on Vysarcian history that Anerith had been reading for the past few weeks. He noticed that she had taken much more of an interest in her historical studies—especially in the form of Vysarcian history—since Demitri's departure.

No one was truly sure where Demitri had gone. Some said that he was sent to represent the Spire on a voyage to Rokuus, in hopes of recruiting some of the foreign mystics into the ranks of the academy. Anerith—and Xavia, for that matter—refused to believe that. There were also rumors circulating that Demitri was fed to the demons inhabiting the lowest reaches of the Spire. Anerith remembered laughing aloud when he heard that little tale. Xavia did not find it amusing.

Whatever true purpose Vanghrel had originally required of Anerith, Demitri was now fulfilling. Anerith believed that the task Vanghrel had asked of him—to act as courier to Aevenore—was merely an afterthought. Anerith knew he had said something wrong during their meeting, and, because of his hesitation, Vanghrel decided to give the task to Demitri instead.

Xavia looked up from her reading as Anerith approached. "I thought you'd be gone by now," she said nonchalantly, her blue eyes vibrant in the sunlight.

Here is why Demitri could not deny the task, Anerith thought. She was such a beautiful reason to desire power. Anerith had trouble looking into her eyes and accepting the fact that he was given the offer to impress her first, but missed his chance. But he was not Demitri. He had other aspirations that were not motivated by a mere lovely face.

"I am to depart on the eve," Anerith said calmly. "The Luminary has made arrangements for me to stay in some inn at Three Rivers." He looked around for any Vigilants and saw none. "Though, I am not supposed to speak of it…"

Xavia nodded and moved her robes over to give Anerith a seat. "Do you know what it's about?" she asked, ignoring Anerith's resistance. "The message to Aevenroe."

Vanghrel had given Anerith a sealed envelope that he was instructed to place only in the hands of King Luther Garrowin. Anerith had no idea what it concerned, and to be honest, he did not care. He knew it did not concern him and it would be useless to worry about it. Xavia, on the other hand, would have opened it by now, Anerith was sure.

He sat down. "I'm not sure. Probably something to do with funding." He hoped the matter would end there.

Fortunately for Anerith, Rutherford approached and sat on the bench on the other side of Xavia.

"Did you hear?" Rutherford began, eager to relay the next batch of Spire gossip heard in the dining hall. "Demitri got sent off to help fight the drakes in Neveren!"

Anerith snorted. "Is that right?"

Xavia closed her book. "Who said that?"

"Ursin," Rutherford said, producing a butter biscuit from his robes and biting into it. "He said he saw Demitri leaving the Spire the night before last on one of the Luminary's wyverns, heading toward the mountains. Ursin's father runs a miner's guild in Kingsforge and he said his father sent him word that drakes have been raiding the mines there. He said that the Luminary had to send some sort of aid to keep an alliance with Aevenore." He took another bite of his biscuit. "But…drakes!"

Xavia turned to Anerith. "What if that's what the message is, Anerith? Let's see."

Anerith recoiled. "What? You're going to believe Rutherford and Ursin? Ursin says his mother used to be a Rhelklander!"

"She was!" Rutherford exclaimed, spraying biscuit crumbs.

Xavia ignored them both. "What if there really are drakes in the mountains and Demitri was sent there?"

The notion seemed outlandish to Anerith, but he was not close-minded enough to totally brush aside the possibility. He just did not like giving into the curiosity of his paranoid friends. "I can't open the message, Xavia. Vanghrel would find out."

She glared.

"What are you guys talking about?" Rutherford asked as he finished his biscuit. "Oh dammit!" he said, noticing Xavia's book. "Do we have that evaluation on Skall today?"

Xavia nodded, setting the book aside.

Rutherford brushed the crumbs off of his robes. "You know, Laz says that Demitri is one of Skall's descendants. That's why Vanghrel sent him away."

Anerith rubbed his head. "So Demitri is the Son of Chaos now? Destined to bring about the Days of Astasia?" He looked at Xavia. "You know, this is not the best company to keep with a curious mind like yours."

Xavia didn't smile. "Why are you here, Anerith? You don't seem to care about power, magic, or even the happenings of the institution to which you belong."

Rutherford's eyes widened and he looked as if he were about to slip away from the confrontation, but he stalled.

Anerith knew he should not press the matter. The sun was setting.

"I'll be going," Anerith said, gathering up his robes. He reached inside the pouch at his belt to grasp the sealed message. "Good luck on the evaluation...and whatever else you get yourselves into."

Before he could leave, Xavia added, "Don't follow all of the rules, Anerith. That's how things stay hidden."

Anerith refused look back. He didn't want her face to be in his mind for his next few days of travel. Instead, he stalked away to collect his pack. Before he could even reach the dormitories, a Vigilant appeared before him. Anerith could never tell one Vigilant from the other. This one led a horse and carried a heavy sack in addition to his bow and two short blades.

"Adept Zathon," the Vigilant said, "I am Nyjien. The Luminary sent me to see to your departure." He handed Anerith his supplies and helped him mount the horse.

Anerith decided to look back at Xavia before leaving, but she was nowhere to be seen. His hand still clutched the message, but he did not open it.

CHAPTER 12: UNINVITED GUESTS

Lockrian Woods, southern Terrace, along
the shores of the Chasmere Sea

After a couple days of reflection and reluctance, Raiken eventually reconvened with the council to surrender the Greenstone to Fyrachel. Abandoning all he had known for the past few years had been a lot easier than he thought, but Raiken had always been a child of change. Ever since he had fled Melbrook, he felt more at home without a home.

The forest felt different to Raiken without the Greenstone hanging around his neck. It felt lonely and cold. After meeting with the council, he spent most of the morning wandering, trying to reconcile his thoughts on leaving Lockrian. He had long felt restrained in the woods, unable to explore the rest of the world as he had when he was working in Quayhaven. Despite the constant danger and uncertainty he had felt as a thief in the ports, those were some of his most pleasant memories. They were a different kind of pleasant, not at all like the serene harmony he felt in Lockrian. The unrestrained sense of freedom he had taken for granted before coming to Lockrian was slowly rekindling inside of him.

The Greenstone had bound him here, but now he was free from those shackles.

Valcorse called out behind him, descending from the trees. Raiken turned to watch the falcon weave his way through the tight branches and the curtains of leaves. While Raiken would have once been able to interpret the bird's calls, that connection was now broken, their link through Lockri now in the hands of Fyrechel. That didn't stop the bird from finding perch on Raiken's arm.

"I was afraid you wouldn't find me," Raiken said, reaching into a pouch at his belt to produce a small bit of uncooked meat. Valcorse took it without question. "I need your help. I think she's hiding from me in the Glade. She knows I can't find it now…"

The Glade of Mists was at the heart of Lockrian Woods, and it was the only way to enter the underground labyrinth of Heartheald, where Lockri's soul rested. And, even though it was in the center of the woods, the Glade was impossible to find unless one was permitted by Lockri or led by one of his children: dryad, embrechaun, or beast.

Valcorse finished the meat and rustled his feathers, as if considering the request. He took to the air and Raiken followed.

The Glade of Mists was a bizarre place, even by Raiken's standards, and he had seen many marvels in his short life. Though it was called a glade, it more resembled a forest all its own. The clearing wasn't as tightly packed with trees and brush as the rest of Lockrian, but it wasn't entirely a glade. The arching trees formed a high canopy, shading the Glade of Mists from the sun, making it seem unnaturally dark.

As Raiken entered, he saw the familiar mists that gave the glade its name. They roiled along the forest floor, playing tricks on unfamiliar eyes. Even though Raiken had frequented this place during his stay in the forest, without the Greenstone, his vision became lost in the dancing lights and swallowing gloom that filled the Glade of Mists.

"Gwyn," he called out, trying to follow Valcorse's distant calls. "I know you're here. Don't make me stumble around; I might grab something inappropriate…" He jested, as he usually did to conceal his emotions, but a sudden wave of foreboding began to wash over him with the billowing mists. He had forgotten how dreadful this place could be without the guidance of Lockri. "Gwyn?"

"If you've come looking for a guide," a voice called out, "turn back. I am not permitted to allow outsiders into this place."

Raiken laughed, but it was weak and nervous. He tried to follow the voice, even though it seemed to come from four different directions. "Is that what I am to you now? An outsider?"

"What else can you be?" she asked, acidly. "I know nothing outside of these woods."

Raiken tasted the irony in those words. They were partially the reason he was leaving. Yet, hearing her voice again made him never want to leave.

Gwyn suddenly appeared through the mists. She wore her leathers and her short bow across her back, just like she had the first time he met her. Back then, Raiken had thought of her as a precious thing that he would never be able to attain. Only now did he realize he had been absolutely right.

"Did you come to say goodbye?" she asked, avoiding his eyes. Raiken could tell she had been crying. "I think your bird could have delivered the message."

Raiken felt poisoned by her mood. He didn't want to prolong this pain. "Gwyn, I don't belong here anymore. We both knew that I wouldn't be here forever. It's just—"

"Do you remember when you first left the forest?" Gwyn interrupted, finally meeting Raiken's eyes. "You took the Greenstone into the Bandary Caves up north to help bring down that grek lord Maudreus..."

Raiken forced a smile. "I almost didn't come back." That was when he had first felt the Greenstone's seductive power.

As doubtful he had always been of the gods and their magicks, Raiken felt an undeniable connection to a force more powerful than he could comprehend. The Greenstone created that link between himself and Lockri, and each time Raiken pulled at the threads of Lockri's power, he felt that thick, sickening resistance of the Balance. Even in his crystallized state, Lockri refused to empower Chaos by giving all of his power to a mortal.

Raiken didn't have to worry about such things anymore. His only concern was the embrechaun standing before him—beautiful as the day he met her—and the tears running down her cheeks.

"Therrus knew about it," she said, wiping the tears away. "He has many scouts working for him, and he never wanted the council to let you stay here, even after all you and Sebastian had done. So he had you watched vigilantly. When he found out you left, he was going to use the information to convince the council to exile you from Lockrian." She bit her lip for a moment, the tears still coming. "But I...before he called the council, I went to him..." She buried her face in her hands, sobbing.

She didn't need to go on. Given her reaction, Raiken knew that she had done something she was ashamed of in order to keep Therrus from going to the council. A sudden rage began to boil inside of him, and he reached up for the Greenstone to calm himself, forgetting that it was no longer there. He envisioned strangling Therrus and throwing him into the Chasmere Sea. He imagined turning away from Gwyn right then, without another word, but he couldn't. He knew she had done whatever it was to keep him here. She at least deserved a goodbye.

"He said..." Gwyn continued between sobs. "He said he would never go to the council..."

Everything that Raiken wanted to say was caught in his

throat. He wanted to tell Gwyn that it didn't matter, that she didn't have to explain. He wanted to hold her. But mostly, he wanted to be away from here, and to not have to deal with such an exhausting mix of emotions. What he had once thought was pure and good was now falling apart, and he didn't want to be around to watch it crumble.

Gwyn dried her eyes and looked up into Raiken's again. "But it doesn't matter. You're leaving anyway…"

Silence lingered between them, hanging in the surrounding mists.

Raiken wasn't sure if it was a residual effect of wearing the Greenstone for years, or if it was because he stood above Lockri's tomb, but he suddenly felt a sense of dread that usually only came to him when Valcorse brought dire news.

Gwyn's eyes suddenly shifted, feeling the same presence as Raiken, and she looked up into the trees.

Valcorse's cry could be heard before he appeared through the haze. He circled, calling for Raiken's attention.

"Can you feel that?" Gwyn asked. "Raiken?"

"Yes," Raiken said, surprised that he did. "We have to hurry."

They followed Valcorse south, toward the shore. As they made their way further from the Glade of Mists, Raiken felt his link between himself and the falcon fading. To make matters worse, Gwyn had returned to her normal self, darting between the trees, making it difficult for Raiken to keep pace with her. Without the Greenstone, Raiken felt sluggish and unsure of his footing in the forest. It was a nauseating feeling, like being drunk and knowing he could walk, but unable to actually do so. Despite his handicap, Raiken fell back to the instincts he relied on as a thief: his own.

They neared the South Brim quickly, slowing their pace as they reached the wood's edge. Though Raiken's link to Valcorse was weakening, he still felt the urgency that drew them to the shore. As he and Gwyn peered through the thinning leaves of Lockrian Woods, he saw what drove them here.

Werelings. Dozens of them. They crowded the beach, snarling at each other and establishing control between packs. The beasts gathered around the remnants of a ship that had just washed up on the shore. They appeared to be on the verge of tearing each other apart over whatever remains they had found.

Gwyn spoke Raiken's own thoughts of the shipwreck. "Do you think anyone could have survived?"

"If they did, they won't survive much longer." Raiken crept closer to the beach, staying hidden behind the high brush. Gwyn followed, resting a hand on Raiken's wrist as he drew his daggers.

Their eyes met, and Raiken saw her doubt. She was unsure that he would stand a chance against these beasts without the Greenstone. Raiken gently brushed her hand away. Although the Greenstone did heighten his senses and reflexes, he had spent many years knife-fighting rival rogues and drunkards in Quayhaven. Raiken was confident that he could handle a bunch of three-feet-tall wolf-men without the help of a fallen angel.

Valcorse landed on a rock close by. Out of habit, Raiken attempted to send the bird out to distract the werelings. Gwyn, seeing Raiken's inability to reach the bird, leaned over and gave the command. Raiken ground his teeth, still getting used to the lack of Lockri's presence. Regardless, he peered around the rock, gripping his daggers.

"Let me get some help," Gwyn whispered, laying a hand on his shoulder.

He shook his head. "Whatever is out there would be gone before we returned."

The werelings were in a tight huddle. Raiken waited for Valcorse to sweep in before bursting from his crouch. As the bird dove, letting out a shrill cry, Raiken leapt out of hiding, running full speed toward the gathering. Gwyn was already loosing arrows from her hiding spot. Though her missiles found their marks, and werelings were dropping dead around him, Raiken still felt as if he were fighting alone.

Valcorse provided a distraction while Gwyn scattered the pack and Raiken sprinted across the sandy beach. He let fly one of his smaller knives. His aim was shaken by his stride and the blade flew wide of its mark. He cursed and slashed at an approaching wereling. He ended it quickly with a dagger through the throat, but in its death throes the vile creature knocked Raiken over.

This is not good, Raiken thought to himself in a panic, tumbling to the ground. He struggled to get the body off of him, but before he could free himself, another wereling armed with a long staff gave him a blow to the side. *Not good at all*. He groaned and kicked out to trip the beast as he heard the others approaching.

"Gwyn!" he cried out, sensing his imminent demise.

The pack came at him on all fours, slavering and growling. Some fell under Gwyn's arrows, but there were too many for her to pick off. They were on Raiken before he had time to get to his feet.

Raiken cut at one of them with his dagger and caught it in the ribs, opening the beast's side. It fell dying, but another beast took the opportunity to grab Raiken's arm in its claws, tearing the scout's flesh. Raiken cried out, dropping his dagger. Three others had circled around him when Raiken heard Gwyn cry out.

Just when Raiken thought he was about to be torn apart, he heard a chorus of whinnying death cries accompanied by the sickening sounds of crunching bone. The werelings surrounding Raiken were also distracted, looking toward the South Brim where the cries sounded.

A lone figure stood above the broken bodies of the dying werelings that had scrambled up the beach toward the hidden archer. It was not Gwyn. The hulking figure stood firmly, blood covering its gnarled fists. It was a living tree, or at least it looked like one.

Audrea let out a terrible growl, challenging the remaining werelings. The dryad was in her true form, terrible to behold. She raised her thick arms, covered in her bark-like skin, and sounded her challenge again. The werelings poised to feast on Raiken could not resist that challenge, and they broke off to test themselves against the dryad. Raiken took the opportunity to trip two of them and end them with his blades. The others scrambled toward Audrea.

In spite of her massive form, the dryad moved gracefully as she descended the hill to the beach to meet the remaining pack. They immediately leapt on top of her, their fangs flashing. They bit and clawed but nothing could pierce her natural armor. Audrea grabbed a large wereling off her back in a single fist and slammed it to the ground with a sickening crunch. She dispatched of the others similarly and the beach finally quieted.

The momentary silence was soon broken by a sudden burst of flame that cracked and sizzled upon Audrea's flesh. The dryad let out a scream of pain and fell to the ground, trying to smother the fire.

Raiken got to his feet, his eyes darting to find the source of the flame; a tricky wereling with flaming arrows? Or perhaps bottles of fire oil? Yet all he saw was a grey wereling, armed with a long staff, standing alone. In one hand he held a flame which seemed to burn in midair.

The wereling was laughing. Before Raiken could question this strange scene, the creature flicked his wrist and the flame launched toward Raiken's chest. The fireball was too fast to dodge and Raiken took the entirety of the blast. The force of it knocked him back into the woods, and when he landed, his vest was aflame. He cursed aloud and rolled over to put out the fire.

What in the foul reaches of Nekriark was that?! Raiken thought, trying to stand and ready himself against another attack. The wereling was still on the hill, weaving his hands and growling in some rhythmic melody. Raiken looked over to Audrea and Gwyn for answers, but they shared the same disbelieving look. Raiken reached for a knife from his boot and waited. Behind the wereling, Valcorse descended. Raiken waited for the right moment, and when the bird dug its beak into the werelings' neck, Raiken loosed his knife and buried it in the wereling's chest. The wereling's fire sparked and died, smoke billowing from his claw-like hands as he fell.

Silence fell over the beach once more. Raiken felt his chest. His hair had been burnt away and his vest was ruined, but at least his skin had not been severely burned. His flesh felt sore and hot, and Raiken was sure it would bruise. He walked over to the embrechaun and dryad. Gwyn was helping Audrea stand, a much more manageable task now that the dryad had returned to her human form. Raiken tried not to look at her naked body, but it was exceptionally difficult when dryads could assume such exquisite forms.

"Are you alright?" Raiken asked, wondering the same about himself. He felt more tired than he should. He thought he could handle all of those werelings himself, even without the Greenstone. He still had some things to get used to.

Audrea didn't seem to hear him. "That wereling was a shaman..." her eyes narrowed. "But how?"

"Shamans disappeared with the druids," Gwyn said, staring distantly at the dead wereling. "The Balance took their powers."

Both ebrechaun and dryad fell silent.

"Did we miss the Coming of the Days or something?" Raiken asked ruefully. "The council always told me that I should never even think about tapping into Lockri's true powers, because it would bring about the Days. Yet this furry little bastard can summon fireballs freely? I didn't feel a quiver in the Balance, did you?" Raiken wandered off to find his thrown blades, visibly irritated.

"It's not possible, Audrea," Gwyn asked. "Is it?"

"I would say no," the dryad began, "if I had not seen it with my own eyes." Audrea strode toward the fallen wereling sorcerer. Raiken and Gwyn quickly joined her. As the dryad inspected the body, she opened up its clawed fist and let out a gasp.

"What?" Raiken knelt over, looking in its hand himself. He picked out a broken black stone, holding it up. "This? It's a stone, not a ball of fire."

"It can't be," Audrea said, backing away sharply. "That came from Vhaltas..."

Raiken looked at it, flipping the stone over in his hand. A faint script was carved into it, but the stone was cracked, and Raiken couldn't discern the text. "Then how did a wereling come by it?"

Gwyn stared at the stone, wondering the same thing. After a moment, her eyes caught something else. A body lay near the shore where the werelings had gathered. It was no wereling corpse. Gwyn left Raiken and Audrea to inspect the stone so she could get a closer look at the body.

As she neared, she saw that among the remains of the broken ship was a battered young man, still breathing.

The council met in Fyrechel's underground manor rather than in the shelter located in the center of Druid's Grove. All but Therrus were present, for which Raiken was relieved. After hearing Gwyn's story and nearly dying at the hands of the werelings, a confrontation with Therrus was the last thing Raiken desired.

The boy's body was laid in a chamber with a spare bed and a lockable door, as ordered by the Heiress. Gwyn and Genis inspected the boy, who had been identified by Raiken as a Pendaran sailor.

"Only a trader from Pendara would wear a heavy coat like that so far south," he had said, a little disdainfully. "If they didn't have their fashion, they'd be no better than pirates."

Raiken stood with Fyrechel and observed the boy's effects laid out on a table. There was a finely forged rapier, which looked like it belonged to nobility, a few pieces of parchment that had been washed of ink by the saltwater, a compass, and a sea chart that marked many different stops along the Alakais Coast to the east, where the ruins of the Fell Peoples' domain were. The black stone rested menacingly nearby.

"No one else was found?" Fyrechel asked, disbelievingly.

Raiken shook his head. "It's no wonder he wrecked. You can't captain a ship all by yourself, not even if you're Captain Ellyrah. Even he needed skeletons to work the oars."

Fyrechel ignored the jest. "And no ship would survive Levithrom's Teeth. The reefs would bring down any ship, no matter the crew."

"So, his ship was either attacked by pirates and he was left for dead," Raiken speculated. "Or he went mad, murdered his crew, ate their remains, and steered his ship into the Teeth..."

The boy moaned suddenly, causing Genis to yelp and Gywn to gasp. Fyrechel's voice suddenly boomed.

"Odarin mel'arana comain." Her voice was distant and embracing, like a swirling wind. Everyone was left in silence.

"Heiress..." whispered Audrea, nursing her wounds in a chair at the far end of the chamber. She stood up, expectation in her eyes. "We were sworn not to."

"What happened?" Raiken walked over to the boy. He was still motionless. "Was he waking?" He turned to Gwyn.

She bit her lip.

"He might have been," Genis said, "but he won't now."

Raiken turned to the Heriess. "What is going on? What did you do?"

"Something that I should not have been able to do," she replied. "I called to Lockri for dream pollen to keep the boy from waking. Lockri should not have answered..."

"What is this?" Raiken burst out suddenly. "Hairy shamans, dryad witches...before we know it, I'm going to start changing into Lockri's hound during the full moon!"

"Heiress," Audrea said weakly. "We swore never to speak those words."

Gwyn stepped closer to the boy. He was still breathing.

"It's the language of Uldagard, child," Genis interjected, stroking the gray patch of hair growing from his chin. "It is spoken every day in the worship of Lockri."

"But certain things should not be asked for, Genis," replied Fyrechel. "And I should not have done it. However, this boy should not be awake. Something possesses him; I can feel it."

"And that stone is from Vhaltas..." Genis said, sounding fairly intrigued.

"Is that why everyone seems to suddenly be a wizard?" Raiken asked, scratching his neck. "Because this fool was possessed on Vhaltas? If he's just a cultist, we should slit his throat and give him back to the sea."

"No!" Gwyn exclaimed suddenly.

Raiken looked at her apologetically. "I just mean..."

"No," Fyrechel agreed. "We should keep him safe here until we have time to consider all of this. He should sleep for another day or so, if the spell worked. And if it did indeed work..."

"Then we are in incredible danger," Genis finished. "The only way that spell would have worked is if the Balance was shifted heavily to one side by a meddling force."

"Look." Gwyn said weakly.

All eyes turned to the boy. Gwyn had opened up his hand, and on the palm was scorched flesh. Raiken went to the table to retrieve the black stone and placed it in the boy's hand. It fit the shape of the burned flesh perfectly.

"The Shackle of Flame," Genis said matter-of-factly. "Which means that this boy was in the Stratovault."

"Which means we will need a priest," added Fyrechel, turning to Raiken.

Raiken looked up. "That would take days."

"We don't have days," the dryad said, turning around.

Again, Raiken tried not to look at her backside through the thin silk robe she wore.

"Does your twin know much about exorcism?" Genis asked Raiken, almost excitedly.

Raiken nodded. "We spent some time in Vysarc…"

"Oh my," Genis said, smiling with enthusiasm. "Do bring him here promptly."

Fyrechel walked back in with the Greenstone in her hands. She handed it to Raiken. "Here. You will need this to navigate the Burrow Gates."

Raiken reached out hesitantly. "Are the laws changing suddenly?" He clutched the Greenstone before the dryad could answer.

"In times of war," Fyrechel said, "laws begin to lose their meaning."

"War?" Gwyn asked. "With whom?"

Fyrechel ignored the question. "Take the Shackle with you. The priests will be able to confirm or deny our own suspicions. Let us hope they are unfounded…"

Raiken put the Greenstone on and instantly felt Valcorse's presence above the dryad's keep. He called out to the bird and felt an answer. The feeling was intoxicating, but soon broken by the touch of a delicate hand on his arm. He looked down and saw Gwyn's green hand close his fist around the Shackle.

"Bring it back," she said plainly, her eyes staring deep into his. Raiken knew she simply meant, *come back*.

"If anything happens," Raiken told everyone, but most importantly Gwyn. He didn't want her emotions on his conscience. "I will send the stone back with Valcorse."

Gwyn bowed her head and returned to the boy sailor. He didn't specify which stone, but Gwyn knew.

It is better this way, Raiken thought. *I should not leave her with hope when I have none to spare.*

Raiken turned to leave, calling on the Greenstone to show him the path to the forbidden ways of the Burrow Gates.

CHAPTER 13: THE EURHEBORN
Celendas, the kingdom of Eurheby

Cedric did not drink on the night his father announced the reinstitution of the Eurheborn, and he drank very little each night that followed. Something had awoken inside of him that now filled that void. A sense of adventure and the threat of impending doom had enlivened him. Now, he spent nearly every waking hour in the sword yard.

"Loosen your grip," Tanith instructed from behind his visor. "Your hands will tire and stiffen if you hold your sword like that."

"Not if I don't have to hold it that long," Cedric jested, circling the captain. His royal armor was baking him under the rising sun, but it did not slow him down. He was a weasel in the sword yard; no one could catch him.

Cedric lunged again, bringing his blunt-edged, two-handed greatsword down toward the captain. Tanith easily stepped aside and made to counter, not realizing the prince's attack was a feint. Cedric brought the sword back around to catch the captain in the leg, knocking him onto his back.

The sword yard had gradually become crowded, many of the guards wanting to see their captain spar with the prince. They all cheered when Cedric took him down.

Cedric removed his phoenix helm and helped Tanith to his feet. "I think that was the first time I ever disarmed you, Captain."

Tanith removed his own helm, revealing the hint of a smile

in return. "Was the fight not over, you would have lost your grip on that sword of yours."

Cedric laughed, but he knew Tanith was right. His hands ached. He was not altogether accustomed to wielding a greatsword yet. They were far heavier and more awkward than a normal longsword or bastard sword. Yet, Cedric was determined to follow the Galvian tradition of the Dragon's Dance: a fighting style that specialized in broader and longer weapons used to fend off blows from beasts larger than men.

Much larger.

"You are adapting quickly to that blade," Tanith said, nodding to the practice steel that Cedric held. "It took me the better part of six months to become accustomed to the weight of one of those when I first started learning the Dance."

"I've spent the last few years of my life stealing barrels of mead from the Lock & Key," Cedric said, spinning the blade. "I'm stronger than I look. Besides, there isn't much else for me to do in the castle besides drink and duel. Usually, I do both."

Tanith nodded, still betraying a slight grin. Cedric never saw the captain smile much, but he always enjoyed the man's company. Tanith did not always cater to the nobility, which the prince found refreshing. He was young and able-bodied, and capable in his position. Cedric aspired to be as self-assured and reliant as Tanith Elton.

Cedric was suddenly reminded of the time when he was eleven, and Tanith was first elevated to his high position in the Tower Guard. The king's distant cousin of House Rose was in Celendas for the winter, and his drunken conduct raised quite a stir with the local merchants. Cedric rode with his father to gather his troublesome cousin, only to find young Tanith Elton dragging the unconscious form of Batrim Rose from the Lock &

Key with a long rope.

"Back to your posts, louts!" Tanith now shouted to the convened guardsmen, bringing the prince back from his memories. He turned to Cedric. "We should be off as well. Your father has called for another council this morning."

Cedric nodded. "He's assembling the Eurheborn from the knights that answered the ravens. All the barons and dukes have sent their sons, but father has not asked me."

"You are not a knight, Cedric," Tanith said plainly, throwing his huge sword over his shoulder into its sheath. "You are a prince. Your place is here."

"My father's place is here," Cedric snapped acidly. "He is king; the throne is his. I should be able to defend my inheritance while I am still capable. Besides, was King Ausfred's son not a member of the Eurheborn?"

Tanith turned to the prince. "Those were different times, your highness. And besides, do not aspire to be like Vesper Galvian. He may have been your great uncle, but he nearly brought the kingdom down on itself. Your grandfather ruled in Ausfred's absence, as was his duty, and Vesper nearly killed him for his desire to take the throne. That one mishap led to the disbanding of the Eurheborn." Tanith stiffened, obviously uncomfortable with the lecturing tone he had suddenly taken on. "If you'll excuse me, your highness, I must prepare for council."

Cedric left the yard and made his way to the royal armory in silent contemplation. As the young squire Bensly tended to the prince's armor, Cedric looked at himself in the mirror. His reflection appeared much older than he felt today. He sighed as Bensly deftly removed his bracers, thinking about how the boy was almost half his age. Cedric's eyes wandered, looking to escape the feeling of dormancy. Above the mirror was a large painting of

Sir Thaley Rone, one of the founding knights of the Eurheborn. Thaley wore a lavish suit of gilded purple armor, similar to the one Bensly was removing from Cedric.

"Do you know the story about Sir Rone?" Cedric asked Bensly, not entirely sure why.

The boy was much more talkative than the other youths of the court, and Cedric enjoyed that about him. "Which one would that be, your highness? The one about the lady, or the one about his sword of stone?" Bensly removed Cedric's leggings and hung them neatly on the rack behind him.

Cedric stretched, enjoying the unrestrained mobility that his armor did not allow. "Neither. I mean the story of his father."

Bensly stood up from his knees, his floppy brown hair was pasted across his sweaty brow. "Correct me if I am wrong, your highness, but wasn't Sir Rone a low-born bastard?"

The prince nodded as he removed his own bracers. "So they say. The stories always tell that Sir Rone was raised in the forests to the north, near the Rhelklands. They say he was abandoned and that he learned to fight by battling with barbarians during his youth."

Bensly picked up a tourney sword from the weapon rack behind him and flourished it into a graceful thrust. "And he dueled with a clan chief twice his age, running him through and buying his own freedom."

Cedric chuckled. "The stories tell a lot of things." He sat down in a cushioned seat against the wall. "However, there is truth in every story. Sir Rone was not abandoned. His father was a Celecian monk that served in the abbeys outside of the Regencies. He forbade his son to touch a sword. So, when Rone grew old enough, he fled his home and traveled south, where he could fight dragons and find glory."

Bensly lowered his tourney sword, seeming to lose enthusiasm. "I had never heard that."

Cedric stared up to the painting of Sir Rone. "Then you certainly never heard how his father and the other monks tracked Rone down on the borders of the Rhelklands, half-dead. They took him back to the abbey and locked him up in a cell to keep him from running again. After a while, his father felt that his son was lusting after glory as a direct result of his more carnal desires. So, like most Celecian monks of that time, Rone's father had him castrated."

Bensly cringed, half-crossing his legs where he stood.

Cedric smirked. "That kept Rone subdued for awhile. But one day, Rhelklanders raided the abbey, and all the monks were slaughtered. Rone survived only because he was doing missionary work in the Brindle Swales. When he returned, he reclaimed his sword and set out once more, this time for vengeance as well as glory."

"Is that true?" Bensly asked wide-eyed. "Was Sir Rone a eunuch?"

Cedric gave the likeness of Sir Thaley Rone one last look, seeing something of his own reflection in that painting. "I have something I must do," Cedric said, leaving the squire alone with his crushed perception of a favored childhood knight.

Geldra wiped the sweat from his brow as he pushed into the king's royal study. Alastair Galvian was alone, poised over his great table that stretched the entirety of the study. Ancient records and parchments were spread before the king.

Alastair looked up as the high councilor closed the doors.

"Lucrid's balls, Geldra," Alastair cursed wearily, looking at the disheveled old man. "Did you have to take the stairs? You look like you've just walked through the Abyss."

Geldra shuffled toward the king. "I'm sorry, your majesty. There were some things that needed attending. But I believe the knights and nobles have all gathered in the small council. They await your presence."

The king adjusted his heavy robe and made sure the Phoenix Crown still rested atop his head. He organized the collected records of the Eurheborn's deeds that were spread across the table. As he rolled up a stack of parchments, Geldra noticed an old map of the Demonscale Heights in Neveren. Before he could inquire about its purpose, the doors of the study were suddenly thrown open again.

Prince Cedric Galvian entered, sweaty and out of breath.

"Cedric," the king stated sternly, "I expect you are aware that the small council is ready to convene. Do you require a few draughts of rheystone milk?"

Cedric took the jab in stride, his face stern. "Father, I have a request that I would ask of you before we attend council. Let me kneel with the Eurheborn. Let me ride to Aevenore with the knights of Celendas and take part in the defense of our kingdom. I cannot sit here while our collective fates are held in jeopardy."

Alastair sighed.

Cedric sensed his father's reservations. "I know I am not a knight, but knights must be led by nobility. Let me lead the Eurheborn in your name, father."

"No, Cedric," the king said bluntly. "You will not go with the Eurheborn."

The words stabbed Cedric in the heart. He wanted to tell his father about all the hours he spent in the sword yard with

Tanith, but he knew it wouldn't matter. His father was stubborn when it came to matters of the crown. Typically, those were the matters that Cedric usually cared very little about. But not this time. "Father, please. I can't stay here. Not with everything that's happening."

The king gathered his documents. "The council is ready, Cedric."

Cedric knew there was no swaying his father on this matter. Suddenly, he felt the need to find a drink, quickly. The one thing that he was never denied. He turned and left.

Geldra moved close to the king. "The prince is ruthless with a sword, your majesty. I have seen him in training with Captain Elton. Maybe it would be wise to reconsider his request."

The king shook his head. He returned to the table and uncovered the map of Demonscale. "I have other, more pressing matters for my son to tend to."

There was a long silence while the king stared at the map and Geldra awaited an explanation. "Your majesty?"

"King Ausfred left a detailed account of his campaigns in Demonscale," the king said. "I have studied these accounts rigorously for the last two days and I feel confident that I can navigate the way to Scorn where the Dragonsbane resides."

"The Dragonsbane?" Geldra asked, the faintest hint of excitement finding its way into his voice. "You are not suggesting that you will be going after it?"

"I am suggesting that, Geldra. And Cedric is coming with me. That is why I cannot afford for him to leave with the Eurheborn." The king strode toward the doors. "I have great need of him."

Geldra protested. "Your majesty, you must reconsider this plan. The greks, the drakes…it is much too dangerous."

The king pivoted sharply. "If we do not act now, then mountains will no longer divide this kingdom from those dangers." He opened the doors. "Come, Geldra. The Eurheborn await. They must ride for Aevenore tonight."

When the king departed, a wicked grin spread across Geldra's face and the color slowly faded from his eyes. "The sooner they ride, the better."

The council chamber was as silent as a burial ceremony. Willem and Serra Conrad sat quietly, dressed in lively red tunics that did not reflect their moods. They had not joined the other nobles in drinks the night prior, still mourning the loss of their sister. Lacey Renevere also sat at the table wearing the green of Lumbridge with two green-cloaked rangers on either side of him. Ashton Hale of Delethas and Geoff Peln from the Stills sat on the other side of the table next to three vacant chairs.

"I can't speak for all of you here," Peln began, breaking the silence while setting down his drained tankard. "But my blood is boiling. I never thought I'd live to see the day. Dragons," he grunted a laugh. "I thank Celecy that those bastards showed up."

The statement brought disbelieving stares from around the table.

Peln refilled his tankard with a pitcher of wine he had nearly finished himself. "Now at least I know that I haven't been Dancin' all these years for no damned reason." He laughed louder this time, raising his tankard to the others. Geoff Peln was a large man, in more ways than one. He was broad of shoulder and thick of arm, but he had an equally impressive belly that threatened to burst his sword belt, which might be why he preferred a large warhammer these days. He was dressed in a simple tunic of dark blue, with the moon and stars of House Goodnight.

Ashton Hale was the first to share the laugh, probably because he was the only member of the council competing with Geoff's drink. Leif Ghalahan joined in and raised his own drink in response. His older brother Erik sat in silent contemplation, obviously not sharing the same high spirits as Leif. The brothers both had the same long, straight black hair and wore the deep red and green colors of House Rose, one of the more influential families to the north. Rumors said that the nobles of House Rose were Spearitans, being so close to the city of Parity, but the rumor was not openly discussed.

Raymun Landover and Kable Orton were the remaining attendees, and they both raised their drinks with Leif and Peln. They were the youngest nobles called to council, both being just a year younger than Lacey Renevere and both just newly knighted. The seat next to them, reserved for the prince, was vacant.

After a few more moments of mixed merriment and mourning, the chamber doors were opened and the envoys from Aevenore entered with the king and his councilor. Tanith Elton followed and closed the doors behind them. The king's eyes fell on the empty chair next to Raymun and Kable. He stared sadly at the seat for a brief moment. After proper introductions, the council was seated and the king commenced the meeting.

"Recent events have brought this council together," Alastair began. "The tragedies of our past are slowly creeping into our time, and they must be met before they consume our prosperity. Many of you have no doubt heard the rumors." He looked around the table, as if accusing one of them of spreading the stories. "Drakes, the dragonspawn, have been sighted in Neveren. They have openly assaulted our kingdom by taking the life of one of our beloved noble daughters, and in return, Celendas shall strike back with the very weapon that ended the dragons' reign before."

All of the gathered nobles sat in their chairs straight and proud, with the exception of Tanith Elton, who seemed to be displeased.

"For the first time since the Dark Wing Rebellion," Alastair continued, "the Eurheborn shall ride once more. King Garrowin has requested aid in his campaign against the dragonkind, and Celendas shall heed that call. The Eurheborn shall depart at once, accompanying these envoys to Aevenore. However, since the Eurheborn have traditionally been self-governed, any one of you may refuse this charge. Are there any objections?"

"Aye," Tanith said defiantly. All eyes turned to him.

The king had obviously expected this response and nodded. "Speak, Captain."

Tanith stood up. "Everyone here must know the history of this kingdom. One of its darkest days was when the Eurheborn nearly destroyed the Galvian hierarchy. When Ausfred died and Prince Vesper wanted the throne, the knighthood, which had no leadership, followed the Black Wing and nearly killed the rightful heir—had it not been for the Tower Guard.

"The Eurheborn was dissolved for good reason. And I have yet to see a good enough reason to—"

"Our sister is dead!" Willem shouted, nearly knocking his chair over as he stood. "Those demons slaughtered her!" Serra pulled his brother back down into his chair.

Tanith looked at Willem and lowered his eyes. "I understand your grief, but I fear the Eurheborn will create political disharmony in the kingdom, and this charge will lead to the weakening of Celendas. Our own walls must be guarded."

The king drew his sword suddenly. The metallic hiss quieted all other noise in the chamber. "Kneel before me, Captain." Tanith did so, his jaw clenched.

The king rested the sword on Tanith's armored shoulder. "I, Alastair Galvian III, hereby assign Tower Guard Captain Tanith Elton the duties of Lord Commander of the Eurheborn."

The statement clearly shocked the council.

"Let it be known," the king continued, "that Lord Commander Tanith Elton is the first Lord Commander of this sovereign knighthood. The decisions regarding the Eurheborn will fall upon these shoulders that I now anoint with the power and authority of the Phoenix Throne."

Alastiar sheathed his blade. No one spoke. Tanith did not raise his head.

"The decision is yours, Lord Commander," Alastair said to Tanith. "This council is adjourned." With that, the king walked out of the council, Geldra quick behind him. The envoys from Aevenore and the newly appointed Eurheborn remained. All eyes fell upon the Lord Commander who still rested on his knee.

Peln was the first to speak. "So, are we going to make history or what?" He took another drink.

Tanith Elton arose and looked upon his knights. He could see no other choice.

CHAPTER 14: HERESY ON HOMECOMING

Melbrook, in the heart of Terrace

Sebastian found Vincent where the old priest spent most of his time when he was able to be up on his feet: the gardens. Vincent was bent over a patch of branquils that were just starting to blossom. As Sebastian approached, he paused to watch the experienced gardener. The sight saddened him. Vincent had always been an old man in Sebastian's eyes, even from his earliest childhood memories. Though once upon a time he had been much more vigorous—training Sebastian how to wield a mace and hammer properly and applauding Raiken's constant tumbling antics. Those were Sebastian's fondest memories, and in those memories, Vincent was a strong and capable man, the kind of man any young boy would want as a father. Now, hunched and withered, he was like a man waiting to die, but too stubborn to do so.

"Martin," Vincent said without turning or standing up, "I think the branquils could use some more water."

Sebastian frowned. *He's forgotten again.* "Father, it is me, Sebastian. Martin is away in Wynnstead. Do you remember?"

Vincent straightened and looked at Sebastian. "Ah, Sebastian. Pardon an old man's memory. The branquils are blooming. It shall be a dire summer."

It was said that if branquils bloomed before mid-spring, it was an ill omen sent by Celecy foretelling a dry and hot summer.

"I have never seen them bloom this early," Vincent said.

"Not in all my life…"

Sebastian joined the old priest, the two of them watching over the garden in silence. Sebastian wondered what would happen to the gardens if he ever left. None of the other priests gave the plants the same kind of attention as Vincent, and Sebastian and Raiken were the only ones that Vincent had ever trained in proper botany. Now Raiken was gone and probably never coming back. If Vincent was not here and Sebastian left, the garden would surely wither and die.

"Sebastian," Vincent said, breaking the sad silence. "I am near the Shore. My body is tired and the Black Sea is calling. I shall not be here to see the summer. If it is indeed a dire one, I would like to know that someone would be here to tend to the gardens."

Sebastian nodded. He knew this time would come, when he must either take on his expected responsibilities or hold on to his fading dreams of becoming a knight. He thought about such things often. Sebastian was by no means a child, like the boys with their heads in the clouds and their hearts longing for glory. Yet, he wasn't an old priest either, sitting in a church to comfort those who would seek counsel. He had spent the last few years of his life dreading this decision. Part of him hoped he would never have to face it, but here he was.

Before Sebastian could respond, the back doors of the church were thrown open. Grayson, a young cook from The Raine Song, came rushing through the garden.

"Careful!" Sebastian called out, seeing that the boy was about to trample a patch of remedy leaves. He cringed inside, feeling like he was already taking on Vincent's role as warden of the gardens.

Grayson nervously dodged the leaves, nearly falling over.

"Father Vincent, we need a healer!"

"What's happened?" Vincent asked, bracing himself on Sebastian's arm.

Grayson was trying to catch his breath. "It's Vance, Father. One of the girls tried to kill him! Came after him with a knife, she did. If Lennick hadn't been there to stop her, she would have gutted him for sure!"

Vincent gripped Sebastian's arm. "Come, let us see to him."

Grayson hurried back into the church with Sebastian and Vincent close behind. Inside, a small group of onlookers huddled around Vance, who was lying on the ground, coughing and bleeding. More voices could be heard outside the front doors. Sebastian helped Vincent over to the bleeding man.

"Give him some room," the older priest commanded. "You are not a pack of vultures." When the crowd parted, Sebastian could see the severity of Vance's condition. There were multiple stab wounds around his chest, oozing blood. If none of those wounds pierced his lungs it would be a miracle. Although, considering it was Vance, miracle might be deemed too strong a word. Vincent knelt down.

"She…she is a witch!" Vance said between fits of coughing. "She must…must be burned…" He spat up blood.

"Keep your mouth shut," Vincent commanded, placing his withered hands over the wounds. He whispered something and made Vance arch his back. Sebastian began to lead Grayson and the others out of the church. This was the kind of healing that did not call for an audience. After closing the doors, Sebastian ran out to the garden to pick the necessary herbs. When he returned, Vance's coughing had become much less violent.

"Once he's healed, he may want to join the Sect of

Halcyon," Vincent commented, taking the herbs and grabbing the mortar and pestle off of the table near the altar. "He keeps mumbling about witchery and corruption." While he ground up the herbs, Sebastian retrieved some cloth and water to clean the wounds. As they applied herbal staunches, Vance's coughing subsided completely and his breathing slowed. Sebastian was amazed to see that none of the knife wounds had hit any major organs. Or if they had, Vincent had asked the Mistress of Acrivas for the power to heal the wounds. Such a favor was not asked lightly, and Sebastian was not sure if Vincent had risked it for a man such as Vance. He did not press the matter.

"Burn her," Vance mumbled, his eyes flicking open slightly. "She is…the Corruptor's whore…"

"Who?" Sebastian asked.

The voices outside were rising.

Vance opened his eyes, and in them Sebastian saw only loathing. "Laurel Darcy."

Sebastian threw the doors of the church open and dashed through the gathered crowd. People were huddled around both the church and the tavern. Sebastian ran, dodging some bystanders and knocking others over in his haste. He reached the Raine Song and nearly tore the door off its hinges as he rushed in.

Inside was dark, the only light coming from a flickering lantern at the bar. Even in the shadows, Sebastian saw her, backed into a corner with a bloodied knife held between herself and Lennick, who was bleeding from his arm. Laurel bled too from a wound above her right eyebrow. And her clothes were torn, as if some wild animal had attacked her, but she made no move to cover herself. The shadows of the tavern shrouded her face and Sebastian could not make out her expression, though he could feel the desperation it conveyed.

Lennick turned toward Sebstian. "Thank the Four," he said, hurrying over to the priest. "She's gone mad, Sebastian. She was with Vance in the back room for a moment, and the next thing I hear is Vance screaming like the Mad Count Ribald. He came hobbling out, bleeding like a slaughtered lamb all over my floors, and then she tried to finish him off." Lennick took a step toward the door, obviously leaving this for Sebastian to handle. "I tried to stop her, but she sliced my arm open. She kept screaming 'He promised me!' over and over. I think that bastard Vance spurned her."

Sebastian found that prospect completely improbable. Vance would have stabbed himself in the chest for a chance to bed Laurel. As Lennick went out the door and began to ward off the curious patrons outside, Sebastian carefully moved toward Laurel.

"Alright, back away, people," Lennick said, "Melly, get away from the window!" The doors shut, drowning out the rest.

Sebastian approached Laurel, who still held out the bloodied knife, shaking. "Laurel? It's me, Sebastian. Please, tell me what happened?"

Laurel didn't answer.

"Did he hurt you?" Sebastian asked, stepping toward her slowly. "I know you wouldn't have attacked him without cause. I know he is a—"

A slashing knife cut Sebastian off. It caught him on the arm, same as Lennick. He leapt back, covering the wound. Looking up, he saw that Laurel had come out of the shadows to make the attack, and her eyes looked completely white.

"He promised me!" she shouted, tears streaming down her face.

Sebastian stared into the two vacant orbs that used to be

the loveliest eyes in Melbrook, slowly remembering something terrible. *And he shall cloud the vision of those desiring his power,* Sebastian thought, a quote from the mythos book entitled *The Descent of Archangel Saradys.* The book chronicled Sol Saradys' fall from archangel to Corruptor. *His promises shall bind, and his will shall blind.* Sebastian whispered a prayer to Lucrid the Defender.

"He promised me," Laurel said weakly, her voice hoarse from fevered shouting.

"Listen to me, Laurel," Sebastian said, ignoring the pain from his arm. "You have been lied to. He has come to you in a time of weakness. You did not have a choice, but you do now. Do not listen to him!" While he spoke, he reached out to places that he had not dared to go since he faced the darkness of Vysarc. He reached for powers that most mortals knew to stay away from, and he tried to repel the grip that the Corruptor had on Laurel.

A wave of dread washed over Sebastian and fire licked at the corners of his eyes. His body felt thick and awkward, as if he were trying to wade through mud. The feeling nearly made him sick, but he fought through, thinking of nothing but purging Laurel of her dark possession.

After a moment of silence between them, Laurel suddenly started murmuring incomprehensively and Sebastian felt the world fall away around him. He fell into a waking dream and he saw Laurel kneeling before a flaming throne. Upon the throne sat a terrible figure that could be none other than the Corruptor, yet his hands were severed.

"She came to me," the figure said, staring at the bleeding stumps that used to be his hands. "The marons brought her before me, but she brought with her the desire of killing that fool." The figure arose, standing tall and magnificent. "However, I shall give her back to you. You have done me service in attempting to exorcise me from her. The Balance slowly shifts in my favor. I am not without generosity, priest." The laugh that came from the figure shrank Sebastian. It devoured him.

The flames quickly died and the tavern returned around him. Laurel sat on the ground, looking confused and half asleep. She saw Sebastian standing before her, and then looked down to realize she wore almost nothing. She attempted to cover herself with her torn clothing until she saw the bloody knife in her hands. Her eyes widened as it fell to the floor.

"It was a dream," she said, trying to convince herself. She looked up to the priest. "It had to be a dream."

Sebastian went over and cradled her in his arms. "It was a dream," he answered.

She fainted as soon as her head fell onto his shoulder. Sebastian covered her in a spare blanket from the inn and carried her to the church, shielding her from the gawking crowd that followed.

He laid her in his own room, where Vance would not find her when he awoke. He locked her in his chambers and returned to the chapel. Vincent was still there with Vance, who now looked to be sleeping peacefully.

"How is he?" Sebastian asked.

"Still yammering about heresy and such," Vincent said, annoyed. He wiped his brow with a damp cloth. "But how about our witch?"

"It was no witch," Sebastian said. "Laurel had a dream..."

Vincent dropped the cloth back into the bloody water basin and turned toward Sebastian. "A dream, eh? A bad one I take it..."

Sebastian nodded. "I had one, too. At least, I think it was a dream, or some kind of hallucination. I..." Sebastian paused, unable to look Vincent in the eyes. "I'm sorry, Father. I tried to channel Lucrid to purge Laurel of whatever was plaguing her. I know I shouldn't have…"

Vincent placed a hand on Sebastian's shoulder. "I may be old, Sebastian, but I am not blind. You love her. And you would do anything to keep her safe. I would have done the same thing. In fact, I have…"

"But her eyes, Father," Sebastian began. "They were…"

"Not her own," Vincent finished for him, not needing an explanation. "White as death, they used to call it. But death is more pure, if you ask me."

Sebastian gave him a questioning look. There was no way Vincent could have seen his confrontation with Laurel. "How…"

Vincent motioned for Sebastian to have a seat in one of the pews. Vance began moaning quietly near the altar. The sedation of the herbs was no doubt slowly wearing off, but the priests ignored him. "I received a raven a few days ago from Mydraise," Vincent began, leaning his head back and closing his eyes, as he did when he was burdened with something. "I did not think much of it at the time. The Council of Mydraise is the Faith's most notorious collection of paranoid priests and cardinals. They chase devils from every corner of the Tripartite."

"What was the message, Father?" Sebastian asked impatiently.

Vincent hesitated. "Cardinal Delayne cautioned all factions of the Faith that the Cult of the Burning One was growing in strength. He claimed that he dreamt of the Corruptor, who he believed had risen to power in the Revery. Unfortunately, such a claim was taken lightly, as no one wanted to actually believe it. For if it is true…"

"Father," Sebastian began, folding his hands in prayer.

"My dream…I think I saw the Corruptor. On a throne of fire, and his hands were severed…"

The latter detail brought a reaction to Vincent's face that Sebastian had never seen in the old man. Fear.

Vance suddenly screamed. "Witch! Burn her!" He sat straight up, his wounds no longer bleeding. "Where is she?" His wide eyes darted frantically.

"Relax you fool," Vincent said, annoyed. He and Sebastian both went over to restrain him. "You nearly died. Stay down."

"Where is she, Father?" he asked indignantly, trying to stand up. "I want to see her punished. That harlot nearly killed me!"

"That's enough!" shouted Sebastian, grabbing Vance by his bloody tunic. "She is not well and you will stay away from her. Do not pretend her actions were undeserved." Fury flamed in Sebastian's eyes.

"Get off of me!" He shoved Sebastian back, knocking over Vincent who let out a painful grunt. Vance got up to run, but he didn't get very far. From the back door of the church, a figure slid over and jammed an elbow into Vance's back, knocking the man down in a scream of agony. The figure, clad in dirty leather and covered in what looked like green cobwebs, knelt over Vance, shoving a knee into his back.

Sebastian helped Vincent up and gave his brother a bitter smile. "That was unnecessary."

"Did I come at a bad time?" Raiken asked, picking off the stringy residue from the Burrow Gates as Vance struggled below him.

CHAPTER 15: NO ESCAPE

The Hall of Mayrs, somewhere in the Revery

Donovan Marlowe knelt next to Sol Saradys' throne, his eyes fixed on the stump that used to hold the Corruptor's left hand. On the other side of the throne knelt a young man in a black robe, his hair streaked with white. Donovan stared at the Corruptor's other phantom Hand. *"Shades,"* the wind seemed to whisper. But Donovan felt no wind here.

Donovan let his eyes wander. He was in a great hall with no visible walls, and only hazy blackness above. There were wisps of flame flickering in the darkness and small gangly creatures darting in and out of the hall. Below the throne's raised dais was a collection of bodies. Somehow, Donovan knew that they were dreamers. *Am I dreaming too?* he wondered. *I must be.* Poised upon the chest of their respective dreamers, sat one of the ugly little creatures.

The body he pearched upon began to wake, twitching and moaning. The creature quickly scuttled off. The waking dreamer was an older man dressed in royal robes. When he opened his eyes, he beheld the Corruptor in awe.

"My lord," he hissed, rising to his feet.

Sol Saradys arose from the flaming throne, his two new Hands rising with him and following. Donovan felt like he was being dragged by unseen bonds, unable to resist the Corruptor's silent command. The man with the white-streaked hair could not resist either and they followed the Burning One—his obedient shades.

"Geldra," Sol Saradys' voice boomed as he reached the edge of the dais. "It is a bit early for you to be wandering the Revery. The sun still hangs over Celendas, does it not?"

The man called Geldra bowed. "Yes, my lord. Although in a way it could be said that the sun is beginning to set on the Phoenix City." When Geldra looked back up, a wicked grin spread across his face.

Sol Saradys crossed his arms; flesh had begun to materialize upon the living flames of his body and he assumed the form of a man, be it a crimson-skinned man of unnaturally grotesque beauty. "So the king has spread his forces, has he? Predictable. Tell me, does he send aid to the north to fight the Rhelks?"

Geldra's smile widened as he nodded.

Sol Saradys' laugh shook the great hall. "Fighting the very forces that rise against me. Perhaps I should reward this king rather than obliterate his domain." He laughed again, letting his arms drop to his side. Donovan felt his chest burn and tighten, as if a fiery fist had wrapped itself around his heart. The white-haired man groaned in pain as well, telling Donovan that he was not the only one in such agony. "No, Celendas shall fall. With Lockri still in power in his cursed woods, the Valice will be the best course into Lorendale."

"There is more," Geldra began, his smile fading into a malicious grin. "The king fears that the drakes are pronouncing the return of Adratheon. He plans on venturing into the mountains with his son to reclaim the Dragonsbane."

The grip on Donovan's heart subsided and he let out a long gasp of relief. This drew the attention of Geldra, but the old man's eyes quickly darted back to Sol Saradys, as if he were afraid of shunning the Corruptor by looking upon his mortal Hands.

"Adratheon," Sol Saradys said, his face betraying no

emotion. "The black dragon could prove useful. The king mustn't be allowed to depart on this quest of his. You are to postpone him until the ships arrive."

Suddenly, the black walls of the hall faded into a landscape that Donovan had not yet forgotten. Vhaltas rose up around them: the dead forests, the flaming heights of the Stratovault, and the rising worship fires attended by cultists. The scene flew by as if the inhabitants of the hall were birds taking wing over the Burning Isles. They flew over the shore and remained high above a strange ceremony.

"The cults have not yet united," Sol Saradys explained in a disembodied voice. "However, enough have come together to raise the sunken remnants of Ellyrah's cursed fleet." The shore was lined with ashen-robed figures, all chanting and swaying in unison. An enormous fire was built, and the waves crashing against the rocks of the jagged shore fell into rhythm with the snapping flames of the fire. The sea began to churn violently, and after a few moments of chanting, black sails arose from the bubbling waters. The cultists on the shore then began to exult.

Donovan knew the stories about Captain Ellyrah and his undead fleet. He raided all the lands of Athland, and even the realms beyond the Black Sea, with his crew that defied death. He was granted immortality by Nekriark and the power to command the dead, and in return he was to sow devastation wherever the winds took him. After the Balance denied him his powers, he descended into the depths of the Chasmere Sea, only to return with the Days of Astasia. Now, his fleet arose from the waters, to help bring the Days and herald the Corruptor's return.

The scene faded away. Sol Saradys clenched his fists once more and Donovan and the white-haired right Hand both groaned.

"My lord, your hands..." Geldra finally said with a desperate quiver in his voice.

Sol Saradys looked at his stumps. He raised them high, pulling his mortal Hands with them. Both men dangled in midair with Sol Saradys' phantom fingers wrapped around their hearts. "These meddlers freed my hands by removing the Shackle that bound them," Sol Saradys explained, as if it were humorous to him. "However, my champion, fortunate enough to be in the Revery at such a time, took my hands with him. I had no choice but to take these two as my new Hands—my Shades. Otherwise, that fool Sinder would wield my powers to his own accord." Sol Saradys lowered his Hands. "And I cannot abide by that, as much as I would like to witness it. We are too close to Astasia."

"So, you have chosen your Hands?" Geldra asked excitedly.

"Chosen is a strong word," Sol Saradys returned to his throne. "I had no intention of leaving the Revery until they intervened. So it was only right that I should have them carry out my campaign. Let the fall of the Balance be their doing."

Geldra laughed with the Corruptor.

And Donovan slowly faded from the Revery to the sound of that terrible laughter.

Druid's Grove, Lockrian Woods

Donovan awoke drenched in sweat. He was panting, exhausted, but he couldn't remember why. He couldn't remember anything. His heart raced as his mind tried to piece together who and where he was. *I'm a sailor*, Donovan told himself. His eyes adjusted to the soft green light illuminating the room. He was lying on a bed of what looked like leaves but felt like silk. The room was shaded, light spilling in through slender windows on the walls and through the thatched roof above. He could see trees outside. *I'm in a forest hut...or something.*

The room smelled of earth, yet looked as elegant as a royal chamber. Donovan pushed back the silken green covers. He was bare from the waist up. He wore simple brown trousers and no shoes. As he sat up, he felt a sharp pain from his left hand. He grimaced and looked at the burned skin on his palm. Again, he had no memory of what had caused it.

"Did you dream?" said a voice from within the chamber.

Donovan started, nearly falling off the bed. His eyes darted in all directions, but he didn't see anyone. "I... I don't remember."

Suddenly, two emerald orbs appeared from one of the darkened corners of the room. They were eyes. Donovan quickly realized why he hadn't seen anyone. The figure that now revealed itself was a girl with dark green skin and a similarly colored tree cat in her lap, purring furiously. She sat on one of the windowsills, easily blending in with the earthen environment of the chamber. A short bow leaned against the wall, not far from reach.

"That is what you said the first time you woke up," the figure said, turning away from him to stare at the forest outside. "However, you thrashed in your sleep as if marons had taken you."

Donovan stared at her for a long moment, not knowing if he should speak or even move. She was beautiful, there was no doubt, but she looked...unnatural somehow. After a long moment of staring, realization and memory came to Donovan simultaneously. *She's an embrechaun.* The thought terrified him.

The only stories he heard about embrechauns came from Anochra, a haunted forest where any man foolish enough to follow the nymph songs into the trees would never return. Embrechauns were known to be fierce and vengeful creatures, deadly with their bows and deceitful with their tongues.

When she turned back to him, he recoiled clumsily.

"Oh, not again..." she sighed.

Donovan ignored her, beginning to scan the room, looking for anything he could use to fend off this fiendish she-devil.

"Look," she said, moving from her seat. The cat on her lap meowed defiantly as it hopped down and fled into a darkened corner. "We've been through all this before. You are not in Anochra, I am not interested in drinking your blood, and no, you cannot leave."

"Why not?" Donovan asked in response to the last statement, still not believing the other two.

The embrechaun stood up and reached for her bow. "Because you brought something terrible into these woods..."

Donovan stopped listening. He saw a hint of light from a cracked door across the chamber and leapt to his feet. With lightning speed that surprised even him, Donovan was out of the bed and through the door before the embrechaun could protest. As he entered the hallway, he heard her hurrying after him, shouting. He slammed the door behind him, latched the metal lock, and searched his surroundings. The embrechaun started banging on the door and shouting "Fyrechel!" Donovan ignored the foreign curses. He was in a long hall with many doors. He didn't have much time to decide, so he leapt through the nearest open door.

The room he chose was as small as the room he had just left, but there was no bed. Instead, there were wooden chests lining the walls and shelves that stored all kinds of bottles and vials containing strange glowing liquids. Something caught his eye at the far end of the room: a glisten of silver. He crossed the room and found his rapier resting atop his black sailing coat. He recognized they were his and he didn't question how he knew. He grabbed the rapier and headed for the door, but something terrible stepped into the doorframe to block his way.

A tree. Or at least, it looked like a tree. The hulking figure was delicate yet strong, graceful yet brutish. He knew it to be a dryad. Even his fading memory could not erase the tales he heard as a child about dryads crushing invading lumberjacks and the greks that burned down their forests. They were the fury of the wild. The dryad stared at Donovan with glowing yellow eyes that spoke of pure hatred.

Donovan knew his blade to be useless against it, so he scanned the room. The windows were covered, and he couldn't tell what kind of height he was at. He'd have to risk the fall.

"Audrea!" a voice said from the hall—the embrechaun's. "Do not harm him! The Heiress commands it!"

Donovan took advantage of the distraction and leapt toward the window. His body crushed the elegantly carved window frame and he closed his eyes to brace for his landing.

But it never came.

He opened his eyes and he saw that he was tangled in vines growing from every direction. He turned and looked back up into the room. The dryad stood at the window, its hands curled into gnarled fists, both of them glowing with a faint green aura. The vines tensed and relaxed with the dryad's heavy breathing. They held him in place tightly and he couldn't move without them clenching him all the harder.

"Do not struggle," the embrechaun said, appearing from

the doorway. "Audrea has expressed great interest in disposing of you after what you brought here. Do not give her an excuse."

Donovan felt hot tears welling in his eyes, and it infuriated him. "What did I do to be kept prisoner here? Whatever it is, I don't remember! Please, let me go!"

"Where will you go?" the embrechaun asked.

Donovan could not answer.

She gave him a sad look. "You have done something terrible, Donovan. And we cannot let you go. Especially since you can't remember."

Donovan ignored the embrechaun and began to attempt to free his rapier so he could cut his way out of here. As he struggled, the vines tightened and stifled his breathing.

"Audrea, no!" the embrechaun cried.

The vines wrenched the air out of Donovan's chest and his eyes began to roll back into his head. The terrible forest prison began to fade away and a flaming throne slowly took form in the blackness of his mind. As the embrechaun's voice faded, a new sound took its place—a dark laughter promising Donovan a chance to remember. It was a promise of vengeance.

CHAPTER 16: A STORM COMES FOR CELENDAS

Delethas, the southern port of Celendas in Eurheby

Normally when he wanted to retreat from within the castle walls, Cedric would venture out to The Lock & Key or The Red Feather Inn, or he would go up north to visit Raymun at the Landover Estates. However, both of his primary drinking companions had departed with the Eurheborn the day before. So instead, Cedric donned a brown hooded riding cloak to conceal his face and left the walls of Celendas, heading south for Delethas. He took the ferry down to the ports before the morning council had commenced and he hadn't returned since. With the coin he brought with him, he had bought a room in The Ten Tankards and kept himself inebriated for the past day and a half. He was not looking to sober up anytime soon.

He sat in a corner while the sailors began to filter in. As the sun set and work died down on the docks, the seats filled up fast in The Ten Tankards. The bartender, Kristofer, hurried about the common room, his portly face turning red as he tried to keep the patrons at their drink. As tankards emptied, conversations began to flood the bar and Cedric couldn't help but overhear them. Many of the sailors spoke of the same thing.

"That bastard-king DeSatho can't deny us passage! He has no right!"

"I've lost me three bags o' currents in the last three days since his traders stopped bringin' their silks. There ain't many other ships that go to Rokuus, so he better start sendin' his merchants soon. That is, unless he wants a war on his hands."

"Aye, I don't doubt King Galvian wouldn't be looking for a reason to gut old Benedict for the death of his son."

Cedric drank deep.

"King DeSatho never laid a finger on the prince!"

"Nay, but he kept his priests at bay when the boy took ill."

"Ah, Brick, you've the wits of a box of shit. No priest coulda saved him."

"Not unless they cut the Prince of Doom from the womb."

This brought a wave of laughter.

"The Prince of Doom from the womb! That's fit for a bard's song!" The laughter continued.

Cedric could barely taste his drink anymore. The words rekindled the fury that he had been trying to drown. He got up to leave.

"Aye, it's no doubt we've got the barbarians lookin' to bring down the Hilt and cultists lurking in the sewers. This world isn't fit to be around much longer. The Prince of Doom is the child of Astasia, says I."

Before Cedric made it to the door, he saw the man who spoke those words. He was an old, gnarled deckhand that looked like every other dockworker Cedric had ever seen and smelled as if he had just gone bathing in a pile of horse excrement. Seeing him laugh at his expense enraged the prince, and before Cedric realized, he was walking toward the drunkard with a clenched fist and intoxicated pride.

Cedric smashed his gloved fist into the side of the man's head, creating a sickening noise. The prince could feel his knuckles crack as they collided with the side of the man's skull. The drunkard fell over with a grunt of pain, but he was back on his feet in the blink of an eye. Most of the taverns of Delethas were known for their brawls, so naturally any frequent visitor knew how to handle an assault. The prince now wished he had remembered that earlier.

The man smashed Cedric in the face with a plate from the table. Cedric's hood flew back and his long, dark hair spilled out. It was noble hair, not a tangled mass like most of the dockworkers and sailors of Delethas. Cedric held a hand to his bloodied face and then felt another blow to his stomach.

Even through the ringing in his ears, he heard another man yell. "Haldron, *no!*"

Cedric fell to one knee. For a long moment he heard or felt nothing but the pain from his face and stomach. He felt like he would be sick. There wasn't much in his stomach except for two-current mead and even cheaper wine, and it was thrashing about now, ready to out. After a moment, Cedric realized that either he had gone deaf, or the entire tavern had fallen silent. As he opened his eyes and wiped away the blood, he could see that the latter was true. All conversations about DeSatho's no-sail decree and the Prince of Doom had halted. All eyes were on the prince of Celendas.

Cedric slowly got to his feet, trying not to shake. As he rose, all the sailors, minstrels, deckhands, dockworkers, serving girls, and even portly Kristofer slowly took a knee in reverence. The man called Haldron rested on both his knees with his head bowed.

"A thousand pardons, milord," he said in a voice choked with tears. "I had no idea…"

Cedric wiped his bloodied glove onto his riding cloak. A long, awkward moment passed where no one spoke or moved. They awaited the prince's response to what could only be considered an act of treason by Haldron. Cedric had no intention of punishing this man for defending himself. However, he did feel a bit vengeful.

Without thinking, he threw his leg out and kicked the old man in the face. A gasp rose in the tavern, as if the prince had just lopped off his head. Cedric did not wait to hear more. As Haldron fell backwards, the prince flew out the door, pushing several patrons out of his way.

Outside, a storm was brewing. Thunder rumbled as Cedric tore down the crowded streets, throwing his hood back up. As he did so, he silently wished that he were another man, a normal man. Not a prince. A normal man would not run from a simple brawl. A normal man would not need to hide himself to pass through the docks. A normal man might be able to earn his way to knighthood, rather than being born into the silver chains of royalty. His anger only worsened when he realized he was crying.

After several blocks of running in a direction he didn't remember choosing, Cedric realized that he had reached the harbor. Dozens of ships rocked lightly in the steady waves of the anchorage, swarming with sailors and deckhands as they finished up the evening's duties. Many of the sailors sang slurred songs and struggled to keep their footing, while a fair amount of others had already passed out on the docks, fortunate enough not to roll off into the sea and drown in their drunken states.

Seeing the ships gave Cedric a sudden idea. He scanned the docks for a high-ranking sailor—a captain. He found one near a ship that was just dropping anchor. The ship was one of the finer vessels in the port and the man he placed as captain wore a long red coat trimmed with gold. His black hat was ornamented with the crossed oars of the Sea Farer's Guild. Cedric knew the guild to be located in Quayhaven, only a few days' ride from the kingdom city of Aevenore.

If he could sail away now, he might be able to meet the Eurheborn as they reached Aevenore. Without his father present, no one could deny him entry into the order.

"Excuse me," Cedric called to the captain in a feigned western accent. "Is this your ship?"

"We ain't got no goods," the captain called back, not bothering to turn around. "Pendara won't let no ships through the Valice on account of the storms. Though if you ask me, I'd think DeSatho was trying to clear the ways for his own ships."

Cedric was about to pull back his hood to see if he could convince this man that it was a matter of the crown that the prince be taken to Quayhaven immediately, but before he could further consider the option, a commotion arose on deck.

"Get your blistered hands off of me; this is a fifty current shirt!" a melodious voice shouted.

"Cap!" another voice yelled over the first. "We got a stowaway!"

The captain ignored Cedric and trotted toward the ship. "Let's have 'em!"

Two figures appeared at the rails of the ship. One of them was a burly sailor, wearing only a weathered pair of brown trousers with a red sash tied around his head. The other was a much more elegantly dressed gentleman, presumably a noble. He wore a deep crimson shirt laced up at the neck and fine leather pants. The sailor held him by his arm and in his other hand he carried what must have been the stowaway's possessions: a pack and a harp case.

"You!" the captain snarled accusingly.

"I must say, Captain," the finely dressed man began, "the accommodations on your ship leave much to be desired."

"I oughta have your tongue out, boy!" the captain cursed, pointing a stubby finger at the man. "Better yet, maybe we head back into the Valice and toss you over so you can swim back to Pendara and face the king's justice!"

That seemed to drain the color from the man's face.

The captain motioned for the sailor to get the man off of his ship. The sailor threw the possessions onto the dock. As they sailed through the air, Cedric cringed, knowing an expensive harp when he saw one, even in its case. The stowaway assaulted the sailor with a stream of curses as his effects flew through the air. Cedric moved to catch the harp. He managed to position himself under the spinning case, but it was awkwardly shaped and when he caught it he was knocked off balance. His hood was thrown back as he landed on his backside.

Everything happened so fast Cedric didn't have time to think. He felt slightly embarrassed having fallen over, but when he rose to his feet, he received the same response he had experienced at The Ten Tankards.

"Your majesty…" the captain began, kneeling and bowing his head.

The burly sailor was kneeling as well. The stowaway hardly noticed. He was hurrying down the plank toward his cherished harp case, still cursing the man who had carelessly tossed it.

"That thing is worth more than your life, you sea-snorting—"

The stowaway stopped short as he reached Cedric. As the stranger stared slack-jawed at the prince of Celendas, Cedric realized he was no stranger.

"Jaryd Fawn?" Cedric asked.

This washed away the shocked look on Jaryd's face and

he smiled. "I am honored that you remember my name, lord prince. Last time I came through Celendas, you nearly dropped me down the lift shaft."

That memory brought a smile to Cedric's face. Of all the bards that passed through Eurheby, Jaryd Fawn was by far the most memorable. He sang Ausfred's Final Flight so beautifully that even King Alastair wept when he heard it.

Cedric handed the bard his harp case and turned to the captain. "There must be some misunderstanding here, Captain. Surely you do not treat court bards with such hostility."

The captain looked up, clearly abashed. "I humbly apologize, my lord. This here man was on the run from DeSatho's Shore Guard. I didn't want no trouble aboard the *Maiden Breaker*."

"He killed a girl!" shouted the kneeling sailor up on the deck. "We could not give him passage, but he snuck aboard anyway."

Cedric turned to the bard; his royal blood began to flow and sober him. "Is this true?"

Jaryd leaned in closer to the prince. "Forgive my forwardness, my lord, but these are matters we should perhaps discuss in private. I believe there are worse evils in Pendara than a dead whore—evils that might very well threaten your kingdom..."

Cedric raised an eyebrow. *Another evil?* He didn't have time to question it, though. The sky erupted, and rain began to pour violently.

"Come," Cedric said, gathering the bard's things. "I have a room at The Ten Tankards. We can talk there."

Jaryd didn't move. His eyes were cast toward the far horizon of the Valice.

Cedric turned and saw what caught the bard's attention.

Through the heavy rain and the darkening clouds, sails as black as night came toward Delethas.

"Those aren't trading ships, are they?" asked Cedric, already knowing the answer.

The captain had risen to his feet. "Those sails…I'd heard stories, but…." he trailed off.

The sailor leapt down from the deck of the *Maiden Breaker* and shielded his eyes from the rain. "Those can't be sails. No ship can fly that fast…"

Cedric felt a tug on his arm. Jaryd pulled him close.

"Take me to the king. Now."

Cedric did not ask questions. Something dreadful was coming, heralded by those black sails. He pulled up his hood and helped Jaryd with his things. They left the captain and crew of the *Maiden Breaker* to watch the haunting ships approach.

Jaryd clearly knew his way through Delethas, winding through back alleys and cutting through cramped buildings. Cedric had spent half his life in the ports and he still had no idea what paths they were taking. Soon, they approached the gates where merchants were busy covering their goods in their wagons, and commoners were scuttling off to take shelter from the rain. Only two guards stood sentry at the gates. They dropped their spears to block the way as Jaryd and Cedric approached.

"We are heading for Celendas," Cedric said, trying to catch his breath.

"No one leaves," said one of the guards.

Cedric, in no mood for this, threw back his hood. "I am the prince of Celendas; now you will step aside."

"Come now," Jaryd added. "If you hadn't noticed, it is quite wet out."

The guards did not move. One of them made a sound that

could have been laughter. The other one simply repeated: "No one leaves."

"Did you not hear me?" Cedric demanded, stepping closer to the guard's face. A helmet covered most of the guard's features except his eyes. "I am Prince Cedric Galvian. You *will* step aside!"

"No," the guard said.

Jaryd let out a grunt just then, his harp case falling to the ground and splashing into a puddle of mud.

Cedric felt a sudden blow to the back of his skull. He staggered. In the fading reflection of the guard's steel helmet, he thought he saw another figure behind him with a large axe handle held high. Cedric heard the sound of Jaryd slumping to the ground, followed by the sound of his harp case cracking under the weight of his body. As his own vision started to blur, Cedric caught a glimpse of the guard's eyes staring blankly at him.

Even in the darkness of the storm, he could see they were as white as death.

CHAPTER 17: A CHANGE OF COURSE

Triarch, east of the Silver Spire and south of Melbrook

The small town of Triarch was usually called Three Rivers, since the Fareashen name, pronounced *Tree-ark*, did not exactly roll off of the western tongue. The name roughly meant "three becomes one," which was appropriate for a town built upon the convergence of the Glimmeraine, the Serek, and the Branton rivers. Because the town was nearly right in the center of Terrace, it was a convenient rest spot for anyone traveling between Quayhaven, Aevenore, or the mountains. Anerith learned this to be true, as he met many diverse and interesting people during his short stay in the Waterside Inn.

There was an old free knight that rented the room next to Anerith's named Sir Alliston Preal who had just returned from Rokuus. He sat at the table next to Anerith in the common room with a host of young men. Like Anerith, Sir Alliston was on his way to Aevenore to seek council with the king, and he was quick to share his concerns with anyone who listened.

"Dragons!" Sir Alliston had insisted, after draining his seventh tankard of the Waterside's cheapest ale. His speech had begun to slur. "The dragons of Rathaine are stirring from their slumber. The mystics in Jekro say they have been sleeping for sixty years, but I saw one with my own eyes!"

One of the younger men at Sir Alliston's table whispered something to one of his companions that brought a few laughs. He was a handsome young lord from the Silver Coast with long blonde hair. His name was Crispin VonAnthony, and Anerith did not care for him in the least. In the short time that Anerith had known him, Crispin had ridiculed nearly every person in the common room of the Waterside, including the young bard from Crestly, the short and pudgy barmaid who Anerith thought was pretty, and Anerith himself, on account of his "witch robes."

"Tell me, sir knight," Crispin said to Sir Alliston, "did these dragons travel with a pack of unicorns? Or maybe a flock of pixies?"

His companions, two freckle-faced brothers dressed in the sunburst yellow of Romney nobility, snickered faithfully.

Sir Alliston drank again, seemingly oblivious to the mockery that Crispin was making of his tale. "Na. A flock of drakes...foul dragonspawn." The old balding knight rubbed his eyes, as if the memory pained him. "They came at night, when we could not see. You know, in the moonlands, they do not light fires at night. It offends their gods. So the dark wings came unnoticed, began burning the city, and the empress summoned spirits from the beyond to defend Jekro..." Sir Alliston trailed off, looking like he was falling asleep.

"Summoned spirits, did she?" Crispin asked, laughing. "Is that why I woke up and felt a little lighter this morning? I thought it was the shit that I took the night before, not because some narrow-eyed sorceress shifted the Balance on me..." More laughter ensued.

"That noble windsack there is a VonAnthony," said a whispered voice in Anerith's ear, interrupting his eavesdropping. Anerith nearly fell out of his chair in surprise. He was so intent on Sir Alliston's tale that he had not realized someone had joined his table. She was an older woman, with a hooked nose and a stained purple hood over her wiry hair. Anerith could smell drink on her breath. "Not to be trusted, them. Witches and warlocks they are, praising the Burning One. But I don't have to tell you."

Anerith gave her a confused look, noticeably leaning away from her. "Pardon me? Perhaps you have mistaken me for somebody else..."

She gave him an equally confused look, "Well, you're from the Spire, ain't ya? I figured you would know the name well. Helena VonAnthony made quite a stir during her time in the Spire." She narrowed her eyes on Anerith and added, "That might have been a little before your time, lad, but surely you have seen her husband, the baron, lurking around the Spire."

Anerith shook his head. Anerith had of course seen the baron in the Spire courtyard, but he had not given it much thought. Nobles came and went, but only nosey students like Xavia and Rutherford bothered keeping track of their appointments.

Again, the old woman looked surprised, giving Anerith a suspicious raised eyebrow. Her eyes were cold blue, and they darted from Anerith to Crispin VonAnthony, who was buying Sir Alliston another round of drinks so he might ridicule him some more. Her eyes fell back on Anerith.

"I see the Luminary has been keeping his secrets then," she licked her lips, leaning in closer. From the wild look in her eyes, Anerith was afraid that she might try and kiss him. She stopped inches away from his face, her hot, rancid breath thick enough to taste. "There was a time when his students studied openly...the secrets of the world, secrets of Chaos. But, some of the students began to surpass their teachers, going mad in the process." Her eyes widened. "They always went mad. You see, mortals cannot ever hope to grasp the enormity of the flowing powers in the world." She nodded toward Crispin with a wry grin. "And that fella's family has made an awful name for themselves trying to do so."

Anerith took a nervous drink, hoping the woman would tire of this tirade and leave him be. She did not move, meaning he would have to be the one to leave, which he was fine with. He hadn't planned on leaving for Aevenore until morning, but he suddenly felt the urge to be back in the Spire, away from these doomsayers. The sooner he departed for the kingdom city the better, it seemed. These sounded like dangerous times to be traveling alone at night, but he would risk it if it meant being far from this woman.

Much to Anerith's dismay, the woman continued. "Not Lord and Lady VonAnthony from Quayhaven, mind you. They are sensible folk." She thought about that. "Well...more sensible and wary than young Crispin's aunt and uncle in Wynnstead, I should say. You see, Wynnstead was founded after the Shackling, when the world was healing. But dark forces lurked, and the Ways to the Abyss were not altogether closed. The Calluses, they call them: shifting boundaries between our world and the demon realm. And both Wynnstead and the Silver Spire were built upon them."

Suddenly, Crispin let out another mocking laugh from his table, startling Anerith who had suddenly become intent on the woman's words.

The old woman didn't seem to notice. "Some say that Gabriel VonAnthony took a demon bride that he found in the Calluses, deep in the Wynnstead crypts." She let out a clucking sound that Anerith assumed was laughter. "Believe that if you will, but old Sierra will not. She knows better. Gabriel married himself a witch, one that was not afraid to lay with demons. That is how he came to power: through his demon-loving wife." Sierra said that last part a little too loudly, and some of the other conversations in the Waterside halted, including Crispin VonAnthony's. She continued on, unaware. "She learned witchcraft in the Spire, and learned how to walk the Revery without sleeping. Blasphemous!"

Anerith made to get up, but Sierra reached out with her withered hand and grabbed his wrist, holding him in place. Her strength was surprising.

"That is how she died, I tell ye," she said, none too quietly. "She tried to take on the Dream Lord himself. She learned the secrets of the Spire and she thought she could succeed where the old Luminary had failed. But corruption took her," she laughed.

Crispin VonAnthony was standing at Anerith's table now, his eyes narrowed on old Sierra. He wobbled on his feet, clearly drunk. "So they let harlots in here now, do they?" His eyes darted to Anerith. "You, witch robes, keep your whore quiet or I'm going to let Sir Dragonslayer over there take her for a ride." He took a drink from his goblet.

Behind him, Sir Alliston's head was buried in the nook of his arm. He was fast asleep.

"How fares your dear aunt, my lord?" Sierra asked maliciously. She rose to her feet, barely standing taller than Anerith even as he sat.

Crispin stopped mid drink, gave her an angry look over his glass, and then quickly threw the remaining contents of his goblet in her face. He most certainly would have done more had his companions not restrained him, telling him they did not wish to spend the night in the constable's quarters. They dragged him out of the common room.

"Watch out for the Sect, you witch!" Crispin yelled. "Both of you! I know people and..." his voice faded away as the door shut behind him.

Anerith was on his feet, ready to go to his room and lock the door. Sierra grabbed his wrist again, turning him to face her.

"You truly do not know of the terrible things that happen below the Spire?" she asked, her face dripping with wine. She didn't wait for an answer. "Even as we speak, the baron is attempting to free his wife's spirit from the grip of the Abyss, using dark words given to him by the Spire. Should he succeed, it will lead to dark days indeed." Her pupils were so wide that it made her eyes look entirely black. "Not only will the Balance bring Chaos upon us, but the Sect of Halcyon will be forced to break any allegiance they have with the Spire and put all of its students to death like they did in the early days." She squeezed Anerith's wrist tightly. "Do not let the secrets of the Spire consume you all!"

Anerith pulled his arm away from her, finally breaking her grip. She didn't follow him as he retreated from the common room. She merely watched him leave, never blinking.

Anerith did indeed go straight to his room and locked the door behind him. He packed his things that night, hoping to depart the Waterside as soon as the sun rose. Once he was ready, he sat on his bed and attempted to read some more from *The History of Vysarc: From Kaneya to Rhavael*. But as he read, the words lost all their meaning. His mind was far too preoccupied, so he set the text aside and lay on his back.

A few moments later, he realized he held Vanghrel's message in his hand, between thumb and forefinger, so as not to crush the envelope. He held it so tight his hand had nearly lost all feeling. He must have been holding it since Sierra had approached him. The envelope was still sealed.

Slowly, as he thought about Sierra and the sealed message, he fell into a disturbing, dream-filled sleep.

He dreamt of Vysarc. The underground empire looked exactly how he had imagined. The ceilings were high and every structure was ornamented with symbols of death and Abyssal worship. Wyverns soared from perch to perch high above, appearing as granite statues between flights. With the exception of those macabre creatures, Anerith was alone in the city, walking the cobbled streets in silence. Every now and again, he would pass a skeleton sitting on a stone bench, or a corpse floating in a pool, but there was no sign of life.

He wandered through the wide streets, across massive bridges, and under enormous arches, not sure of his purpose. When he finally reached his destination, he woke up.

The sun was shining through his window, pouring light down onto the sealed envelope in his hand. He sat up and gathered his things, not wanting to dwell on his dream or the night before. He only wanted to be done with his task. However, as he departed the Waterside Inn and walked through Triarch, his thumb couldn't help but explore the small wax seal on the envelope.

Making his way to the large stone bridge that led out of town, Anerith felt a cold sensation trickle down his spine. It was then that he looked around and saw all the watchful eyes following him. He hadn't bothered noticing when he first arrived to Triarch, but now he could see it. Everyone watched him with suspicion. The stable boys stopped their playing as he passed, watching the stranger in robes with anticipation. The baker was setting up his cart for the morning, but he wheeled it back into his shop as Anerith approached. Sierra's words had opened his eyes, but he did not stop to stare in return.

What if Xavia was right all along? Anerith thought. What if there really were deadly secrets in the Spire that he had simply ignored because he didn't want to face them? Because they would lead to questions of faith and doubt, and he did not want to take a stance in things he did not truly understand.

He tried to shake the thought of Xavia's words, and those that Sierra had spoke, and the watchful eyes that accused him of things he had never done. As he crossed the bridge out of Triarch and he came to the crossroad, he stopped. The sign pointing east read "To Aevenore." He knew that was where he should go. After a moment, his feet began to carry him west instead, toward "The Silver Coast," towards Wynnstead.

I'll make the same time if I cut through the Aevenwood, he thought to himself, not considering the ever-apparent dangers of the woods. *I'll still reach Aevenore.*

His thumb ran over the Luminary's wax seal again. He couldn't resist thinking about everything that message held, how much it could tell him. He dared not open the envelope. Doing so would earn him Vanghrel's wrath. However, if he stumbled into Wynnstead and recovered a lost text that belonged to the Silver Spire, well, that might just earn him a little favor. Maybe next time he'd be chosen for a task that would impress Xavia.

Not that he cared about that of course, but Wynnstead was on his way in any case. He was tired of turning away from the secrets of the Spire.

CHAPTER 18: A SUDDEN REQUIEM

Melbrook, on the outskirts of the Aevenwood

Raiken sat in an empty pew—in an empty church—still covered in mossy cobwebs. He held the Greenstone in his cupped hands, staring into its depths. He could feel the same sickening sluggishness that had come over him when the council had taken the stone. Part of him was thrilled to have the shard back in his possession; he had worn it for so long that it felt like an extension of himself. However, another part of him felt hesitant to embrace its charms again. He did not want to be gifted with anything anymore. He did not want to be Lockri's pet; he wanted to be Raiken Belrouse.

Whatever that meant.

His eyes drifted away from the Greenstone as he took notice of the church around him for the first time. The Burrow Gates had exhausted him, so he had slept while Sebastian and Vincent escorted Vance from the church. Sebastian then retreated to tend to an ill woman while Vincent was no doubt in the gardens. He suddenly felt like he never left. Looking around, he realized how little the church had changed since he was a boy. The altar depicting the Heavens and Abyss still held all the miniature gods, angels, and Underlords of his youth. The arrangement told Raiken someone had just recited the tale of Lockri's Flight. Raiken chuckled at the irony.

"Are you well, my lord?" The voice came from beside him in the aisle. A sneaky young girl dressed in acolyte attire looked at him expectantly.

Raiken wondered how the girl had crept up on him, but when he reached up with his left hand to touch the Greenstone, he realized it was in his other hand, no longer around his neck. He laughed again.

"Shall I get a priest, my lord?" the girl asked worriedly.

"No," Raiken said, putting the Greenstone back around his neck. Instantly, he felt the familiar rush of adrenaline. "That won't be necessary." He made to get up, but stopped halfway, and looked back at the girl. She was a pretty young thing with blonde hair and sapphire eyes. Those eyes reminded Raiken of his childhood. *She could be of an age when I ran away*, he thought. "What is your name?" he asked her, sitting back down.

"Kassandria," she said, obediently. She bowed her head slightly and added, "My lord."

Raiken waved the salutation away. "No more *my lords*. I am lord of nothing. I am an exile."

Kassandria raised an eyebrow. "An exile of what, my lord?"

Raiken gave her a stern look.

She smiled and threw a hand over her mouth. "Sir," she corrected herself.

"I am no knight, either," Raiken said with a grin. "Call me Raiken. Tell me, how old are you?"

"I will be thirteen years, come fall," she said proudly.

"And how long have you been with the church?"

The question seemed to take her by surprise. She hesitated. "Well, I have always been with the Faith. Before I came here, I was an orphan in the Fifth Star Church in Aevenore. Why do you ask?"

Raiken raised an eyebrow. "Are you happy?"

"Here?" she asked, still a little bewildered. "I am taken

care of and they have always treated me well."

Raiken smiled. "But that's not what you want, is it?"

She looked at him with eyes that had not yet seen the beauty and terror of the world, and Raiken could see a small hint of doubt in them. He didn't need the Greenstone to navigate the workings of a young mind kept in a cozy prison. He stood up and leaned closer to her.

"I know. I was an orphan, too."

"And not the most well-behaved," Vincent said as he entered, leaning on his cane. Silently, he hobbled down the aisle looking every year his age. When he reached Raiken and the girl, he smiled and laid a hand on Kassandria's shoulder. "I believe Seeley has prepared a fresh batch of cinnamon muffins. And they had the audacity to overpower the aroma of my dragoneye syringas." He produced a few currents from his robes. "Perhaps you would be so kind as to dispose of such a nuisance."

Kassandria gave Raiken a quick glance before taking the coins and bowing her leave. "Thank you, Father."

"Do not let them suffer," Vincent said to her as she left. "Give them a swift demise."

Raiken waited for the old man to look at him, but Vincent didn't. Instead he sat down in the pew behind Raiken. Raiken stood in the aisle now, not sure of what to say. Vincent Cruland represented everything that he had abandoned.

Fortunately, Vincent spoke first. "I have heard tales of your deeds in Lockrian. The Emerald Scout…he is a hero fit for the Chronicles."

Raiken was looking for a hint of mockery in the old man's voice, but he found none. "I did not know the Chronicles glorified the deeds of heathens."

"Raiken, please."

"Is that not what you said?" Raiken asked, a surprising anger rising in him. His errand, and the black stone in his pouch, did not seem to matter much to him right now. "Is that not what you called Lockri and the embrechauns?"

"I was angry," Vincent said tiredly. "Do not tell me that you have not done unwise things out of anger." He gave Raiken a pointed look.

That silenced him. Raiken lowered his head and saw that he had been holding the Greenstone during his outburst.

"You always liked the tales of Lockri," Vincent said reminiscently. "I find it no surprise that you would be drawn to him eventually. However, I hope you realize the dangers that lie in the powers you wield."

"I do not wield any powers," Raiken said defensively. Though it was true that he felt more in tune with his senses while wearing the Greenstone, he was no conjurer.

Vincent nodded slowly with a knowing smile on his face. "You may not realize it yet, but you possess true power, Raiken. I do not speak of powers such as channeling the Heavens like in the tales of the cleric Darrance Stow. Or calling on the elements like Fereign the Grey. But power nonetheless, all power comes at a price. It may not seem like much of a price when you can already feel the pulling of such powers, but it is a price that must still be paid. And, if the stories of Darrance and Fereign tell us nothing more than the dangers of power, let them remind us that the Balance is more than just an idea placed in our little minds to keep us from misbehaving." He looked at Raiken with tired old eyes, full of wisdom. "It is an idea placed in our little minds to remind us that we are not gods. We must respect the powers that surround us." Vincent's eyes fell onto the Greenstone. "And the powers that can corrupt us."

Raiken did not know how to take the warning.

"So, what brings you here?" Vincent asked, quickly switching subjects.

Suddenly, Raiken's thoughts returned to the black stone in his pouch, to the unconscious boy in the woods. However, now he was unsure if he wanted to approach the matter with Vincent. He was an old man, and Raiken did not care to worry him unnecessarily. Also, he would not mind being away from the priest's calculating eyes for a bit. "It is a matter I must discuss with my brother," Raiken said.

Vincent nodded, rising from his seat. He turned and narrowed his eyes at Raiken. "In these past few years, your brother has come to bear burdens that were not meant for him." The look that Vincent gave Raiken made it clear what he really meant. *You left him. You left him to clean up your mess and to handle the duties that were meant for both of you.* "If you bring him another, I would have it from you first."

Raiken considered that for a moment. He couldn't let old grudges get in the way of his current task. The old priest was right. Raiken had let Sebastian clean up after him for far too long.

Raiken motioned for Vincent to sit back down next to him. Raiken pulled the black stone from his pouch. Even holding the thing gave him a sense of dread and anxiety that he could not explain. He quickly handed it to Vincent.

As Vincent took the stone and examined it, Raiken told him of the events that took place in Lockrian. He told him of the wereling shaman, the shipwreck, the young captain, and his dangerous trek through the Burrow Gates. During it all, Vincent did not take his eyes or hands off of the black stone. He rolled it between his fingers, and traced the intricate scripture that ran to its jagged edges, unreadable. His old eyes bore through the menacing aura that the stone emanated, looking for something.

When Raiken finished his tale, there was a long silence, filled only by distant voices beyond the church's doors.

"That is the trouble with raising twins," Vincent said, breaking that silence with a wistful voice. He closed his fist around the black stone. "They will either bring you twice the joy you are entitled to, or…" He trailed off.

Sebastian's heavy footsteps could be heard from the stairs leading down to the antechamber outside the church proper.

Vincent opened his hand. "This is half of the *kropal*: the Shackle of Flame. It was used to bind Sol Saradys' hands after his defeat in the War of the Scales." His eyes did not leave the stone. "If this…"

Vincent left Raiken hanging on those words as Sebastian opened the doors and entered. He looked like he hadn't slept in days; his eyes were rimmed with red and his shoulders hung heavily.

"What are you doing here?" Sebastian asked his brother, not wasting any time on pleasantries.

Raiken turned from Vincent. The expression on his face spoke of many things, not the least of which was fear.

Sebastian turned to Vincent and saw the stone he was holding. Suddenly, his own face reflected his brother's. "Is that…?"

Before Vincent could answer, the front doors behind Sebastian were thrown open and a young member of Melbrook's militia rushed in. He wore the sigil of Duke Berrymore on his surcoat: the branched berries of his namesake. The bloodied man stumbled to the floor, dropping his spear.

"Father!" he cried urgently. "There is devilry at work!"

Sebastian helped the man to his feet. "It is under control, Aidron. She has been confined and the madness has left her."

Aidron gave Sebastian a blank stare. "No, no woman, my lord. 'Tis a man, taken by the Corruptor! Walking in death!" His eyes held pure terror.

"Where?" Sebastian asked as Raiken rushed to his side.

"At the old mill," Aidron said, picking up his spear to lean on. "We locked him in there, but...Kevin and Bailey..."

Sebastian gave Vincent a look.

"Go," Vincent urged. He closed his fist around the stone. "I have some reading to do..."

Raiken called for his falcon as they left the church, a dagger in each hand. "To answer your question, brother, I just came to warn you that the world is ending. I'll tell you all about it after we take care of the walking dead."

The old mill was on the borders of the Aevenwood, far from Melbrook. Long ago, it had been used by the Finch family of bakers until raids from the forest became too frequent. Seeley Finch had since constructed a new mill closer to the Second Wrought Bridge in town. The old building near the Aevenwood had become somewhat of a landmark—an unfortunate hangout for brigands and knaves.

Raiken remembered the place quite vividly, as any man remembers the place where he took his first woman.

The twins arrived to find the door barricaded with barrels and broken crates. They could see no movement inside the mill.

"Maybe Aidron spent a little too much time singin' in the Raine," Raiken suggested with a whisper, as he peered through the cracks of the outer walls.

Sebastian walked around the back of the mill, where the

ground gave way to the Glimmeraine River. There was a set of stairs leading down to the basement door, which hung open, swaying in the calm wind. Sebastian motioned for Raiken to follow him, but when he turned around his brother was gone.

"Raiken!" he hissed in a low voice. There was no reply. He made to head back around the mill to look for his brother, but suddenly heard a sickening noise coming from the basement door.

He knew it to be the sound of Kevin and Bailey's demise, rising above the gentle flow of the Glimmeraine.

Sebastian pulled the mace from his belt and crept down the stairs. He reached the door and peered inside. Light from upstairs dripped in between the floorboards. Sebastian could see a hunched figure in the center of the basement, kept busy by a pool of dark blood and the remains of two militiamen. A familiar coldness crept up Sebastian's spine, a feeling he hadn't experienced since Vysarc.

He was frozen there for a moment, watching the dark figure devour Kevin and Bailey, unsure if what he saw was real. He wanted to rush forward and bury his mace into the back of the figure's skull. Instead he watched, waiting.

Suddenly, a loud crack brought Sebastian out of his trance. The floorboards gave way and Raiken fell down from the floor above, smashing to the ground at Sebastian's feet. The gory sounds ceased as the hunched man turned and rose. Sebastian could see in the faint light that the man's face was badly scarred, but something else had claimed his life. Yet, something even worse had given it back to him. His burned face was familiar to Sebastian but he did not have time to dwell on it.

The pile of rubble at Sebastian's feet moved, and Raiken's foot lashed out and kicked the door open, exposing Sebastian to the walking dead man. Raiken tried to stand up, but cried out in pain, holding his back.

"Damn all the termites to their own private hell!" Raiken exclaimed, throwing the decayed wood off of him with his one free hand.

Amidst the clatter of infested wood, the dead man began to shamble toward the twins, letting out an eerie moan that spoke of hunger. Sebastian quickly helped his brother to his feet, pulling him out into the sunlight.

"Celecy's tits!" Raiken cursed, finally noticing their undead adversary, "the boy was not lying!" He struggled to catch his footing, clumsily drawing his daggers in the process. "What is going on here, brother?"

Sebastian stepped forward to meet the shambling man, no longer paralyzed by the fear that overcame him earlier. Whoever the man coming at him had once been, he was a man no longer. Sebastian's faith obligated him to give the corrupted mortal vessel release. He did so, burying his weapon into that burned face.

A disgusting gurgle ended the profane being's life, its soulless body collapsing onto the pile of splintered wood. Raiken stared for a long moment. "I thought that might be more exciting."

Sebastian did not reply. The Belrouse brothers stared over the dead, both in silent contemplation.

As was his fashion, Raiken broken the silence again. "Have I been gone too long? Is this a common occurrence in Terrace these days?"

Sebastian ignored him, kneeling to inspect the corpse. It took one look at the man's tunic for Sebastian to remember.

"This man was one of VonAnthony's. His name was Toland," Sebastian said, noticing the baron's sigil beneath the gore that covered Toland's tunic. "He burned his face saving a child from a fire…"

"VonAnthony of Wynnstead?" Raiken asked. "What's he doing this side of the Aevenwood, undead and eating people?"

Thoughts of his fellow priest, Martin, raced through Sebastian's mind. He looked to Raiken. "There was a requiem… and VonAnthony's wife. They say she was a witch…"

Raiken raised an eyebrow. "We better go. I hear it's rude to arrive late to a requiem."

Sebastian shook his head. "I have to return to Melbrook. Laurel is in trouble…"

"What if more of these come?" Raiken asked, pointing to Toland's mutilated body. "All of Melbrook will be in trouble."

Sebastian knew his brother was right. However, he also knew that there was something in Wynnstead that he did not want to face. Fortunately, one thought reassured him as he watched Raiken dust himself off and head toward the woods.

For now, he would not have to face anything alone.

CHAPTER 19: BLACK SAILS

Celendas, the Phoenix City of Eurheby

High up in his chambers, King Alastair added more oil to his lamp, wondering why young Camry hadn't been by. Not that he minded, as the welcomed silence gave him time to contemplate the dark days ahead. However, he did find it rather strange. Geldra's young ward usually stopped by at least once a night to carry messages either to or from the high councilor, who preferred not to take the lifts. Yet, for some reason, he had been left alone all night. *These are strange times*, he reassured himself. Trying not to dwell on it, Alastair turned the knob on the lamp to better illuminate the map upon his table.

Demonscale Heights was a wasteland, looking sinister even on parchment. On most maps, the region was little more than a gap between the three lands of Eurheby, Terrace, and the Rhelklands. However, the scholars of the Phoenix Keep held much more accurate maps. The old cartographers of Celendas were famous for sending their scouts to the farthest reaches of Athland so that they could compile the most comprehensive and inclusive maps available in the Tripartite. The libraries of Celendas contained a collection of maps and charts that rivaled even the massive *Sorenthion's Atlas of the Known World*, all recorded copies of which had been lost in the siege of Candrella.

Alastair drank his wine, taking a moment to savor it— something he neglected to do normally. As he stared at the course that he had drawn out, he couldn't help but wonder if this would be the last night he would enjoy such luxuries. That thought did not scare him. Ever since his decision to take Cedric into the mountains on their quest to find the Dragonsbane, he had little room in his heart for dread or apprehension, since anxiety had already staked a claim.

As he set his wine aside, a knock sounded at the door.

"Come," the king announced, standing for the first time in hours. Stretching his limbs was ecstasy.

Geldra slid into the room, opening the door only slightly so the king could not see the slain guards that lay outside his chambers. Myron and Kessley both lay facedown in pools of blood that flowed from their slashed necks. Geldra closed the door behind him to shield the king from that grisly view.

"Your majesty," Geldra said. "I have come to consult you on your coming journey."

Alastair rubbed his eyes. "Very well, Geldra." He turned his back to the high councilor and returned to his maps. "I mean to head northwest, toward Holthurst. The Stairs lead up into the caves, which will be much easier than traveling over the mountains." He ran a hand through his hair. "Although, there are sure to be a few tribes of greks lurking about, at the very least. Perhaps Duke Jerome will have some men to spare." He thought on that for a moment. "In any case, the hardest task will be finding a way into Scorn."

Geldra slowly came forward, stepping silently. He reached the king, sitting again at his table, drinking wine and prattling on about his quest. Geldra crept close and reached into his robe, producing a small dagger.

Alastair set down his empty wineglass and turned to find the high councilor breaking the wax seal of a scroll with a small dagger. It was a royal decree. "What is that?"

Geldra unrolled the scroll to show the king. "It is to

legitimize my regency in your absence, your majesty. I pray to Celecy that it shall be a short one." He handed the document to the king, slightly smiling, still holding the dagger in his other hand.

"Yes," Alastair said, filling his wineglass again and reaching for his quill. "Forgive me, Geldra. It is late and I am weary." He scrawled his name on the parchment and reached for one of the burning candles nearby. He let the red wax fall, spattering like blood onto the parchment. After enough collected, he let it cool while he stood up again to pace around his chambers. His balcony doors were left open and the spring breeze blew in to ruffle the curtains, but not enough to extinguish the candlelight. "Tell me, Geldra, do you feel a change in the wind?"

Geldra stared at the wax cooling, his smile widening. "Yes, your majesty. Change is coming..." He gripped the dagger tightly.

Alastair walked out on his balcony, letting the winds of change wash over him. "For the better, I hope," he said, before his eyes fell upon the distant flames of Delethas and the black sails that rocked menacingly on the waves.

Geldra pressed the king's seal into the wax as he heard Alastair curse from the balcony. He quickly rolled up the parchment and stuck it into his robes. Then, he went to tend to his king.

Delethas, just outside of Celendas

Cedric's leg felt numb from kicking at the iron bars of his cell. One of the bars had begun to move, but only slightly. Cedric cursed and sat down on the cold, stone floor across from the bard, who had been sitting cozily for nearly the entirety of their imprisonment, humming wordless melodies.

"You know, a little help would be nice," Cedric said angrily as he tried to rub the feeling back into his leg.

"I am with you in spirit," Jaryd said between melodies. His eyes were closed in concentration.

Cedric had had enough. "This is no time for song, gleeman! You said you had news that concerns Celendas. Now, if you will not help me get us out of here, you will give me the news."

Jaryd continued humming.

Cedric got to his feet and grabbed the bard by his tunic, lifting him up to face him. "Now!"

Jaryd gave the prince a look of disbelief, as if he had just been slapped across the face. He pushed Cedric away. "Back! Listen, boy, those ships are a part of the Burning One's fleet. Now, unless you want to rot here while your kingdom falls to the Corruptor, you will give me a moment's peace." He quickly returned to his trance-like humming.

The prince, unfamiliar with being treated like a common ruffian, took a moment to regain his composure. He left the bard to his curious business as he continued to kick at the iron bars. Just as he thought one was loosening more, a shout came from the stairs.

"Oy! Stop that racket!" A shadow stretched down the stairs, dancing in the torchlight above. The dungeon was far below Delethas, in the old constable's keep. Cedric knew that much, but he had yet to figure out why he had been thrown in here. After a moment, the guard appeared—the same man that barred his escape from Delethas.

"Let me out of here," Cedric demanded. "You have no

right to keep me. I am your prince!"

The guard did not respond. He only removed his helmet, revealing greasy hair plastered to his forehead and eyes that were not his own.

Cedric suddenly felt the pain from the back of his head again. Those putrid white eyes were the last thing he had seen before waking up in this prison.

"What is wrong with his eyes?" Cedric asked the bard, receiving only a hummed melody in response.

The guard approached the iron bars, a cruel grin on his face. The smile looked forced, as if a puppet master pulled at phantom strings from the corners of the guard's mouth. His eyes flinched repeatedly, like something pained him.

"He will let us out," Jaryd said, rising to his feet. "This one doesn't worship the Burning One. He was just caught on a bad day." He began to whistle the same melody that he had been humming before, and the guard responded by raising a hand to his head.

Jaryd moved like lightening, grabbing the guard's head through the bars and then slamming it into the iron. The guard fell limply to the floor. Jaryd reached for the unconscious man's belt and produced the keys, quickly finding the right one for the cell.

Before Cedric could inquire as to what had just happened, the door to the cell was thrown open.

Jaryd picked up the guard's sword and gave it to Cedric. "Let's go find my harp."

They made their way quickly up the stairs, Jaryd leading. *This must not be his first time in a cell*, Cedric thought, but he did not speak the assumption. His mind was suddenly focused on the cries he began hearing from above.

"What's happening?" he asked Jaryd between heaving breaths.

"Come on; we have to hurry," was all Cedric got from the bard.

Soon, they reached the top level of the old constable's keep. The great stone building was deserted, just like below, but shadows danced on the walls as lightning flashed through the windows. Cedric gripped the guard's sword tightly as he followed Jaryd to the entrance. The bard pushed the heavy wooden door open enough so they could see outside.

What they saw was absolute chaos.

The old constable's keep was on a great hill at the northernmost gates of Delethas, and from where they stood, Cedric and Jaryd could see that those gates were thrown open and waves of ashen-robed figures were gathering there.

Other shapes ran through the streets below, dark figures that skittered about on four limbs. They appeared more or less human, despite the thick hair that grew over their bodies. They chased after fleeing townsfolk—those who had not already been slaughtered—snapping at their heels and toying with them in their pursuit. There were some small skirmishes between surviving guardsmen and the invaders, but they were shortly ended.

It looked like every building was engulfed in flames. Townsfolk fell to their knees and wept or tore at their hair. Some of their eyes had gone white. Most of the ashen-robed figures did not pay much heed to the townsfolk, with the exception of those invaders with horns growing from their heads. Those terrible figures wielded great mauls and crude axes and made short work of any townsfolk who attempted to flee the city.

They were all amassing to march on Celendas.

Cedric attempted to push Jaryd aside, his sword raised to fight, but the bard quickly closed the door and kept the prince from racing to his death.

"Stand aside, coward!" Cedric said, ready to face the devils outside, knowing full well that he would die in the process.

"Quiet!" Jaryd hissed as his face twisted in anger. "How will we get to the king with you dead? I am not well-versed in dragging corpses. I tend to leave them behind for the wolves."

"The city is falling!" Cedric exclaimed.

"I can see that," Jaryd retorted. "But we need to get to Celendas. We have no hope of surviving here, and we can't leave by sea...there are too many ships."

"What do you suggest?" Cedric asked, clearly trying to restrain himself from pummeling his unlikely companion.

Jaryd raised a finger to his lips. Amidst the sounds of Delethas falling, Cedric heard two constrained voices. But this wasn't the same suffering sounds from the streets. This was laughter.

They both returned to the door and opened it slightly. Close by outside, against the wall of the keep, there were two robed figures in the shadows. One of them was moving awkwardly. Cedric narrowed his eyes, straining against the rain and darkening night. He could hardly make them out. But, as one of the robed figures was knocked back against the wall, Cedric could see flesh between the two. There was a third figure—a woman—confined between them. She was restrained by the figure against the wall, a hand over her mouth and an arm around her neck. The other figure tried to grapple her legs, but she kicked wildly.

Before Cedric knew it, Jaryd had already slipped out of the keep and was creeping along the shadows of the wall. The prince followed, trying to keep his footing in the mud. They were an arm's length away from the figures when lightening crashed. One of them tried to shout, but Jaryd dove on him before he could utter a sound. Out of pure instinct, Cedric leapt at the other one, his sword raised to strike and his eyes closed.

He thought of the sword yard, facing the hulking Tanith Elton in armor. *Left foot back, right foot wide, bring the sword down across your chest,* he thought to himself. When he opened his eyes, he saw a dying man at his feet, bleeding in the rain. He looked over and saw Jaryd dragging his kill by the feet toward the keep's door. The freed woman was watching in shocked disbelief, luckily not making a sound.

"Come on, love" Jaryd said to her in a whisper. "These boys owe you an apology. Help us collect it."

She stared at the bard, still motionless. Cedric slid the sword into his belt and began to drag the other body toward the keep. After a moment or two, the woman stood up to help. Jaryd gave her his cloak to cover herself, and they soon managed to get the bodies into the keep.

Once inside, Jaryd disrobed the one he had been dragging, and fit the robe over his own clothes. Cedric did the same with his, not asking any questions. The woman sat on the ground, collecting herself.

"They are soulless...their eyes..." she kept saying to herself.

"You know who these men are, don't you?" Cedric asked Jaryd, tying the robe.

The bard nodded. "From Vhaltas. They serve the Burning One and they herald the Days of Astasia." He searched the dead man for any weapons, finding a short dagger and small pouch. "If we sneak into Celendas with them, we may be able to find a way to the keep."

"Join ranks with the enemy?"

"Did you say the Burning One?" the woman interjected.

They both turned to her now. She was an older woman, more beautiful than plain.

"He came to me in a dream," she said, staring at nothing in particular. "He told me to join him, that he would bring me currents and jewels. But I know the Burning One and his lies, and I told him to steer right off." She shivered. "But my husband… my Randle, he had dreams too. And he told me he would do anything to get our children away from the ports." Her mouth hung open, and she looked at Cedric. "…our children."

Cedric stepped toward her, not knowing how to comfort her.

"We must hurry," Jaryd said, peering out the door. "They are moving."

Cedric took her hand and she looked up at him. Her eyes widened, recognition suddenly coming to her. "Your majesty?"

"We will stop them," Cedric promised, squeezing her hand.

"Lovely," Jaryd said. "I'll make a song of it. Now come on!"

Once outside, Cedric and Jaryd made their way to the stables unnoticed. Figures in robes ran everywhere, none of them questioned by the eyeless men with the flaming staves that seemed to command the army. Cedric and Jaryd saddled two horses and made their way around the wall toward the port, where they easily slipped into the fields. They rode toward Celendas. Not far behind them marched the army of Sol Saradys.

Cedric and Jaryd reached Celendas to find it nearly as ravaged as Delethas. However, the people of the kingdom city fought neither beasts nor robed men; they fought amongst themselves. The guards that tried valiantly to keep the peace were severely outnumbered.

The prince and the bard came in through the south gate, along the Celedine Canal. Usually, Riverside would be crowded with trade carts and hollering merchants at this hour, but as Cedric and Jaryd rode under the archways and into the market streets, the crowd that had gathered did not shout about the price of grains or bread. They shouted things about the Burning One, about Astasia, and about things Cedric did not even understand. But he followed the bard's galloping horse through those streets, past people he once knew that now had white eyes and no sense of decency.

"Where are your knights?" Jaryd shouted back to the prince as their horses turned a corner. "They need to be gathered!"

Cedric thought about the colorful Eurheborn riding out of the city without him. "The Tower Guard is all that remains. To the keep!"

As they made their way through the crowded streets, their horses whinnied and shouldered a path through the madness. There were faces Cedric knew. Marl Keys of The Lock & Key wielded a broken bottle against two drunkards, two pairs of white eyes. They overtook him as Cedric rode by, shoving the broken bottle into his throat. He also saw Ralt Bridger, the popular baker, hitting an old woman in tattered robes with a rolling pin. He held a bloody cleaver in his other hand. Beggars had come out from the shadowed alleyways and were running into abandoned shops and taverns to raid the storerooms. The prince and bard rode past the Temple of the Lady and Cedric saw Cardinal Carthys hanging by his neck, his body stripped of any mark of his order, aside from the Tear of Celecy necklace that was now lodged in a place that very much defiled its sanctity. The Cardinal's body swayed in the breeze, and ashen-robed figures were tearing the temple apart from the outside. The rumored Sect of Halcyon was nowhere to be seen as their sworn villains openly opposed a beacon of Order in the world.

Is this truly Astasia? Cedric wondered to himself. The stories all said that brother would turn on brother and all would tremble before the powers of Chaos when the Days came. And as he watched the madness that surrounded him, he could not see any other explanation.

The Days of Astasia had truly come.

The Phoenix Gates rose above the rooftops of Riverside as Jaryd and Cedric crossed the bridge. The enormous gates were opened, but the madness of Riverside had not yet made it to the keep. Or so it seemed. Cedric could see a few armored figures scrambling for horses, their purple cloaks flapping violently behind them.

"There!" Cedric cried, pointing toward the barracks. Jaryd rode ahead in that direction, but Cedric's eyes were suddenly drawn to the towers, the highest of which had flames licking at its peak. Time seemed to slow down, and the screams of Riverside faded into an eerie silence. The only thing that he saw was the flames, climbing toward the sky.

"Father!" he cried out, kicking his horse with all his strength. It let out an unearthly shriek and bolted toward the keep, flying past Jaryd. The Tower Guard barely even noticed the prince, as they were preparing for the riots that they knew would soon reach the keep's walls. Cedric leapt from his horse and scrambled into the keep, drawing his sword clumsily. He threw the doors open to find a score of dead bodies in the main hall: guards and servants both, their throats opened wide to spill their lifeblood. Scattered fires were blazing and the smell of burning flesh was in the air.

Cedric raced toward the lifts, although he knew they would be of no help. Jaryd was shouting something behind him, but Cedric could not hear anything except for his own blood thundering in his ears. When he arrived at the lift's controls, he saw Durrek's young, lifeless body slumped over the pulley locks, a small dagger in his back. Cedric cursed and kicked the locks, hoping they would loosen, but he saw that they were broken, the lift box shattered a few floors above.

Jaryd grabbed him by the shoulder. "Where is the king?"

"I don't know," Cedric said, shaking the bard's hand off of him. He made to run toward the stairs, but a choked voice called to him.

"Cedric..."

The prince whirled and saw his father, crumpled in a shadowed corner of the lift well. The king gripped a scroll in one hand, and held the Phoenix Crown in the other.

"Father!" The prince rushed to the king's side, hot tears already in his eyes. "What happened?"

The king tried to crawl, but his legs were in a gruesome knot, white bone sticking out from his flesh. "That traitor..." he coughed and a splatter of blood hit the floor, "he ruined the lift...I tried to jump across....the stairs..." He began coughing violently, barely able to speak.

"Father, let me get you to a horse," Cedric began to move the king, but Alastair let out an agonizing howl, coughing all the more.

Jaryd knelt by the prince. "He would not make it, Cedric. We must away. The cult will be here soon."

"Not without my father!" Cedric said angrily, glaring at

the bard. "This is the king of Celendas!"

Alastair handed Cedric the crown. "You... must go..." he also pushed the scroll toward his son. "The...the Dragonsbane... it is the only hope."

Cedric set them both aside, tears now falling freely. "We will find it together, father. Be strong! I need your help!"

"I am...done..." the king said weakly. "The sword...it is the only hope. If this is...is the end. Celendas will need to face the dragons. It is...our..." his eyes flickered and rolled back into his head. His body went limp in Cedric's arms.

A mix of anger, despair, and utter devastation drove Cedric into a catatonic silence as he stared at his father's dead body. His heart seemed to shrivel and collapse in his chest. He could not breathe.

A clamor arose from beyond the keep's open doors. A voice shouted "Intruders!" Jaryd knelt to help the prince up.

"We must go! They are breeching the walls!" The bard tugged at the prince's arms.

Cedric was unresponsive.

The bard turned the prince to face him, forcing him to drop his father. "The king has ordered you to pick up that crown and rule in his stead! We must away if you wish to ever carry on his name!"

This made the prince blink, finally taking notice of the shouts outside. He looked at the bard and wiped the tears from his face. Picking up the scroll and the crown, he stood up. "Let us make haste."

The bard eagerly obliged, rushing toward the doors.

"Wait," Cedric said, looking back at his father's body. He turned and ran back into the keep.

"Where are you going?" Jaryd asked incredulously,

following the prince regardless.

Cedric threw open the doors to the throne room and placed the Phoenix Crown on its throne. "I will return for this."

After a moment of silence, they both ran back out the doors to their horses.

"Where do we go, your majesty?" Jaryd asked, staring out at the oncoming tide of corruption. The Tower Guard had closed and barred the gates, but they would not hold. "I am starting to feel unwelcome here."

Cedric unrolled the parchment and stared at it for a moment. "Into the mountains," he said finally.

With that they both kicked their horses and rode toward their fate.

CHAPTER 20: SECRETS OF THE SPIRE

The Silver Spire, West Terrace

Xavia waited on Rutherford—a frequent activity that she never enjoyed. Either the coward feared the Vigilants might spot him leaving his room, or he had fallen asleep by accident. He was nothing if not unreliable. As she waited, she impatiently flipped through a few more pages of a book she had found in the Adjurers' Library entitled *Book of the Druids: Before Loren's Coming and Beyond*. It was a fascinating volume that chronicled the history—as told by the druids of Lockri—of the northern lands before Loren the Conqueror established the empire of Lorendale. However, she wasn't currently interested in either history or reading; she wanted to carry out what she and Rutherford had planned earlier that evening.

Even so, as Xavia flipped through the pages, her thumb marked a section she had returned to repeatedly. It was an entry written by the druid Kruaeus, who witnessed the very first moment of the Vysarcian Empire's rapid decline. She couldn't help but read it again.

The dryads had warned us of dark days ahead. Lockri had grown restless again, turning hounds against their masters and leading once pure embrechauns into corruption. Anochra had become unsafe and the council had decided to move Lockri's Rest to the south, through the Burrow Gates. So, I was dispatched to the west with a handful of other druids to scout the borders of the Rhelklands and Vysarc in case either the barbarians or the greyfolk decided to move against our people during their weakened state. Phenlo, Durisa, and Elik took the northern dales while Vestrin took the Dread Moon Hills to the south. I was left with the Ravages.

For days I wandered, until I reached the western borders of the dark forests. There I saw the Wound. The Dead Plains dominated the lands from the Ravages to the Arcarrion Sea. Stretched for miles before me, was the trail of what appeared to be a dark boulder. The Vysarcian legions surrounded it, their thralls hard at work digging at the head of the massive trail. They were digging for the source of the Wound: a star from beyond the Black Seas where only Chaos resides. I know this only because I was later able to study the Archgeist's journals after the fall of Vysarc.

The Archgeist himself, Rhaveal the Vanquished, sat atop his krodin at the head of the Wound. Krodins were the only beasts foul enough to serve the Vysarcians: fat, lizard-like creatures that moved as slow as cattle.

I crept forward, ready to turn and find the quickest Burrow Gate in the Ravages and report whatever foul deed was happening below to the dryads. Then, a rider came from the west with a horde of Vysarcian soldiers chasing after it. A clamor arose and soon the rider was surrounded. I leapt down from my vantage and readied my bow, heedlessly charging toward the Wound. As I neared, I saw that the rider was a woman with a child in her arms. My instincts took over. I climbed the ridge and launched an arrow toward the Archgeist's chest, who was now reaching toward the woman. The arrow found its mark, burying itself into the Archgeist's black heart. If only Rhavael the Vanquished could be destroyed so easily…

In moments, the legions turned, and the undead soldiers marched toward me. The rider ran from them, holding her baby outward. As she neared the Wound,

*she threw the child to me. I caught it and begged her to
leap as well. Alas, she did not. She turned and faced over
fifty of the undead with nothing more than a knife.*

*I did not watch her die. I took the child and I ran, never looking
back. I would later regret not killing the woman myself, had I
known her true fate then. However, I raised the child, Roganna,
by myself in Anochra, refusing to leave the forest despite its
dangers. When she was old enough, I told Roganna about her
mother and the Wound. She swore vengeance on the Vysarcian
Empire, but I kept her as far away from the Dead Plains as possible
for as long as I could. However, years later I was taken prisoner
in the underground city of Vysarc, when the druids united with
the knights of the Lorenguard to strike back at the atrocities that
had been carried out by Rhavael's son, Skall. Many of us were
tortured to death, but I was kept alive to suffer. The Vysarcians
were expert surgeons that put their craft to work in dark ways,
prolonging life when it should rightfully end. I should have
died down there, but I was saved when the city began to fall.*

*My rescuer was none other than Skall, the Son of Chaos,
and my own daughter Roganna, who had slain Rhavael herself.
We escaped the city as it caved in on itself; the mindless thralls
turned against their masters and the Vysarcians were devoured. I
learned later that Skall was not to blame for the terrible things he
had done. Rhavael had made a pact with a terrible Burning Priest
named Pulasia, who was a master of deception. He had helped
Rhavael call the black star from beyond, the heart of which they
used on Roganna's mother to impregnate her with the essence
of pure Chaos. In doing so, they created a source of dark energy
that was not restrained by the Balance. Rhavael's son would be
the most terrible sorcerer the world had seen since Sol Saradys.*

However, young Skall knew nothing of his dark birth.

The Archgeist used Pulasia's power to impart his own will upon his son, forcing him to do terrible things. And if it had not been for Roganna killing him, the Archgeist would soon have completed the ritual that would transfer his accursed spirit into his son's body permanently.

If that were to happen, the world would have returned to Astasia once again.

Xavia continued reading, but she could no longer comprehend the words. She was fixated on Skall's name, the Son of Chaos. She could not let go of the rumors that surrounded Demitri's departure. Nearly everyone now said that Demitri was Skall's descendant, sent to battle the drakes in the mountains. Part of Xavia wanted to deny it—the part of her that knew the subject was only raised because Mereth had been teaching them about Skall lately. But that part of her was quieted by her optimistic side, hoping that Demitri was in fact destined for some greatness beyond the complacency she had become so accustomed to seeing at the Spire.

Suddenly, Rutherford slid into her room, closing the door behind him. He pressed his back nervously against the door as if he had just avoided being eaten by a dragon in the halls. His face had gone white.

Xavia set the book aside. "You're late," she said, rising to her feet.

Rutherford did not respond. He tensed, still leaning against the door, and looked at her. His eyes looked completely white. Xavia blinked and looked again. Whatever lack of color she saw in his eyes was now replaced with the usual, oblivious brown orbs that widened and drank in the candlelight of her room.

"I…" Rutherford began, blinking rapidly. "I must have been having a nightmare," he said, unsure.

"A nightmare," Xavia asked. "Walking in your sleep now, are you?"

He just looked at her, still scared.

"What kind of nightmare?" she asked.

He finally looked away, shaking his head. "It's madness, really. Not something I'd like to believe, and I'd rather not dwell on it. Demitri was in it, wearing the black robes of the Entrusted. But he knelt next to a burning throne. And an angel sat on the throne. Not a rightful angel, but one that had broken its wings and grown horns. It looked like the frescos of Sol Saradys that you see in the church." He tried to laugh a little.

"Well," Xavia said, "you're awake now. And we need to go. The Luminary hasn't been out of his study in days. I want to check the door."

Rutherford stared, knowing exactly what door she meant. But he did not argue. He did not seem to be in a terribly willful mood.

They left her room. Xavia locked her door behind her and wondered if she should tell Rutherford that she had a dream very similar to the one he described.

But she didn't have any time to ponder on it. A black shadow moved up behind them and grabbed both of them by their robes, dragging them down the hall. As Xavia cried out and resisted, she saw bodies slumped on the ground. They were all Vigilants.

The shadows clawed at her and she slipped into the same dream.

Not knowing why exactly, Vanghrel had fallen asleep holding a map of the Revery. It was an old Therrecian artifact, older than the very first graves of Vysarc, and it held the power to guide a dreamer through the Revery. The only reason that Vanghrel had brought it up from his storage below was to keep it out of the hands of Myriad, who would no doubt use it to rally more of his demons through the Revery. But, with his dreams being what they had been of late, Vanghrel could not be more grateful to have the map in his possession.

That night, the Revery was alive with the chanting of marons, praising their new lord and his new dominion over the dreamlands. Vanghrel had crept across broken castles, majestic cities, terrible caverns, and haunted forests on his way to the Hall of Mayrs. He did not know why he wanted to get there, but he knew he had to. When he arrived, he saw what he feared: Sol Saradys standing before the gates, surrounded by dreamers, all with marons upon their chests crying out for their souls.

The Burning One spoke with thunder, his voice giving thousands of different orders at once.

"Perhaps you would like a taste of his power as well," said a voice from beside Vanghrel.

Vanghrel spun around to face a maron—though not face-to-face, as the marons were very short. The creature was pale-skinned and dressed in finery, contrasting the marons that he saw in the distance. He knew that marons could appear any way they pleased in the Revery.

"It is quite intoxicating, as we have found," the maron finished with a smile.

Vanghrel scowled at the demon. "I have no desire for such power, fiend, so save your breath for those weak of heart. I am Luminary of the Silver Spire. I do not bow down to promises of power, not while I have power of my own." He turned back to watch Sol Saradys speak his will to the dreamers.

The maron raised its crimson eyebrows, clearly impressed. "We have the Luminary here, do we?" He smiled. "Tell me, lord headmaster, do you only hold such power so long as it stays a secret to the world?"

Vanghrel turned sharply back to the maron, his eyes narrowed.

The maron just kept smiling. "Being what I am, and living where I do, I know a lot about secrets. So allow me to give you a piece of advice, Luminary. Secrets are weapons ready to be unsheathed against you. And your darkest secrets—those that are kept in the back of your mind—are the ones that hate you the most. They await the day that they might destroy you for keeping them hidden."

Vanghrel closed his eyes tightly, trying to wake himself. The little demon's words were unsettling him, and he had no desire to remain in the Revery for much longer. It was getting cold.

The dream fell away.

Vanghrel sat up quickly in his bed, his hand clenching the map of the Revery tightly. The first thing he saw was Demitri, sitting in the large chair next to his scribing table. The young Entrusted hardly seemed to notice Vanghrel wake up; he was busy reading one of the Luminary's journals.

"Demitri?" he asked, wondering if he made a wrong turn and was still in the dreamlands.

"I always thought you might have been conspiring with forces outside of the Spire," Demitri said, turning a page in the journal. "But I would have never guessed that you were in league with forces from beyond our world." He closed the book and looked at the Luminary. His eyes were not white. "The Sect of Halcyon, the Spearitans, the Faith, the Regency, Nekriark's legions…who doesn't know of the power this place holds? Aside from the very students that learn within its walls, of course."

Vanghrel's eyes darted around the room. There were demons lurking in every shadow, he could see their green, red, and purple eyes glowing in the weak candlelight. Myriad must have opened the Calluses, sensing the Balance weakening.

"What are you doing up here?" he asked Demitri, addressing the question to all those watching eyes as well.

Demitri stood up, his black robes parted by the breeze from the open balcony. His chest was scarred with intricate lines: flames and swirling patterns that seemed to form scripture. There was a dreadful aura about him.

"How long did you plan on keeping all your magicks locked up from the world?" Demitri asked, his voice sounding very similar to one Vanghrel had just heard in his dream. Demitri smiled. "Do not mistake me. I do quite appreciate the deception. It was my Left Hand that brought mistrust and betrayal to this realm, and I always enjoy a good show of it." Demitri clenched his right hand. "But when it is used against me, I do find it quite tiresome."

Vanghrel watched the eyes in the shadows, considering what this subordinate boy was saying to him. It didn't take the Luminary long to realize with whose voice Demitri spoke.

"Against you?" Vanghrel said through his yellow teeth. "If anything, I have been your loyal servant."

"*Do not,*" Sol Saradys' voice boomed suddenly through Demitri, his right hand rising up to point at the Luminary, "pretend that I know not your every fear and desire, old man, all your lies and secrets. You know who I am, and you know what I am capable of." A small flame flickered into life in his left hand.

Vanghrel did not flinch, even though the demons from the shadows began to creep into the candlelight, surrounding his bed. "And do not pretend, Corruptor, that you hold any power over me. Not while the Shackles still bind you."

Demitri paused, lowering his hand. His smile returned as the flame in his hand crackled and died. "We understand each other, lord Luminary. We could shake the Balance to its foundation should we war with one another, but that is not what either one of us desires. Surely you must be of some use to me, a sorcerer of your power. So what I suggest is: carry out whatever sinister plans you have been hatching over the years, and carry them out yourself. You alone will recover the Shackles. No more lackeys; no more Entrusted." Finally, Demitri let his smile fade, replacing it with a scowl. "There will be no more trust."

"And if I do not obey?" Vanghrel asked, not submitting to the demigod that stood before him. A strange sense of bravery had overcome him with the Burning One's sudden shift in demeanor.

Demitri tilted his head, as if the question was incredulous. "I may not have the power to destroy you yet, mortal, but as you might have noticed, the legions below are no longer bound to you. They are free to devour you if need be." Demitri raised his hands, both of them burning bright red, as if they were about to burst into flames. "The Balance sways; surely you must feel it. Magic is escaping its bonds. Look." He nodded at Vanghrel's hands.

Apprehensively, Vanghrel looked down. Demitri was right. His hands were both covered in a thin layer of frost that was slowly climbing up his arms, misting as it went. He was clenching his fists so tight that he hadn't even noticed. As he relaxed his hands, the ice cracked and fell away, the map to the Revery dropping onto his bed with the icy shards.

Vanghrel's sour expression finally softened. It had been so many years since he dared channel any magic that he almost forgot how exhilarating it could be. Sickening, to be sure, but exhilarating. He looked up at Demitri, as if for the first time.

Demitri's smile returned. "Terrible, isn't it? Feeling the power at your command, but being unable to freely wield it. You feel the restraint, don't you? The fear? Only I can bring that down, sorcerer." Demitri threw off his robe, his upper body now glowing red in the moonlight. "You will serve me."

Vanghrel finally heard the whispers of Sol Saradys that had been spreading across Lorendale—opening his mind to the Corruptor's promises.

The doors to Vanghrel's chambers were suddenly thrown open and Mereth Augana, the Adjurer of Ancient Lore and Archaic Symbology, walked in. The demons took back to the shadows. Mereth looked at the scene before her in surprise, but when she turned to see Vanghrel on his knees upon the bed, she gave him a willful grin before turning to Demitri. "The remaining students are gathered in the great hall, my lord. They await your instruction."

Demitri's sinewy body relaxed, the red glow fading. He nodded and looked to Vanghrel. "You will leave this place tonight, Vanghrel Thondrane, and you will not return unless you bring me the Shackles. If you try to defy me, I will unleash your darkest secrets upon you. The secrets that now belong to me."

Demitri Dryce, the new Luminary of the Silver Spire, walked out of the room, his Entrusted robes left forgotten on the floor. The demons then returned to the shadows—their eyes fading into the darkness—and Mereth left with the same insolent look on her old face. It took some time for Vanghrel to gather himself and cross the room to his bookshelf. He pulled two large volumes from the shelf and let them fell to the floor in a heap, falling apart as they hit the ground. He then reached back into the recess of the shelf and pulled out a black leather-bound volume that was covered in thick layers of dust. He blew on the cover to reveal the title wrought in cold iron.

Where Dragons Die.

Vanghrel tucked it under his arm and threw on his heavy robes. He walked out to the balcony and whistled sharply. As he waited for his wyvern, Guyul, he looked out across the lands far below. They were dark, green, and peaceful. He imagined that land wreathed in flames, the likes of which could only be summoned by the Burning One. For the first time that he could remember, he felt a chill of pure fear creep up his spine.

Guyul screeched as he made to perch on the balcony, the wind from his wings nearly knocking Vanghrel over. He lashed his great talons and took hold of the balcony's rail, kneeling so that his master could mount him.

For a moment, Vanghrel hesitated, passing his old, withered hand over the wyvern's scales with what seemed like genuine affection.

"The time has come, old friend," Vanghrel said, hefting the heavy book under his arm and gripping the wyvern's saddle. "We are given night, so we must bring the Dawn." He pulled himself into the saddle. "Come, we ride for Demonscale. There is only one heart black enough to stand with me against corruption." Guyul took to the air with another shriek.

"And he is the only ally I have left."

CHAPTER 21: A PATH TO SCORN
Demonscale Heights, the edge of oblivion

Anathu stared down at the dead rodent in his hands with a mixture of disgust and ravishing hunger. His mouth was nearly as dry as the land around him, and he hadn't eaten anything other than moss and leaves for days. He was about to resort to eating the scorched earth under his feet when he had come across a murder of crows, all pecking at a rodent hole. Anathu shooed them away and claimed their feast as his own, picking up the eviscerated critter by its remaining leg. He sat and stared at it for a long time before biting into it, wondering just how he had gotten here and where he was going. His memory was like a lettered parchment covered in spilt ink. Only certain parts of it made sense to him; the rest was shrouded in blackness.

"You need to eat," Locksley warned. His sad eyes stared eagerly at the meager meal in Anathu's hands.

The sound of falling rocks startled Anathu, and he raced for the cover of a small ridge, tucking his meal and young Locksley into his heavy black coat. He surveyed the dark valley. Aside from a few dead trees and scavenging crows, he did not see anything. After a few more moments of watching the deadness of the Demonscale Heights, Anathu relaxed and huddled into the black rocks, releasing the boy from his grasp. His stomach rumbled again. He looked down at Locksley, a bizarre mix of guilt and responsibility washing over him as he lifted the rancid sustenance toward the boy.

Locksley shook his head. "No, you must eat. It's your turn."

Anathu had sacrificed every scrap of food they had come across to feed the boy. Strangely though, he never saw Locksley actually eat. His companion would merely wrap up whatever morsel they found and shove it into his rough tunic. This time, the boy flatly refused the offering. "You need to be strong," was all he would say in response.

Surrendering to his ravenous hunger, Anathu closed his eyes and bit into the mangled rodent, its thick blood and brittle bones making a sickening noise that almost made him gag. Fortunately, his stomach was too empty to throw up. Anathu took a few more bites and threw the remains into the rocks, trying not to see or smell what was left of the thing.

Now that his hunger was partially sated, and the sun was slowly rising over the mountains, Anathu returned his thoughts to why he was in these blasted lands, and what he should do with the boy that would not leave his side. No one traveled through Demonscale; it was far too dangerous. Where was he going? He could not remember. He thought he remembered a voice whispering to him, but that must have been a dream. There was no one else around—only Locksley, who rarely even spoke.

Anathu's eyes were constantly drawn to Scorn: the great stone spire that rose from the center of Demonscale. He was nearing it. Something inside told him that the dark monument was his destination, although he could not reason why.

While his mind wandered, Anathu rested his eyes. Even with his fading memory, he knew that he had not slept in a long time. Locksley quickly huddled under Anathu's heavy coat, brushing his wily hair against Anathu's face. The smell of the boy reminded Anathu of something from another life: a life of ease and harmony, of mountains and forests. He was reminded of a life he never had a chance to live. "You'll never catch me, big brother!" Locksley shrieked in that life, where their father shouldered his axe and wiped the noonday sweat from his brow, smiling as he watched the children play at Bag the Brigands and Catch the Caveworm. "Don't go far now, boys! Mother will worry!"

The dream that felt like a memory left as quickly as it had come. Despite his tired eyes, Anathu fought to keep the agonizingly pleasant vision from returning—afraid that if he lingered on it, he might truly accept it as part of his past. But Locksley's easy breathing made it hard for him to fight the encroaching slumber. Within moments, he was in the Revery, reliving a memory that this time he was entirely sure was not his own. Yet he felt every surge of pain. And pleasure.

The caves were collapsing as the black dragon crawled its way across the gaping chasm that divided its lair. Its wings were both broken and bleeding, and several of its claws were missing, black blood pouring from the wounds. It continued to pull itself toward the altar that rose high into the mists of the towering cave. The altar was a grotesque monument of slaughter; human bodies were impaled, severed, gorged, broken, desecrated, and defiled in every way imaginable.

The dragon dragged its dying body toward that altar as if it were the only thing that mattered to him. It stood for everything that mattered in the world: love, hate, desire, mortality, and purpose.

From the mouth of the cave, the king charged in, his purple armor gleaming in the pale moonlight, the Dragonsbane held in one hand and a shield with the golden phoenix of Celendas emblazoned upon it in the other. The Eurheborn did not follow him, most of the knights having perished in Adratheon's flames before the dragon was brought down.

Ausfred Galvian held the great Dragonsbane as if it were as light as a dagger. "Stand before me, you devil!" he bellowed. "I would see your eyes when I cut out your black heart!" His voice echoed in the chamber like a choir, as if all the ghost kings of Celendas that had been slain by Adratheon sang the challenge together.

But the dragon kept clawing its way toward his cherished altar. Adratheon knew of the Dragonsbane's accursed power; if Ausfred managed to cleave his heart in two with the sword, he would no longer be able return to the Mortal Realms. His body would die forever if his heart was divided, and only that damnable blade could do such a thing.

"Face me!" Ausfred repeated, tossing his shield aside and following the trail of dark blood.

Just as he was nearing the chasm where Adratheon's altar stood, Ausfred caught sight of the wicked monument. He stared at the naked and contorted bodies that made up the altar, their painful deaths reflecting in his old, hard eyes. But it was not despair that gave the king pause; it was pure hatred and fury, and he ground his teeth and charged the dying Adratheon.

The dragon neared the altar, his body slowly shrinking in size: the black scales gave way to tanned flesh, his wings crumbled away, and his talons became human hands with the bloodied remains of fingers. And still he clawed toward the altar, now a thin, naked man when he once was a magnificently terrible black dragon.

As Ausfred raised the Dragonsbane to end the reign of Adratheon, the man that had once been a dragon reached up and pulled back a heavy cloak from the altar to reveal a hidden body. The mutilated figure underneath that cloak made Ausfred Galvian stop dead. It was his daughter, Princess Abigail, ravaged and barely recognizable except for the ornately forged circlet of woven gold and silver that she had always worn atop her head. Although now it was wrapped around her neck and twisted, cutting into her flesh.

The king choked, his knees buckling. "Abby…"

Adratheon took advantage of the distraction and leapt at the king, burying one of his mutating, clawed hands into Ausfred's side through a chink in his armor. "She is beautiful," Adratheon whispered into his ear.

Ausfred screamed in torment, pushing the dragon away. "You heartless bastard!" He reached out a gauntleted hand and seized the dragon's neck. "Why?! Why have you no heart?" Tears rolled down the old king's face.

"You will never understand, mortal," Adratheon said through gasping breaths. He wore an arrogant smile that held a hint of compassion. "You will never realize the beauty of futility, the majesty of death. You cannot live through it." Adratheon began laughing and choking as the king tightened his grip. "I built this altar for you, for your kind. So you might understand how much I love…how much I hate…"

Ausfred cursed through his grinding teeth, trying to crush Adratheon's neck, but the dragon stopped fighting. The king threw the man down, raising the Dragonsbane once more until a sharp pain constricted him. He screamed in agony and grabbed his side. His wound was now pouring blood. It was surely fatal.

"My work is done, your majesty," Adratheon said cruelly, rising to his knees. With both arms outreached in an embrace he added, "Give me mortality…"

The king bellowed against the pain and with both hands raised the sword, burying it into the black heart of Adratheon.

Anathu jerked awake, instinctively checking his body for any wounds. He breathed easier when he found none, realizing it had all been a dream, even though it had felt so real and eerily familiar. As he opened his eyes, torchlight blinded him. Night had fallen, and apparently Anathu had an audience before him.

"Yeah, he's a live one," someone said in a guttural voice.

Another voice said something in a language that Anathu didn't comprehend. It sounded more like a dog barking than actual speech, but he knew there was meaning behind the noises. He sat up, blinking and shielding his eyes, backing up against the rocks.

A figure stepped in front of the torchlight. He was a twisted man...no, not a man, a grek—the foul creatures that had taken over Candrella many years ago. Despite his memory gaps, Anathu knew that rogue bands of greks lurked in the mountains.

The approaching figure spoke again, grunting and gnashing his teeth. And then another figure stepped up behind the grek, this one a man. His was the voice that spoke the common tongue.

"Surely he didn't know that he was trespassing, Thurg," the man said to the grek while flashing Anathu a devilish grin. He was an older man, middle-aged at least. His dirty hair was thinning and his beard was frayed. It looked like he only had a couple of teeth left. However, his dress did not match his unkempt appearance. He wore a nobleman's shirt, probably swiped from a murdered traveler, and a nice pair of velvet pants. The scabbard at his side was empty because his sword was drawn and pointed at Anathu. "I am quite certain that this stranger would be willing to pay a reasonable toll to make amends for such a discrepancy."

Anathu realized the man was talking to him. "I don't have any currents," he said hoarsely. His voice felt like he had been screaming for hours. Perhaps he had been during his dream. Suddenly, he realized there was no sign of Locksley. He turned his head and searched, but saw only blackness beyond the ring of torchlight. "Where's the boy?"

The grek looked at the well-dressed man for an interpretation, but the man just frowned and shook his head.

It was then that Anathu's eyes adjusted to the light and saw that a wide circle of greks stood outside of the torchlight, surrounding him.

The man raised his sword, ignoring Anathu's query. "It's a shame. We are quite hungry. If you hadn't noticed, not much grows in these lands. Coin is usually the only thing we find that sates our hunger." He lowered the sword again, pointing it at Anathu's throat. "However, you may still be able to feed us..."

The man said something else, but another voice in Anathu's head had drowned it out.

It sounded like laughter.

From a distant cliff, the Revenants watched the confrontation below. Feignly Moss was crouched low, straining his eyes. He could only see the burning torch, not the figures around its circle of light. Unlike Shaith and Dora, Feignly was not a true Vysarcian. He was not raised in the depths of the world where darkness reigned, so he could not see what Dora and Shaith now saw. The two Vysarcians had onyx eyes that drank the darkness, able to witness the scene before them perfectly.

"What's going on?" Feignly asked, getting visibly impatient.

"Quiet down," Dora commanded. "The greks are surrounding him."

"How many?" he asked.

"Too many," answered Shaith, inching her way toward the edge of the cliff.

Feignly stood up and produced a long knife. "Well then, we better get on with it. We can't let them kill him."

Dora held up a hand. "We cannot interfere. My father's book says that he must not know his purpose, or else he would never carry it out."

Feignly scoffed. "Does your father's book say what we are to do if he is eaten by greks? Perhaps we shall just follow the beasts around and collect their leavings and piece him back together?"

"Enough!" hissed Dora, angrily. "We've come this far, Feignly. If you wish to be paid, you will obey my commands, as you promised our house patron. We watch and wait, just as we have for the last three years." Dora looked down at her ring, the red stone glinting in the pale moonlight. "Soon, Adratheon will be ours."

Feignly did not give in. "But you said when the fury takes him, he won't remember what he's done. How would he remember if we helped him, then?"

Before Dora could answer, a shriek came from the torch-lit scene below. The Revenants huddled near the edge to watch as Anathu lost himself to his father's rage.

The torchlight went out in a wash of blood.

The Revenants watched the slaughter. Even Feignly, who could not even see what happened below, watched with a wicked smile on his face, his ears filled with the sounds of greks dying in anguish. It was all over in a matter of moments.

"Come on," Dora said, closing the book she had been reading and gathering her things. "We must reach Scorn as soon as he does."

Of course, Anathu could not remember where he was going, but the large dark spire of rock called to him. So he walked. He felt satisfied about something. In one hand, he carried the head of an old man, held by a tuft of dirty hair. Anathu dropped it, hoping it wasn't important.

The voices still called to him.

Come to me...this is what you are after...your legacy lies in Scorn...

A small hand suddenly slipped into Anathu's, ignoring the dripping gore. Anathu looked down and saw Locksley, staring wide-eyed up at him. "Sorry. I ran. I was scared." The boy looked down, ashamed.

Anathu didn't question the boy. Something inside him told him it was futile. After what seemed like hours of walking in silence, the two wandering souls reached the foot of the towering spire known as Scorn. As Anathu approached, the voice grew louder and more demanding, urging him onward.

"Fly," Locksley said playfully, pointing into the hazy darkness above. Anathu looked up as well.

A dark cloud brewed overhead, descending upon them. Anathu wanted to run, but he was frozen in place, fear and anxiety raging inside of him. The voices told him that he would soon understand everything, and Locksley's presence gave him hope and strength. So he let the darkness wash over him.

As it did, he realized it was not a storm cloud, but a flock of bat-like creatures, covered in scales with leathery wings. They flew all about him, circling and clawing at him. Soon, he was in the air with them and they carried him up and up. The same vivid dream came to him as he let the drakes carry him home.

CHAPTER 22: EXCELLENT TIMING

Castle Berrymore, North Terrace

The High Sectary of Halcyon rarely wore the trappings of his order: mask, brimmed cap, and dark coat. Normally, he adorned himself in his family's colors and devices, like a respectable noble. For in public, he was known only as Warrell Stane, the last surviving heir of the legendary House Stane in northern Terrace. He was not commonly regarded as the commanding general of an underground fraternity on a mission to rid the world of corruption. That would just not hold in casual conversation. However, those who knew Stane well in the political world knew of the unspoken influence he carried with his position in the Sect of Halcyon.

Currently, Stane waited while Duke Stanton Berrymore read over the various reports that had been submitted to the Sect of Halcyon over the past few days. The High Sectary sat patiently at the duke's long table, tracing a finger along the deep scar that ran from his missing earlobe to the corner of his smirking mouth. He took a drink of the duke's robust Rokuusian amber, watching as Stanton's slovenly face went from annoyance, to worry, and finally to disbelief.

"These cannot be true?" said the duke, although the doubt in his voice made it clear that he had already decided that they were, in fact, very true. Rumors had come in from all over Terrace of witchcraft in secluded farming communities and disappearances all around the Silverlands—namely around the Silver Spire. Other reports mentioned the walking dead, Chaos worship, and other perverse acts performed in public. All of the claims spoke of dark days ahead for Stanton Berrymore.

"I wish I could say that they weren't," Stane said, setting down his wine. "But the reports are too numerous, and our agents do not lie. Corruption is creeping through our lands, and the cult is spreading their foul mistruths that their lord will arise once more."

Stanton set the parchment down on the table, rubbing his thick, stubby hands together as if to wring them free of the taint the foul news carried. He and Stane shared a moment of silence in the great hall of Castle Berrymore, alone except for the great knightly statues that lined the walls. Stanton stared at those statues, considering something before he spoke.

"What would you have of me?" he asked the High Sectary.

Stane took another long drink and considered the question. "Authority."

Stanton ran a hand through the wisps of hair that remained on his balding head. "Authority," he repeated, not quite a question.

"As you may know," Stane began, "the king is not completely supportive of the Sect's methods in dealing with heretics and corruptors, especially not in sight of the masses behind Aevenore's walls. However, he turns a blind eye to happenings beyond those walls, granted we do not interfere with the outlying nobility." He motioned toward the duke. "Thus, if you give me the authority to answer to the documented crimes, the Sect will restore order to your lands."

The duke's eyes were still transfixed on his grand statues. "This is madness, Warrell. Do not take offense when I tell you that I doubt the legitimacy of these claims." His eyes fell on the parchment. "Demonic possession, Astasia, drakes…" He looked up to the High Sectary. "You know that our relationship is not of a pious nature, Stane, and you know me to be a man of the Faith—a true Son of Celecy. So when people start accusing crones of witchcraft and whores of lying with demons, I cannot not use those claims to justify war."

Stane poured himself more wine and smiled slightly through his graying beard. "We live in war, my lord, regardless of your beliefs. The Balance holds our realm in sway, there is no denying that. We are ever at war with Chaos." He drank, letting the words sink in. "Besides, this has nothing to do with religion, yours or mine. The majority of these reports come from towns under your domain. Your people are scared and demand action to be taken. And if you want to keep your lands, action *must* be taken."

The duke finally poured himself some wine. His eyes fell upon the parchment once again. "I have been to the Moonlands, Warrell," he said quietly, as if to himself. "I have *seen* dragons. I have faced armies of greks and seen the terrors of old Vysarc." He drank and shook his head. "But these…these are not tangible enemies to face. These are rumors! Gossip. How can I believe these claims to be true?"

"Perhaps you will believe this," Stane said, finishing his wine. "King Garrowin appointed you to this position as little more than a formality for your years of service in his knighthood. You hold little power in the court, and even the lowest barons of Eurheby own more land than you. However, if I am not mistaken, you are an eligible suitor to wed the king's daughter, Alyssa."

This caught Stanton's attention and he turned, raising an eyebrow. It was no secret that he aimed to marry the princess. King Luther had yet to birth a male heir and Stanton was favored to marry into the nobility. However, this did not mean he did not face heavy competition among the other nobles.

Stane continued. "How apt do you think the king will be to marry his beautiful daughter to the duke of a rebelling peasantry?"

Stanton drank as the High Sectary continued.

"On the contrary, would he not favor a duke that took action and stamped out the seeds of corruption before they blossomed into complete anarchy?"

The duke set his drink down and cracked his knuckles. He looked as if he were about to speak, but a commotion arose from the doors behind him that turned his and Stane's attention from their conversation. A disheveled nobleman stumbled in, pulling his arm away from a struggling guardsman.

"Get your hands off of me, you bastard!" the nobleman shouted. "Do you know not who I am? I am Vance Mandary! The duke's cousin!"

The duke got up to meet Vance, raising a hand to stay his guardsmen. "Cousin, what is the meaning of this?"

Vance immediately dove into his story of how a barmaid in Melbrook had seduced him into the back room of the Raine Song and tried to kill him in the name of Sol Saradys. Vance wept as he told the story, making himself the perfect martyr of a dramatic tragedy.

Stane waited until the story was done before he approached Stanton. "My, *ahem*, men will be heading toward the Silver Spire on the morn. Perhaps you would like us to tend to things in Melbrook? It is on the way…"

Stanton put an arm around his cousin, comforting him while giving the High Sectary a look of complete submission. "I will have the documents drawn up. You have full authority."

Warrell Stane could have hugged the young Mandary brat for his excellent timing. But instead, he turned on his heels and made for the door, writing his own legend in his head as the man who brought about Astasia.

CHAPTER 23: WRATH DIVINE

The Aevenwood, just outside Wynnstead

Neither Sebastian nor Raiken were strangers to the twisting paths of the Aevenwood, where they had spent much of their youth.

"Remember when..." Raiken asked through winded breaths, "we used to...only pretend to...quest in these woods?" He grunted as leapt over a fallen branch. "Those...were the days."

Sebastian was in no mood to talk. His mind was racing between one crisis and the next: Laurel's wellbeing, her attack on Vance, the walking dead, his estranged brother. It was enough to make a man lose sight of his course, something Sebastian could not let himself do.

The sky darkened as they neared Wynnstead, a storm rolling in that set the appropriate mood for their journey. Thunder rumbled after quick flashes of lightning and a chill wind blew in from the hills.

"I hope the old baron still keeps a hot kettle," Raiken commented as he stared up into the sky, jumping over a tangled root in the process. "He used to mix his teas with mulled wine, remember that?"

Sebastian was confused for a moment, wondering why Raiken thought that old Grevin VonAnthony was still baron. Then he remembered that his brother had not likely been keeping up with the happenings of Wynnstead's governing family. A new baron had taken up residence in Wynnstead since they were children. "Grevin died," Sebastian said flatly. "Then, his son mysteriously died, and now his grandson, Gabriel, is the baron of West Terrace. You should send your bird out more often."

Valcorse cawed and Raiken shrugged, falling a little behind his brother.

It was then that Sebastian slowed down. The thought of the baron reminded him of Martin's trip to Wynnstead and Vincent's harsh words against the baron's wife, Helena. He decided to tell Raiken about it, secretly wondering if any of it was connected to the dead man who walked by some foul sorcery.

"There was a witch in the Spire named Helena," Raiken said when Sebastian had finished his tale, catching his breath as they slowed their pace. "Well, they said she was a witch. She used to come to the ports in Quayhaven and ask pointed questions about old relics from Therrec and Vysarc, things that manipulated dreams. I wonder if that's the same Helena?"

Sebastian stopped as the rooftops of Wynnstead came into view. *Vincent said that she had died a blasphemous death*, Sebastian thought, *and that he had seen her in the Revery*. None of it made any sense to Sebastian at the moment, though. Too many thoughts occupied his mind and he didn't have the time to sort through them all just yet.

A distant howl sounded, followed by more thunder.

"We might as well go and ask him," Raiken said, ducking under a low branch and heading toward the town.

Sebastian felt a sense of foreboding as he stared at the grey skyline that hung over the rooftops of Wynnstead. But he was sure it was just his rapid thoughts, and the fact that he and his brother had just encountered a restless—a term the church used for the undead. Sebastian and Raiken had fought many restless in Vysarc, but this was different. This was in their home, their world.

He hurried after Raiken.

They broke through the border of the woods as the storm gained momentum. The wind was now howling and small drops of rain fell from the violent sky. Raiken was already at the town gates, if they could rightfully be called gates. Baron VonAnthony liked to present himself as high nobility, so he had elegant waist-high metal fences built around Wynnstead, with small gates that were usually guarded. Sebastian found it curious that they weren't guarded now. Raiken leapt the short fence easily and made his way up the hill toward Wynnstead.

Sebastian followed hesitantly, his eyes noticing strange things. There was no activity on the road, which was very odd. Merchants heading to Triarch, the Silver Spire, and Quayhaven frequently traveled the roads leading south out of Wynnstead. And even with the encroaching storm, Sebastian found it curious that he and his brother were the only people to be seen.

As Sebastian ascended the hill to join his brother, he noticed that Raiken must have realized the same thing.

"Where is everyone?" he asked, his bird settling on his shoulder. The rain was lessening, but the clouds remained dark. A calm before the storm.

Sebastian stood next to his brother and looked down on the streets of Wynnstead. They were completely deserted. The Becklund Stables on the edge of town held the only signs of life that the twins could see: several horses in a gated field that flicked their tails and grazed amongst the long, swaying strands of grass. Even the Silver Moon Inn looked as if it hadn't seen a visitor in ages.

They continued down the hill into town. As they walked through the tightly knit streets of Wynnstead, it felt like a dream. All the shops and homes looked to be locked up as if it were a holiday, but there was no joy in the air. Instead, it was utter dread that lingered upon every step that the twins took. After passing several abandoned buildings, Raiken stopped suddenly, looking down.

Sebastian walked around him to see that Raiken was gripping the Greenstone, his eyes distant and concentrating.

"Someone else is here," Raiken whispered, shrugging Valcorse off of his shoulder. The falcon took to the air silently, flying toward the baron's manor upon a distant hill at the far end of town. "I can sense...something. Something terrible."

Sebastian frowned, knowing that the Greenstone did not lie. He didn't exactly approve of his brother using such an artifact, but this was no time for a lecture. Especially in light of the thing he had done in the Raine Song—asking such a thing of the gods. Besides, Sebastian did not even have the chance to scold his brother. Raiken bolted.

"Raiken, wait!" Sebastian called out.

But Raiken had already taken off toward the baron's manor at a full sprint, his daggers drawn. Sebastian followed, reaching for his mace.

The gates to the baron's manor were wide open, as were the front doors. Raiken was already up the veranda stairs and poised at the threshold when Sebastian finally caught up.

"Wait!" Sebastian called, feeling a heavy sense of dread as the storm began to rage once more, the rain now coming down in sheets.

However, Raiken had already stopped. Something had caught his attention and he stood frozen, looking into the baron's manor. All Sebastian could see was a flickering light that came from the open doors. He quickly climbed the stairs and saw, much to his horror, what had caused Raiken to stop short.

Inside, in the vast foyer of the manor, Baron Gabriel

VonAnthony's body hung limp, swaying lightly from a rope that had been tied to the stairway railing overhead.

For a long moment, Raiken and Sebastian stood hypnotized by the slowly swaying body. The body's shadow swelled and died as it passed over the single lantern that lit the room.

A flash of lightning, immediately followed by deafening thunder, jolted them both out of their trance. Raiken would have fallen backward down the stairs if Sebastian weren't there to catch him.

"Ugh...so," Raiken said, collecting himself, "that's the new baron, huh?" His hand went back to the Greenstone. "I don't think he's the one I sensed."

Sebastian couldn't help himself this time. "You shouldn't listen to that *thing* so much, Raiken. Vincent says you can only take on so much of Lockri before—"

Raiken silenced him with a raised hand, not even turning to look at him. "This is not the time, brother." He walked into the foyer, Sebastian following with a scowl.

The manor was in shambles. It looked like someone had torn the place apart looking for something: books were thrown from their shelves in the other rooms, the dining room table was turned over, and below the baron's dangling feet there was parchment scattered all over the floor, spattered with blood.

Sebastian knelt down and gathered a few pages, moving toward the lantern so he could read the scribbled writing. With a quick glance over a few pages, Sebastian could clearly tell that they were journal entries written by a troubled man. Raiken read over his shoulder, an old habit that Sebastian despised. The oldest page that Sebastian could find read:

I carry with me a black conscious, one that I must give to the light by expelling these thoughts from my mind. I have not seen my lady wife for nearly three days. I cannot help but worry. She dwells too deep in the Spire and trusts the Luminary more than she ought to. However, I should not complain. She has become increasingly accomplished during her time under Vanghrel's tutelage, and her abilities have been quite integral to my quick succession. Through a dark pact that I was unwillingly a part of, Helena has become able to wander the Revery on her own accord. The secrets that we mortals dream are invaluable, far beyond my own imagining.

The rest of the page was covered in splotches of ink and splatters of blood, making it unreadable.

Sebastian tried to read the next page, but it was in even worse condition.

"I have heard of shamans in Therrec that are able to manipulate dreams," Raiken said, swatting away the baron's feet as they dangled in front of his face. "Mayrmancers they are called. I wonder if old Helena finally found her way over to the Peninsula and learned a few tricks of her own." Raiken scratched his head for a moment before reflexively grabbing the Greenstone. He heard something.

"Listen to this," Sebastian said, holding up another piece of parchment and reading it aloud. "Today Helena told me that she had met him again, in the same valley that the shamans had guided her to. She said that he was horrible and wonderful to look upon, wreathed in flames with rotting wings upon his back. He told her that everything she desired would be hers, should she help him in his rebellion. And even though I feared to associate with such unknown forces, I could not let Helena go it alone."

Raiken was walking away as Sebastian read. His eyes were set on a door at the end of a hall. He still had the Greenstone in one hand and a dagger in the other.

Sebastian continued reading. "We have pledged ourselves to the Burning One, and he has been most gracious..." Sebastian let the words sink in. "Vincent was right..." He shuffled through the parchment some more until he found an entry that looked to be the most recent—the blood upon it was still wet. "Here," he said, assuming Raiken was still hunched over his shoulder. "He writes that Helena died while trying to assist Sol Saradys in the Revery. Her spirit became trapped and..." his eyes darted across the hastily-scrawled handwriting. "He went to the Spire. The Luminary gave him a tome that would allow him to return her soul to her body. But only if..." Sebastian's eyes widened as he read the words. "Oh no..."

Raiken approached the door. He could hear the rattle of chains accompanied by a guttural moaning. Sebastian kept reading.

"He thought he could bring her back...by necromancy. As if the fall of Vysarc taught this world nothing..."

Raiken let go of the Greenstone and reached for the doorknob.

"And he used his people as payment, the entire town." The last words the baron wrote were *flesh for flesh*.

Just as Raiken turned the doorknob, a voice came from above them.

"Do not open that door!"

Sebastian stood up, bumping his head on the baron's dangling feet. Raiken spun around, a small knife appearing in his hand, poised to throw. A robed figure with a large tome descended the stairs. His hood was drawn back to reveal his long hair.

"His wife is in there," the stranger said, nodding toward the door that Raiken was at. "What's left of her, at least." A thud sounded from beyond the door as if in response. "And he's done something terrible here," he said, pointing toward Gabriel's limp body.

"Who are you?" Sebastian asked, eyeing the young man's robes.

"He's from the Spire," Raiken said, his knife still raised. "Probably one of Helena's goons."

"My name is Anerith," the stranger said, stopping halfway down the stairs when he saw the glint of Raiken's knife. "Anerith Zathon. I am an Adept from the Silver Spire, but I never knew Helena. I never met her. She was before my time. I have only heard of her."

"What are you doing here?" Sebastian asked.

The question took Anerith by surprise. "I...I heard something about the baron." He looked down at the heavy tome that he held under his arm. "And something about the Spire."

Lightning flashed. It was now raining violently, pounding on the roof above.

"Maybe you know what he did here?" Sebastian asked accusingly, holding up the baron's journal entries. "Tell me, do they teach necromancy at the Spire these days?"

Anerith shook his head.

Raiken stepped up next to his brother. "So, you just happen to stumble into this town with the same tome that this sorry flop took from the Spire, and you don't know anything about what's going on?"

Anerith gave them both a disbelieving look. "I honestly do not know what happened here. I was sent to Aevenore to deliver a message for the Luminary. But I heard things about the baron...things that I have discovered to be true. That is what brought me here."

"That tome," Sebastian said, nodding to the large volume under Anerith's arm. "Is that what I think it is?"

Anerith held it out, walking down a few more steps. Lightning flashed again, reflecting off the brass lettering on the cover for the brothers to see.

Permissions of Nekriark.

Raiken scowled. "That bastard!" He turned to Sebastian furiously. "We nearly got ourselves killed in Vysarc trying to destroy the remnants of that book, and the Luminary's been keeping a copy of it under his wrinkled ass!" Raiken stepped forward as if to retrieve the book, but Sebastian caught his wrist.

"Don't touch it, Raiken. And you drop it," he said to Anerith. "The writing of the Abyss has power over mortals, even if they don't read it."

Anerith let the book fall from his hands, watching it tumble down the stairs as if it were about to burst into flame. Raiken walked over to it after it had landed on its spine, open. He kicked it closed.

"What else are you wizards hiding there?" Raiken asked.

Anerith just gave him a stupefied look.

"Have you seen a priest of the Circle anywhere?" Sebastian asked. "His name is Martin."

Anerith shook his head. "I only arrived here just before the storm. I haven't seen anyone except for," Anerith nodded toward the baron, and his eyes moved to rest on the door down the hall. He then looked at the scattered parchment. "I think the rest of the townsfolk are in the crypts..." Anerith trailed off, as if the words tasted terrible in his mouth.

"Right," Raiken said. "Well then, let us ask Lady Nekriark how that requiem went." He turned and headed down the hall. Sebastian and Anerith had no choice but to follow him.

"I read what he did," Anerith said to Sebastian. "It should not have been possible…to kill that many people. What kind of magic is that?"

"Chaos," replied Sebastian. "Gabriel gathered this entire town into the crypts under the pretense that they were honoring the dead. A requiem is a time of submission, and in the presence of so many submissive mortals, Chaos can do great and terrible things." Sebastian spoke the old teachings as if he were at a Recitation. It took him a moment to realize the reality of what he was saying, and when he did he added, "The question is, what kind of fool allows himself to wield such powers?" They both looked over their shoulders at the hanging baron. Sebastian felt a sadness that almost outweighed his growing anger. "He loved her," Sebastian added, his eyes falling to *Permissions of Nekriark*. "He would have done anything to save her." He thought of Laurel and of the power he had drawn from. He shook his head and turned away as Raiken was opening the door.

The sight beyond the door caught the three men's breath in their throats.

Helena VonAnthony sat in a corner with iron manacles around her wrists and ankles, chaining her to the wall. She wore a formal white dress, stained down the front with blood, gore, and vomit. Her eyes were whiter than her dress.

Lightning crashed once more, flashing eerie shadows across the walls. Helena began to struggle to her feet, moaning hungrily as her white eyes fell on the three intruders.

Sebastian stepped forward. "For this?" he asked angrily. He turned back toward the baron whose body still swayed with the blowing curtains. "You killed them all! For this?" Sebastian was shouting now, pointing at the chained, restless corpse of Helena.

Raiken and Anerith stood frozen, unsure of what to do now.

But they didn't have to wonder for too long. Sebastian suddenly darted away from them toward Helena, his mace raised to strike. Neither of his companions tried to stop him; they just watched as Sebastian's mace sunk into Helena's decayed skull, splattering putrid gore all over the floor and wall. Sebastian did not stop when she fell. He continued to bludgeon what was quickly becoming more a pile of rotten flesh, bone, and gore and less the resemblance of human remains. It wasn't until Raiken heard the distant, piercing cry of Valcorse that he went over to stop his brother. He placed a hand on Sebastian's shoulder, startling him.

"I think she's learned her lesson," Raiken said, raising a hand to cover his nose as he looked over Sebastian's shoulder.

Sebastian shrugged his brother's hand off and made to continue his work, but Raiken grabbed his wrist.

"Wait!" he said, raising a finger to his mouth, signaling silence. "Something's wrong…"

"Do you think so, Raiken?" Sebastian asked sarcastically, scowling at the gruesome remains of Helena VonAnthony. He couldn't help but spit upon them before turning away.

Valcorse called again from outside, but the bird could not be seen through the downpour.

Raiken walked toward the foyer, the Greenstone shimmering in the growing darkness. Before he reached the front doors, they were thrown open by a gust of powerful wind. Raiken was nearly thrown off his feet by its force. Anerith and Sebastian ran over to brace him.

When they recovered, Anerith pointed toward the foyer with wide eyes. Valcorse had flown into the manor, finding perch on the banister of the stairs. But Anerith was pointing just below the bird, on the floor. *Permissions of Nekriark* had been blown open, its pages flipping wildly.

"Don't let it open!" Sebastian shouted, now throwing his brother out of the way and rushing toward the tome. Raiken fell to the ground with a crash, his eyes fixed on the book as well. All three men knew the dangers of an open tome, especially one devoted to the foul teachings of Nekriark.

But Sebastian was not quick enough. Beneath the swaying shadow of Gabriel VonAnthony, the flipping pages stopped abruptly. The script on the open pages began to emanate a faint and eerie black glow. Sebastian froze, unable to do anything except read those words.

"...and those that bow in prayer to the Underlords
shall sacrifice their lifeforce in order to awaken the Intended
by the powers of Chaos. The Intended shall arise under
your command, restored in body by the grace of Nekriark.
Furthermore, unless the Sacrificed are properly and individually
anointed and burned to ash, they too shall rise under
your command upon the next day darkened by storm. The
Sacrificed and the Intended shall seek sustenance immediately,
and only living mortal flesh shall sate their hunger."

Sebastian had read the spell before, back in Vysarc. However, while the words were familiar to him, the sickly feeling that washed over him was not. It was a feeling of utter doom, the opposite of what he had felt when he banished Sol Saradys from Laurel's mind. It was a power that was not tempting him, but challenging him.

It was Chaos.

Lightning crashed again outside. It was getting closer, the following thunder shaking Sebastian's stomach.

"We should leave here," Anerith said quietly, his eyes

fixed on the tome, whose pages seemed to defy the violent gusts of winds that now threatened to blow Gablriel out of his noose. "I feel something terrible."

Raiken was on his feet now, the Greenstone shinning vibrantly and bathing the foyer in an emerald haze. Though it drew Anerith's eyes from the tome, the soothing light did not ease any of the terror in his eyes.

"Something's coming," Raiken said, watching Valcorse shake the rain from his feathers. Raiken moved swiftly to close the doors, but an arm reached out from the darkness and a rotting hand clutched Raiken's neck.

And then the brewing storm unleashed.

Groans sounded in unison as shadowy figures spilled in from the door, windows, and even up from the floor. Countless townsfolk that Sebastian had known since he was a child stumbled toward him.

Lady Veirk who had baked him rheystone cookies on New Season came in through the window by the stairs, crashing through the stained glass. Her head was tilted to one side as if she had no strength or desire to use her neck. But her eyes fixed on Sebastian immediately, bile running from the corners of her mouth. Cameron Dills, a young carpenter who had crafted a sign for Vincent's gardens, groped for Raiken as he tried to pry the restless from his throat. Trudy Becket, a once-lovely maid now turned pale and horrible reached up from the splintered wood floor and grabbed Anerith's ankle.

Anerith fell over, shouting and reaching for Sebastian. Shaking away the disbelief and letting adrenaline take over, Sebastian pushed Lady Veirk back out the window and brought his mace down on Trudy Becket's wrist. Her small arm put up no resistance, turning to mush under the weight of the weapon.

Anerith shook the severed hand off of his ankle, watching in terrified suspense as it fell to the ground with a sickening splat.

Sebastian turned to help Raiken, but his brother had already broken free of his attackers and was now trying to secure the doors. Sebastian looked at the shattered windows and the undead fists that were now punching up through the floor.

"It's no use!" Sebastian told Raiken, helping Anerith to his feet. "We can't stay here!" He reached out to grab Raiken's shoulder.

As Sebastian made to pull his brother back, he paused at the broken window frame, something catching the corner of his eye. He turned to stare eye-to-eye with a fellow priest.

"Martin!" Sebastian exclaimed, but the wayward priest stumbled through the window grasping for Sebastian. As Martin got to his feet, Sebastian grabbed him by the shoulders and threw him against the wall. "Martin! It's me! Sebastian! Wake up! Don't listen to him!"

Martin bared his blood-stained teeth, snapping and groping at Sebastian, not comprehending.

"We don't have time for this, brother!" Raiken said, holding the door while Anerith tried to keep the other restless away with a long floorboard.

Sebastian didn't hear. He tried to restrain Martin's hands as he placed his palm on Martin's head.

Sebastian spoke softly, but his voice boomed as if it came from the sky. *"Lucrid, the Defender, I ask this of you knowingly."*

"Sebastian!" Raiken shouted, the doors creaking under the weight of the restless.

"Purge this Mortal of villainy; banish him of misrule."

"Brother!" Raiken yelled angrily, the stone around his neck burning like green fire. "This is no time for prayer!"

Yet the gods did not answer. Martin sunk his teeth into Sebastian's forearm. A vile pain shot through Sebastian's arm and he threw Martin to the ground. "Burn you!" Sebastian swore, swinging his mace at Martin's head as he tried to get up. The sickening thud that followed laid Martin to rest. But the fires of fury inside of Sebastian were just beginning to kindle.

"Brother!" Raiken called, his arm jabbing violently through the cracked doors. "These things are not dying!" He pulled back his dagger, slick with dark blood. "We cannot stay here."

Sebastian ground his teeth, tasting the acrid taint of blood in his mouth. He spat it out and looked around. There was no safe exit, a thought that oddly relieved Sebastian. He had no desire to walk away from this. He quickly ran up the stairs, leaving Anerith and Raiken to hold the door.

"Sebastian!" Raiken yelled.

But Sebastian did not stop. He reached the top of the stairs and took a small bag of ceremonial ashes from his belt. With a quick spin, he made a rough sacred circle and knelt inside it.

"Brother!" Raiken exclaimed before he and Anerith were knocked off their feet as the doors were finally thrust open. As a restless stumbled toward him, Anerith spoke a foreign word and a jagged stream of bright light came down from the sky, exploding at his feet and knocking the restless from the veranda. A second bolt of lightning struck and the entire veranda was turned into a cloud of splintered wood.

Raiken, forgetting his brother for a moment, stared wide-eyed at Anerith, looking for some sort of explanation. But as the young man from the Spire turned, Raiken could see that Anerith was as surprised as he.

"What did you do?" Raiken asked. Anerith just shook his head in disbelief. The moans of the restless coming from below made them both get to their feet and scramble for the stairs.

They reached Sebastian and heard his whispered prayer: "By the Hammer and Flame, the Spear and the Blade, for this I pray. Grant me the power to purify…to end this blasphemy." He repeated this over and over again, lost in a trance.

"Brother, come!" Raiken insisted. "We can get out through the back." There were some restless that were already shambling up the stairs, reaching out with lifeless arms, but Sebastian gave no indication that he noticed. He continued his prayer.

Raiken reached out for Sebastian, the Greenstone glowing brilliantly as it dangled from his neck, crossing into the sacred circle. At that moment, Sebastian's chanting stopped. It seemed like time stood still. The rain stopped, the restless moans hushed, and the doom that they all felt melted away. Outside, the clouds parted, letting free a sudden burst of sunlight that brought a chorus of unearthly howls from the restless surrounding the manor. A moment later, Anerith, Raiken, and Sebastian shielded their eyes from the heavenly light as the world came down around them.

Raiken and Anerith both struggled to drag Sebastian out of the ruined manor. Dead bodies littered the ground. As Raiken heard Valcorse call from the clear blue sky above, he threw off the last bit of the manor's rooftop and saw the cataclysm that his brother had unleashed.

The sky was crystal clear, a bright white sun shining down on the three of them. There was no sign of a storm. It was magnificent.

However, below that pristine skyline, Wynnstead lay in

absolute ruin. Nothing stood. The blast that had come with the sunlight leveled every building and structure, leaving the earth below completely scorched.

"He did it," Raiken said, staring at the ruined land. "He broke the Balance." He laughed nervously in sheer disbelief, without blinking an eye. "I always told him he had a bad temper."

CHAPTER 24: A REASON FOR TREASON

Port Laras, Pendara

"Let us pass!" the sailor urged, his speech slurred by heavy drink. "We have the right to sail!"

"Back, the lot of you!" the commander of the guard ordered, pushing the drunken sailor away with the butt of his halberd. "The ports are closed until the storms pass!"

The fallen sailor spat as the rest of the protestors helped him to his feet.

"It's been three days, and we haven't seen no cloud in the sky!" one of the older sea merchants shouted, followed by a hearty agreement from the others crowded around the gates to Port Laras.

But the commander and the other members of the Port Laras Shore Guard ignored their cries. They stood stalwart in their shining blue armor, their halberds held ready to defend the gates if it should come to blows.

"The king wants us to die!" one of the sailors whined from the rear, followed by another shout of encouragement. "He speaks with the cultists! I have seen those robed bastards in his castle! His mind is poisoned by the Burning One!"

"Hold that tongue," the commander snarled, "unless you mean to lose it!"

The arguing continued. It had been nearing a breaking point since the day before, when one of Pendara's respected merchants, Captain Kless, was hauled off in irons for attempting to return to his ship. Since then, the sailors had become bolder in their protests, and now the entire harbor was on the verge of a riot.

Queen Amarie DeSatho watched the encounter from her balcony. The evening chill was settling in and she pulled her shawl tighter around her shoulders. The wind tousled her unkempt hair, but she made no attempt to brush it from her face. Her eyes were rimmed with red, a result of countless tears and lack of sleep. After taking a deep breath, she turned from the sight below—a sight that might very well signal the fall of her kingdom—and returned to the bedside where her youngest daughter lay dying.

Reyna let out a weak cough, still not opening her oval eyes. Her usually lively face had gone a pale shade of grey, and her lips looked nearly white. Small clumps of her auburn hair had fallen out recently, and with each passing day she looked more and more like a corpse. Amarie stifled another sob of grief and took Reyna's tiny hand in her own.

Abney Donnar, the royal healer, dabbed at Reyna's lips with a wet cloth. He too looked on the verge of tears, but he kept his composure as best he could so as not to upset the queen. "Your majesty, I have made this case known to your lord husband, but he refuses to open the harbor. We do not have the treatment here inside the castle, nor do we have access to the priests of the Circle. As you know, the Spearitans do not practice divine healing and they refuse to have any priests that do so in their domain."

Amarie sniffed, wiping her nose with the back of her hand. She did not respond. Her eyes were fixed on her ailing daughter.

Abney continued as he rubbed his boney, stubble-covered jaw. "I have had council with the apothecaries, and they are all certain that the princess has been poisoned somehow."

This caught the queen's attention. She turned to face Abney with a look of both hope and anger. "My Reyna, poisoned? Who would do such a thing?"

Abney shook his head, mopping at Reyna's brow. She moaned quietly in her sleep. "Pendara has many enemies..." Abney offered.

"You mean the king has many enemies," Amarie hissed, instinctively looking toward the open door to make sure none of her husband's hooded visitors were wandering around—those strangers that had begun to appear the day after the New Season banquet. The sudden thought of that night gave the queen an epiphany. "Abney," she said, in a much calmer voice, "do you think it possible that Reyna was poisoned at the feast? Many of our liege lords were there, perhaps one of them..." but the queen trailed off as Abney shook his head.

"Pardon me for saying, your highness," Abney said, "but Reyna would be dead by now if that were the case. This poison is deadly and cruel. It moves slowly enough through the blood that it makes the victim suffer, but it surely would have claimed her life if it were in her veins for that long." Abney shrugged and pondered for a moment. "However, it is hard to say for a certainty. The apothecaries assure me that this poison is exotic to our lands, so curing it will not be easy."

Amarie bit her lip, still holding Reyna's hand tightly, forcing herself not to weep. I *have to be strong for her*, she thought, *her father will not*. "You know of this poison, Abney?"

The old healer shook his head. "Assassins bring all manner of deadly poisons to Lorendale, some from Rokuus, some from Aushua, though none of our scholars have the means to study them. We cannot grow such plants here, and I'd not like to imagine who would grow them, if given the liberty."

The queen dried her eyes, unable to stop the tears anymore. "So, we know nothing of what is killing my daughter?"

Abney inched toward the queen, nearly falling out of his seat. "That is not entirely true, your majesty. The apothecaries believe this poison did indeed come from Aushua. Now, we only need to appeal to the king so that—"

"Aushua?" the queen asked, jerking her head up suddenly.

Abney nodded quickly, taken aback by the queen's reaction.

Amarie thought of the feast again, of the bard singing to her husband's Aushuin mistress. Then she remembered hearing news of the girl's murder and the bard's disappearance. A dark thought occurred to her.

"You have long lived in this castle," Amarie said quietly. "Tell me, Abney, do you know the ways below? Where the king's councilor lurks?"

Abney stiffened and suddenly looked over his shoulder, also looking for any robed visitors.

Satisfied no one was around, he nodded to the queen.

The stench below the castle was once unbearable, but after what seemed like several months in his confined prison, Durion knew no other smell in the world. It was almost comforting, since the smell only permeated in the dungeon halls. If he could smell the dungeons, then he wasn't in the torture chambers below, smelling his own death on the edge of every passing minute.

Durion's dark, olive skin was grimy and slick with blood; gashes covered his withering body, but his face held a hint of accomplishment. Among the shrieks and sickening sounds from the halls, Durion sat tall like a man bathed in the subtle sedation of vengeance.

A robed figure appeared before Durion, and slender hands appeared from beneath heavy sleeves to grasp the rusty bars that imprisoned him. Durion blinked, expecting that at any moment his cage would be opened and he would be exposed to whatever hellish ritual that the Cult of the Burning One had in store for him this day.

But the figure only stood there, gripping the bars that divided them.

Finally, Durion looked up from the figure's shadow that flickered in the faint torchlight. He saw that the cultist's hood was thrown back, and the face was not one that he would have ever expected.

"Has she passed on?" Durion asked, his thick Aushuin accent turned raspy by days of starvation and thirst.

Queen Amarie did not hesitate. "Your daughter has, but mine has not."

"Give it one more day, your majesty. Some children resist the poison, for a time."

"Look into my eyes," the queen demanded. Durion calmly did as he was told. Her eyes were still red and fresh tears were finding their way down her cheeks. But her face was stern, as unflinching as the Aushuin prisoner's.

"What would you have of me, queen? Do not ask me to suffer, as I have given all that I care to in this life."

Amarie knelt down on the grimy floor so she could look Durion in the eyes. "I want you to listen to a tale, one that you might not care to hear, but one you must know so that your daughter's death can be justly avenged."

"I know that it has already, queen," he said, leaning his

head back against the wall. "In my land, blood is repaid with blood. My daughter may rest in the Gardens now, far from this cruel world."

"You are not in Aushua," the queen said vehemently. "You are in Pendara—where vengeance is always misguided. You are here because the king pays old debts to the Cult and your daughter warmed his bed. Now, will you kindly hear my tale?"

Durion lowered his eyes to meet the queen's.

Amarie's voice softened but it still carried a hint of malice. "Years ago, there was a princess born to a selfish king that never wanted her, never loved her. Before she had even seen her first year in this world, the king tried to swap her for a bastard born son that he had spawned with a seaside whore, hoping that he might pass the child off as his heir. Seven years later, the princess would be lying upon her death bed, dying for the king that never once held her, or protected her, or…" The queen lost her composure and began to cry openly, bowing her head to hide her tears.

Durion watched her weep, his eyes unchanging and his face wearing the same placid expression. After a moment of choked sobs, the queen continued.

"She would become a pawn used to reap much deserved vengeance on the king. However, the selfish king would not mourn her death. In fact, he found it a relief, as he would not have to marry his kingdom away to a nobleman that did not bear the DeSatho name." Amarie slowly raised her gaze to meet Durion's once more. "But her mother loved the princess so much that she would offer vengeance on the king…" she produced a key from the wide sleeve of her robe. "…even at the cost of treason."

Durion held the queen's gaze, not even looking at the key. His tongue slowly wet his lips, but he said nothing.

"I do not know how you poisoned my daughter, Durion,"

the queen said. "But given the circumstances, I know why you would do such a thing. Your daughter was defiled by a foul man, and justice is called for. However, I ask you to carry out that justice directly." Tears continued to flow down the queen's cheeks, but her face remained hard. "Do not take my daughter because a cruel man took your own."

Durion finally let his eyes fall to the key in the queen's hands. "We Aushuins have shadows that float through your kingdoms, assassins and reapers. If you release me, I will locate the one that poisoned your daughter, and before the sun sets she will be free from Celecy's awaiting embrace. For a time, as all mortals are cursed with the inevitable encounter." He looked back up into her eyes. "But your husband shall suffer, that I promise you."

The queen's eyes flashed with what could have been a glint of hope.

Jassily Constance read the message again and then crumpled it up and threw it into the hearth. The blazing fire quickly swallowed the parchment. It had been three days since King DeSatho had denied Jassily the men that he had previously been promised, and with the harbor being shut down and the arrival of the king's robed emissaries, Jassily could do nothing more than confine himself to his quarters. He had a growing suspicion that the king was associating himself with cultists, but such a thing was too crass to inquire about. Why would the king risk his reputation by harboring madmen from the Burning Isles? He walked over to the long table in his room and poured himself some wine.

Suddenly, a soft rap came from his door. Jassily unsheathed the dagger at his belt and set down his wine. He moved carefully toward the door.

"Who calls?" Jassily asked, pressing his ear against the door.

There was no answer. Jassily bit his lip, hesitating. After a long moment, he cracked the door open to see if he was truly imagining things.

He was not. There was a slender figure in an ashen robe at his door. He hid the dagger behind his back and waited for the stranger to address him. Instead, the figure squeezed in through the open door, pushing Jassily aside. Fearing something foul was afoot, Jassily quickly closed the door and grabbed the figure from behind, pressing his dagger against their neck.

"What is the meaning of this?" Jassily demanded.

"Is this how you honor the queen in her own castle?"

Jassily quickly let the figure go and Amarie turned around, throwing back her hood. Jassily fell to his knee immediately, dropping his dagger to the floor.

"Your highness, forgive me. I feared…the king's guests…"

"I fear them as well," the queen said quickly. "But do stand up. We must hurry."

"My queen?" Jassily looked up, confused.

"I understand you need men for the Reclamation," Amarie said, taking Jassily's hand and helping him up. "I also understand that the king has denied you them because he will need his men to carry out whatever vile plans he has made with the cultists. However, the king has become increasingly oblivious to the happenings of the kingdom, and I have gathered more men than he promised you. They are loyal to me and ready to leave the city on my command."

Jassily stared slack-jawed at the queen, unsure of what to

make of this treason.

"I only ask one thing in return," the queen said sternly.

"Whatever you require."

"You will take me and my daughters with you north, far away from Pendara and the Tripartite."

Jassily bowed to the queen. "I am yours to command, your majesty."

"Please," she said, taking his hand, "call me Amarie"

Benedict DeSatho arose from the bed, his portly body slick with sweat, glistening in the surrounding candlelight. Behind him, a naked girl—paler and very much younger than his former mistress—struggled to clothe herself as the king poured a decanter of wine. He did not offer any to her.

"Begone," he ordered, and she happily obliged, dressing herself as she made her way toward the door. The king looked down at the ring he wore on his left hand. The black stone shimmered eerily, and he felt a wave of comfort wash over him. "I must be going mad," he said quietly before taking another drink.

The sound of sliding stone came from behind the king.

"Quarris," Benedict said between drinks. "I told you that I did not care for you to use those passageways."

"Pardon the intrusion, your majesty," Quarris said in his raspy voice, emerging from the shadows of the king's vast chamber, "but the ceremony is about to begin. Celendas has fallen into our lord's hands, and the priests will need to anoint you as the Ascender of the new empire."

Benedict swallowed the wine. It tasted sour tonight. "Very

well. May I dress myself, or will the cultists need to take their pleasure of me as they do of my prisoners?"

Quarris did not laugh at the jest. "I will wait below."

"There is no need," Benedict said, setting down his wine and throwing a thick, blue robe over his hairy back. "Lead the way."

The two traveled through the narrow passageways of the castle in silence, descending down into the depths below. The waves of the sea could be heard faintly through the rocks as they neared their destination. Finally, the king spoke.

"Your visitors have raised a lot of questions," Benedict said, speaking of the cultists. "The city is on the verge of a riot, yet you let them wander around freely."

"As I have told you, your majesty," Quarris said in his hoarse voice, "the Isles are no longer safe. There has been a division in the cult, caused by an act that was intended to unify the warring tribes. Our champion, Sinder, was denied the aspect of Sol Saradys that was intended for him, and he has rallied those that are loyal to him to seek out the Shades."

"The Shades?" Benedict asked. "They are chasing ghosts on the Isles?"

Quarris finally stopped descending the stairs and turned to the king. "Not ghosts, Shades: the shadows of celestial beings. All angels, demons, and gods cast shadows that can devour mortals. These shadows carry the influence of those that cast them, and mortals who bathe themselves in such shadows can become Shades. Shades carry with them the echoes of godly powers...as well as the flaws that come with those powers."

The king raised a skeptical eyebrow, "So, you mean to tell me that your chosen vessel could not become Sol Saradys' right Hand because someone else beat him to the punch?" The king chuckled. "No pun intended, of course, my dear Quarris."

Quarris' glass eye twitched. "The Binding Ritual that was intended to turn Sinder into a Shade was stolen from our priests in Andira before they could have it translated. Whoever was responsible must have taken it to Vhaltas, recovered the other half of the text, and carried out the ritual before Sinder could. Thus, Sol Saradys' power has been unleashed upon our world, and the cult has been divided once more."

The king scowled, setting aside his skepticism on account of the dire look in Quarris' one good eye. "Is that not what you wanted? Sol Saradys freed?"

Quarris stepped closer. "You do not understand, your majesty. Both of Sol Saradys' hands have been freed. His left hand, the subtle hand that deceived Lockri, works against Sol Saradys, and now the Shade possessed by that hand is free to use the Corruptor's powers against him."

Benedict stared at the man, scratching his jaw, obviously confused.

Quarris leaned even closer, but the king did not recoil. "The Burning One became the Lord of Corruption because he himself was corrupted. He was born of both angel and demon blood. Prythene, the Realm of Fire, is tainted with Chaos; flames cannot be given Order as fire is Chaotic in nature. Upon the Divisions of the Heavens, demons found their way into Prythene and many of them coupled with angels. Only one offspring survived such a coupling."

The king finally let his gaze fall. "So, whoever found the ritual to free Sol Saradys' left hand is the Shade that will oppose the Burning One?"

Quarris shook his head. "That is not known. All we know for sure is that Sol Saradys' hands have been freed by someone outside of the cult."

"So where does that leave us?" Benedict asked, motioning to the wall that divided the two of them from the waters of the Valice. "Do we still set sail for Celendas, or do we not know which Shade rules there?"

"The right Hand is responsible," Quarris said, turning around to continue his descent. "The left would not operate so openly. We must consult the other priests regarding this matter. You will be our emperor, but we shall remain your advisors."

Benedict rolled his eyes. A moment later, he nearly stumbled over Quarris, who had abruptly stopped. They had reached the bottom of the stairs, and in the room beyond, Benedict could see why the old man had stopped short.

Quarris' tables were covered in blood and the bodies of the other priests were sprawled out in grotesque positions, their insides spilling out onto the floor. For a moment, the scene reminded the king of an abattoir he had visited as a child where great whales were slaughtered. But that moment was brief, for the stench of death brought the king's mind back to a very real moment of absolute horror.

His future empire was already toppling.

The king did not have time to dwell on the thought, as a foot caught him square in the back and forced him forward. He fell violently atop Quarris, the old man crying out as the overweight king forced him to the stone floor.

The king rolled over in time to see a dark-skinned man kneel over Quarris and draw a silver blade across his throat. Blood splattered across the killer's face.

Quarris' cry was cut short, and in between his dying coughs Benedict could hear him ask, "You're...the Shade?"

The killer stood up, looking down on Quarris. "I am a

shadow."

Benedict sat up quickly. He felt a sharp pain in his wrist and he knew it was broken. He could not get away. The killer's eyes were now on him, and the king could tell that it was one of his Aushuin prisoners.

The Aushuin neared Benedict until his thin shadow swallowed the king.

"Mercy!" Benedict cried out, "Have mercy!"

Durion smiled. "Do not fear, king. I shall provide you with the same mercy you have shown me and my kind."

King Benedict DeSatho's anguished screams were drowned out by the crashing waves of the sea.

CHAPTER 25: A NIGHTMARE TO REMEMBER
The Revery

Donovan Marlowe stared into Sol Saradys' eyes. Those fiery red orbs held his gaze for what seemed like an infinitely long period of time. In that time, Donovan felt a nostalgic sense of vengeance creeping into his soul.

"You have a choice," the Corruptor finally said, his eyes unblinking, his words like soothing fire. "You can give into that burning desire that you feel within your chest at this very moment and embrace my power—a power that no one in your world can even fathom—or you can remain as you are." The angel of corruption leaned back in his throne, bringing his arm up. Flames licked out from his stump and formed a hand, clenching to make a fist. He smiled and settled the fiery fist under his chin. "Oblivious. Living in Lockri's prison."

Donovan saw no sign of the Burning One's white-haired right Hand. The Hall of Mayrs was empty. He was alone with the Lord of Corruption.

"How does it feel?" Sol Saradys asked his left Hand—his Shade. "Oblivion. Mortality. I would dream of such things if I did not rule in nightmares." This brought a smile to the Corruptor's face. "Such a mysterious curse…mortality. I once held court with Adratheon, the Black Dread, when he was but a hatchling. He told me that he envied every aspect of mortality: the frailness of it, its passing pleasures." He paused. "Though he is utterly insane, even for a dragon, I found his musing on the subject fascinating."

Donovan wanted to turn away, but he could not. He had no control over himself in this place. He was the Corruptor's instrument. Although, why did it feel like he was being persuaded into something, and not forced? That question seemed much too heavy for Donovan to grasp just now, with Sol Saradys' eyes burning into him.

"You offer resistance," Sol Saradys said. "I have been searching your soul for a reason why, but what I find does not explain…" he trailed off, his face giving signs of contemplation. "Since you will not remember this conversation, allow me to divulge to you the secrets of my power. Corruption feeds off weakness. Because I was born of corruption—and I was too weak to resist it in Prythene—it has become an ever-growing force inside of me, writhing and begging for release. I have no doubt you can learn the rest of that story from any shoeless priest wandering Athland. However, what you might not learn from such deficient minds is that mortals were graced with a quality that we angels and demons lacked."

Sol Saradys leaned forward, his flaming eyes searching for something in Donovan's.

"Willpower," Donovan said, not even realizing it.

A smile spread across Sol Saradys' crimson face, that beautiful and flawless human face.

"Remarkable," he said, his red eyes unblinking. He raised his burning hand and with a flourish of his fingers he produced a sudden spark. "A flame that burns quickest burns brightest. Another flame can burn forever, but never as bright. That sudden, bright flame will be forgotten, dying out, unable to cast light on the ruin of worlds." Sol Saradys' smile seemed to almost fade, but he held it, just as he held Donovan's gaze.

It was another long moment before he added, "The

brevity of mortality can breed the most powerful of resolves. In your case, however, I cannot fathom why you deny what I offer. Perhaps you forget too much…" Sol Saradys motioned with his hand of flame and, from the darkness, a maron skittered toward the throne. It approached and sat down next to Donovan, its eyes staring hungrily up at its master's left Hand.

"You will remember, Donovan," Sol Saradys said, his voice already fading into the darkness that was now swallowing Donovan. "You will remember the day that you began to dream of fire."

Donovan remembered the dream immediately, but he could not wake from it.

The waves of the Valice crashed against the hull of The Godless Swan. *A young Donovan held tightly to the rail, barely able to see over it. An older man approached the boy, wobbling from the force of the waves. Under his arm he carried a scribe's ledger.*

"Careful, Donovan!" Einrist said, bracing himself on the rail and nearly dropping his ledger into the sea below. "Your parents would be quite amiss if you fed the krakens of Chasmere upon their return voyage!"

Donovan brushed his shaggy hair out of his eyes. "There are no more krakens," he said, standing on his toes and watching the ship cut through the waves. "Father said the hydreks hunted them all to extinction and he has sailed as far as the Terraquin Sea."

Einrist laughed, setting his ledger down on the deck and grasping the rail with both hands. "Well, hydreks are no better than krakens, my boy. But, your father would know. I have never traveled with a finer pair of captains than your parents, Donovan."

Donovan finally let go of the railing and turned toward the old scribe. "Will you be leaving us at Pendara?"

Einrist's smile lost a bit of its kindness as he nervously looked over his shoulder. "We shall see. Jonah and Felyse can no doubt make these journeys without me; as you know, I am not the best of sailors."

Donovan looked down at Einrist's ledger. "But surely the paladins will pay well for what you found in Aushua. Will you not find more in Andira when we sail again?"

Einrist's smile faded instantly. He reached down and picked up his ledger, not taking his eyes off of the boy. After a moment, his smile returned, but it was only a mask. He even faked a laugh. "Have you been eavesdropping again, Donovan? You know how the captain feels about such behavior."

As if in response, Captain Jonah Marlowe appeared from below deck. He was donning his long black coat. On his waist, he wore the rapier that Donovan was destined to inherit.

"Lower the sails!" the captain shouted, pointing with his gloved hands toward two crewmen who sat about drinking. "Prepare the anchor! The harbor is near!"

Donovan went to help, but Jonah caught him, lifting the boy into the air easily. "Not you, mate. You head below. Help your mother secure the holdings."

Donovan squirmed from his father's grasp, laughing. The captain tousled his son's hair and let him down. But as he walked away, Donovan made it only halfway down the stairs before turning to watch as the scribe approached the captain.

"The boy knows our business," Einrist said.

"Of course he does," Jonah said incredulously. "He's been on every one of our excursions and he has the ears of a hawk. Why does it concern you?"

"I would prefer it if he didn't speak of such things on deck,"

Einrist said, looking around and not seeing Donovan's hidden head. "We are not altogether honest merchants in all of this."

Jonah laughed. "Not sure about you, Einrist, but none of us ever claimed to be honest. The Spearitans can have all of their relics; they mean nothing me. I don't think anyone on this ship believes in the neutrality of the Archbason. Her currents, however, are something that I will always have faith in." Jonah slapped Einrist on the back as he made his way toward the stern.

The scribe straightened his white hair and Donovan feared Einrist may have caught a glimpse of him, so he quickly ducked his head below deck. He waited a moment before looking out again to see where they were about to make port.

The Godless Swan dropped anchor about a league from Port Laras. A large Spearitan galley waited for them there, a discovery that Captain Jonah did not hide his distaste of. "Not in front of the harbor! Do they intend to ruin my business?" However, a small vessel disembarked from the galley and swiftly made for The Godless Swan. Donovan watched as a young man in brilliant pearl armor commanded two monks to row the small craft. The monks boarded The Godless Swan first, helping the younger man in armor. Two other rowboats approached behind them, both carrying many more armored paladins.

Captain Jonah did not hesitate. "What is the meaning of this?"

Einrist approached the paladin, clutching his ledger. "Sir Cain, I was instructed to meet you in Parity, at the cathedral."

Lucas Cain was an exceptionally young paladin, his long blonde hair flowing over his pearl-armored and white-cloaked shoulders. In his hands he held a magnificent spear and on his hip he wore a longsword. He let his gaze move from the captain to the scribe. Felyse and Donovan had now joined the rest of the crew on deck, but the paladin paid them no mind. His eyes held on Einrist. "It has come to the Archbason's attention that you have been playing her false. I am here to deliver justice to the *heretics. The Balance will have retaliation for your crimes."*

Captain Jonah stepped forward, turning to the scribe. "Einrist! What is this about?"

Einrist shrank back, his eyes fixed on the paladin.

"He has sold relics to the Silver Spire," Lucas Cain said flatly, "tainting those items with Chaos. They are lost to us now, and he will pay the price of heresy." The other paladins were now onboard, severely outnumbering the crew of The Godless Swan, *their swords drawn.*

Felyse spoke, stepping up to clutch her husband's arm, hiding Donovan behind her. "Please, not in front of the child. If you must, take the scribe to your Archbason. Let him pay for his crimes in Parity."

Einrist turned toward Felyse, his shocked expression turning into a scowl.

"Better yet," Jonah offered. "Let us sail for Parity ourselves. We will answer to your Archbason's judgment there." Jonah narrowed his eyes at Cain. "You are a Knight of the Scales, Sir. Such unchivalrous behavior reflects poorly on your entire order."

The young knight turned to the captain, his face cool and confident. "Heresy does not call for chivalry, Captain," he turned to Felyse, "and the scribe is not the only heretic aboard this ship. As far as the Archbason is concerned, the entire crew of The Godless Swan *is guilty of crimes against her Chapel. However, Captains, her holiness will not be the one to deal the Balance's justice." He motioned for the other paladins to move forward. "Such deceit has no place in Parity."*

"Wait!" Einrist finally cried out, halting the approaching paladins. "Sir Cain, if I may…" he stepped forward, opening his ledger.

Lucas did not stop the scribe. He stepped behind the line of paladins and motioned for the scribe to show him. The crew of The Godless Swan *could not hear what the scribe was telling the paladin, nor could they see the contents of the ledger. Though when Donovan looked up at his father's face, he could tell that Jonah knew very well what was written in that ledger.*

After a brief conversation, Lucas looked thoughtful, staring out to sea. Finally he nodded and Einrist closed the ledger, stepping back toward the rail. Lucas turned back toward the crew.

"Einrist will be taken back to Parity to further explain his findings in Aushua. The rest of you will burn in the name of the Balance." The bluntness of the statement nearly knocked young Donovan over. The boy stared at Lucas Cain's careless face. The paladin couldn't have been more than ten years older than Donovan, but Cain's eyes held a cold malice that was beyond his years.

The line of paladins approached, some producing ropes while others raised their swords threateningly.

Donovan's parents begged for their son to be spared, but the executioners paid no heed. It was only Einrist's voice that stayed their advance.

"Sir Cain," the scribe shouted. "The boy."

Lucas turned and stared at Donovan for the first time. "Bring him."

As the torches were lit and the small boat made its way toward the Spearitan ship with Einrist and Donovan aboard, the scene started to fade. A voice that sounded like a slow moan of agony became clearer.

"It's not real, Donovan," the voice said. "Wake up."

But Sol Saradys could be heard over that foreign voice, getting the last laugh.

Donovan's eyes shot open. The first thing he saw was Gwyndalin, bathed in a soft emerald light. She sat cross-legged in a chair next to him. Donovan's limbs were bound to his bed. He opened his mouth to speak, but the embrechaun cut him off.

"I know," she said, rolling her eyes. "You don't know me, you think you're in Anochra and that I want to drink your blood, and you don't remember—"

"Gwyn?" Donovan said, squinting his eyes and groaning. "How long was I asleep?"

Gwyndalin's eyes widened and she drew back from Donovan. The tree cat that sat in her lap stretched and leapt to the floor with a defiant meow.

Donovan tried to get up and realized that he was bound. "I'm not going to run this time, Gwyn."

But Gwyndalin didn't move to unbind him. She leaned closer, staring into his eyes. "You remember?"

"My head hurts," said Donovan. "But, I remember...fire." He opened his eyes and turned to Gwyndalin. "I did something terrible." His eyes were wide with the innocence of youth.

Gwyndalin still stared at him in disbelief.

Tears were welling in the corners of his eyes, but his face remained hard. "I'm afraid I'll forget again."

Gwyndalin began undoing Donovan's bindings. She took both of his hands into her own and stared into his eyes. Something in those eyes reminded her of Raiken. "As long as you have something to hold onto, you will always remember." She turned Donovan's left hand palm up so he could see the dark scar where the *kropal* had burned him.

"You have a choice, Donovan."

CHAPTER 26: DRAGONSBANE

Scorn, in the heart of Demonscale Heights

Anathu woke up and, for the first time in a long time, he remembered. He sat up, his back aching. *From the fight*, he thought to himself, remembering the grek bandits that tried to rob him in Demonscale. The blood still stained his hands. Anathu sat there, clenching and unclenching his fists, freely turning them from talon-like claws to human hands. His flesh transformed freely. He was in control of them now. He was not lost like he had been back in Crestly.

He remembered.

As the drakes began to squawk at him, he remembered more and more. He was a miner in Crestly, although he was a stranger there to everyone, having come in from the mountains where he had slain his family. *My family*, Anathu thought, letting the images of a mountain man, his disapproving wife, and their laughing son come into his mind. They had taken him in, cared for him. But when his dark past took his thoughts, he had lost himself in a rage.

"I killed them," Anathu whispered, the soft words echoing off the stone walls. His tainted soul did not allow him to dwell on that thought just now.

Anathu stood up, his eyes quickly adjusting to the dark. The cave was enormous, just like in his dream. Drakes fluttered around in the darkness above while others lurked in the shadows below. The entire cave was alive with black scales and leathery wings. And they all watched Anathu, as if awaiting his command.

There were stairs ahead, rising up high into the swallowing shadows. Anathu could see movement up there, and the drakes squawked their disapproval of whatever those flittering shadows were. Anathu felt as if the drakes were crying out for his protection.

How can I understand them? Anathu asked himself.

Because I am of their kind, his mind answered.

That sudden thought brought back the scene from his dreams. They were not scenes from his own memories, but memories of Adratheon. Anathu knew then that he was in the cave from his dream: Adratheon's tomb—Scorn.

Anathu strode away from the encircling drakes and took the first step.

Feignly Moss was not the one complaining this time. He ascended the earthen stairs with ease, finding handholds and footholds from seemingly nowhere. With his lithe body, he made the climb look like a practiced dance. Meanwhile, Shaith and Dora struggled far behind.

"Why can't we be of dragon blood?" Shaith asked irritably. "I'd gladly be clawed to shreds by drakes if they agreed to fly me up this accursed mountain."

Dora spat in response, watching it soar down into the blackness below. Not even her Vysarcian eyes could make out the ground from this height. "Thanks to Father, we know of this stair. Ausfred and his stupid knights had to climb the walls of the mountain to get to Adratheon's lair."

Shaith turned away from Dora, rolling her eyes. "Thank you ever so much, Pulasia," she said under her breath. "If it weren't for your bloody book, I'd still be home in the Depths, with the family's pillaged wines, making love to Andrys and Losk." She spat as well.

Dora shouted again, not hearing Shaith's curses, "The man who gave me my father's book also told me of this place. He said he came here often while Adratheon lived. Unfortunately, he never told me much about actually accessing the tombs above. Thinking back, I should have inquired…"

Shaith stopped climbing. "Gave you the book? Who gave it to you?"

Dora grunted, almost losing her grip. "Remember that old man from the Silver Spire that visited the Depths?"

"Come on!" Feignly shouted from above, a few rocks falling from his shifting feet. He wore his normal smile. "I think I smell dragons!"

Anathu neared the top of the stairs, but even then, the shadows did not recede. They were alive, guarding whatever lay beyond. It was then that the voices returned.

Come to me, my son…all those questions…come and claim your answers…

The voices spoke over each other, making the words difficult to understand. Anathu just urged himself on, trying to ignore them. As he reached the top of the stair, the voices began to fade away, giving him a quick respite.

It was short-lived.

Anathu almost stumbled over backwards when the ghosts appeared. Gliding from the shadows, they appeared as armored men, pale and translucent. Anathu found his footing, recoiling but not fleeing. He stared at the dead men with a building rage that he could not find reason for.

The ghosts wore elegant armor and winged crowns from Celendas: dead kings. The closest ghost, with long hair flowing from his fleshless head, reached out toward Anathu, his bone hand held up to stay the intruder.

"Do not come!" the voice commanded. *"You will find only your ruin!"*

Anathu threw out his arm defensively. The phantom's hand dissipated like mist, its body turning into a cloud of dust that quickly dissolved. Anathu blinked and the rest of the ghosts were gone as well. He stood alone in the dark cavern. He took another step up the stairs and a ghost leapt from the shadows once more.

"King Argus commands you to yield, villain!" The dead king wore a tattered old cloak that was held in place by a jeweled phoenix brooch at the neck. *"Do not heed the call!"*

Anathu growled and lashed out, this time with taloned hands, sending the specter back to the netherworld. He walked briskly into the welcoming dark, baring his lengthening teeth. Ghosts came and he blinked them away, slashing at them when necessary. Soon he began to run, screaming against the surging voices in his head. They were wailing whispers, driving him to the brink of his deteriorating sanity. Finally, he found silence. He slowed his run and saw that he had found his way into his dream.

He was in a cave with nothing overhead—only oblivion. Before him was a rocky platform that fell off about twenty feet from where he stood. The chasm looked like it descended all the way into the Abyss, and only a small bridge of rock connected Anathu's side to the one beyond. Yet, none of the surrounding hazards mattered to Anathu. His eyes were fixed on the lake of blood on the other side of the chasm that ran off into the underworld like some gruesome waterfall. The blood was infinitely dark, much like his own. That thought seemed to drive away his uncertainty, replacing the feeling with a warm sense of nostalgia. He closed his eyes.

When he opened them, he was somewhere else...

The cabin was not decorated—it was built for necessity. A stack of firewood rested in the corner, where spiders and rats were known to dwell. An axe hung above the dinner table. This was the only home Anathu had ever known.

He stood behind a corner, gripping the splintered wood with his bloodied, childish hands. The argument arising was newborn, but Anathu knew every word...

"He doesn't belong here!" she shouted, a familiar scowl marring her face like some scar from a recent tragedy. She held a bloodied bundle to her breast, the glimmer of restrained tears in the corner of her eyes. "It will only get worse."

Mother...

The man only scratched his neck. "We'll bury him in the hills. That was his place." His eyes held both grief and desperation. "I shall mourn for the beast with you, woman, but do not ask me to abandon the boy. He has no one."

"Maybe for good reason!" the woman shouted. "Today, it's a dog, but what about tomorrow? What if your son—"

"Don't!" the man shouted, frightening the young Anathu that watched vigilantly from his hiding spot. The wayward boy mouthed the words as they escaped his father's mouth. "He loves Locksley; he would never harm him!"

Before the woman could respond with the hurtful words that Anathu had blocked from his elusive memory, the scene faded. The room did not change, just the time. Day had turned to night, life to death.

Anathu stood, shaking with unrestrained rage. The people he called Mother and Father were laid in a mutilated heap at his feet, their blood soaking into the simple floor of their simple home. The memory was fading quickly, as Anathu's furious eyes fell on the fiery red hair of his young brother. The dead boy that should have stayed in bed—the ghost that had led him to remember...

When Anathu opened his eyes, the gruesome scene had returned to the past. His heart felt acidic, as if it were corroding his soul. There was nothing left for him, so he put the memory behind and crossed the chasm. As he reached the other side, he knelt down beside the pool of blood. He saw his reflection on the dark red surface. His face looked twisted, not like he remembered. His eyes were black holes and his forehead sloped down above them to form a menacing scowl. Had he always looked like this? He couldn't say for sure. Then, as he stared into the blood, his face began to take on a different shape. The pool rippled and something began to emerge. Anathu rose to his feet, prepared to face whatever came at him from the bloody depths. But when the shape emerged, Anathu's heart slowed and his body tensed.

The drake was smaller than a bat, newborn. It squeaked as it crawled from the blood that birthed it. Anathu immediately knelt down and took the drake into his hands. It squirmed, but it did not fight. It rubbed its beak-like snout against Anathu's cruel fingers. In that moment, the uncertainty that was growing within Anathu fell away like shattered glass. He knew, without hesitation, that he had come home, and he held his brethren within his hands. The dreams and memories haunting him were of a past forged out of fantasy. This was real.

Anathu saw more shapes arise from the gruesome bath, more drakes born from the blood of Adratheon. The drake in Anathu's hand nibbled at him, so he set it down on the rocky floor. It spread its little wings and balanced itself, stumbling to the edge of the pool where it drank of the blood.

Anathu watched the rippling pool, his gaze drawn deeper into the cave. In the darkness beyond, he saw a tiered altar from which the blood flowed. He approached and climbed it slowly, not taking his eyes off of what lay atop that altar. The grisly edifice from his dream rose from the top of the altar, all its bodies turned to bones. And at the foot of the horrific monument lay Adratheon, the Black Tyrant of Demonscale.

Anathu reached the top of the altar, staring down at the dragon's body. It was a man's body. Even though he had died sixty years prior, Adratheon's flesh remained as if he had died only moments ago. The Dragonsbane was buried nearly hilt deep in Adratheon's chest, pinning the dragon to the altar. From that gaping wound, the blood flowed down the altar, forming the pool below.

Anathu reached down to touch the blood. As he felt its warmth, Adartheon's head rose, his eyes wide.

"*My blood is in your veins,*" Adratheon spoke.

Anathu nearly fell off the altar. When he blinked, he saw that Adratheon was still dead, his eyes closed. But the blood was still on his hands.

"Is he asleep?" a voice asked from behind.

Anathu spun quickly, raising his claws to strike. But the red-haired boy did not attack; he merely peered over the dead body of Anathu's father.

"Can we wake him up?" Locksley asked.

Feignly felt the mountain shake. They were near the top, and the drakes had begun to soar all around them. He nearly lost his grip as he braced himself with one hand while the other swiped at a drake with his knife.

"These damned things need to find easier prey," Feignly said, looking back to see if Shaith and Dora still followed. They were further down the narrowing stair, but they were keeping the drakes at bay better than he was. "Bloody witches," he mumbled to himself.

"The dragonborn must have found the blade," Dora said, hugging Pulasia's tome while she reached for a rock to hold onto. "We must hurry. Adratheon's heart will now begin to heal, and once it does, I will not be able to use the stone."

"Then move your ass," Shaith said from behind her. "I can strike fear into the hearts of these babes, but I'd rather not test my resolve against their mother."

Feignly stumbled backward on the stair as another drake dove at him, his laughter echoing throughout Demonscale.

With eyes closed, Anathu held onto the Dragonsbane as his mind replayed the dream. He saw Ausfred Galvian drive the sword into Adratheon's chest, nearly cleaving the black heart in two. Anathu felt the pain, and he let out a deathly howl. A winged figure on a flaming throne laughed menacingly from above. The dream flashed by and, despite the pain, Anathu opened his eyes. Even worse than that pain was the absolute certainty that he now knew who he was: the son of Adratheon, a dragonspawn.

"*Anathu, we are one,*" said Adratheon's voice, echoing in Anathu's mind. "*You must cleanse the blade or we both shall perish!*"

Anathu, still screaming, tore the blade from his father's chest. Locksley smiled from the shadows, his malicious face fading into the swallowing darkness. As he departed, an ancient voice came from his young, ghostly lips, "Go, my son. Make me proud…"

CHAPTER 27: THE NEW LUMINARY
The Revery

Demitri did not dream of the burning throne or Sol Saradys. Instead, he dreamt he was a stranger, lost in the woods, rubbing a scar on his left hand. He wandered through the green, uncertain of where he was going or what it was that beckoned him deeper into the woods. It was a feeling of lust, but not the impure obsessions he was used to.

Then, she appeared. Her green skin was devoured by the surrounding leaves, making her barely visible. She called to him, pulling at his heart in the same way that Sol Saradys did with his fiery fist. Demitri followed, not sure why, other than he felt compelled to do so. He followed her through the dense forest until they came upon a misty glade where a deep calm settled in his bones. Demitri parted the leaves and stepped further into the dream.

There she was, standing upon the ruined stump of a once-mighty tree.

She motioned for him to come closer. As he did, she reached up and unlaced the fastenings of her leathers over her shoulder. Her clothing fell away, as if carried by the nonexistent wind. Moonlight soaked into her bare, emerald flesh and Demitri was pulled further toward her.

As he neared, he saw Xavia's face on the embrechaun's body. Demitri approached her, but as he reached out, she leapt off the tree stump and ran. He followed.

They ran through the glade, the mists thickening. Demitri

chased her into an enormous tree that opened up like a cave. He descended the wooden stairs, led by a soft glow that emanated from the mysterious creature he pursued. When he reached the bottom, he navigated a labyrinth of earthen corridors, fighting his way through living vines and vicious hounds, all the while screaming for Xavia.

He caught up to her in a great chamber, bathed in emerald light. It was not the girl that illuminated the earthen palace. The light came from a large jewel that floated in the center of the chamber suspended by invisible chains.

There was no question in Demitri's mind: this was Lockri's Rest, and the jewel had to be Greenheart—the only weapon against the coming corruption.

Demitri stared into the stone's depths, seeing ages pass by in an instant. He watched as Lockri and Sol Saradys crossed the Black Sea. He watched as Sol Saradys wrecked havoc on Lorendale, enslaving mortals and binding them to his will. He saw Lockri mold the earth, embrace dryads, and paint the world in vivid color. Visions flashed before him of Lockri shifting into a hound, his fury unleashed on the greks as they invaded his forests. He wept as Lockri corrupted his own children in order to defend the forests. Demitri watched as the world returned to Astasia in the blink of an eye.

A howl tore Demitri's gaze from the brilliant green stone and the torrential scenes that pulsated within it. He turned to see the girl transform into a beast before his very eyes. Coarse green fur began to grow all over her body, her pointed ears grew larger, her nostrils flared, and her jaw widened. A green light shot out from the Greenheart and enveloped her, raising her off the ground.

She looked at Demitri then, as an abrupt moment of calm

embraced her. It lasted only a moment, but Demitri felt a lifetime of torment in her eyes. Xavia's face twisted in pain as she morphed into a hound of Lockri—a corrupted being of Uldagard. Demitri shouted defiantly and reached out to shatter Lockri's heart. As he laid his hand on it, his flesh seared…but the Greenheart cracked and acrid smoke fissured from its jagged wound.

Demitri felt the aspect of Lockri seep into him: the primal lust and the unrestrained fury of the wild. He screamed and tried to force the aspect out of him, twisting it to his will, pushing it back into the Greenheart. However, only corruption fed into the Greenheart.

Demitri opened his eyes and stared into the cracked emerald. He saw his reflection, but he was not himself. He was Sol Saradys' left Hand, and, reflected in the Greenheart, Demitri saw that fiery hand clench into a smoldering fist.

The Burning One's will had been done.

The emerald light intensified, and Xavia's scream made Demitri's ears bleed. The chamber seemed to swell under the pressure until a moment of complete silence made time stand still.

And then the Greenheart shattered.

The Silver Spire

Demitri sat up, gasping for breath. He was in the Luminary's bedchambers, the entire room lit by the crimson glow emanating from the scars on his body. His skin looked like it was about to burst into flames. As he slowly gained control of his breathing, the light faded.

Something stirred next to him.

Xavia rolled over, rubbing her eyes. Demitri held his breath, watching her as the moonlight traced the delicate curves of her body. She was not green. She was not an embrechaun. When she opened her white eyes, he also saw that she was not his.

With a smile, Xavia reached over to stroke Demitri's shoulder. He turned away, nearly cringing at the touch. It was a rare occasion when he had so much control over his own mind, but right now, he was Demitri Dryce, and the woman lying next to him was nothing more than Sol Saradys' whore.

"Demitri," she said in a husky voice, her hands suddenly all over his body.

Demitri threw away her advances. He said a word in a strange language and reached for his tattered black robes. When he stood up, the color slowly returned to Xavia's eyes. She quickly took in her surroundings, her eyes wide and confused. She saw that she was naked and she quickly covered herself.

"Demitri?" she asked, panicked. "What's going on?"

"You were right all along, Xavia," Demitri said, not looking at her. He slid his robes on. "The old man had a world of secrets: demons below the Spire, magic coursing through the tower's very stones, and a plan to dominate the entire world. I've seen the truth behind this place, and I only had to sell my soul." His shoulders rose and slumped as if he were laughing. "The irony is…I never cared about secrets. Only you…"

Xavia leaned over to see Demitri's face, which was turned away from her. "Demitri, what are you talking about?" She reached out for him.

Demitri stepped away before her hand reached him. He spun around, his skin glowing faintly red in the early sunlight. His eyes narrowed. "You have a lust," he said, his voice crawling beneath Xavia's skin. He was changing before her very eyes. He looked terrible, godlike. "You would serve me well…"

Xavia recoiled again, shrinking into the bed and trying not to cry.

Demitri reached up and pulled at his whitening hair. "No! Not her. You said she would be mine!"

The outburst was short-lived. Demitri returned to his terrible presence, straightening and smiling at Xavia. "He has spirit left. That is good." He stepped closer to her, his skin smoldering. "I did promise him. And he shall have you." He reached out for her. "I always deliver what I promise."

Just then, a pounding came from the door. The corruption faded from Demitri's face. He stood up, backing away from Xavia.

"I won't let him have you…"

Demitri left a confused Xavia in the bedchamber and went to the door. Mereth's clenched fist was raised to knock again as the door swung open. She was wearing the elaborate robes of Grand Adjurer that were once worn by Marakus.

"Yes?" Demitri asked, irritated.

Mereth nodded in stern reverence. "Luminary, I am sorry to disturb you. But I thought it pressing."

Demitri stared at the woman, struggling to remember why she wore the Grand Adjurer's robes. His memory bled into his dreams, and Sol Saradys dominated that realm. Whenever he managed to gain control over his mind, it took him awhile to comprehend his own knowledge. After a moment, it all came back to him. Dream or not, Demitri remembered Grand Adjurer Marakus standing up against Vanghrel's demons as they overran the Spire. The old man was flayed and strung up from the Adjurer's Tower as a warning. Since then, Mereth claimed the position of Grand Adjurer, and Demitri could not think of a more cunning woman for the job. *Aside from Xavia...*he thought.

"Luminary?"

Demitri shook his head, feeling the nausea of Sol Saradys' influence growing stronger. "What is it, Grand Adjurer?"

"The remaining students have been gathered and lessons can soon begin. However, there have been...distractions." Mereth leaned in closer and whispered. "The Nekrians are growing restless. They lurk in every shadow of the Spire, grabbing students and whispering blasphemies in their ears. Myriad has no control over them."

"I do," Demitri said, irritated. "And they shall play an important role in my conquests, so I grant them certain liberties." He eyed Mereth threateningly. "Will you have trouble performing your duties under such conditions? Because I assure you... demons will abound when I bring Astasia."

Mereth swallowed and shook her head, struggling to maintain her cold exterior. "I do not question your logic, Luminary. However, if you want to have an army of warlocks, necromancers, and corruptionists, I must be given time to train them. Myriad must understand this."

"Enough," Demitri said, waving a careless hand. "I will speak to him." With that, he closed the door, wondering if Myriad could answer a few things about the Greenheart as well. He clenched his right fist tightly, feeling the reassuring presence of the broken *kropal* in his grasp.

Demitri strode down the seemingly countless stairs, refusing to take Vanghrel's much quicker portals leading to the

Calluses below the Spire. He wanted time to familiarize himself with his surroundings again, including his own skin. Still, while he longed to distance himself from Sol Saradys' inescapable influence, he used the Corruptor's power to enthrall Xavia, who followed close behind him, wearing only a slip of a robe. He had promised himself he wouldn't use his new abilities for such purposes, yet he could no longer look into her true eyes, so full of innocence and confusion.

At the moment, he preferred them devoid of all remembrance of his past life.

"Is it true that the old man built this tower on rifts between our Realms and the Abyss?" she asked excitedly.

Demitri smiled, deigning to turn around and look at her. If he only heard her voice, he could imagine her as she once was. "Yes. The Calluses. During the War of the Scales, many gates were opened between the Realms. The Heavens were nearly rent asunder when the angels became corrupted, following Lockri's descent to our world. Nekriark nearly swallowed Athland in its entirety." His smile widened and his voice lowered. "Those were the days."

He heard Xavia chuckle softly.

Demitri continued. "The Ways between Nekriark and our world were closed after the Shackling, but some demons remained when those scars began to heal. Their presence poisons the land, preventing the Ways to fully close. Chaos seeps from those wounds, binding the Nekrians to the caves below the Spire. Vanghrel somehow learned of their presence and built his tower on top of the Calluses, harnessing the demons and their Chaos magic."

He finally turned around to face Xavia, Sol Saradys' fingers creeping up his spine. "And now they're ours."

The smile that spread across Xavia's face was entirely devoid of humanity.

The two continued downward into the darkness below, Demitri savoring the chance to unveil the Spire's mysteries to his love while Xavia let the Corruptor's influence awaken her thirst for power. When they reached the threshold of the Calluses, their surroundings began to shift, the fading of illusions. Demitri wasn't sure if it was an effect from the Chaos magic that lingered down here or his own perception fading as Sol Saradys began to take over once more.

"You do me great honor, Luminary," a voice hissed from the void. "The previous proprietor of the Spire never visited his lowly servants so close to our element."

Myriad emerged from the shadows.

Demitri focused, striving to stay fully conscious for this exchange. "I have a request, Myriad."

"We are yours to command, Luminary." The small figure knelt down in an elaborate bow.

Demitri turned to Xavia, whose smile gripped his heart in a grasp much colder than the Corruptor's. "If you would excuse us, I am sure there are many wonders for you to witness down here."

Xavia wandered off without hesitation.

"She is quite beautiful," Myriad said, watching her saunter into the mists. "For a mortal."

"You are to keep your demons in check, Myriad," Demitri said, his voice brooking no argument. "The Days are upon us. Ancient powers writhe, waiting to be harnessed, and I need my students trained accordingly."

Myriad raised a horned eyebrow. "Trained? By whom, exactly? The Adjurers? With all due respect, Luminary, I cannot count one who has ever even tasted magic, let alone wielded it. My legions will test your flock and weed out the unworthy, and when the time has come, I shall instruct the remainder in the old ways."

"That was not a suggestion," Demitri stated flatly, his vision slowly darkening.

Myriad smiled. "Of course not, Luminary, I overstepped. It is only...the Balance wavers. I have felt it ever since your arrival. It buckles under the weight of forgotten presences. Powers are rising in this world: the Unshackling of your Hands, a wayward boon from the Heavens...I dream of the Four and Lockri interfering. The remaining Shackles must be gathered and destroyed if we hope to win this war. Each stone destroyed will unleash new magicks upon the world."

Demtiri stared into the writhing mists, reminding him of his own dream. He spoke the words with the Corruptor's voice. "The Greenheart."

Myriad's eyes widened in sudden realization. "Indeed, my lord. I had not thought...yes! The Gates can be breached now!"

Demitri scowled, images racing through his mind: the Corruptor's memories.

"The Burrow Gates," Myriad hissed, sensing Demitri's confusion. "Lockri built them to unite his scattered forests, but he dug too close to Nekriark. That is how we first infiltrated Athland, through the fool's own portals! However, when he sacrificed himself during the Shackling, he warded the Gates, keeping malign blighters—such as myself—from invading the forests. But now, as Chaos seeps from the Calluses, it weakens those wards."

Demitri saw visions of a past that was not his own: Sol Saradys whispering into Lockri's ear, Corruption flooding into his naive heart. His dream suddenly made sense to him. The Greenheart already held corruption.

Myriad smiled, as if he were inside Demitri's head and saw the same visions. "The Greenheart is the one Shackle that already bears corruption. It will be the easiest for you to break. Lockri never chose a mortal vessel, since he put his love and faith into the land itself. Mereketh and Evathayne both chose to take mortal form, much like yourself...or, your patron, Sol Saradys..."

Demitri sighed and motioned for Myriad to continue.

"But Lockri never chose a mortal form, his influence and power resides in the stone itself. Break the Greenheart, break Lockri."

The image of the Greenheart being shattered by his own corrupted hand made Demitri smile wickedly, but the smile wasn't entirely his.

CHAPTER 28: THE PRINCE AND THE PARIAH

The Eurhebine Plains, western Eurheby

The trek across the Eurhebine Plains was exhausting, mentally and physically. The landscape was a scatter of plateaus and ridges with small collections of skeletal trees. Cedric had refused to stop until he and Jaryd had reached the borders of Holthurst, and even then he only gave them time to water their mounts and stretch their limbs before pressing on again. They rode hard for nearly an entire day after crossing into Holthurst until the prince's horse finally refused to carry him anymore. Cedric and Jaryd both dismounted and continued on foot.

The prince walked in silence, trying to keep ahead of the bard and his incessant singing. Cedric's resolve was withering, and hearing Jaryd's seemingly unaffected morale projected through song only seemed to anger him all the more. He could not look back—the burning towers of Celendas wracked him with grief—and he could not look up to the mountains ahead without his heart filling with dread at the thought of what he must do when he got there. So he kept his eyes downcast, seeking to withdraw into himself.

However, his present company did not make that task easy.

"To doom we ride under acrid skies, into the blackened wastes," Jaryd sang, his soft voice seeming to echo unnaturally on the wind. *"The dragon's breath shall be our death—"*

"Perhaps!" Cedric shouted, finally turning around. "Our company could deal with a bit of silence, Jaryd? What say you?"

Jaryd smiled. "I say silence is for the grave, my lord." He had an arm around his horse, as if he were singing only to the beast. His mood had remained the same since they left Celendas and it was slowly wearing down Cedric's fragile resolve.

The prince's world had been utterly destroyed a matter of hours ago and the devastation could not take full effect so long as the bard's melodic voice followed him with every step he took.

As soon as the prince turned around to continue his pace, the bard began again.

"*Black sails came that baleful day, to light once more the Phoenix Flames, but through the gloom the Prince of Doom —*"

The bard's voice stopped abruptly as Cedric spun around, his hand on his sword hilt and his eyes narrowed on Jaryd.

"You will not call me that," Cedric said, his face reddening with restrained fury. "And you will cease this absurd merriment. Celendas has fallen! My father is dead! The world is coming apart, and it is no time for song!"

Jaryd stared blankly at the prince for a long moment, as if he were waiting for Cedric to draw his sword. But after the moment passed, a warm smile spread across the minstrel's face.

Cedric stepped forward. "Do you mock me, bard?"

"Of course not, my prince," Jaryd said, producing a wineskin from his belt. "It's only..." He took a long drink, his eyes staring into the sky as he swallowed. "In the face of such devastation, what do we have besides song?" He looked back at Cedric, his smile gone and his eyes hard. "Ask yourself, Cedric: would we have made it this far in silence?"

Cedric's own gaze shifted from the bard abruptly and he quickly drew his blade, throwing the bard to the ground. Jaryd rolled away to land on his back, watching as the prince charged toward three robed strangers that had suddenly scrambled over a nearby ridge in a frenzied dash toward him and Cedric. They wore the same ashen robes as the invaders of Celendas. Cedric easily hewed one of them down, spattering blood across the long grass, but more appeared over another ridge near the woods.

"Cultists," Jaryd hissed, reaching for his dagger. But all he found was the wineskin at his belt, and when he brought his hand up it was covered in Rokuusian amber. It looked like blood in the fading sunlight. His eyes darted quickly and he saw his weapon on his horse's saddle as the beast thrashed and made to run away at the smell of spilt blood.

"Jaryd!" The prince had been knocked over by a cultist that had apparently thrown himself on Cedric's sword. The slumped body now lay on top of the prince, pinning him down as two more cultists approached. The assailants shrieked wildly in the Abyssal tongue.

Jaryd got to his feet and scrambled for his horse before it fled. He reached it just in time, grabbing the reins to calm the animal down. He threw open the saddle bag, but instead of grabbing his dagger, he drew out his harp. Jaryd turned around and ran his fingers across the strings. It was like a roll of thunder, the final note piercing the sounds of battle like a stone shattering a mountain of glass. The cultists fell to their knees, their hands over the ears.

The prince looked up and saw Jaryd standing on a nearby rock, his fingers gliding over the harp. He sang in a strange language that Cedric had never heard before. It was beautiful, but terrifying. It took Cedric a moment to realize that the cultists were now writhing on the ground, tearing at their ears, Jaryd's music clearly tormenting them. Cedric, however, felt a burst of strength. Sudden pride and valor filled his heart. He struggled and lifted the dead cultist off of him, wiping his sword on those soiled, ashen robes. He stood tall, letting the bard's music paint the world around him in hues of heroism and glorious battle. He felt ready to take on the Burning One himself. His eyes narrowed on the cultists that now struggled to their feet, drawing crude weapons from their robes. With Jaryd's music inspiring every parry and thrust, Cedric made short work of the Corruptor's zealots, leaving only one alive, the one who surrendered his weapon in tears.

Jaryd's music began to fade away as the heat of battle died. Cedric stepped over to the weeping cultist, throwing back the man's hood.

No, the woman's hood.

A middle-aged woman wept at the prince's feet, her hands bloodied and her face branded with malign marks of the Corruptor. She held out her hands to the prince.

"Please," she said between sobs, her voice raspy as if she hadn't spoken in days. "He promised…"

"Who?" Cedric asked with a raised sword, already knowing the answer.

She only wept.

Cedric made to grab her, but a hand caught his wrist. He turned to face Jaryd, a soft smile on the bard's face.

"Well done, your majesty," the bard said, letting go of Cedric's wrist. "Let me tend to this. Please, see to the horses."

Cedric made to refuse, but he looked back at the pathetic woman. Something underneath all the hatred he felt for her made him pity her even more. He turned away before he was tempted to cut her in half and strode toward the horses, which were both whinnying in the field below the ridge.

After Cedric calmed the beasts down, he turned to see Jaryd sitting next to the woman, playing his harp. The prince couldn't hear the song; it was played only for her. He lost sight of the two when he neared the ridge, and by the time he crested it, the woman was gone and Jaryd was polishing his harp with one of the dead cultist's robes.

"Where is she?" Cedric asked incredulously.

"I wouldn't worry about old Edith," Jaryd said, not looking up. "She's done a terrible thing, but the grief that she will now have to live with is more than adequate punishment for her transgressions."

Cedric blinked, not sure whether to feel anger or relief. "What in Dhullas are you talking about? Her people razed my city! And you let her go?"

Jaryd stood up, shouldering his harp and giving the prince a strange look. "Do you break the swords of your enemies, Cedric? Or do you take those swords and arm your own people?"

Cedric didn't know how to answer that.

"Corruption destroyed Celendas, your majesty, not a bunch of fools in foul-smelling robes. Mortals without enough willpower to fight his influence are the swords of Sol Saradys. He promises ecstasy, he promises love, his corruption flows into your heart and blackens everything you most desire and he uses those elements to forge his weapon. Some people aren't strong enough to face the cruelties of this world, and they fall to their knees, offering their ever-capable vessels as a leather hilt for Sol Saradys to wrap his fiery fingers around. And if given the chance to disarm him, would you choose to destroy that sword or turn it against him?"

Cedric still had no answer for the bard, but he felt a surge of unexplained guilt creep though him. "Was she...possessed?"

Jaryd reached his horse and motioned for the prince to continue their journey. "Edith was taken in by the cult. Her husband left her and their family for a dockside whore. Her son died a year ago and her daughter was given a bastard by a local noble who raped her. These people are easily turned to the Burning One, who promises them relief from their troubles. How can we fully blame them?" Jaryd motioned to the dead cultists behind them. "If this is all we were given in the world, wouldn't you perk up your ears to an archangel who promised you a bit more?"

Cedric wanted to reject the notion, but he felt it a bit childish, so he kept his mouth shut, with his eyes now fixed on the mountains ahead—a sight he loathed much less now, after such an encounter.

After almost a league of silence, Cedric finally asked the question that was burning in his mind. "What was that song you played? I felt something..."

Jaryd drank from his wineskin, emptying it before he answered. "Some mortals are arrogant enough to think that they are responsible for the magic of song. It is no secret that music is the most powerful force in the world. It is the only magic that has an effect on us all: mortals, gods, angels, demons." He stared into the sky again. "Men do write songs, but some songs are older than us all. Some songs created us. We walk within Celecy's music, Cedric, and every melody that we hear carries an echo of her First Song."

Cedric considered that for a moment. He had heard stories about legendary minstrels who learned the music of the Heavens, able to banish demons by performing one of Celecy's songs. Before Cedric could think on it more, he asked, "How did you learn that song?"

Jaryd's eyes were now on the mountains ahead, and he didn't answer for a long time. When he did, he said, "Some songs can't be learned, your majesty, just as every bard can't create a masterpiece to be remembered by." He tossed the empty wineskin to the ground. "Not every bard can hear the Heavens." Jaryd smiled, cocking an eyebrow as he looked over at the prince. "My theory, though…I'm just that good."

Jaryd and Cedric both reasoned that it would be wise if they avoided any stops along their way to Neveren. White Rock looked as if it had not been invaded, but as Jaryd said, with Sol Saradys' powers of corruption, it was not always easy to tell friend from foe. Also, Jaryd admitted to tiring easily after such performances, and until he got some proper rest, he would be worthless in another encounter. So, they avoided the duke's keep and took the more difficult paths into the mountains. They did not meet any more resistance in the form of cultists, though they did encounter the tracks left by a band of greks. The foul creatures were easily avoided. Cedric knew that greks wouldn't dare approach armed travelers unless they outnumbered them five to one, and tribes of more than a few greks rarely thrived.

Their trek into Neveren was difficult, as the horses had trouble finding footing through many of the paths, and soon Cedric and Jaryd were forced to dismount. By the time they reached the borders of Demonscale, they had to tether their mounts to a cave with a spring nearby.

"I hope we live through this, if only to ensure we can lead these marvelous beasts back to open fields," Jaryd said, patting his horse on the neck.

They gathered their gear and, after a brief meal of dried meat and berries, they descended into the tunnels leading into Demonscale. The map Cedric's father gave him led them through the darkened passageways without much difficulty. Jaryd made a torch from a dried log, a sleeve of his travel coat, and flint and tinder from his pack. They encountered some of the known terrors of Demonscale in those passageways: huge bats, an enormous cave worm, and a couple of dead greks. Fortunately, Cedric only had to brandish his sword against the worm, which fled back into the shadows once the prince sliced open its side.

After navigating the twisting labyrinth of the underground, they emerged to see a fiery sky above and the blackened wastes of Demonscale below.

"The one place in Athland that I've never been," Jaryd said, extinguishing the torch in the ashen dirt. "Can't say I'm going to be quick to return either."

"Come on," Cedric said, his eyes fixed on the tower of stone known as Scorn.

They walked in silence, both travelers actively on their guard for any malign beast out for their blood. They reached the foothills of Scorn sooner than either of them expected. Before they could even think about how they would ever climb such a tall spire of rock, Jaryd pointed up.

"I say, is that a falling cloud?"

Cedric looked up. It did indeed look like a black cloud was descending from the peak of Scorn. It began to take shape, and when Cedric saw the flapping, leathery wings he threw himself and Jaryd to the ground. "Drakes!"

The ravenous cloud swooped over where their heads had been, almost crashing to the ground. But the dragonspawn wheeled back into the sky at the last moment, leaving behind only a shadowed figure that landed on the ground in an explosion of blackened earth.

Cedric rolled over, coughing as a blistering cloud of dust assaulted his eyes, mouth, and nose. He waved the grey mists away and watched as the dark figure rose to its feet. Its back was to him, and Cedric could see a greatsword across its shoulders, swathed in tattered, black leather.

Jaryd rolled over as well, cursing under his breath. His voice could barely be heard over the screeching drakes above. The bard saw the black figure just as it began to stride away from them. His eyes narrowed on the sword. "Is that...?" the bard's question trailed off as the prince got to his feet.

"Halt!" Cedric shouted, starting toward the stranger. "I say, stop in the name of the king!" He began to draw his sword.

The stranger was unresponsive, keeping a steady pace toward the western horizon. Cedric finally reached him and placed a hand on his shoulder. Jaryd saw the stranger spin around, a handful of knives slashing out at the prince. Not knives, claws.

Cedric fell to his knees, grabbing the side of his face. Blood sprayed onto the blackened earth.

"How dare you!" Jaryd shouted in a mocking tone, scrambling to his feet. "You have struck the king of Celendas!"

The stranger turned away and kept walking.

Jaryd reached Cedric, helping the prince to his feet. He saw the slashes on prince's face and cringed. "Was that a grek?"

Cedric looked at the blood on his hand, and then back to Jaryd. He shook his head, narrowing his eyes. He pushed the bard aside and spun his sword, gripping it with both hands.

"Wait!" Jaryd warned. "That sword he carries..."

The rest of the world faded away as the prince charged after the stranger. He leapt into the air, his sword raised over his head. But as he came down, the man spun, quick as lightning, and an enormous sword caught the prince's blow.

Cedric's eyes widened when his feet hit the ground and he saw the Dragonsbane against his own steel. Before he could say anything, he was thrown back with incredible force, almost losing his grip on his own blade. He landed hard on his back, coughing in pain. The stranger now loomed over him, the Dragonsbane in his hands. He was of a height with Cedric, his hair black as night and his eyes blood red with inhuman rage. He wore a tattered black coat as if he had been nearly clawed to death by drakes.

"Ah," said Jaryd, brandishing his harp, "the sons are left to finish their father's deeds."

Cedric turned to the bard in confusion. "Who's son?"

"This fool has saved us a trip, your majesty," Jaryd said, his fingers already dancing. "He brings us your father's sword. And only one man other than a Galvian heir could wield such a blade."

Cedric got to his feet, confusion still painted across his face. He stared at the stranger while the sky darkened. As the drakes began to descend behind the stranger, it looked as if the man standing before him had wings. And then realization came.

The Dragonsbane was forged from Galvian blood, as well as drops of dragon blood. And it was said only Galvians could wield it, because they sacrificed their own blood in the forging. But dragon blood coursed through the dark steel as well.

Cedric gripped his sword tightly and stared at the dragon's child. Jaryd's music enveloped him, forcing the rest of the world to drop away. All that mattered to the prince right now was his rightful sword, held in the hands of a savage.

"I will have that sword, fiend," Cedric warned. "Whether or not I have to pry it from your dead fingers, well...that is your choice."

The stranger said nothing. Jaryd's song was the only sound that hung between them, and as the bard's fingers quickened, Cedric's courage mounted. The prince charged.

The dragon's child met the blow, and their own dance began. Jaryd followed the duel, his voice beginning to strain as he tried to continue the song. His melodies were accented by the clashing crescendos of steel, and his fingers could barely keep up with the speed. Jaryd watched in disbelief as the prince's blade became a blur, delivering blow after blow that the dragon's child could barely parry with the larger Dragonsbane.

After a time, Jaryd felt his fingers beginning to cramp. The frantic speed of the swordfight was hard for him to keep up with in his exhausted state. Eventually he missed a note, causing Cedric to miss a step. The dragon's child swung the Dragonsbane with enough force to disarm the prince, knocking the smaller sword into the dirt.

Jaryd fell to a knee, his energy completely drained. "Gah!" He dropped his harp.

Cedric lost his balance and fell to the ground, landing awkwardly on his wrist. The sounds of bones breaking ceased Jaryd's music—an unresolved melody. The prince cried out and rolled onto his back, watching as the stranger approached. The dragon's child raised the Dragonsbane to finish off the Prince of Doom.

Cedric closed his eyes tightly, whispering. "I'm sorry, Father."

The shrieking of steel meeting steel forced his eyes open.

He saw the stranger's face, contorted, struggling against a blade almost as wide as the Dragonsbane: a blade that saved Cedric's life.

The prince rolled away to see if Jaryd had come to his

rescue, but he could see that the bard knelt only a few feet away from him, staring wide-eyed at the sword that caught the Dragonsbane. Cedric looked up to find a new figure towering above him. It was a hulking Rhelklander, the biggest man Cedric had ever seen. His face was buried in long, bushy hair and a thick brown beard, yet his burning eyes could be seen through the tangled mess. And they were fixed on the dragon's child.

"Fight him, Anathu," the Rhelklander said. "Do not let his words devour you!"

This amazed Cedric even more. He was raised on the notion that Rhelklanders could not speak. They were savage barbarians that lived only to kill each other. And what did he mean by his words? *Is the dragon's child a minion of Sol Saradys?* Cedric wondered. Too many questions ran through his mind, but they were soon drowned in the wave of pain that took him when he tried to get up, foolishly forgetting his broken wrist.

After a long moment of grating steel, the Rhelklander threw Anathu back. With a beastly growl, he charged after him. "Hear me, Anathu! You are not your father! Drop the sword and be free of his madness!"

The man called Anathu bared his razor teeth and struck out at the Rhelk, wielding the Dragonsbane as if it were an extension of his body. Cedric cradled his injured arm and got to his feet, stumbling over toward Jaryd. The bard was wiping the sweat from his brow, watching the Rhelklander wear down the enraged dragon's child.

"It's him," Jaryd said in disbelief. "I thought it was a legend…"

Cedric didn't know which man he was talking about, but he helped the bard to his feet. "Come on, we may have to fight again if one of them dies."

"No," Jaryd said. But before he could continue, a horde of screeching drakes descended from the sky.

Jaryd and Cedric both cried out and ducked under their claws. The Rhelklander, hovering over a winded Anathu, turned to see the approaching drakes. Anathu took advantage of the distraction and burst into a dead sprint, heading westward with the Dragonsbane in his bloodied hands.

The hulking Rhelklander bellowed and charged into the swarm of descending drakes. Cedric and Jaryd heard the sounds of their deaths as the cloud of black earth spat out dark blood. When the dust settled, only the Rhelklander stood. The remaining drakes were crying out their retreat as they took to the air.

"You," Jaryd said, helping the prince to his feet, his eyes fixed on the Rhelk. "You're bigger in person. I've dreamt of you."

"And I of you," Skahgerok said, looking at both Cedric and the bard. "Come. We must reach the Burrow Gates. Anathu is heading to cleanse the blade, and we must stop him. But first, we must recover the Shackles of Heaven, or Celendas will be only the first of many kingdoms to fall."

CHAPTER 29: THE THIRD SIGN OF ASTASIA

The Aevenwood, between Wynnstead and Melbrook

The Aevenwood was eerily silent as the three men made their way toward Melbrook. Anerith was on the edge of exhaustion, leaning on a makeshift walking stick he had fashioned from a sturdy branch. He was not used to such physical exertion—and the things he had done in Wynnstead had completely drained him. Sebastian walked as if in a dream, his eyes glazed over and his every step clumsier than the last. Raiken kept ahead of the other two, claiming he needed to scout for any signs of trouble. Sebastian knew it was only a ploy so he wouldn't have to stay behind and talk about what happened in Wynnstead.

After a time, Anerith found his voice. "I've read about the power of prayers, and though I have never seen old divine rituals performed firsthand, is it safe to say that what happened back there was...unnatural?"

Sebastian did not turn around. "You could say that."

Valcorse swooped low and shrieked.

"You *could* say that!" Raiken shouted from ahead, a twisted humor in his voice. "But you could also say that what happened back there is perfectly natural. Is it not natural for a hill to cave in on you if you dig too far into its side?"

Sebastian stopped. "Are you implying, brother, that I meant for that to happen?"

"Why else does one pray," Raiken asked mockingly, "if

not to ask the gods for help?" He leapt off of the rock he was on and swaggered toward Anerith and Sebastian, his eyes fixed on his brother. "We were both in Vysarc, Sebastian. I know you can see threads of the divine world that no other priest can see. But does that give you the right to pull them?"

"I didn't ask for this, Raiken," Sebastian said, anger finding its way into his voice. "And besides, what else could we have done?"

"Run!" Raiken declared, motioning toward Melbrook. "We could have run, like I said. Leave those *things* for the militia to take care of. I'm sure there are a score of knights in Aevenore who would give their manhood to fight off legions of the undead."

Sebastian glared at his brother, and a momentary silence fell between them.

Anerith stepped forward. "You have been to Vysarc?"

The twins ignored their companion, their eyes locked on each other for a long moment. Finally, Sebastian's eyes fell to the Greenstone. "What about you, brother?"

Raiken tucked the stone into his vest.

"I felt your stone when it crossed the circle. I felt Lockri." Sebastian stepped forward. "His savagery empowered that ritual, much like he empowers you. Tell me, does a day go by when you don't use a sacrificed angel's power to your own advantage?"

"That's different," Raiken said, turning around to continue his scouting.

"Is it?" Sebastian answered.

"Yes!" Raiken said, whipping his head around. "I wear a reminder of the Balance around my neck. Lockri gave his soul to maintain the fragile harmony of this world." He pointed a finger at his brother. "And you profaned it."

With that, Raiken disappeared into the trees.

Sebastian stood there for a moment in stunned silence. Behind him, Anerith shifted awkwardly on his feet, not sure if he should follow Raiken and give Sebastian a moment to himself or wait until the uneasiness passed. In the end, he opted to change the topic of contemplation.

"Where are we headed?" Anerith asked.

Sebastian turned and blinked at him, as if seeing Anerith for the first time. "Melbrook," he said, confusion washing from his face. "We can rest in the church and figure out exactly what happened back there." He turned toward the ruin of Wynnstead, shivering at the sight.

Anerith swallowed nervously, his exhaustion plain to see. "What exactly happened back there? I need to know."

Sebastian turned from him and began walking toward the trees Raiken had disappeared into. Anerith had no choice but to fall into step with the priest. Eventually, Sebastian answered his question, his eyes skyward.

"I asked for things that I should not have, at a time when the Four could not refuse me." He looked ahead. "Raiken was right; we should have run."

"I have read little on divine magic," Anerith said. "I don't…I mean, I didn't put much faith in tales of the Balance—Order and Chaos. We learned the theories, but I did not pay heed to the legends of the *Books of Astasia*."

Sebastian stopped suddenly. Valcorse flew low through the trees, crying out a warning.

"Something's wrong!" Sebastian said, sprinting toward the path that Raiken had taken. Anerith followed behind, struggling as his robes got caught up in the hanging overgrowth. He nearly tripped several times trying to keep up with Sebastian, who seemed to be running for his life. As the two reached a clearing where their path merged with two others, a sound like splitting wood cut through the air, and a pain unlike any he had ever felt exploded from Anerith's leg. The young Adept from the Spire fell to the ground screaming.

Sebastian stopped and turned. He saw Anerith on the ground holding a crossbow quarrel protruding from his leg. But before he could run over and assist Anerith, a voice called out to Sebastian from the trees. "Halt there, heathen!"

Sebastian's eyes darted, looking for any sign of the speaker. But all he saw were leaves and shadows. *Bandits*, Sebastian thought to himself.

"We have no coin!" he called to the trees. "Which is fortunate for you, as robbing a cleric of the Four will buy you brigands eternal servitude in the Abyss!"

"Ah," the voice said, softer now and approaching from the east. Sebastian found the source as a figure emerged from the trees. He was cloaked and masked, and Sebastian saw that around his neck hung a silver pendant: the star and halo of the Sect of Halcyon. "And what is the penalty for a self-proclaimed holy man to harbor Chaos?"

Where have I heard that voice? Sebastian wondered to himself.

Several other figures appeared before Sebastian could put a name with the voice. All of the newcomers bore the stars and halos on their surcoats and they all held crossbows trained on Sebastian and Anerith.

Anerith cursed in pain again, seemingly oblivious to the encounter unfolding around him while he continued to try to get to his feet. "Sebastian!"

"Let me tend to him!" Sebastian pleaded with his hands up in submission. "I only need a few herbs…"

"He'll live," the leader said calmly. "For now. I am sure our reputation precedes us, and it is rather well known that heathens do not thrive in the presence of the Sect of Halcyon."

"We are not heathens!" Sebastian responded. "I am a priest of the Sacred Circle, and this is my companion. We are returning to Melbrook for healing." He motioned to Anerith. "Much more urgent healing, thanks to you."

"Not heathens?" the leader asked, stepping closer. "Your church practices heresy and you travel with a warlock from the Spire. And if that weren't enough to damn you, here you are: the only survivors of a ravished hamlet that was the site of an unnatural storm last night. One might marvel at your ability to evade the title of heathen on such accounts, dear priest."

The Sectaries surrounding them spat out curses in agreement.

"However," the leader continued, reaching into a leather pouch at his side, "we remain noble in our campaign to expurgate the taints of Chaos and corruption, so you will have a fair trial. But in the end, you will face the consequences of your atrocities." He produced a handful of fine yellow powder that sifted through his gloved fingers.

Just as Sebastian opened his mouth to dismiss the accusations, a cloud of the man's yellow powder was thrown full in his face. Sebastian coughed and briefly saw the trees of the Aevenwood spin before blackness overwhelmed him.

He was unconscious before he even hit the ground.

Sebastian heard their voices before he fully awoke. At first, they were wordless sounds that came from behind spinning walls, but after a moment, he remembered the Sect of Halcyon from the Aevenwood and recognized the leader's voice. It was then that he began to hear the words. They were discussing executions. He heard the leader's voice above the rest, and the familiarity of that voice stabbed a shard of cold recollection into Sebastian's heart.

Warrell Stane.

He knew the voice reminded him of someone from his past, but it had been years since Sebastian had last heard that righteous windbag speak. Even back then, Sebastian should have known that Warrell would rise quickly in the Sect—he was an excellent speaker and he could rally a mob in the blink of an eye.

Sebastian tried to wipe his watering eyes. It was then he realized his hands were bound behind him. He squinted and took in his surroundings.

He was in a church—his church—seated in a simple chair. The pews had been cleared out of the proper and the altar had been removed. Why the Sect had brought him back to Melbrook, he could not begin to guess. Everything felt like a cruel dream.

The voices became clearer as Sebastian found full consciousness.

"They should be made examples of. Expose them, and then we will search for the remaining stones at the Spire."

"What makes you even think the Luminary has collected them all?"

"It doesn't matter. We face corruption here, and it needs to be dealt with."

"Who are they?" asked a nearby voice that nearly made Sebastian topple the chair he sat in. Anerith was bloodied, bruised, and bound next to him. Yellow powder caked his eyes and the corners of his mouth.

"The Sect of Halcyon," Sebastian said, breathing deep to

overcome the sudden shock. He looked around, making sure none of the other Sectaries were in sight. "Bastard children of the Spearitan Faith. Witch hunters and conspirators, all of them." He struggled with his bindings. "They will no doubt hold us responsible for VonAnthony's atrocities in Wynnstead, which means we face the gallows if we don't get out of here."

"Halcyon," Anerith said, tasting the word. "A time of peace. Harmony."

Sebastian grunted and tried to free his hands as Anerith mused aloud.

"I read of their atrocities in the *Thousand Deaths of Skall*. Not only did they brand him the Son of Chaos and kill him in every way imaginable, but they massacred anyone and everyone that either cared for or had been cared for by him." Anerith stared at the tapestry that adorned the apse at the top of the dais. It was a vibrant image of the Four fending off the Harbingers of Astasia. "How can so much violence ultimately lead to peace?"

Sebastian exhaled in defeat as he failed to free his hands. "They believe it is their job to purge Chaos from our world, including all who would associate themselves with it. That's why we need to get out of here. You're from the Spire, a bastion of Chaos in their eyes. The arcane was corruption's stain on the world according to the *Book of the Sect*."

Sebastian remembered the lightning that had saved Anerith's life back in VonAnthony's manor. And, judging by the morose look that washed over Anerith's face, he remembered as well.

Just then, the doors opened behind them and footsteps rang loudly through the vestibule. Sebastian could hear a gathering outside as harsh voices came in through the open doors. His back was turned toward the entrance so he could not see what the commotion was about. The doors slammed shut.

Warrell Stane strode in front of his prisoners, his mask discarded and his eyes narrowed. He would have been considered a handsome man, if it had not been for the blackened heart that beat in his chest. His long auburn hair rested elegantly on his shoulders, perfectly curled and manicured. The years hung in the corners of his eyes, but his wicked face had a timeless quality to it. The gruesome scar that ran across his cheek was the only thing that belied his civilized demeanor.

"Let us forgo formalities," Stane said plainly, fixing his eyes on Sebastian. "We are not strangers, but I will not associate with heretics. You have been accused of treason, both of you. Against the throne and the Faith. Do you deny these charges?"

"We do," Sebastian said plainly.

Stane nodded and a Sectary stepped forward from behind Sebastian to throw the back of his hand across the priest's face. Sebastian grunted and bit back a curse.

"Perhaps you would like to lie as well?" Stane asked Anerith, his arms behind his back.

Anerith held his tongue, looking over as Sebastian spat blood onto the floor.

"Is this how you found your faith, Warrell?" Sebastian asked mockingly, his voice finding a hint of dark mirth. "You couldn't find true faith until you convinced yourself that all others were a lie. It's no wonder you rose so high in the Sect." He laughed.

Another blow silenced Sebastian.

Stane maintained his calm composure. "If that is all you have to say for yourself, Sebastian Belrouse, I foresee a shortness of breath in your future. The penalty for harboring Chaos and spreading corruption in our realm is the noose. Perhaps you should pray that your townsfolk are easily convinced of your innocence."

Stane's eyes returned to Anerith. "And you. Your master has betrayed us. He has broken any allegiance there might have been between his coven and the Sect by dispatching his agents on such a heinous quest. For that, you will die."

"I don't know what you're talking about!" Anerith declared. "I am only a messenger!"

Stane produced a familiar scroll from his belt and crushed the parchment in his fist. "And we have read your message, warlock. Did the Luminary truly believe that we would turn a traitor to the throne over to him?" The High Sectary let out a wicked, arrogant snort of amusement. "Madness must be claiming him in his years. We know what Benegast was searching for in Therrec, and we know what you came here for."

Stane nodded to the masked Sectary who had struck Sebastian. The man stepped forward and reached into a satchel at his side. Anerith cringed, expecting to see a cruel torture device in his gloved hand, but it was only a silk cloth. If fell open to reveal a jagged black stone.

"No..." Sebastian said weakly, staring at the familiar stone. "Raiken, you bastard."

"Quiet," Stane commanded sternly. He grabbed the stone from the Sectary, cradling the silk, making sure not to let the *kropal* touch his flesh. He presented it to Anerith, his eyes narrowing. "Take a good look, warlock. This is the closest you will ever come to recovering the Shackle of Flame for your dark master. Whatever deal you worked out with the heretics here is no more. Your quest for ruin has come to an end."

Anerith stared at the stone, amazed and dumbfounded. "The Shackles of Heaven."

Stane covered the stone. "Will be presented to King

Garrowin, once we recover the remaining stones."

"They must be returned," Sebastian said with a distant stare. A sudden realization came to him, the terror of it overwhelming. "The Balance is breaking. There is no other way I could have…" He looked up at Stane and at the covered stone. "We must return it. The dead are walking, the Burning One is stirring…Warrell, we—"

"The dead most certainly *are* walking!" Stane shouted suddenly, jamming a finger into Sebastian's face. "And you will answer for such heinous deeds!"

The masked Sectary stepped forward, produced the heavy necromantic tome from VonAnthony's manor, and let it drop to the floor with a thud at Sebastian's feet.

"What did you sell your soul for, Sebastian?" Stane asked, grabbing the priest's chin and forcing him to look him in the eye. His voice became shrill and maniacal. "A black rock and a town of rotting corpses? Was it worth it?"

Sebastian knew there was no use in denying any charges the Sect would lay upon him. They had their minds made up, and there was no swaying a Sectary, especially not one as vile as Warrell Stane. Sebastian stared into the High Sectary's eyes, unflinching.

Stane released Sebastian's chin. "You will pay for your sins, both of you." He turned to leave, motioning for the masked Sectary. "To the gallows."

The gallows were rarely used in Melbrook. They were constructed before Sebastian and Raiken were brought to the church. It was said that they were once used when Sir Brennik

Langle served as the town's constable during the rule of King Frederic Crayce, when hangings were a routine display thought to keep order in the kingdom's surrounding hamlets. More recently, however, they served more as a rookery for crows and pigeons, as well as a crude reminder of more harrowing times.

Sebastian and Anerith were led out through the wide roads of Melbrook, where townsfolk were gathered to hiss and throw various objects at the accused. Sebastian was hit by random onions and small stones, while Anerith took the brunt of the assault, being the mysterious witch bringing trouble from the outside world. He was hit by chunks of brick, mud, flasks of ale, and what smelled like animal excrement.

The march was agonizing, and it crushed Sebastian's soul. They were led by four masked Sectaries that riled the townsfolk, spewing vile lies about the atrocities committed by the priest and his warlock compatriot. Sebastian was horrified to see how many people he knew became so quickly swayed by the mistruths. Many may have just felt pressured enough by the Sect to join the rising mob, but others looked at Sebastian with a pure, seething hatred, as if they had waited years for this moment. The widow Yvette Langley spat on Sebastian as he passed.

"To the Abyss with you!" she shouted. "You betrayed us!"

"Hang 'em high!" called a familiar voice. Sebastian saw that Seeley Finch stood atop a wagon, providing others with stale bread to throw. "Corruptors!"

Sebastian felt his fury rising, accompanied by a shame that was not rightfully his. He knew he did not do the things he was accused of, but thinking back to what had happened in Wynnstead, he could not help but feel guilty of something. Through clenched teeth, he whispered his prayers to the Four, hoping they would show mercy…

...until the gallows came into sight. Hope died then.

Laurel—her face reddened from what must have been days of crying—stood next to Vincent on the small platform, nooses around both of their necks.

"No!" Sebastian screamed, pushing one of the Sectaries out of his way so he could run toward them. He didn't get very far as the other three easily restrained him, raining down blows on his head.

"Leave him alone!" Anerith cried, only to receive a blow from the butt of a crossbow from another Sectary behind him.

"Enough!" Warrell Stane cried out from the front of the procession, his voice muffled behind his mask. With a sweep of his long-sleeved arm, he demanded, "Bring them forward."

Head lolling, Sebastian nearly lost consciousness as the people he had spent his whole life serving cried out for his death. This was the power of fear and uncertainty, and the Sect knew how to wield such weapons with cruel efficiency. Sebastian was dragged onward to the gallows, a limp and bloodied Anerith following close behind.

They were quickly put in line with Laurel and Vincent, nooses fit around their own necks. Sebastian fell to his knees as they fit his noose, no longer able to take in the horrors that surrounded him.

Warrell Stane stood on the platform with the accused. He leaned over to whisper into Sebastian's ear, "You will be the last. I want you to see the deaths that you are responsible for before you kneel at Nekriark's blistered feet."

Sebastian spat out blood. "I'll wait for you...along with all the other dead for which you are responsible."

Stane did not respond. He only smiled wickedly at Sebastian before he turned to address the gathering.

"My fellow men of the Dale, before you stand the accused!" He motioned toward Vincent, who waited impatiently, his eyes betraying no emotion other than anxiety, as if he were going to be late for an appointment. "Father Cruland, servant of Chaos! It was this man who allowed the foul stench of corruption to creep into your very homesteads! His church is a haven for the malign and those who would befoul all that we cherish. He was found harboring a witch!"

He pointed at Laurel, whose composure was also surprisingly calm, despite the evidence of her tears. Her eyes were fixed on Sebastian, and they conveyed more emotion than words could ever do justice. "She let the Burning One's influence take her, bowing to his promises of dark power."

The townsfolk screamed for her swift demise. "Burn her!" "Let's have her head!" "Have the wench bow before me!" Profanities continued until Stane raised his hand to silence them.

"But how did the Corruptor wake from his damned slumber? How did his whispers escape the cursed depths of the Stratovault?"

Some frenzied farmers shouted that Sebastian had seduced Laurel to the malign powers of Chaos. Others said she was an escaped witch from the Spire, and Anerith had come looking for her. But Stane just shook his head each time someone offered a theory. After enough time, the aggressive gathering turned into a wide array of silent stares.

Then, Stane produced the *kropal*, swathed in dark silk.

The whole town gasped in unison.

"It's the Shackle of Flame!" cried a panicked woman. "His Hands are free!"

"Astasia!" someone shouted. "The end is nigh!"

"The Corruptor is free!" became the town's chanting cry.

Stane let the hysteria rise to a dangerous pitch before he raised his hands again to call for silence. "It is true, much to our dismay." He motioned to the church in the distance, its sculpted likeness of the Four dominating the town's rooftops. "This bastion of sacred teaching has fallen in line with the power-hungry ways of the Silver Spire. Together, they are seeking the Shackles of Heaven so they might unleash Sol Saradys on the Mortal Realms once more."

This time, no one shouted obscenities. Everyone's fearful eyes were on the High Sectary of Halcyon, waiting to hear how the end of their world could be prevented.

Warrell Stane took a moment to revel in his control over the gathering, still holding the dark stone for all to see. "But now we have the *kropal*, the Stone of Prythene, and we will gather the remaining Shackles before the forces of Chaos are able to lay one tainted finger on the bindings that hold Sol Saradys where he belongs…in burning damnation!"

The crowd erupted into cheers, as if every maid, child, and old man were a soldier in a righteous army, ready to spill blood for no other reason than to slay their own fear and confusion.

Sebastian watched the people of Melbrook in horror, unable to rationalize the devastation that he had witnessed in the last few hours. He destroyed an entire town with a single prayer, and now he was witnessing another town's demise by the hands of manipulation and lies. He closed his eyes, searching for the strength to pray, but hope had truly rotted away within him. A dark thought occurred to him: he was ready to die.

"Now," Stane continued, "justice is in your hands. If anyone among you can stand for the accused—"

"I will stand for all of 'em, you crooked bastard!"

A commotion broke out as the gathering split in two.

Sebastian looked up and saw a hulking figure approach, his face bloody and bruised. He held a long knife to the throat of a Sectary as he made is his way toward the gallows.

It was Barrid Lupke, the blacksmith that had forged Sebastian's armor, and it seemed he had just escaped his own bondage.

Sebastian rose to his feet, wanting to warn Barrid against such lunacy. The Sect would not answer kindly to threats.

Barrid looked all around. "You blind fools! Are you going to let them string up Vincent?! Walter! He healed your son when he got the molts! And Karin! Vincent prayed with you for days while your husband was away in Rathaine! Do you think it was pure chance that he returned alive?!"

No one responded. They were all too confused or too scared to stand with Barrid.

The blacksmith searched their faces. Unsatisfied, he spat, "You frightened sheep! You might as well be doin' the Corruptor's work!"

"Barrid! Don't!" Sebastian tried to call out, but his voice was too hoarse.

"Master Lupke," began Stane.

"Hold your tongue!" Barrid commanded, spinning around to put his hostage between himself and the Sectaries that surrounded the gallows. "You let them go or I'll slice this boy from ear to ear. Cut 'em down! Even the boy from the Spire. You have no authority here. You are not Joacim, and your accusations are false!" He turned back to the assembly. "Don't you see?! He's using you to—"

The sharp twang of a crossbow loosening its load silenced Barrid, and the blacksmith leapt back as his hostage slumped to the ground, a quarrel sticking out of his neck.

Barrid looked down at the boy's blood that had splattered all over his tunic. Then he looked up to the High Sectary, his anger replaced with shock.

"I do have authority," Stane said calmly, lowering his crossbow. "As I told you before, the Duke has given me full authority in Terrace, and I strike with the king's hammer, not Joacim's. I have authority to punish the wicked and the unworthy." He motioned to the dead Sectary at Barrid's feet. "That boy failed in keeping you contained. The punishment? Death." He motioned to the accused behind him, who all watched in horror. "These foul miscreants seek to spread corruption and work the Burning One's will. Death. And if you seek to interfere with my authority..." Warrell let the unspoken warning hang there.

Barrid looked down at the boy again and then at the knife in his hand. Finally, he let his weary gaze fall on Vincent, Laurel, Anerith, and Sebastian. He locked eyes with Sebastian for a long moment. "I will never believe it, Bash. You are my faith..."

Before Sebastian could respond, Barrid broke into a dead sprint toward Warrell Stane, his knife raised to strike.

"For Uldagard's green and Prythene's flame!" Barrid shouted an old sonnet as his battle cry. "The Acrivas Sea and Sollum's breeze!"

Three crossbows were fired, all of their bolts finding the attacking blacksmith. Barrid fell to his knees, stumbling, choking on blood.

"I will...stand...with the Four," he managed, falling to his back and looking to the sky. "So...I...may...rest with death.... and...not...linger..."

"On," Sebastian finished for him, his eyes clenched shut against the tears.

"Does anyone else wish to stand for the accused?" Stane

asked then.

No one spoke; some didn't even breathe.

"Very well," Stane motioned, and then the world came down around Sebastian.

Vincent was the first to hang, the floor beneath his feet giving way and dropping his old body to his death. Sebastian barely found the strength to scream, and he might have if he didn't hear Vincent's last words before the noose choked him.

Sebastian did scream for Laurel's death, earning him a blow to the back of his neck with what felt like a hammer. His vision blurred as her body swayed. All he could do was thank the cursed Four for at least sparing him the sight of watching her last breaths.

Time stopped when Sebastian opened his eyes again. It was Anerith's turn. The floor gave way, Anerith screamed for mercy...and it came. His body hung suspended in mid-air, the noose around his neck limp, swaying in the calm breeze.

A gasp rose from the crowd and even the Sectaries all took a step back.

Anerith was flying. His eyes were clenched, ready for death, but his body was held safely in midair.

A miracle.

But then Sebastian's thoughts returned to the lightning at the VonAnthony manor and how it had saved Anerith's life then. As he watched the wind caress Anerith's body, Sebastian felt a sudden chill climb his spine. Something he had read in Vysarc suddenly came back to him, and for a moment he thought that he had actually died.

For he was staring at a ghost.

And the elements bowed to Skall's command. He was not born of this world, thus he was not held back by its restraints. Yet he was touched by the power of creation: the power of Celecy. And in her astral blood lies the ability to command the Realms...all Realms.

As the Sect of Halcyon together cried "Witchery!" and rallied the terrified support of Melbrook, Sebastian watched Anerith levitate, wondering if he were watching what all mortals feared the most.

A true sign of Astasia.

CHAPTER 30: WHAT FLAMES CANNOT TOUCH
The Hall of Mayrs, the Revery

They were alone this time, the encroaching shadows of the hall held at bay by the fiery, empty throne. Donovan and Demitri stared at each other for a long time, neither one of them saying anything. There were no gatherings tonight in the Hall of Mayrs, no dreamers coming to supplicate before the new Lord of the Revery. The Burning One was simply not there.

"How can this be?" Donovan asked aloud, unintentionally. He looked away from the throne suddenly, his eyes meeting Demitri's. "Where is he?"

Demitri met his gaze, evaluating Donovan. "He seems to be busy these days. Lands to conquer, a Balance to destroy." He didn't smile. "Who are you? Besides the Left Hand of Chaos, that is."

"I'm a sailor," Donovan said without hesitation, "who sold his soul to a fallen angel in the name of petty vengeance." Donovan's eyes narrowed on Demitri. "But you sold yours for a woman, didn't you?" Donovan grinned slightly when Demitri tensed. "I know you. We are now of the same body."

Demitri's eyes flitted between Donovan and the surrounding darkness. He was growing nervous. "You have the other half of the *kropal*," he said accusingly. "I've dreamt of it."

Donovan shook his head. "I don't have anything, except for maybe a flaming noose around my neck, just like you." He paused for a moment. "Tell me: why did you go after the stone?"

Demitri stared blankly at Donovan. "Like you said, you know me." He glared back into the darkness. "She has more control over me than the Corruptor."

Donovan stared into the same darkness, trying to find Gwyndalin's face. "There are some things that even Sol Saradys can't corrupt."

Silence hung between the two men as they watched the shadowy faces of their lovers appear and disappear in the misty blackness surrounding them.

"What are we?" Donovan asked finally.

"We are the Hands of Chaos," Demitri answered without averting his eyes from Xavia's shadowy, materializing face. "The chosen ones, bound to do the Corruptor's bidding. Many cultists spend their entire lives trying to become what we are, and we are the first. It's an honor—one that I have yet to fully appreciate."

"I was raised on the sea," Donovan said. "There are no gods out there, yet my parents were killed because of them, so I set out to destroy all belief in them. Now I am the instrument of one."

Demitri faced Donovan. "Sol Saradys is no god. He turned from his path. Gods are unwavering; they are what they are. The Corruptor chose his own fate, and he chose one of misrule and deceit. You do know the tale?"

Donovan shook his head. "All I know is what the Spearitan Faith fears."

"Very well," Demitri said, sitting down on the stone floor. "You should know whom you now serve. I am sure you know the stories of Celecy and the Black Seas; she harnessed the Winds and gave life to all. Her children were the rulers of the stars that she aligned and the world that she molded. Celecy watched as her children slowly began to divide, some seeking to ruin her creations and some vowing to keep all in order. This was the birth of Order and Chaos. The wars followed, and I'm sure you know how it ended. The eldest god, Athlas, crafted a cosmic law that drew the borders between the Realms."

"I know this," Donovan said, also finding a seat on the floor. "You're putting me to sleep."

Demitri gave him a mocking look. "You already are asleep. The Realms were also divided into Planes. We are in such a Plane; whenever we sleep, we slip into the Abyssal Realms, where we are given the power to create our own worlds. The Underlords yearned for such powers, so they tempt mortals into their worship by sharing with them their perverse notion of creation."

Donovan motioned for Demitri to continue while stifling a yawn.

"Sol Saradys was the ruler of such a Plane," Demitri continued. "Prythene: the Plane of Fire. All the elements are controlled by Order, so their Planes reside in the Heavenly Realms. However, all the angels that dwelt in the Planes were not altogether pure. One such angel was the result of…unnatural breeding. Sol Saradys came from the blood of angel and demon. He was the first Corrupted."

"And then he tricked Lockri; he schemed and lied, and they sailed the Black Sea and the Balance died," Donovan said in a sing-song voice, quoting an old poem.

"You wanted to know what we are," Demitri said.

Donovan nodded.

"After the Wars of the Balance, Sol Saradys was bound to the Stratovault, which, as we well know, is an unnatural pathway between the Mortal Realms and the Abyss, one of the many that he created during his conquest. He was bound by magical stones which were forged by angels willing to sacrifice themselves to return Order to the world, except for the *kropal*, which was used to bind the Corruptor's hands just to spite him. You see, the stone was crafted in Prythene, where Sol Saradys could not spread his corruption. In this way, the stone prevented him from manipulating mortals, which he so loved to do. The other stones bound his tongue from speaking more than whispers, his eyes from seeing the world he so wanted to conquer, and his ears from hearing his name worshipped. Since he could not be destroyed, lest the Balance be destroyed, he was purged from the world."

"Until we came along..." Donovan said, staring at the ground.

"No," Demitri said, "it should not have been possible, even if we both had the correct halves of the ritual. We might have managed to unbind the Corruptor's hands, but only a Chosen of the Burning One's order would be made a vessel for his Hands. Why would the Corruptor risk splitting his powers between two madmen who have no desire to serve him? Unless...he had no choice."

Suddenly, a roiling mist came in from the shadows, enveloping Donovan and Demitri. They both stood up to flee, but stopped short when they saw a hazy scene take shape. The Corruptor sat on his throne, surrounded by dreamers. He still had his hands. An enormous figure strode into the chamber, an equally enormous sword strapped to his back. His face was covered in ash like a cultist and he wore nothing more than an ashen wrap around his waist and a barbed shoulder sheath holding his sword in place. The man fell to his knees before the throne, speaking unheard words, and after a moment, Sol Saradys began laughing, exulting, and then opened his arms wide as if to offer himself.

The large man rose, shouting angrily. He charged Sol

Saradys, his blade drawn. And when he cut the Corruptor's hands off, they fell to the floor and disappeared just as the sword-wielder turned to mist as well. The scene faded as Sol Saradys let out an unearthly howl that reminded Donovan of that dreadful night in the Stratovault.

The mists receded.

"He had no choice," Demitri repeated. "We *are* his Hands, because he no longer has his own."

Donovan stared down at his left hand. The burn looked as fresh as if he had just touched the *kropal*. "And he can do with us as he pleases. We are his instruments."

"Then where is he?" Demitri asked. "Where has he been?" He gave Donovan a very intense look, a new realization taking shape in his mind. "What if we are in control of him? What if we lead *him* by the hand?"

The question summoned another cloud of smoky blackness. This time, two shapes walked out of the mists: two women of equal beauty.

Gwyndalin wrapped herself around Donovan.

Xavia ran her hands over Demitri's shoulders, kissing him lightly on the neck.

"There are some things that Sol Saradys cannot corrupt," Demitri said, looking into Xavia's eyes. They both began to fade away from the Revery in each other's embrace.

Donovan stared at Gwyndalin, but the apparition quickly dissolved. He was left alone. "There seems to be so few..." he said as he slowly awoke.

Sol Saradys stepped from the shadows and sat on his throne. His laughter echoed through every mortal's nightmare that night.

The Silver Spire

Demitri woke to the sound of birds—not ravens or crows, but colorful moonjays—alighting on his balcony. He rolled over and stretched, the dreams of moments passed were a distant memory. The bed felt cold and he turned to see that Xavia did not lie next to him. He sat up and saw her standing naked in the morning sunlight that poured in through his balcony door. Her eyes were taken by Sol Saradys.

"Leave her," Demitri commanded sternly, rising from the bed. His fists were clenched and flames began to flow through his veins.

"You are correct," Xavia said with a voice that was not her own. "There are some things that I cannot corrupt. I will never have power over love." The very word seemed to weaken the voice. Xavia stepped toward the open sky. "But the absence of it has even more power than I…"

Demitri leapt from the bed, but before he could do or say anything else, Sol Saradys threw Xavia's body over the balcony into the awaiting sunlight.

"No!" Demitri cried, running after her, calling on any power he could imagine. But none would suffice. Blinded by the morning sunlight, he searched for any sign of her survival.

But his love disappeared; it had fallen from the top of the Silver Spire, plummeting to a grisly demise. Among every other sort of pain that Demitri felt at that moment, he felt the cool burn of flaming fingers wriggling their way into his mind, preparing to give their commands.

Demitri had no strength left to resist.

In the Calluses below, Myriad could hear Xavia's death and he whispered his thanks to the Corruptor.

Druid's Grove, Lockrian Woods

In Lockrian, Donovan did not wake up naked and alone, merely naked. Gwyndalin's limbs were entwined with his own, the throes of their nocturnal deeds made plain by the state of Donovan's bedcovers. He could not tell if it was morning or late evening. The shade from the trees and the unearthly glow of Lockrian Woods made the room come alive with shades of emerald and jade.

Gwyndalin's treecat slept at the foot of the bed, purring softly and kicking as it dreamt of whatever pleasures such a beast was entitled to: most likely sleeping.

Donovan laid his head back down, smiling, thinking nothing of fire or Chaos.

CHAPTER 31: THE SON OF SKALL
Melbrook

From his perch above the rooftops, Raiken watched in pure amazement, sharing the same reluctance to breathe as the rest of the gathering. Anerith was held suspended in midair, the noose around his neck swaying lightly in the breeze. His eyes were tightly closed, expecting a sudden shortness of breath.

He was flying.

"Brother," Raiken muttered to himself, shifting his gaze to Sebastian, who knelt on the platform next to Anerith. "Please do not tell me you asked for another...favor."

After another long moment filled with gasps and whispers of Chaos, Stane turned to attend to the crowd. His commanding aura had faded away and Raiken could see, even from this distance, the man was genuinely frightened. Nonetheless, he reached into his coat and produced the *kropal* once more. Wide-eyed, Raiken searched for his own stone to make sure Valcorse was at the ready. It still hung from his neck, radiating emerald fire. From the trees in the distance, the bird took flight silently.

"Fly swift, friend," Raiken whispered weakly, his grip on the Greenstone tightening.

"Chaos!" Stane shouted, pointing at Anerith.

The word made Anerith open his eyes. It took him a moment to realize what was happening, but when he saw what he was doing, his mouth dropped. Even so, he still hung suspended in the air, without the aid of the noose.

"Here is visible evidence that the Spire teaches witchcraft!"

Stane said. "It seduces young mortals to the lure of magicks! And now that the Shackles have been disturbed, black magic is flowing back into our world, thirsting for our destruction!"

The gathering sounded their agreement, crying out ideas for further executions. But they were all silenced as a large falcon swooped down from the skies, swifter than a bolt of lightning. With a shriek, it unleashed its talons and snatched the *kropal* from Stane's raised hand, spraying blood as sharp claws left their mark on the High Sectary's hand. The crowd gasped once more.

"Bring it down!" Stane shouted, cradling his wounded hand. "Bring it down!"

Several Sectaries stepped forward and loosed their crossbows.

On the roofs, Raiken closed his eyes, whispering a chant to Lockri under his breath. It was not something he was fond of doing, but he had never felt so scared for his friend's life. "Do not let him fall," Raiken begged of the Lord of Uldagard. "See him safely home…"

The bolts that flew after Valcorse were shot true, but veered away at the last moment, as if a powerful gust of wind blew them from their course.

"Gods below!" cursed Stane, his face reddening. He spun and pointed accusingly at Anerith. "You! You commune with the elements and twist the wills of beasts! Sorcerer! Cut him down!" Two Sectaries stepped forward to do so, pulling Anerith down from his flight. The young man from the Spire did not resist.

Stane turned to another dumbstruck host of Sectaries. "All of you! Build a pyre! We will burn this blasphemer at the stake!" The crowd voiced their agreement, each scared citizen hanging onto Stane's every word. At a time of such uncertainty, anyone with answers was a worthy savior. They followed the Sectaries around like a rabble of untrained soldiers. Sebastian and his two hanging friends were forgotten in the wave that swept a confused Anerith away to be burned alive.

A pyre was built in no time, fashioned out of debris from the ransacked church. Without delay, Stane commanded Anerith to be tied to the tall stake that rose from the center of the kindling. Some of the men from Melbrook even volunteered to help.

"Please," Anerith cried. "Don't do this! I'm only a messenger!" But his pleas were lost in the shouting of the mob. Everyone in Melbrook crowded around to see the young man burn.

Behind the madness, Sebastian struggled against his bonds. He didn't thrash around, afraid that he would lose his balance and strangle himself in the noose, but nobody paid him any mind now that there was a sorcerer in their midst. Sebastian almost gave up trying to free his wrists from behind his back when he felt the touch of cold steel. It slid between his wrists and the bonds fell away. He spun around to stare into Raiken's eyes, peering over the raised platform with a dagger spinning between his fingers.

Sebastian nearly shouted in surprise, but Raiken raised a finger to his lips, pointing toward the commotion outside the church.

Sebastian slid his neck out of the noose and took a moment to look at the grisly sight of Laurel and Vincent, hanging lifeless. He cringed and turned away, sliding off the platform toward Raiken.

"Come on," Raiken hissed, "into the woods!"

"We can't leave him," Sebastian said, pointing toward Anerith. "He doesn't deserve to die like that. We have to help him!"

The sounds of more gasps drew the twins' attention.

The pyre had been lit, but they could both see that, though the flames danced around their new companion, not one of them touched him. It was as if an invisible sphere surrounded Anerith, protecting him from the fire.

"Looks like he is doing a fine job of avoiding death all by himself," Raiken said sarcastically. "We won't be as lucky," he said, motioning to Laurel and Vincent.

The coldness of the statement enraged Sebastian, but Raiken had already ducked low and headed toward the Aevenwood.

"Wait!" Sebastian hissed. "I need something." Sebastian crouched low and made his way around the platform, heading toward Barrid's smithy.

Raiken cursed under his breath, left with no choice but to follow him.

The smithy was in disarray; all the devices of the Four were torn from the walls and thrown into the furnace and Barrid's tools were scattered about. The Sect had obviously been searching for any reason to incriminate the blacksmith for supporting a heretical order.

"What do you need here?" Raiken asked, clearly annoyed. "We have to get to the Burrows before someone notices you're missing. Some of us can't fly or repel fire."

Sebastian threw one of Barrid's trunks aside and pulled a leather hide from the wall.

"Quiet!" Raiken said in a panicked voice. "They might hear us!"

"Where is it?" Sebastian wondered aloud, ignoring his brother. "He couldn't have let them take it…"

"What?" Raiken asked incredulously. "What is so important in here that's worth risking our lives for? All I see are horseshoes and hammers!"

This caused Sebastian to pause and stand up straight, turning to his brother. "That's it..." He rushed over to the shelf that held all of Barrid's tools. "He probably knew the Sect would search his shop." Sebastian pushed the shelf aside, shoving with his shoulder. It barely budged. "Come on!"

Raiken shrugged and helped him. The shelf slid aside under their combined force revealing behind it a curtain with the Sacred Circle emblazoned on it. Sebastian tore it away and his gleaming blue armor glistened in the light of the dying embers of Barrid's forge.

"We have to sneak out of town quietly and you want to wear a suit of plate mail?" Raiken asked. "I must have gotten the looks *and* the wits."

"Come on," Sebastian said, reaching for the shimmering breastplate. "Help me."

Outside, the Sect had torn Anerith from the stake, extinguishing the flames with water from the well. They bound his mouth to silence his pleas.

"He is immortal!" a woman cried in a horrified voice, "Skall returned! He cannot be killed." Her cries were buried in the voices of the others, but her claim still caught Warrell Stane's ear. He turned to look for her, his eyes frantic and distant as thoughts raced through his mind. He didn't find her.

"Tie him to that tree," Stane commanded, pointing to Anerith and then to a large oak tree in the church's courtyard. "He will die by quarrel!"

The Sectaries obeyed, and in moments Anerith was bound to the tree and seven Sectaries took position in front of him, their crossbows trained on his chest. Without delay, the High Sectary ordered them to fire. But, much like their attempts to bring down Valcorse, their quarrels flew wide of their target, as if a gust of wind had blown them off course at just the right moment.

This time, hardly anyone gasped, as if the event was expected. Many people continued cursing Anerith as some of the burlier men of the town tried to force their way past the line of Sectaries to have their hand at the sorcerer. But, the High Sectary grabbed a crossbow himself and reloaded it, marching toward Anerith as the young Adept winced in painful expectation of the crossbow's quarrel aimed right between his eyes.

A long silent moment passed; no one moved or even dared to breathe. Then, the High Sectary pulled the trigger. The crossbow clicked, followed by the splintering sound of wood cracking, and the broken quarrel went spinning in two different directions.

Warrell Stane threw the broken weapon aside in rage. He made a tight fist and threw it into Anerith's face. Everyone gasped this time, and even the High Sectary took a step back in surprise.

But, when Anerith brought his head up, blood trickled from his bound mouth.

"He can be hurt!" someone cried out.

Stane stared at the man, stepping away from him for fear of some retaliation. But Anerith just breathed heavily, his head down, bleeding. He continually mouthed the word: "Please..."

"But he can't be killed," Stane said, only to himself. "When the Revery falls to Corruption's seed...the Black Wind's son shall rise again..."

"Sir," a masked Sectary said. "What are we to do?"

"He is the Son of Skall," Stane said, staring blindly at an

exhausted Anerith. "He is here to bring our doom...unless we take him to his."

The masked Sectary took off his hat and let it fall to the ground, dropping his crossbow as well. When he took his mask off, there was absolute fear in his young eyes. "Skall could not be killed. He was strangled, stabbed, beaten, poisoned...nothing could kill him. It must be true."

In the distance, well behind the silent gathering, two figures crept into the trees of the Aevenwood. One of them reflected the fading sunlight off of a dazzling suit of impenetrable armor while the other melted into the emerald leaves.

Something that wasn't the sunlight gleaming off of Sebastian's armor flickered in Stane's eyes, a distant memory or thought rekindled. "He wasn't killed. He was cleansed of his impurity."

Anerith looked up, finally meeting the High Sectary's gaze.

"And by drowning this offender of Celecy," Stane continued, turning to the people of Melbrook, "we shall forever prevent Astasia, paving a glorious path toward Halcyon."

Darkness began to swallow Anerith's vision as the town united against him, the High Sectary's words rallying them to his cause. Anerith let exhaustion claim him, hoping he would wake up back in Triarch, and everything that had happened since he left the Spire had been a terrible nightmare given to him by that cruel hag.

But the taste of his own blood lingered in his mouth. And it was real.

And it held frightening power.

CHAPTER 32: THE HANDS OF CHAOS
Druid's Grove, Lockrian Woods

When Donovan awoke, Gwyndalin was gone. There was no sign of her in his room. Even her treecat had fled. He quickly got dressed and headed out into the forest to search for her. The dryads had slowly grown tired of standing guard over him once Donovan learned that he had no hope of ever finding his way out of the forest, so he met no resistance leaving Fyrechel's manor.

Donovan tried to check all of the usual haunts that Gwyndalin had shown him, but without her guidance, he kept winding up back at Druid's Grove. Eventually, he sat down on a stump, hoping that she might return sooner or later. There was no movement in Druid's Grove, and the only sounds came from the rustling of small animals in the trees above. The silence gave Donovan a chance to think about his recent revelations; now that he filled a void inside himself, Sol Saradys could not manipulate him anymore. When his parents were killed, he lost nearly all of himself. He had no strength of will anymore because of the void their deaths had left within him. And the Corruptor fed off of such weakness.

It was her, Donovan thought to himself. She had saved him. She had given him that desire to be a part of this world again. And he loved her for it. He loved her.

That thought struck him like a knife in the back. "I love her," Donovan muttered to himself. He thought of the implications of what he was saying. He loved an embrechaun—a being that could not leave the mystical home she was bound to.

But regardless, he loved her. He stood up at that instant, knowing that he had to find her and tell her.

Then, he heard the baying.

It came from everywhere, the howls of desperate wolves, growling and dying. He tensed, thinking of Gwyndalin in trouble. Without much consideration, he chose a direction and ran. The howls intensified as he made his way through the green. Donovan immediately thought of the werelings. Gwyn had told him about the mutated wolf-men, and Donovan was no stranger to the tales of Murdock Woods. The thought of his savior being mauled to death by such vile creatures only pushed him harder.

After what seemed like only a moment of panic, he reached the border of the forest where the ground dropped off above Murdock Woods. He could see the ocean, and the smell of the sea brought back sudden, strong memories that nearly knocked Donovan over. But he was able to shake off the nostalgia when the smell of bloodshed overpowered the saltwater.

The werelings were everywhere, clawing their way toward the woods in a blind frenzy, but they met the arrows of the embrechauns and the savage fury of the dryads. Even the forest seemed to come alive to prevent their entry. The werelings that were able to push past the defensive line would make it into the woods only to be spat back out again by unseen forces. The creatures were driven by some unnatural purpose. Donovan could see it in their eyes. It was not food or shelter that they sought; it was something much more malign. Something primal.

Donovan quickly ducked into the overgrowth, making his way behind the line of embrechaun scouts to find Gwyndalin. It did not take him long. She was at the center of the defensive line, firing arrows at lightning speed while commanding her kinsmen to do the same. Donovan crouched low to stay out of the embrechauns' line of sight as he made his way to Gwyndalin's side.

"What's going on?" Donovan asked.

Gwyndalin startled and spun, but returned to her bow when she saw it was Donovan. "What are you doing? You shouldn't be here; it's too dangerous."

Donovan searched for a hand weapon, drawing Gwyndalin's long knife from the sheath at her hip. "If I can survive the Burning Isles, I think I can manage this." Donovan looked out and saw that the waves of werelings were thinning. "Looks like you won't need my help, though."

Gwyndalin fired her last arrow, taking down a hulking wereling that had just made his way over the cliff only to fall back down into Murdock. The dryads were taking care of the rest. Soon, the battle was over, and Donovan sheathed Gwyndalin's unspoiled blade.

Once the bodies of the werelings were thrown back over the cliffs, the embrechauns were ordered to return to their normal posts and the dryads returned to the Grove to convene the council.

"They weren't here for food," Donovan said, staring at the blood on the ground. "Something dire drove them here. Not even desperate or frightened beasts will charge into such certain slaughter."

Gwyndalin began collecting her arrows. "A lot of strange things have happened since you came here."

Donovan turned to her, not sure if he should be hurt by her words. But they did sting, especially since he was searching for her to tell her how he felt. "I'm sorry."

Gwyn looked up, compassion in her emerald eyes. "No, it's not your fault. That's not what I meant. It's just...there's so much confusion right now. And the one thing I was certain about is gone…" She shouldered her quiver, now full of arrows. "It's just…"

Donovan could not hold it back anymore. He stepped toward her and lifted her face to his, wrapped his arm around her, and then kissed her. Instantly, he felt her pull back, so he let go, his heart sinking.

"Donovan," she began.

"Let me speak," he interrupted. "Please. I've done something terrible, I know. I feel a dark presence inside of me, clutching my heart, making me forget everything. I know that it's Sol Saradys. I awoke him because I thought I could destroy him, destroy the idea of him and every other false idol worshipped by all the weak-minded mortals of this world." He felt tears welling up. "I was wrong, Gwyn. I was driven by hatred and vengeance. It made me believe that I was indestructible. It made me believe that I had all the answers and had to prove to the world what I knew to be superstition and fear.

"But I became the weak-minded: easy prey for corruption. I cared about petty things such as revenge and justice, a sense of purpose. I lusted for all the things that required power to obtain. And a promise of power can easily be mistaken as a voice of reason." Donovan's eyes became wide suddenly, and he stared into the distance beyond Gwyndalin, where Vhaltas reigned. "And it was him all along, driving me to do his bidding in the guise of vengeance. He has held influence over me for so long…"

Gwyn took another step away from Donovan, crushing a leaf under her foot.

The noise brought Donovan's attention back. His face softened. "But you freed me from his bonds, Gwyndalin. You gave me the one thing that corruption cannot touch." He stepped toward her and held out a hand.

Gwyn held up her own hands and shook her head slightly. "Donovan…"

Before she could finish, a shriek sounded in the air above. A moment later, a falcon dove down toward them, circling down from its height.

"Valcorse!" Gwyn cried, turning away from Donovan.

Donovan knew the bird. Better, he knew of the bird's master. He felt the subtle flickering of flames kindle under his heart. Then, he saw the black stone that fell from the bird's talons into Gwyndalin's small hands.

"Take it to the council," Donovan said sternly. "Now."

Somewhere in the Burrow Gates

"I need a drink," Cedric said, cutting his way through the strange foliage that dangled from the emerald mists. He cradled his wounded arm, which was bound in a split that Jaryd had fashioned for him.

"I wouldn't drink anything down here," Jaryd said, trying to tune his damaged harp as he followed the hulking form of Skahgerok. "They say the River Volkris runs through the Burrow Gates. So unless you think Abyssal waste is a tasty brew, keep away from any streams we come across."

"We won't pass that river," Skahgerok said sternly. It was one of the few things he had said since they passed through the hidden entrance into the Burrow Gates in Demonscale. "I know the ways down here, and we are heading toward Lockri's domain. Volkris does not dare bring its vileness there."

"Though we should be going after the half-blood," Cedric

spat bitterly. Skahgerok did not acknowledge it.

"We're heading in that direction," Jaryd said, in a half-consoling, half-annoyed voice. "Time passes a little differently down here, am I right Skahggy?" The Rhelk didn't answer. "It could seem like a day's worth of travel in the Gates, but only a few moments will pass by above ground." Jaryd stopped plucking his harp for a moment in sudden contemplation. "You know, being a Burrow Gate guide might be a lucrative enterprise…"

"Why are we going to this forest again?" Cedric asked Skahgerok, trying to push past the bard. "You saved my life, and I'm in your debt. But my duty is to my family and our kingdom, and its future rests in the hands of that thing that we let get away."

Skahgerok finally stopped and turned around. "You know the prophecies of Astasia? Olerune's Portents in the *Books of Astasia*?"

Cedric nodded. "What of them?"

"I wrote them," Skahgerok said plainly. "Because I dreamt them. I was given a high seat in the Revery because I helped imprison Sol Saradys six hundred years ago, and now I am a slave to prophecy: cursed to watch the world crumble in countless ways. I am only permitted to leave the Revery and return here when the need is absolutely dire. And now, because some arrogant witch helped the Corruptor overthrow Sand in the Revery, I have been cut off from my dreams. I am blind. And my last vision was of Sol Saradys, once again made flesh, bringing about the Days of Astasia.

"So, the task lain before me is to gather together the individuals capable of helping me restore order to Lorendale: a task that proved easier when I could turn to the Lorenguard. But those days are gone. Candrella has fallen and the kingdom is divided. The world is in a state easily susceptible to corruption.

"Now that the Burning One's Hands have been set free, it means they will undoubtedly be looking to destroy the remaining Shackles of Heaven so that he may be fully released. The first Shackle the Hands will seek is the Greenheart: Lockri's imprisoned soul. His presence prevents the cults from assaulting Aevenore from the shore. Without the Greenheart, Lockrian Woods will fall and neither the embrechauns nor the dryads will have the strength to hold off the legions of Sol Saradys."

Cedric stared in rapt attention, and Jaryd's face was full of excitement, as if Skahgerok had just told them that they were on their way to a tavern that served free ale.

"So, once we ensure the safety of the Greenheart," Skahgerok continued, "then we will recover your sword. We shall have need of it as well."

Cedric nodded.

"We'll be your Lorenguard," Jaryd said smugly, giving Cedric a pat on the back.

"Did you hear that?" Cedric said, ignoring the bard and peeking around the huge form of Skahgerok.

In the distance, two shadows were approaching from another path. Cedric could barely see them through the dense fog, but their voices began to penetrate the gloom. One of them wore armor that clanked and the other was kicking debris noisily.

"We can't just leave him back there!" one of the voices yelled.

"Look, I told you! He can take care of himself. You saw what he did in Wynnstead, and we both saw what he did back there!"

"What about Vincent? Or Laurel?" The figure that just spoke grabbed the other figure and spun him around. "Why couldn't you save them?" His voice cracked with a sad desperation.

Cedric, Jaryd, and Skahgerok crept closer, listening to the argument while they hid behind the twisted trees and rocks.

"He told me not to!" the man that seemed to glow green said, shaking off the armored figure's grasp. "I tried to free him from the church, before the hangings, but he refused!" The man's voice held a lot of emotion as well, as if he were trying not to cry. "He said if I saved him, there would be no chance to save you! If I tried to intervene at all, it should only be on your behalf! No one else!" He pushed the armored man who had suddenly lost his fury. "He made me swear on mother's grave!"

Silence fell between the two.

The green man spat and coughed awkwardly. "We have to return to Lockrian. We've been gone too long. The council will need to hear about what happened." A brilliant green light emanated from a necklace that hung around the man's neck, as if it were guiding them through the Gates.

"Let me guess," Jaryd whispered to Skahgerok, "you had no idea we would run into these two, did you?"

The Rhelklander stood up and walked toward the men. Cedric and Jaryd followed. As they neared the two strangers, they both unsheathed weapons to defend themselves. Once the mists parted, Cedric could see that they had to be brothers; they looked identical.

"You carry a shard of the Greenheart," Skahgerok said to the one in green, raising his hands to show that he meant no harm. "Then, perhaps you know the way to Heartheald."

"You mean you've been leading us around down here with no idea where we are going?" Jaryd asked incredulously.

"This is where we were going," Skahgerok said, motioning to the identical strangers. "Sebastian and Raiken Belrouse, meet the prince of Celendas and his traveling minstrel."

Cedric stared in confusion, but mustered enough courtesy to bow his head in greeting.

"Welcome to the Lorenguard," Jaryd said with an uninspired strum of his harp.

From the shadow of a malicious rock formation in the distance, Demitri watched the meeting with white eyes. Myriad emerged from the shadows as well, clutching a map written in the Abyssal tongue.

"Looks like we won't need the map after all," Myriad hissed.

Demitri narrowed his eyes. "I didn't need it in the first place. I can feel Lockri quivering in his emerald prison. I know the way."

They slithered their way through the shadows toward Lockri's Rest in Heartheald, staying close behind the rabble that called themselves the Lorenguard.

The Council's Chamber, Druid's Grove

"If you are interpreting Raiken's message correctly," Therrus said angrily, "then the boy that you've taken such a liking to should be killed! He is responsible for what is happening!"

Gwyn shot Therrus a malicious look as the rest of the council debated the suggestion. Fyrechel and Audrea were present with Genis, along with two other embrechaun scouts that had fought during the most recent wereling invasion.

"Since when do you care what happens beyond our borders?" Gwyn asked acidly.

"This concerns us," Fyrechel said to Gwyn. "We are

protectors of Lockri's soul—one of the Shackles of Heaven. If the Corruptor seeks to destroy his bindings, our forest will surely be a target."

"The next target," Audrea qualified. "This forest is the only thing that stands between his legions and the heart of Lorendale."

"This thing is fascinating!" Genis said, holding up the returned half of the kropal against the incoming light from above. "The script is old, but it seems to writhe with new energy!"

"Genis has informed us that Celendas has fallen into the hands of the cult," Fyrechel began, ignoring the broan's loud examination. "It is likely that they seek to destroy all the kingdoms of the Tripartite. And our home is on the path to Aevenore. This boy has brought our doom."

"Exactly!" Therrus agreed. "He should be killed!"

"No!" Gwyn cried.

"No," Fyrechel echoed.

Finally, one of the scouts added his voice to the council. "But the werelings and shadow hunters have only increased since the boy has been here. It is as if his corruption calls to them and they seek him out. He must be destroyed."

"His death will not accomplish anything," said Audrea. "We must follow the advice of Genis. He has the most knowledge of werelings, corruption, and the Burning One's cult. He says Donovan is absorbing the corruption that runs through these very woods. His death would not purge such power. He needs to be exiled: given to the forces that seek him out."

Therrus sounded his support, along with the two scouts. Fyrechel also nodded, but Gwyn only stared across the council chamber. Even though both dryads wore their human guises, Gwyn couldn't help but see them in their terrible true forms: malicious spirits of the wild, skin of bark and limbs like cruel talons. She bowed her head.

She could not save him. The council had spoken. The sadness that began to rack her was not spawned from an ill-fated love she had for Donovan. In truth, she did not even truly care for him, not the way he cared for her. Yet, she did give Donovan the strength to fight the Burning One's influence, and if Donovan was to be surrendered, the resistance she offered would have been in vain.

"You can't do this," she blurted out.

Suddenly, the earthen doors of the council chamber were thrown open. Everyone turned to see an enormous man stride through the door's archway. Behind him were four other men. They all entered, and when the emerald light from above lit their shadowy forms, Gwyn forgot all about Donovan and the Burning One.

"Raiken!" She ran to him, darting past the large stranger and Sebastian. She threw her arms around him, and Raiken heedlessly embraced her as well, lifting her easily off the ground.

"We apologize for the intrusion," Skahgerok said boomingly. Fyrechel arose then, her face betraying emotion for the first time in what seemed like a lifetime. Her green eyes were fixed on the Rhelklander.

"Skahgerok?"

He nodded, falling to one knee. "My lady."

She stepped down from her high seat on the council. Something that shimmered like a tear ran down her face. "You are awake."

Jaryd nudged Cedric, nodded toward Audrea, and whispered. "I call the other one with pointy ears."

Skahgerok looked up. "It is time," he warned. "The Balance is threatened. Tell me, where is the broan?"

"Genis?" Fyrechel asked, still a bit shaken. She turned, but Genis was no longer seated. She turned to Audrea. "Where is Genis?"

"We must find him," Skahgerok commanded. "Immediately."

Everyone in the council chamber began to make their way out to begin a search for the broan. Fyrechel grabbed Skahgerok's wrist as he turned to leave and held him there. Once everyone had left the chamber, she pulled him down and pressed her lips firmly to his. She wrapped her arm around his thick neck in a way that said she would never let go.

Donovan wandered through the maze of Lockrian with no destination in mind. Voices whispered to him, telling him ways to make Gwyn love him—to make everyone love him—but he tried not to listen. It wasn't until he heard a new voice that he stopped to take notice.

"You can hear him, can't you?"

Donovan spun around and saw a demon's face peering out from the leaves.

"The Corruptor," the demon continued. "He promises you, doesn't he? Power, love. He is quite convincing. How do you think he convinces thousands of worshipers to live on a mountain of spewing fire?" The little demon stepped out from the underbrush.

"Who are you?" Donovan asked, taking a step back.

"I am a guide," he said. "My name is Genis. I am born of these woods, an elder spirit you could say. My people were here before Lockri's Flight."

"A broan?" Donovan asked skeptically.

"Call us what you will," Genis said with a wave of his hand. "I am here to help you, because you have a destiny to fulfill that is not yet complete." He held out his hand, presenting one half of the Shackle of Flame. "Raiken has returned. Gwyndalin is in love with him, and she thinks not of you."

"Stop," Donovan said, taking a step back, his eyes fixed on the *kropal*. He wanted to reach out and take it. Something compelled him to, but he resisted. "Go away."

"Do you remember?" Genis asked. "How she felt? The sound of her voice whispering in your ear? All those lies she told you only to strip you of your vengeance?"

"Why?" Donovan asked, closing his eyes in pain. "Why... why, Genis?" He opened his eyes, and Sol Saradys stared back at the broan. "I think I was wrong about you." He laughed, reaching out for the *kropal*. "Not that I am unappreciative, but why?"

Genis pulled the Shackle of Flame back out of Donovan's reach. "You were right about everything. I had years to dwell on your words, and I have finally found the wisdom in them. This world is a battlefield drawn out by the glory-seeking Four. We are cursed to fight each other again and again, neither side able to suffer true defeat. Our only peace lies in Astasia."

"So true, dear Genis," Donovan said wickedly, speaking with the Burning One's tongue. "Though I do have an engagement I must make," he reached out for the stone once more. "If you would be so kind."

Genis handed him the *kropal*.

Once Donovan wrapped his fingers around the Shackle of Flame, his eyes returned to normal and he nearly fell over backward. He stared down at Genis with absolute fear and understanding in his eyes. "I know what I have to do, broan.

He...Sol Saradys thinks he can control me, manipulate me. I am his only way to be free. But I am the one that set out to destroy him. And this," he held up the *kropal*, "is the only thing that can end him. I saw it all just now, when he took over; the shades of angels that once walked this world were severed from their heavenly bodies on the day of the Binding. The Shackles are remnants from their old home, and it is their bane." Donovan's eyes darted everywhere. "Take me to the Glade of Mists. We must get to Heartheald."

Genis nodded with a tiny flicker of fear in his eyes.

The Halls of Lockri's Rest, beneath the Glade of Mists

Heartheald was a labyrinth, but Demitri felt the connection to the Greenheart strongly in Lockri's lair, so he followed his instincts.

"I have not been in these halls in a long time," Myriad said, admiring the intricate patterns and designs that adorned the earthen palace. All of the wards were aglow, humming with power as Demitri and Myriad passed each turn in the winding corridors.

Demitri gripped his half of the *kropal* tightly. "I expected to lose my power here. They say the Greenheart protects the shores of Lorendale from corruption. But I feel even stronger down here. I hear *his* voice even clearer."

"Lockri deals in a different type of corruption," Myriad explained. "His love for the forests created an unnatural fury that infects the wilds now. He birthed a wrath that borders on the edge of hatred, which he reserved for all offenders of nature.

His corruption mutates the deepest followers of his ways. Embrechauns turn into vile wolf-folk and the elder race that dwelled in his woods turned into the very trees they worshipped." Myriad shuddered. "And oh, how I hate dryads.

"But you are correct," he continued. "Normally, the Shackles would expel the taint of corruption, such as the guiding words of the Burning One. However, you are a shade, not some blind cultist. You live in the wake of an archangel. You are his Hand. That cannot be purged from you so long as you live." Myriad smiled. "And you cannot die from any mortal blade."

Demitri grinned wickedly. "It's ahead. I feel it."

They wound through several twisting paths until they reached the heart of Lockri's underground palace: the gates to Lockri's Rest. There, the guardians waited patiently.

Two golems stood on either side of the gates leading into Lockri's Rest. They were hulking forms, each standing taller than two men, their heads brushing the mossy ceiling. Their skin was like thick bark and their hands were like carved stone blades. They had the faces of hounds and the limbs of a graceful stag.

As Myriad and Demitri approached, the guardians crouched low to attack, as if they had been waiting their entire existence for this very moment.

"Careful!" Myriad warned, stepping back behind Demitri. "These are elder beings. You must call upon the *kropal* for power, but beware! If you call upon corruption, the Balance will enable them to call upon their own powers!"

Demitri stepped forward. "So be it."

The guardians simultaneously leapt toward the invaders. Myriad darted aside, skittering up the wall and cursing.

Demitri tightened his grip on the *kropal*. A coil of red energy unraveled from the stone, forming a flaming, barbed whip. He then clenched his other hand and it burst into flame. Demitri raised his burning whip and lashed at the nearest guardian. The weapon struck the beast in the face, burning its thick hide. It howled and fell forward, blinded. But the other guardian leapt over its companion, lunging for Demitri.

Myriad spoke some strange tongue from his perch in the high shadows, and it sent a wave of dark energy through Demitri, empowering him.

As the guardian dove for him, Demitri threw out his flaming hand and a ball of fire erupted from it. It struck the guardian, igniting his thick skin, but it didn't faze him. The golem slashed its claws and nearly cut the intruder in half. Blood sprayed across the hall and Demitri was thrown backward. Both guardians were now on their feet, their own hands trailing an emerald mist.

Demitri cursed himself for his brashness. He would surely not survive this battle. "To the Abyss with the Balance!"

"Agreed," said a voice from his side.

Demitri turned and saw the man from his dreams standing next to him. It was Sol Saradys' other Hand—his other shade.

"Let us end it all," Donovan said, suddenly fading from sight. His whole body turned translucent, and then he was gone. Demitri did not hesitate though. He felt an undeniable connection with the man, and he anticipated what was to come.

The new Luminary of the Silver Spire uncoiled his whip again and readied himself. As the guardians approached, he chose the one on the right, and with lightning speed, he lashed the whip around the charging guardian's neck. The other sentry screamed in pain and fell over, a materializing Donovan standing atop its falling form with his hands covered in thick, mossy blood. Demitri pulled as hard as he could on the fiery noose and snapped his attacker's neck.

In just moments of Donovan's arrival, Lockri's guardians lay defeated, leaving his gates open to the Hands of Sol Saradys.

"Shall we?" Donovan asked, motioning forward with bloodied hands. Together they opened the gates. Myriad followed close behind, smiling the smile of a freed being.

The Glade of Mists, above Heartheald

The search party found Genis sitting on a stump playing his pipes in the Glade of Mists. It looked like he had been crying, but he gave a weak smile and lowered his pipes as they approached.

"It is done," he said.

Skahgerok stepped forward to ask what he meant, but when he saw the broan's eyes, he knew. "How could you, Genis?"

"I have watched these people kill each other too long," he said, motioning to the forest, though it was obvious that he meant the world as a whole. "We live by laws that we did not create, and we die for reasons that we do not understand."

"What's happened?" Sebastian asked, stepping forward. "What have you done?"

"He's stolen the *kropal*," Fyrechel answered, "and given it back to the man who brought it here."

Cedric stepped up next to Sebastian. "Where is it? Those stones are our responsibility now. Tell us where he went!"

"The war has begun," Genis said, standing up on the stump. "And there is no time to go chasing after that boy and his stone. He has his own destiny. Kill me if you wish, or punish me. I could have helped prevent this war, but instead I have helped start it."

Everyone fell silent.

Genis continued. "I apologize for betraying you, and I pledge my allegiance to your cause in this war. However, I could not bear to stand aside while this world repeats the same mistakes over and over again. We are in a realm of eternal battle, and unless we fight the greatest war this world has ever seen, we will repeat the cycle." He jumped off of the stump. "Astasia is where we will find our peace."

He walked out of the Glade, and no one stopped him.

"Why would he do this?" Raiken asked suddenly. "Sebastian and I nearly died protecting that thing!"

"He's a traitor," Cedric said sternly. "We executed people for treason in Celendas. Or at least cut off their hands."

"His death won't change anything," Skahgerok said. "He's right though. There isn't enough time right now to go looking for the *kropal*. But we cannot simply sit around and wait for the Greenheart to fall. Raiken, Gwyndalin, we will go into Heartheald. I need a guide and I need the Greenstone" He turned to Sebastian, Jaryd, and Cedric. "The rest of you go with Fyrechel and prepare for an invasion. There is sure to be one. Hopefully, we will return before the black sails come. We must not let this forest fall."

They all nodded. Sebastian and Raiken grasped forearms in farewell. Fyrechel and Skahgerok shared a quick glance. And then they turned to leave the Glade.

"Splitting up the heroes already?" Jaryd asked Sebastian as they followed Fyrechel. "That is a bad idea in almost every story ever told."

As the Glade of Mists fell silent, Skahgerok, Raiken, and Gwyndalin prepared to descend into Lockri's dark depths.

Lockri's Rest

"How do we do this?" Donovan asked as he stared at the enormous stone that was held suspended in the great chamber. The Greenheart was a magnificent sight to behold.

"There are no writings about how to destroy the Shackles," Myriad said, walking around the Greenheart as if looking for a weak point. "It is merely known that each stone is susceptible to the others' power." He stepped forward, squinting. "There is a piece missing here…"

"I dreamt this," Demitri said, staring deep into the Greenheart. It reflected his image, but it was twisted and jagged. He turned to Donovan. "But I was you and I corrupted the Greenheart by merely touching it."

Donovan looked at him and shrugged. He stepped forward and placed his left hand on the stone. It flickered lightly, but nothing else happened. He turned back to Demitri and looked down at his right hand. Demitri understood and put his hand to the stone also. Still nothing happened.

"Ah," Myriad said, "now it comes together…"

The Hands of Sol Saradys gave the demon a confused look and saw that he was looking at their other hands. Both halves of the *kropal* had come alive, a dark glow emitting from them. Instinctively they both raised their halves together. When both halves touched, the world sighed in terrible anticipation.

The Greenheart's emerald light intensified, and then the entire stone began to shake. A crack ran down its middle, and then it began to crumble. Shrieks filled the chamber: the shrieks of Lockri's hidden spirits crying in agony as their lord began to fall apart.

Demitri and Donovan both grit their teeth and held the Shackle of Flame together despite its growing heat. Their flesh sizzled, and still they held on. Myriad chanted in his infernal tongue, his voice barely audible above the piercing sounds of Lockri's demise.

After what seemed like days of torment, the pieces of the Greenheart fell to the chamber floor, each one shattering into dust. Soon, only smoke remained.

They had done it.

"Lockri is dead," Demitri said, surprise and fear in his voice. But still he smiled, turning to the left Hand. But Donovan was nowhere to be seen, and both halves of the *kropal* had vanished with him.

"We are finished here," Myriad said, picking up a handful of Lockri's remains and letting them sift through his fingers. "But there is much work to be done. We must prepare Aevenore for the arrival of your legions."

Within the Halls of Heartheald

"I have to tell you something," Gwyndalin said, grabbing Raiken's wrist and pulling him back a bit as Skahgerok pushed forward. "About the sailor."

Raiken ground his teeth, pulling on the chain that held the Greenstone as if it were choking him. "What about him?"

"I watched over him like you asked me to. I protected him. But every time he dreamed, he would wake up and forget who and where he was."

"Sol Saradys," Raiken said, trying to loosen his necklace. "The boy must have been power-hungry."

"I helped him fight the influence," Gwyn said, looking at her feet as they walked. "I...I had to give him strength."

Raiken stopped and let go of the Greenstone, realization slowly sinking in. He clenched his jaw to bite back what he wanted to say. And then pain shot through him and he fell to a knee. "Gods!"

"Do you feel that?" Skahgerok asked, unsheathing his enormous sword.

The hallways began to shake, mossy stones falling from overhead.

"We are too late!"

Gwyn knelt next to Raiken, pulling him aside to dodge some falling debris. But Raiken screamed in pain, falling onto his back. The Greenstone around his neck was glowing brighter than Gwyn had ever seen.

"What's happening to him?" Gwyn screamed, panicking. She tried to grab the necklace, but the moment she touched it, she pulled her hand back as if it were on fire. "We need to get it off of him!"

"Stand back!" Skahgerok commanded, grabbing Gwyn and pulling her free of Raiken.

"No!" Raiken cried out, arching his back. His whole body began to tense and his skin writhed, as if insects crawled underneath. And then he began to convulse violently.

"It's Lockri!" Skahgerok said, holding Gwyn so she would not race to Raiken's side. "They must have gotten to the Greenheart! That stone around his neck is all that remains of the Shackle, and Lockri must be channeling his remaining life force into it!"

"That will kill him!" Gwyn cried, trying to break free of the Rhelklander's grip. But it was useless. The man was nearly four times her size. She was forced to watch Raiken suffer.

The Emerald Scout thrashed, trying to claw the necklace off. But then his hands began to change and dark green hair sprouted from his arms. His face began to contort, taking the shape of a beast. He opened his mouth to scream, but instead he let out a bestial howl. As his hands grew into claws, he curled into a ball, still moaning in pain. And then he was still for a moment.

Skahgerok relaxed ever so slightly, and that was all Gwyn needed. She burst from his grip and threw herself at Raiken's side. But before she could even touch him, he spun around and leapt up on all fours with lightning speed.

He was a hound of Lockri now, covered in dark green fur, with a stubby, wolf-like snout. His eyes were filled with fury. He swiped at Gwyndalin with a claw, barely missing her face, but raking her shoulder. She fell to the floor, shouting in pain.

Raiken let out a final howl before turning to flee from the halls of Heartheald.

As Skahgerok watched him leave, he wondered if he should be relieved or terrified that Lockri was still alive.

Regardless, they had failed. The forest was doomed to fall once the legions arrived. He sheathed Salvation and scooped up a sobbing Gwyndalin into his arms.

"The war has come," he said, repeating the words of Genis. He looked down at the embrechaun in his arms, seeing in her everything that was good and pure in the world. "But so have the Lorenguard. There is still hope…"

EPILOGUE

At the foot of the Stratovault, Vhaltas

The cavern echoed with the chants of the gathered cultists. "Bring us Chaos, bring us Chaos," was repeated in unison, creating a huge, swaying rhythm that served as the orchestra for the ritual that was about to begin.

There was a massive altar at the back of the cavern, the intricately carved statue of Sol Saradys looming over the Cult of the Burning One's place of worship. Scarlet swayed with the bodies that surrounded him, repeating their words, but his eyes were fixed on the figure of Sol Saradys. He had seen the Burning One depicted in countless terrible forms—a hulking demon surrounded by fire, a dragon with a bloodied maw, a burned man with broken wings—but this statue filled Scarlet with complete awe. In this cavern on Vhaltas, Sol Saradys was a magnificent angel, his wings aflame, screaming at the sky as chains bound him here beneath a mountain of fire.

"You came with the Left Hand, didn't you?" a voice said in a whisper, careful not to break the mounting cacophony of *Bring us Chaos*.

Scarlet turned and saw a woman that somehow looked familiar to him. Her eyes were sunken dark circles and she wore an ashen hood over her dark hair. A man stood behind her, leaning in to hear Scarlet's response. The man had regal features, surely of noble birth. Scarlet nodded, looking around to see if anyone was offended by their speaking during such a sacred rite.

"What was he like?" she asked eagerly.

"We heard he traveled with a sorcerer," the man said excitedly. "The Right Hand!"

Scarlet shook his head. "He traveled with fools, because only fools would follow him. He is a spiteful boy with a dream of greatness. Nothing more."

The response took them both aback. They stared at the ground considering that for a moment. Then the man looked up again.

"Boy or no, he must have been cunning to ruin Sinder's ascension."

"He got lucky," Scarlet said. "He came to prove what he thought was a myth. But after this ritual, we will all prove to him that the power of Sol Saradys is real, and it was meant to be wielded by Sinder."

This made the man smile. "My name is Mathias, and this is Rya. We welcome you to the cult. What made you convert so quickly after attacking our people?"

"Not that we aren't happy to have you," Rya added quickly with a shy smile.

Scarlet stared at them both for a moment, and then turned to the statue of Sol Saradys. The chanting was intensifying around them. "I've done many terrible things in my life. I stole from the elderly and I killed the young without the slightest hesitation. Nothing was sacred to me. But when I came here, Sol Saradys spoke to me. He made me look at myself from a greater distance. It was then I realized that the only reason I did those things was to feel significant in a world that doesn't care in the slightest for me." He turned back to Rya and Mathias. "And the fact that a fallen archangel had taken it upon himself to speak to me, a lying, killing, vile excuse for a man...it was the first time I ever felt truly significant in this world."

Rya and Mathias both nodded with smiling faces, as if they had experienced exactly the same thing.

Suddenly, a drum sounded from the back of the cavern. It was a quickening rhythm that accented the cult's chanting.

"It's beginning!" Rya said, returning to her own chanting and swaying.

Scarlet turned to the front as well, but he pushed forward to see the altar. He could see three burning priests emerge from the shadows behind the statue. Behind them followed a figure covered in intricately decorated armor. The armor plates were huge, Scarlet noticed. No normal man could bear such weight. But as the figure neared the torchlight, Scarlet could see that the man was all muscle, and his flesh seemed to be growing over the armor, as if it were part of his body. It had to be Sinder.

The three priests aligned themselves, two on either end of the altar and one standing in front of it. Sinder took position behind the altar, standing before the statue of the Corruptor. He threw off his ashen cloak and raised his arms high. The chanting rose and fell with his every movement.

Bring us Chaos…bring us Chaos.

The two priests at either side of the altar reached out to grab either one of Sinder's arms. They both clasped manacles around his wrists and lowered them to the altar. They wrapped the chains around the bottom of the altar and secured them together with a strange-looking lock. Scarlet thought it must have been one of those enchanted locks from Rokuus that he could never open.

The priest in front of the altar turned to the gathering and lowered his hood. His eyes had been only recently removed, as the hollows where they once were spouted fresh blood. He reached into his robes and produced an elegant saber, a style of weapon used by the Therrecians along the peninsula. The shamans there tended to use their sabers for religious rites of passage as well. The priest held the curved blade up and it glistened in the torchlight. The drumming grew faster. The chanting grew ever louder.

Without any hesitation, the priest turned and quickly brought the saber down. Blood sprayed from Sinder's left arm as the blade severed it from his chained hand. The only sound that came from Sinder was a sharp inhale of breath. The sword fell again and cut off his other hand as well. Sinder still held his position bent over the altar, blood gushing from the stumps of his wrists.

From either side of the statue, two more priests emerged, both of them carrying trays covered in red silk. The silk writhed as if two creatures were underneath, moving to the rhythm of the drums and chanting. As they reached the altar, the priests that chained Sinder's arms removed the silks. On each tray were the rumored hands of Sol Saradys. Not the traitorous invaders that ruined Sinder's ascension, but the true hands of Sol Saradys: the ones that were meant for the cult's true champion.

Scarlet pushed even further ahead through the swaying crowd, desperate to see the hands. When he was close enough, he saw them as they were lowered to the altar. They were terrible to behold: crimson flesh with elongated fingers that ended in razor sharp tips. And they were nearly as large as half a person each. Fortunately, Sinder was a massively built man, so he would surely be able to bear their weight and size.

The ritual continued as all five priests busied themselves with stitching the hands of an archangel to his unwanted champion. It was a long and grisly process to behold, but the gathering did not waver in its chanting.

The priests even began their own chant, as if they were asking their lord to preserve the man that defied him.

When it was done, the priests arose, their hands and arms covered in blood. But when they raised those arms, the entire congregation fell silent mid-chant.

The priest with the bleeding eye cavities spoke. "The Corruptor's chosen one."

Sinder arose to the cheering of his minions. He raised his new hands, still dripping fresh blood. His eyes were aflame and his face spoke of the terrible energy that now coursed through his veins.

Scarlet couldn't help but cheer as well, caught up in the magic of what he had just witnessed. He knew the man upon that altar had the power to change the world, and he would be part of his army.

Even though tomorrow held the beautiful promise of deliverance for the Cult of the Burning One, Scarlet realized that he did not care. Tomorrow did not matter.

For tonight was the eve of corruption—and tonight he was alive.

TO BE CONTINUED IN BOOK TWO

DRAMATIS PERSONAE

ADRATHEON: The vile black dragon of Demonscale Heights. Responsible for terrorizing Celendas until his eventual defeat at the hands of King Ausfred Galvian and the Dragonsbane.

ALASTAIR GALVIAN: King of Celendas, ruler of Eurheby, and father of Cedric Galvian.

ALLISTON PREAL: A wandering knight just returned from Rokuus.

AMARIE DESATHO: Queen of Port Laras in Pendara, wife of Benedict DeSatho.

ANATHU: A wayward drifter traveling through the Neveren Mountains, with no memory of past.

ANERITH ZATHON: A young Adept at the Silver Spire with a mysterious past.

ASHTON HALE: A knight in service to the Wharfmaster of Port Cray in Delethas.

ATHLAS: One of the Four gods of the Heavenly Realms. Known as the Crafter of the Balance, also commonly referred to as the God of Water, Ruler of Acrivas, and simply the Crafter.

AUDREA: A dryad in service to the Druid's Grove council in Lockrian Woods.

BARRID LUPKE: A blacksmith working in Melbrook, acquaintance of Sebastian Belrouse.

BENEDICT DESATHO: The gluttonous king of Port Laras and ruler of Pendara.

BENEGAST: One of the Luminary's Entrusted, said to have been abducted by the Sect of Halcyon during his quest for the Shackles of Heaven in Therrec.

BRIAR HANSEL: First mate aboard Donovan Marlowe's ship, *The Temptress.*

CARDINAL CARTHYS: The high priest within the Temple of the Lady in Celendas.

CEDRIC GALVIAN: Prince of Celendas, heir to the kingdom of Eurheby.

CELECY: A goddess. The supreme light of creation, known as the Lady. She is the central focus of the Faith and many other religious denominations throughout Athland.

CRISPIN VONANTHONY: A young nobleman from Quayhaven, nephew of Gabriel and Helena.

DEMITRI DRYCE: An Agravite at the Silver Spire and companion of Anerith Zathon. Romantically involved with Xavia Maldroth.

DONOVAN MARLOWE: A merchant sailor from Pendara whose parents were executed by the Spearitans. He has since pledged his life to proving the Balance to be a myth.

DORA: The self-proclaimed daughter of Pulasia. A member of the Revenant Houses of Vysarc and travelling companion of Shaith and Feignly Moss.

DURION: An Aushuin assassin imprisoned and enslaved by King Benedict DeSatho.

EINRIST: An accomplished scribe hired by the Cult of the Burning One to translate the recovered fragments of the Binding Ritual.

ERIK GHALAHAN: A young knight in service to House Rose in northern Eurheby, brother of Leif.

ERROL: A young scribe in service to King Luther Garrowin of Aevenore.

FEIGNLY MOSS: A rogue in service to the Revenant Houses of Vysarc travelling with Shaith and Dora.

FELYSE MARLOWE: Donovan Marlowe's late mother.

FYRECHEL: An elder dryad, known as Heiress to Druid's Grove in Lockrian Woods.

GABRIEL VONANTHONY: Baron of Wynnstead. Husband to the late Helena VonAnthony and known supporter of the Silver Spire.

GELDRA: The aging advisor to King Alastair in Celendas.

GENIS: The last surviving broan. A renegade in service to the Druid's Grove council in Lockrian Woods.

GEOFF PELN: A burly young knight in service to House Goodnight in Eurheby.

GEYER ELLIS: Head treasurer of Celendas.

GWYNDALIN (GWYN): An embrechaun from Lockrian Woods, companion to Raiken Belrouse.

HELENA VONANTHONY: The late Baroness of Wynnstead. Rumors say that she foolishly aided Sol Saradys in usurping the Revery, dying in the process.

JARYD FAWN: A well-known bard hailing from the northern Regencies.

JASSILY CONSTANCE: Ambassador to the Regency—a union of the Remnant Houses in the North, determined to take back the city of Candrella from the ruthless greks.

JOACIM: One of the Four gods of the Heavenly Realms. Known as the Justicer, also commonly referred to as the God of Earth, Ruler of Uldagard, and sometimes the Hammer of Justice.

JONAH MARLOWE: Donovan Marlowe's late father.

KABLE ORTON: A young noble from House Orton in northern Eurheby. A companion of Cedric Galvian.

LACEY RENEVERE: A young, handsome ranger in service to the Ranger's Guild in Lumbridge.

LAUREL DARCY: A serving girl working at The Raine Song tavern in Melbrook. She is secretly in love with Sebastian Belrouse.

LEIF GHALAHAN: A young knight in service to House Rose in northern Eurheby, brother of Erik.

LENNICK: The proprietor of The Raine Song tavern in Melbrook.

LOCKRI: Former Archangel of Uldagard, blamed for assisting Sol Saradys in bringing corruption to the world. Lockri now exists as the large, enchanted stone known as the Greenheart, also known as the Shackle of the Earth.

LOREN THE FIRST: Former emperor and founder of Lorendale. Founded the kingdom city of Candrella and quelled the uprising of the Vysarcian Empire.

LUCRID: One of the Four gods of the Heavenly Realms. Known as the Defender, also commonly referred to as the God of Air, Ruler of Sollum, and sometimes The Blade of Winged Glory.

LUTHER GARROWIN: King of Aevenore and ruler of Terrace. He is known to be a paranoid monarch, always expecting rebellion or treachery within his kingdom.

MARAKUS: A Grand Adjurer who teaches at the Silver Spire.

MARTIN: A priest of the Sacred Circle Church in Melbrook.

MATHIAS: A young member of the Cult of the Burning One. Romantically linked to Rya Kindell.

MERETH AUGANA: Adjurer of Ancient Lore and Archaic Symbology at the Silver Spire.

MYRIAD: A demon lurking in the depths of the Silver Spire who has made a dark pact with Vanghrel.

NOL: Captain of the Guard in command of Logan's Hilt, serving the kingdom of Eurheby.

NYJIEN KAST: A Vigilant at the Silver Spire, originally from the Quiet Isles of Rokuus.

OLERUNE: One of the Four gods of the Heavenly Realms. Known as the Enlightener, also commonly referred to as the God of Fire, Ruler of Prythene, and sometimes The Flame of Truth.

QUARRIS FELGUN: Advisor to King Benedict DeSatho. Secretly a member of the Cult of the Burning One.

PULASIA: A dead priest devoted to Sol Saradys, aided the Vysarcian Archgeist Rhavael in creating Skall.

RAIKEN BELROUSE: A former thief from Quayhaven now living in Lockrian Woods as the Emerald Scout, the bearer of the Greenstone. Twin brother of Sebastian Belrouse.

RAYMUN LANDOVER: A young noble from House Landover in northern Eurheby. Cedric Galvian's closest companion.

RENNIG: A military advisor in service to King Luther Garrowin of Aevenore.

RHAVAEL: The last Archgeist of Vysarc, father/creator of Skall.

RUTHERFORD: An Alchemist at the Silver Spire. A companion of Anerith Zathon, Xavia Maldroth, and Demitri Dryce.

RYA KINDELL: One of the Entrusted from the Silver Spire, sent to recover the Shackles of Heaven. During her quest she fell in love with Mathias, who swayed her into joining the Cult of the Burning One.

SCARLET: An assassin working for Donovan Marlowe's crew aboard *The Temptress*.

SAND: Former ruler of the Revery—the dreamlands linked to the Abyssal Realms. Was overthrown by Sol Saradys through the aid of Helena VonAnthony.

SEBASTIAN BELROUSE: A priest of the Sacred Circle Church in Melbrook. Twin brother of Raiken Belrouse.

SERRA CONRAD: Eldest son of the Duke of Holthurst in Eurheby.

SHAITH: A member of the Revenant Houses of Vysarc. Travelling companion of Dora and Feignly Moss.

SIERRA: An old crone that lingers around the town of Triarch.

SINDER: The Cult of the Burning One's chosen champion whose body is destined to become the Corruptor's vessel.

SKAHGEROK: A Rhelklander that aided the Four in binding Sol Saradys to the Stratovault, bringing the end of the War of the Scales. After the Shackling, the Four gave Skahgerok immortal life.

SKALL: A mysterious figure that caused the fall of the Vysarcian Empire. Known as the Son of Chaos, Skall was said to have been born from a fallen star summoned by the Vysarcian Archgeist Rhavael. Because of his origins, he was able to wield phenomenal power without disturbing the Balance. It is a common belief that Skall's descendant will herald the coming of the Days of Astasia.

SOL SARADYS: The former archangel of Prythene who descended from the Heavenly Realms to bring corruption to Athland. He is known as the Corruptor, the Burning One, and the new Lord of the Revery.

STANTON BERRYMORE: The Duke of Romney, a small duchy in northern Terrace. Cousin of Vance Mandary.

STROMAN HALE: Wharfmaster of Port Cray in Delethas, and father of Ashton Hale.

TANITH ELTON: Captain of the Tower Guard in Celendas. Cedric Galvian's instructor and friend.

THERRUS: A malevolent embrechaun in Lockrian Woods who constantly seeks Raiken Belrouse's demise. A senior member of the Druid's Grove council.

TOLAND: A gruff old knight in service to Baron Gabriel VonAnthony. His face is noticeably burned.

VALCORSE: A falcon, Raiken Belrouse's companion.

VANGHREL THONDRANE: The Luminary of the Silver Spire. His age, origins, and founding of the Silver Spire remain a mystery.

VANCE MANDARY: A pompous young nobleman that frequents The Raine Song tavern in Melbrook. Duke Stanton Berrymore's cousin.

VINCENT CRULAND: An elderly priest of the Sacred Circle Church in Melbrook. Adopted father of Sebastian and Raiken Belrouse.

WARRELL STANE: The High Sectary of the Sect of Halcyon, a fanatical sub-faction of the Faith dedicated to the eradication of Chaos and corruption.

WILLEM CONRAD: Youngest son of the Duke of Holthurst in Eurheby.

XAVIA MALDROTH: A young Adept at the Silver Spire and companion of Anerith Zathon. Romantically involved with Demitri Dryce. Leads frequent, late-night excursions within the Silver Spire to uncover a rumored conspiracy involving the Luminary.

ABOUT THE AUTHOR

Brady Sadler is a graduate of Purdue University in Indiana with a degree in Creative Writing. In addition to being an author, he is also a sloppy drummer, addicted gamer, embarrassing father, and incompetent chef. Brady lives in the frozen north of Minnesota with his lovely wife Sarah, their daughter Rylie, and their two cats.

CPSIA information can be obtained
at www.ICGtesting.com
Printed in the USA
BVOW03s1340050917
493997BV00014B/28/P